THEY WERE FIGHTING
FOR THEIR LIVES, THEIR DREAMS,
AND THE FATE OF A NEW WORLD.

JANET MACLEOD. Despoiled by English soldiers before she fled Scotland, she now met the terror of war with a bravery born of love for her husband, their children, and their land.

MATHEW MACLEOD. He had fought the English in Scotland. Now he rallied to the French cause in the defense of his new homeland . . . until shot in the leg by a woman.

MEGGAN O'FLYNN. Lovely English spy—and daughter of a man who once loved Janet—she sabotaged the French, but could not betray the Macleods in their time of gravest peril.

ROBERT MACLEAN. Janet's younger brother, captured in childhood by Mohawks, was a stalwart young adventurer equally at his ease in battle or a boudoir.

MARGUERITE LUPIEN. The exquisite French doll who captured Robert's heart, but suffered a tragedy that drove Janet to kill a man with her own hands.

ANGELIQUE COMEAU. A flawless alabaster beauty, exiled with the Acadians from Nova Scotia, abandoned in New Orleans, she surrendered to Robert's desire, and his offer of marriage.

Other Avon Books by
Dennis Adair and Janet Rosenstock

KANATA: BOOK I: THE STORY OF CANADA

Coming Soon
THUNDERGATE: BOOK III: THE STORY OF CANADA

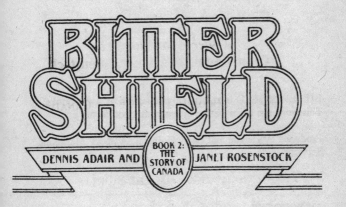

BITTER SHIELD

BOOK 2:
THE STORY OF CANADA

DENNIS ADAIR AND JANET ROSENSTOCK

AVON
PUBLISHERS OF BARD, CAMELOT, DISCUS AND FLARE BOOKS

BITTER SHIELD is an original publication of Avon Books. This work has never before appeared in book form.

Produced by Helene and Larry Hoffman, Authors' Marketing Services

AVON BOOKS
A division of
The Hearst Corporation
959 Eighth Avenue
New York, New York 10019

First Avon Printing, February, 1982

AVON TRADEMARK REG. U. S. PAT. OFF. AND IN
OTHER COUNTRIES, MARCA REGISTRADA, HECHO EN
U. S. A.

Printed in the U. S. A.

WFH 10 9 8 7 6 5 4 3 2 1

ACKNOWLEDGMENTS

Among the reference books used in the preparation of this novel were the following: *New France, the Last Stage 1744–1760* by George F. Stanley; *Quebec 1759, the Siege and the Battle* by C. P. Stacey; *The Picture Gallery of Canadian History* by Charles William Jefferys; *Daily Life in Early Canada* by Raymond Douville; and *Cities of Canada* by George Nader.

Century of Conflict: The Struggle Between the French and British in Colonial America by Joseph Lister Rutledge; *Forts of Canada: The Conflicts, Sieges and Battles that Forged a Great Nation* by Leslie Hannon; and *Ill-Starred General: Braddock of the Coldstream Guards* by Lee McCardell.

The authors would gratefully like to acknowledge the work of Jay Myers, the historian and researcher who worked with us on *Bitter Shield*.

We would like to thank Bob Wyatt, Vice President, Editorial Director of Avon Books for his encouragement, Normand Gervais, Bill Connor and the entire Avon sales staff for their untiring work and Sabra Elliott, Roger Bilheimer, and the publicity staff for the excellent promotion of this series.

CHAPTER I

March 1754

During March the weather in southern Quebec alternated between icy rain and heavy wet snow. The entire space between the front door of the Deschamps house and the river was a patterned network of puddles. Each of the miniature pools was covered with a thin layer of ice so that on contact the first sensation one got was the illusion of breaking through thin glass and the second was the unpleasant reality of sinking three or four inches into cold mud.

It was the season of the thaw, and the trees in the woods dripped water from their branches, the outer walls of the barn were streaked with moisture marks from dissolving icicles, and the wide rambling roof of the main house creaked under the burden of melting snow. Periodically, a clump of loosened snow would slide down the sloping roof and fall to the ground, sounding like an eerie human groan in the room below.

Janet Macleod looked up, startled by the sound of one more snowslide. Then, laughing at her own edginess, she flopped the last batch of dough down on the wood table and began kneading it. The other five loaves were lined up and covered with damp cloths.

This is the last one, she thought with relief. They would all rise overnight and be ready for baking in the morning. Fresh-baked bread! It was the best of all early-morning aromas.

"All in bed!" Madame Tremblay announced triumphantly as she entered the kitchen, wiping her hands on her apron.

"Little devils! They always want one more story! Two days in this house and I'm storied out!"

Janet doubled her fist and hit the dough, then she stretched it, testing its elasticity. "Where's Jacques?"

Madame Tremblay laughed heartily. She was a short, round woman, and when she laughed her two chins moved up and down as if they were made of jelly. "That son of mine is already asleep! He goes to bed earlier than the babies!"

Janet smiled. "Why not? He gets up with the sun and works all day."

"He's a good boy," Madame Tremblay agreed.

Janet lifted the dough, pulled it, and tossed it once again on the floured table. It was hard to think of Jacques Tremblay as a boy. He was a strapping young man of twenty-four, only a year younger than she, as a matter of fact.

"I really appreciate your staying with us while Mathew and Robert are in Trois Rivières." Janet looked fondly at Madame Tremblay. Over the years she had come to count on Madame and Jacques, and so had Mathew. Janet and Mathew found that managing Maurice Deschamps' seigneurie was no easy task. It had grown immensely in both size and productivity. Four new tenant farms had been added to the estate, bringing the number of habitant families to twelve.

The homes of the habitants, however, were half a mile down the dirt road, leaving the house of the seigneur, Maurice Deschamps, the most isolated in the community.

Madame Tremblay positioned herself on a high stool. Her many skirts—Madame always wore at least four in

2

the winter—fell about her as she perched, leaning one arm on the sinkboard for balance.

"It's always so quiet when the children have gone to bed!"

Janet sighed. Madame was quite right. The house took on a deathly silence once the six children were tucked in and asleep. It was always after supper and after the children had gone to bed that Janet missed Mathew and Robert most.

"What do you hear from Monsieur Deschamps?" Madame Tremblay inquired. "Is he still with that . . . that woman?"

Janet began shaping the dough into a proper loaf. "I'm afraid so," she answered without looking up. Maurice was a legend with the habitants—a never-ending source of conversation and entertainment. His desertion of the seigneurie and his children to live in a brothel was a matter of general disgust. Unlike their absent seigneur—and for that matter, most of Quebec's upper class—the habitants were quiet, family-loving, decent, and deeply religious. The idea of a married man having a mistress—even if his wife was permanently deranged—was intolerable. The habitants were the puritans of New France.

"It looks ready," Madame Tremblay said, referring to the loaf. "You're fussing over it. Aren't you ready for bed?"

Janet eyed the perfectly shaped loaf of dark bread. Madame was right, it was ready. Janet lifted it carefully and placed it next to the others, covering it with the damp cloth so the outside would not dry out overnight.

"I always have trouble sleeping when Mathew's away," Janet admitted. "Especially this time of year—the house makes so much noise."

Madame Tremblay laughed. "I'm here! Jacques is here! And six children! Two of whom are big boys now."

"You're right." Janet smiled again. Pierre Deschamps was ten and René nine.

3

Madame climbed down off the stool and yawned. "I'm tired even if you're not!"

Janet picked up the candle holder. "I imagine I'll be able to sleep."

The two women left the warmth of the kitchen. Jacques was sound asleep on the sofa in the parlor. Madame had covered him with a quilt as if he were a small child. "Should we wake him?" Janet asked. "There's more than one extra bed upstairs."

Madame shook her head. "He'll be fine down here."

The two women climbed the winding staircase in silence. The house was still, utterly still.

"Good night," Janet said, opening the door to the spare bedroom for Madame Tremblay. "Sleep well." Janet held the candle till Madame had lit the one in the spare room, then she moved down the hall to her own bed chamber where Helena, her three-month-old, slept peacefully in her hand-carved cradle.

Janet looked around for a moment, then went back down the hall. She opened the door to her boys' room and peeked in. Two-year-old Mat Macleod was on his back, his mouth open and the quilt on the floor. Janet set down the candle and covered him, kissing him lightly on the cheek. She glanced at four-year-old Andrew Macleod. He was huddled beneath his coverings with only his nose visible.

Janet stepped out of the room and closed the door. She passed Pierre and René Deschamps' room without looking in on them, but she stopped in front of six-year-old Madelaine Deschamps' room and opened the door a crack. The dark-haired little beauty was sleeping peacefully. Janet sighed and returned to her own bed chamber. Her excuses for postponing getting into bed had run out.

Janet pulled the puffy, down-filled quilt up around her neck and listened. "Just more snow falling," she said to herself as she turned restlessly onto her side.

Opening her eyes wider, Janet rolled onto her back

4

again and looked up at the dark ceiling. How long have I been asleep? she asked herself. Long enough to have been sleeping soundly when the falling snow woke me, she thought.

Janet shook her head. It was, she reckoned, three or four in the morning.

Through the window she could see that there was no light in the eastern sky, and the silence told her that the crows, who always made such a commotion in the hour before dawn, were still asleep.

Janet lay awake, realizing it would be difficult to get back to sleep. She missed Mathew's warm body on the other side of the bed. But she comforted herself by listening to Helena's rhythmic breathing. The newest addition to the Macleod clan was sleeping on her stomach, rear end up in the air, her legs folded beneath her.

Janet stretched out and touched the foot of the canopied bed with her toes, then tried to relax again. But it was no use. The house groaned beneath its load of wet snow as the beams expanded and contracted.

"I'm silly," Janet said aloud to herself. Distracted, she patted the empty space beside her on the bed. It was only because Mathew was gone for a few days. . . .

Janet closed her eyes, determined to go back to sleep. Moments passed, and she felt herself growing numb as sleep began to overtake her. Then she heard a noise that made her sit bolt upright in bed, her heart pounding. It could not have been snow! It sounded for all the world like someone walking on the roof!

Janet tensed and strained all her senses. She listened while trying to rationalize the sound—it could have been a lumbering raccoon in search of food—then Janet heard it again. It was too heavy for a raccoon!

Janet slid out of bed and wrapped her heavy winter robe about her. She slipped into her shoes, tiptoed to the window, and peered out into the dark night.

"Oh, my God!" She gasped and ran toward the bedside commode. She took out the pistol, checked

5

quickly to see if it was loaded, and thrust it into her robe's sash. Then Janet carefully lifted Helena out of the cradle and fled into the darkened hallway.

She ran down the hall and into Pierre and René's room. Sitting down on the edge of Pierre's bed, she jostled the sleeping boy to consciousness, whispering urgently, "Wake up all the children! Quietly—no candles! Tell them to bring their blankets. Bring them downstairs at once!"

Pierre rubbed the sleep from his large brown eyes and tumbled from his bed.

"Hurry!" Janet pleaded. "I saw them! They're out there!" She could feel herself shaking. "Wake Madame Tremblay, too! Quietly—hurry!"

Still carrying the baby, Janet hurried down the stairs in the darkness. In the parlor, Jacques Tremblay was sprawled out like a sleeping giant. His mouth was open, and he punctuated each loud snore with a snort. Janet gripped his shoulder and shook him.

"Jacques! Jacques!"

Jacques brown eyes snapped open. "Sshhh!" Janet cautioned. "I heard noises on the roof—"

Jacques shook his head. "Snow," he pronounced sleepily.

"Not snow, I saw them!" Janet's green eyes were wide. Jacques tensed immediately, forcing himself completely awake.

"How many?"

"I don't know, I only saw one."

Jacques got up and pulled on his breeches. "Get the guns!" he whispered urgently.

Pierre was leading the way down the stairs. Holding Mat and Andrew by the hand, he was followed by Madelaine Deschamps and Madame Tremblay.

Janet handed Helena to Madelaine, who carefully took the sleeping baby in her arms.

Janet ran quickly into the kitchen and in the darkness fumbled about for the extra ammunition. There were four muskets in the gun rack and another over the mantel in the parlor. She stuffed a candle and some flint

6

into her pocket and, cursing the awkward length of the long muskets, hurried back to the others.

Madame Tremblay already had the other musket off the mantel and was loading it.

Janet handed a musket to Jacques and one to Pierre.

"Load the fifth musket," Jacques told Pierre. "Have it ready."

Helena opened her eyes and threatened to begin crying. "Rock her, Madelaine, hold her close!" Janet looked around anxiously. "You children go to the cellar. You know the hiding place, go and stay there till I tell you to come back!"

"I'm old enough to stay!" Pierre protested. "I can shoot straight!"

"You go to the cellar!" Janet whispered authoritatively.

But Jacques' hand was on her shoulder. "He's right," Jacques confirmed. "There are four windows, we need four muskets."

Janet hesitated for only a second, then she nodded in agreement. "Off with you!" she whispered to the other children.

Jacques pressed a musket into her hands and motioned her toward one of the windows. "Don't waste ammunition," he cautioned her. "Shoot only if you have a good target!"

Jacques pointed Pierre off toward the window in the dining room, then he and his mother moved toward the ones in the parlor.

Jacques edged the draperies away from the window frame slightly and looked out through the shutters into the blackness of the night. As the shifting clouds were blown across the sky, the moon momentarily illuminated the flat, treeless area between the house and the river. Jacques quite clearly saw the half-naked figure sprinting toward the woods.

"They're out there all right!"

Janet looked into the blackness and saw nothing. She thought of the children for a second. The hiding place cut into the cellar wall was, in reality, a tunnel that led to a trap door in the dense woods on the other side of the house. She shuddered at the thought of the helpless baby; she ought to be with her child. But she had to be here. Not even four defenders were enough!

René knows what to do, Janet told herself. He's old enough and brave enough. He'd leave the children in the tunnel if he had to and run through the woods to the village for the habitant militia if it became necessary.

Janet trembled. But what if he didn't make it? So many farms had been burned. So many families massacred in the sporadic Indian raids. When Mathew had finished the tunnel last year, they had rehearsed the plan. Janet thought about it and said a small prayer for René. Let him remember, let all the children remember what they'd been taught.

A horrible, ungodly shriek broke through the silence of the night. It was followed by another and then another.

"Here they come!" Janet heard Jacques' words just as she saw the first fire arrow flying toward the bedroom windows upstairs.

Janet heard Jacques fire, and she heard the return fire from the attackers. One of them was running toward the house, shooting. Janet took aim and fired her musket. The figure spun around crazily and fell on his face. Janet's mouth opened, and a sickening feeling of dazed shock swept over her as she realized she had just killed a human being.

"Good shot!" Jacques yelled in praise.

More fire arrows hurtled toward the upstairs windows, and the sound of breaking glass indicated that they had found their mark.

Again the hideous, blood-curdling sound of the Mohawk war-cry rang through the air. Janet shuddered, then composed herself and fired again.

"They're falling back!" Jacques said. "Didn't expect return fire!" He paused and peered into the darkness. "But they'll be back."

He was correct. Soon one of the warriors emerged

from the woods and then another and another. They ran across the front yard, some carrying torches, others shooting burning arrows or firing muskets.

Jacques picked off one of the leaders with a single shot. Then, seemingly angered by the loss of another of their number, the Mohawks hurtled their torches into the upstairs windows and fell back into the woods.

Janet fired once more as the figures retreated, and another fell dead at the base of the large pine tree. Pierre hit another and cried out as he did so.

The rooms began to fill with acrid smoke. The draft from the broken windows was feeding the fires, and they were burning quickly, forming a gigantic blaze. Smoke smarted Janet's eyes.

"We've got to get out of here!" Jacques was coughing and beginning to gasp. "Through the cellar! Hurry— they'll charge again!"

Janet, Jacques, Madame Tremblay, and Pierre ran through the dark house and down into the pitch blackness of the cellar. Janet bolted the cellar door behind them. She fumbled in her pocket for the candle and flint. In a second the taper was lit, casting strange shadows on the crude, unfinished walls of the root cellar.

Janet led the way to the tunnel door and swung it open. The four of them then crowded into the passageway, and Janet bolted the second door behind them.

"René!" Janet hissed into the tunnel, but the only reply was a whimper from one of the younger children.

They edged along the wall of the tunnel, and Janet sighed with relief when she saw the four younger children huddled beneath the trapdoor that led out into the woods. Madelaine was holding Helena in her arms, Mat and Andrew were crouched at her side.

"Where's René?" Janet took Helena from Madelaine and held the infant to her breast, automatically rocking her so she wouldn't cry.

"He's gone for help," Madelaine pointed upward to the trapdoor. She was terrified to the verge of tears, though trying to act brave.

9

Pierre climbed up and bolted the trapdoor, which had been left open because René could not lock it from the outside and Madelaine was too short to reach it.

Janet closed her eyes and let out her breath. The thought of a nine-year-old running through the woods to the village was frightening. She pictured René running right into the arms of a ferocious Mohawk warrior, and hideous images of the child being scalped ran through her mind. Janet pressed Helena to her even tighter and shivered with fear for René.

Pierre placed a warm hand on Janet's arm. "He'll be all right . . . these are his woods, he's lived here all his life."

"Sshhh!" Jacques cautioned as he pointed up toward the trapdoor. He raised his musket and trained it on the door while Madame Tremblay aimed her musket down the passageway that led to the house. "When we don't come running out of the house, they'll start looking. They know people don't stay in burning houses."

Helena let out a cry, and Janet quickly opened her nightdress and held the baby to her teat, allowing her to suckle in hopes that she might go back to sleep.

Jacques blew out the candle. "They might see the light around the door."

On the ground above them, they could hear the treading of feet.

An eternity seemed to pass as they huddled in the damp, cold blackness of the tunnel. Madelaine held Mat and Andrew to her for both comfort and warmth. Madame Tremblay breathed heavily, and so did Jacques. He and Pierre were tense and at the ready. If anyone opened the door at the far end of the tunnel, he would be framed in the light—there would be something to shoot at.

Janet's eyes remained closed. She could feel Helena's strong hungry pull at her breast, and she could hear her own heart beating in the silence. She remembered Mathew building the tunnel: "When they burn houses, the occupants are forced out and killed. This tunnel,"

10

he assured her, "will bring us where we cannot be easily attacked."

At the time, Janet had thought Mathew was only exercising his frustrated engineering talents. She had never dreamed that the day would come when her life and the lives of the children would depend upon Mathew's foresight.

More time passed and the only sound came from the breathing of the tunnel's occupants.

Then Janet's fleeting thoughts were interrupted by a sudden pounding from above—someone was trying to loosen the trapdoor from the outside!

Each of them stood frozen—there was digging.

"Keep your musket on the passageway from the house," Jacques told his mother. "You too, Pierre!" Jacques spoke in a low whisper, nudging Janet with his arm.

Janet carefully withdrew Helena from her breast and breathed a sigh of relief. Helena had drifted back into sleep. She handed the baby to Madelaine. Then she pulled the pistol from her sash, judging it the better weapon for the range.

"Someone's trying to force it up," Jacques whispered.

"What if it's René trying to get back in?"

Jacques shook his head. "No, he'd give a signal . . . it's not René."

The trapdoor suddenly gave way under the pressure of some sort of wedge. The bolt snapped and the door flew up, allowing a whoosh of cold night air to sweep into the musty tunnel.

All Janet saw was the blur of a figure—a man whose mouth was agape and whose tomahawk struck Jacques' musket as the gun was discharged into the savage's face, blowing it to bits and scattering morsels of skin and blood on those below.

Janet staggered against the tunnel's wall as two more Indians dove through the opening, wrestling Jacques to the floor, screaming their unholy shrieks.

11

Pierre whirled around and shot wildly. Madelaine let out an ear-shattering scream, and Janet saw that one of the Indians had his tomahawk poised over the girl and Helena.

Janet lifted her skirt and kicked the Indian's rear end, causing him to twirl about slightly off balance; she fired the pistol at point-blank range, and the Indian staggered backward and fell on top of the howling children.

Madame Tremblay fired too, and the Indian who was wrestling with Jacques tumbled off him and lay sprawled on the floor.

Janet leaned against the wall, panting, while Pierre pulled the dead Indian off the younger children. The Mohawk warrior was heavy, and it took a series of pulls, jerks, and kicks to get him off the terrified but otherwise unharmed children.

Janet looked up. No more Indians came through the trapdoor. Vaguely, through her shock, she heard gunfire outside.

Madelaine, blood-spattered and shaking, struggled to her feet, and instinctively Janet held out her arms, taking the crying Helena from her. "Oh, my baby, my poor baby!" Janet hugged the child to her, and tears began to run down her face.

Jacques kicked himself clear of the body that had fallen on him. His arm was bleeding and he clutched it where the Indian's tomahawk had grazed him. Madame Tremblay and Pierre both stood stark still, peering expectantly toward the trapdoor.

"Is that all of them?" The deep, husky, French voice was shouting from somewhere above them, somewhere out in the night.

"Mon Dieu!" another voice exclaimed. Then through her trance, Janet heard them calling her name. "Madame Macleod! Madame Macleod!"

"Down here!" Madame Tremblay's voice rang out in answer.

The face that peered into the tunnel through the

12

trapdoor was that of Monsieur Vachon, head of the local militia. Behind him, René looked down into the tunnel anxiously.

"It's all right!" Monsieur Vachon assured them. "Come on!" He extended a long hairy arm into the hole, and Jacques lifted Madelaine up toward Vachon, who gripped her and carried her out. After Madelaine, Mat and Andrew climbed out, then Helena was passed upward. Then Janet, Jacques, Madame Tremblay, and finally Pierre struggled upward.

Janet stood and stared at the once-magnificent house. Flames from within lapped through the broken windows and the open door. Fire was eating the fine drapes and the imported furnishings. The barn was ablaze, too. "Oh, God!" was all Janet could say.

"We got most of the animals out," Monsieur Vachon informed her. But then he added sadly, "The house is a total loss."

Janet felt sick and dizzy as the men from the surrounding farms—the tenant farmers of the Deschamps estate—helped her into the wagon with the children.

Janet held Helena and felt Madelaine against her arm. She was barely aware of the long jerky ride down the rutted road toward the village. Her eyes were fastened on the smoke from the house and barn, which rose curling into the predawn sky.

When Janet blinked her eyes open, the sun was streaming through the upstairs window of the Tremblay house. Mathew was sitting on the edge of the bed, rubbing her hand. His face was weary and tense, tired from the long trip and filled with anxiety.

"Oh, Mathew!" Janet squeezed his hand, and he in turn pressed hers. Janet drew herself up in bed and pulled Mathew to her; his arms went around her as he kissed her neck, her hair, and finally her mouth.

"I can't leave you here!" Mathew kept repeating.

Janet eased away from him and sought his eyes. "Leave?"

Mathew looked intense. "I'm going to take you and the children to Quebec City—you must stay with the children in Quebec City."

Janet embraced her husband and buried her face in his chest. "My place is with you! I belong with you!"

Mathew held her to himself for a time, then drew her back gently and stroked her beautiful russet hair. "I'm going to be working on the frontier forts . . . I'm an engineer, engineers are needed desperately."

"That's why you went to Trois Rivières?"

Mathew nodded. Janet searched his face with her green eyes. Over the past few years he had done odd jobs for the army when life on the Deschamps seigneurie had made him restless. Now he had gone to Trois Rivières to arrange for permanent work.

"We'll come with you," Janet said softly.

"Not this time," Mathew was shaking his head. "It's too far."

"I belong to you—with you!" Janet clung to Mathew.

But Mathew still shook his head. "Maurice will want the children where he can see them, with his mother in Quebec City. Robert has to finish school. The children are too young . . ." Mathew spun out a hundred and one reasons. Janet leaned against him, listening. She felt torn and shaken. She could not be parted from the Deschamps children any more than she could be parted from her own.

"I won't be gone long," Mathew was saying. "It's important. Janet, the frontier forts have to be strengthened. These constant Indian raids are pure harassment. They have to be stopped—and the British have to be stopped, too."

Janet could hear the pure stubbornness in Mathew's voice. He was always like that, he always had been. He refused to live off her fortune, and he had made it clear that their stay on the Deschamps seigneurie was only temporary.

Mathew lifted her chin and cupped it in his hand. Then he leaned over and kissed her deeply, moving his lips against hers. It was a long kiss, and when he

14

withdrew, Mathew looked at her seriously. "We were meant to be together," he told her. "And we will be soon. We have to find our own place, the right place . . . where nothing and no one can ever separate us."

Janet felt Mathew's large strong hands on her back. He massaged her gently, and she felt herself relax in his arms. "How long will you be gone?"

"Only over the summer," he assured her.

"Then you'll come back?"

"I couldn't leave you for longer. I wouldn't leave, but I know you'll be safe in Quebec City—really safe so I won't have to worry."

Mathew's eyes were soft and warm and filled with love as he lowered her to the bed with another kiss.

Janet wrapped her arms around him and sighed contentedly.

Mathew would do what he felt he had to. And if Mathew Macleod were any different, any less stubborn, she couldn't love him the way she did. He was driven by his fierce Scots pride, by the need to build a place of his own and a fortune of his own.

"I love you," Janet murmured. "You're stubborn and I love you."

Mathew looked into Janet's jade-green eyes. They were placid now, but he knew they could burn with a rare fire. Janet was a woman among women; she could defend herself and her children, and she was as strong and willful as she was beautiful. "I love you, too," he answered, pressing her downward and slipping his hand into her nightdress.

Janet closed her eyes and moaned as he lightly touched the tips of her breasts with one hand and undid the ribbons on her nightdress with the other, pulling it down.

Mathew's mouth touched her skin, and he began kissing her everywhere. "I love you, I always will," he was saying. Mathew parted Janet's legs and stroked her lovely long white thighs as she held him close, running her hands sensuously over his back.

They made love slowly and tenderly, bringing each

other to full pleasure, finding joy in each other's passion. "We're together even when we're apart," Mathew whispered. "No one, nothing can ever really separate us . . ."

Richard O'Flynn was acknowledged by his superiors at the Ministry of War as an ingenious spy and a chameleon of many disguises for His Majesty's Government, and by certain others as an extraordinary lover.

O'Flynn's old friend, Admiral George Anson, had once puzzled over O'Flynn's appearance: "Why don't you get old like the rest of us?"

O'Flynn had laughed and replied: "Adventure keeps you young—a change of venue or of personality adds years." It was true. In his time O'Flynn had been a sea captain, a soldier, a privateer, an Irish Catholic priest, an Anglican minister, an actor, a barrister, and a waiter. He had been in and out of prison, in and out of favor. But this year, this month—July 1754—Richard O'Flynn was in favor.

Nevertheless, at the moment Richard O'Flynn felt every one of his forty-five years. If things were going well in his profession, they were not going well at home. Not that Diedre could help being ill: his worry was anything but Diedre's fault.

Richard quickened his pace and caught a glimpse of himself in the glass window of a shop. Even though it was a distorted image, it revealed a tall, straight man, who boasted a full head of hair, graying fashionably at his sideburns. No, the age he felt this afternoon was not apparent in his appearance—his eyes still held a special glint and his skin was still taut and free of wrinkles. What he felt was an age of the soul, a weariness of the inner man.

Richard O'Flynn rounded the windswept corner and entered Grosvenor Square. Carriages in search of passengers moved lethargically around the cobbled square while restless horses gave forth with an occasional neigh as they shook their well-groomed manes and beat out a clockwork tune with their hooves.

Richard smiled to himself. Grosvenor Square was a façade! A façade just like his life, he reflected. Built by the famous architect William Shepherd, the group of homes on the north side of the square featured a grand pavilion centerpiece that boasted tall, graceful columns. They created the impression of being one great mansion, though they were, in reality, five separate and rather narrow houses.

Indeed, although the street was exceptionally wide and the whole area had a wonderful spacious quality, all the houses on the square were narrow. They all seemed to be what they were not. "Just as I seem to be what I am not," Richard said under his breath.

He surveyed the scene—the houses, the park in the center—and it was almost as if he were seeing it for the first time, even though he had lived in this aristocratic neighborhood for many years.

When Richard noticed the doctor's carriage outside his home, he bounded across the square and up the steps two at a time.

"Ellie!" Richard's voice boomed out as soon as he was inside, shattering the silence. In a moment, the scampering little maid appeared, a worried expression on her diminutive face. She made a quick half-bow and held out her arms to receive Richard's cloak. Like everyone and everything in the house, Ellie was disheveled. Strands of dark hair peeked out from beneath her white dust cap, and her face was drawn and pale.

"Doctor's here," Ellie motioned upstairs.

Richard turned quickly and climbed the winding staircase. He had summoned the doctor only an hour ago, though he knew he should have done it sooner. He had rushed home to meet the doctor, and now a sense of apprehension mixed with vague feelings of guilt filled him.

Diedre had developed the fever the previous evening and in the middle of the night became violently sick to her stomach. Half-asleep, Richard had gotten out of bed and fetched the chamber pot. Diedre had retched

17

violently into it several times, finally collapsing white-faced against the pillows.

"I'll fetch the doctor," Richard offered.

But Diedre was adamant. "It's nothing, nothing . . . I'll be fine in the morning."

In the morning Richard had risen and dressed. There was an important meeting at the Ministry. Diedre was nestled under the covers, and though she was still pale, her breathing seemed normal and her expression seemed peaceful. Richard had gone off to the meeting.

At midday, a messenger had arrived from home to tell him that Diedre was burning with fever. Richard sent the messenger to fetch the doctor and hurried to finish up at the Ministry.

Richard flung open the door of the bed chamber. His eyes fell immediately on Diedre, who lay against the dark covers, her face flushed with fever, her eyes closed.

"Diedre?" Richard reached the bed in four large steps. Diedre opened her glazed eyes and looked up at him.

"Diedre!" Richard sank to his knees alongside the bed and took Diedre's hands in his. She blinked up at him and then licked her dry lips with a thickly fur-coated tongue. Richard could feel an unnatural warmth in her hands.

He lifted his eyes to Dr. Monroe, who stood on the far side of the room by the window. The doctor shifted nervously from one foot to the other.

"What is it?" Richard questioned. "What's wrong with her?"

The doctor took his handkerchief out of his pocket and wiped his brow, then motioned for Richard to follow him out into the hallway. Richard bent down and kissed Diedre's burning cheek. "I'll be back, my darling."

Once in the hall, Dr. Monroe pulled the bedroom door shut. The doctor looked worn, Richard thought. And he somehow seemed evasive.

Dr. Monroe stared at the floor, seeking some neutral spot on which to focus. "I've sent for your clergyman," he mumbled.

Richard seized the doctor's shoulders, forcing the elderly man to look at him. "What's wrong with her?"

"Cholera," the doctor answered.

The word cut through Richard O'Flynn like a lethal sword. "Cholera!" Richard's eyes closed, his mouth was slightly open.

"I'm sorry," the doctor stumbled.

Richard rubbed his face with his hand. Cholera was the final pronouncement of a death sentence. Thoughts crowded his mind—there were things he should ask the doctor, things he had to say to Diedre! There were a thousand things to confess, a lifetime of duplicity.

"How long?" Richard asked, even though speaking the words sent a new wave of pain through him.

"A day, perhaps two . . ."

Richard felt the strength drain out of him. Diedre was dying.

"I suggest you summon the family," the doctor advised.

"The family" consisted of one daughter, Megan.

"Yes," Richard answered numbly. "I'll send for Megan."

"I've left what medicine I have with the maid," the doctor said, then feeling he ought to offer some hope, added, "There are some who make it."

Richard shook his head. Diedre would not be among them. She had been frail and unwell for years.

The doctor turned, and Richard watched him head down the hall and descend the stairs. As he turned to go back to Diedre's side, Richard was besieged with memories as well as guilt.

He had left Diedre many times over the years and he had been anything but faithful. There had been other women, women taken wherever he found them. There had also been one special woman—Janet Cameron. He had come close to leaving Diedre for Janet Cameron, very close indeed. But in his heart Richard had always nourished a special feeling for Diedre; it was something he could not define.

When they had been married, Richard had prayed for strong sons. But after Megan's birth, Diedre could have no more children and Richard had accepted that. Diedre had always been Richard's stability; she was the one person with whom he did not have to act, the one person with whom he could be himself.

He returned to the bed chamber and looked down into his wife's face. "Oh, my darling," he whispered faintly. Diedre's beautiful heart-shaped face was lined with pain, and her once coal-black hair was streaked with gray and damp with perspiration. Richard gently ran his hand down her long white throat. Diedre had wonderful skin, skin like porcelain. She had been like a doll, finely featured and beautifully proportioned, until age had overtaken her, age and illness.

Richard watched Diedre and cursed himself for even thinking of Janet Cameron. But what man was faithful? He rationalized his actions—he had been more faithful than most men. He had never flaunted a mistress before Diedre, never told her of the others, never caused her any pain. But his vocation had certainly caused her untold anxiety.

Richard lifted Diedre slightly and cradled her in his arms. "I love you," he whispered over and over.

Diedre opened her eyes and finally managed to speak. "Watch over Megan," she pleaded, then added, "I love you, too."

"You'll be fine," Richard lied.

Diedre shook her head weakly. "Don't lie to me anymore, I know this disease." Hot tears filled her magnificent blue eyes and rolled down her cheeks. She shook against him and her fingers dug into his sleeve. "I'm afraid," she murmured. "Oh, Richard, I'm afraid of death!"

CHAPTER II

June 28, 1754

The Monongahela River began in the western part of the Virginia Colony and flowed like a sinuous ribbon in a northerly direction for over one-hundred miles into Pennsylvania. There, the Monongahela joined with the Allegheny River to form the headwaters of the mighty Ohio.

The men of the Virginia Colony who had followed the Monongahela north called the area of its headwaters the Ohio Territory.

But the French, who had claimed the area in the mid-1600s, considered it part of New France. The French recognized its importance as a geographical link to the much larger region they also claimed—the Louisiana Territory.

In 1673, two canoes filled with *voyageurs*—water-traveling fur traders out of Quebec—had gone as far as the St. Francis River. Their leader had been the French explorer, Louis Joliet. Nine years later René Robert, the Sieur de la Salle, led another such group all the way to the delta of the Mississippi River. La Salle immediately realized the military importance of the delta so he claimed the entire Mississippi basin for France. From that time onward, fur traders based in Quebec traveled the rivers and established a chain of frontier forts and small settlements: Saint Louis, Saint Genevieve, Prairie du Chien, Fort Detroit, Fort Niagara, Fort Ontario, and Fort Duquesne, which was located on the fork of the Monongahela and the Allegheny. There were also French forts to the east, stretching all the way to Louisbourg. But despite the chain of forts that guarded New France and enabled the French to control the rivers, they had few settlements. The land was still empty.

"Possession is nine-tenths of the law," a Virginia leader intoned. And the Virginians were on the move. The Ohio Territory was the gateway to western expansion, or so it seemed to Virginia militiaman Christopher Gist.

Below Christopher Gist in the valley of the two rivers, the breezes of late June rippled through the long grass and rustled the leaves of the trees on the adjacent rolling hills. The fertile ground of the valley was still spongy and slightly muddy from the spring rains. But the air was fresh, the sky was clear, and the sun shined warmly in the clearings.

Militiaman Gist straightened up, sitting tall in the saddle and stretching. He and his Seneca Indian companion, Eagle Feather, had broken out of the deep woods and paused momentarily to listen. In the distance, they could hear the sounds of axes hitting tree trunks and the rhythmic humming of saws.

The two men were a study in contrast. Gist was tall with dark hair, thick dark eyebrows, and clear blue eyes. Eagle Feather was squat but broad of shoulder. His dark darting eyes took in everything at once, and he had heard the commotion of the woodsmen long before he and Gist had emerged into the clearing.

Eagle Feather motioned silently to the left. The noise came from some distance, from an area around the protrusion of the bluff where road crews worked to clear a path—an artery wide enough to accommodate

22

the ox-driven supply carts that carried food, men, and weapons north.

Wordlessly, Gist and Eagle Feather followed the sounds, letting out a holler of identification before they got too close to the tense men whose work carried them outside the immediate protection of the Virginia militia stationed at Fort Necessity.

As Eagle Feather and Gist approached, men with axes and saws scattered along both sides of the path. They shouted and yelled out greetings, for Gist was well-known and widely acknowledged as the "best damn scout around."

"What's happening?" one of the men called out. "Did you find the Frenchies?"

"Where are the Canadians?" another questioned.

Christopher reined in his big mare and paused long enough to greet Militiaman Henry Thomson, who was in charge of the road crew. Thomson stood in the middle of the path. Gist's intelligent-eyed chestnut mare twitched her tail.

Thomson looked up expectantly, petting the mare's nose to calm her. "What's your news of the Frenchies?" Thomson's face was drawn with fatigue. Like the others on the crew, he was hungry and apprehensive beneath his outward bravado.

Christopher made a motion with his head. "They're on the march, headed in this direction." Christopher glanced around. "Have our reinforcements arrived?"

Thomson frowned. "More men arrived, but not the food supplies to go with them. We're already short of flour. We'll go hungry if we get penned up."

Gist sucked his lip and shook his head. He had not brought Thomson the news he wanted to hear. Thomson in turn told Gist what he didn't want to hear. Reinforcements without added supplies were no good; they were practically an added liability.

Christopher Gist scowled. "I've got to deliver my news to Colonel Washington immediately. I suggest you and your men pack it in, head back to the fort."

With those words of advice, Gist let out his horse's

reins and nudged the ready animal. He and Eagle Feather galloped off toward Fort Necessity.

They weaved in and out among the hewn tree stumps along the would-be road. One had to keep a careful lookout for deep ruts, and on either side of the trail there were large rocks and boulders that stood like gaunt soldiers guarding these foothills of the Alleghenys. In the distance one could see the taller mountains looming up on the horizon; they cast deep purple shadows across the valley. The air carried the aroma of freshly chopped wood—hemlock, maple, birch. As Christopher Gist and Eagle Feather loped down the other side of the hill, Christopher's mind was clouded with the seriousness of the message he carried and he could not help wondering how the young colonel would react.

Gist had known Washington before his promotion. And to Gist's way of thinking, the youthful colonel displayed considerable arrogance when dealing with others—that special kind of official arrogance that bordered on pomposity. His conceit had grown in the weeks since he had received his field commission—that lovely little scrap of paper with the official seal that turned Militiaman George Washington into Colonel George Washington.

Gist's thoughts wandered back to the last time he had brought Washington a dispatch. It informed Washington of a "French presence nearby."

That was back in May when the spring rains still poured forth from the dark sky and the ground was rutted and muddy, so muddy that in some places a man could sink in up to his ankles.

Washington had taken that May dispatch and read it over and over. Then he had ordered forty of his men to prepare to move out of Fort Necessity by night. In the early morning hours of May 28, Washington and his men had surprised a group of French troops and attacked them without provocation. Ten of the French were killed, including their commander, Ensign Joseph

Coulon de Villiers de Jumonville. Twenty-eight others had been captured.

This "success" had left Washington with some dangerous misconceptions—or so it seemed to Gist. Washington seemed to believe he was able to do more than merely protect those who were building the forts. He toyed with the absurd idea of securing the entire Ohio Valley with only one-hundred-and-twenty men.

If Gist closed his eyes, he could picture the man now. Those pale blue eyes of young Colonel Washington would look down his nose, the long aristocratic nose that would always crinkle when Washington sniffed his brandy before lifting the glass to his lips. "The French can't fight!" he would intone. Washington had said it all too often. But he believed it even if Gist didn't. After all, the French had been surprised by the attack. The French and the Virginia Colony were not, yet, at war.

Gist shook his head and muttered as he speculated on the future. The advancing French troops offered a more serious threat than that group in May. Adding to this threat was a commander who underestimated the enemy. That could be fatal.

The two riders had been going downhill gradually, and as they entered the forested area, they continued to ride in silence. After a time, the forest receded, and as quickly as it had swallowed them up, it opened onto the vast grassy area called Great Meadows. The horses sensed they were close to home and put their heads down and surged forward down the rolling hill toward Fort Necessity.

Gist could see a single shaft of gray smoke floating straight up from the barracks. The fort had been constructed hastily, and four of its buildings were made of roughly hewn logs imperfectly notched together. The stockade and the ramparts, which might have offered greater protection, were incomplete, and the fort itself was badly situated on boggy ground with the forest stretching out and up on all three sides.

Gist swore under his breath. Every time he looked at

the insecure fort he felt sick. It was ill-designed, badly located, and incomplete. Washington could call it Fort Necessity if he wanted to, but Gist called it Fort Vulnerable. If the decision were his, Gist thought to himself, he would scrap the whole mess and start over. The ground was indefensible and just plain unhealthy: too damp, too dark, and too insect-ridden.

The noonday sun had begun to dry up the morning dew, and the grasshoppers and mosquitoes surged about. Eagle Feather had drawn up his kerchief to cover his face partially against the insects. Over to one side, there was a mud flat where hungry bloodsuckers swarmed thickly in spite of the early hour. They attacked both man and horse, sometimes flying straight into the eyes in their quest for tender flesh.

As they drew closer to the fort, Christopher Gist took off his hat and waved it in the air, yelling, "Scouts-a-coming!"

It was a precaution born of experience. More than a few returning scouts and their Indian companions had been shot by terrified, trigger-happy guards. Unhappily, the Virginians were good shots even when frightened. If they lacked judgment, they didn't lack skill.

Gist and Eagle Feather drew in their horses and looked up toward the sentry tower. "Scout Militiaman Gist to report to Colonel Washington!"

The answer that came from the sentry was unintelligible, but the gates of the fort were presently flung open, revealing stacks of unstored supplies and hastily erected tents, as well as too many horses tied to the hitching post near the water trough.

The fort was bursting at its unfinished seams. Three companies of Virginia militiamen and an independent company of regulars from South Carolina had joined Washington's one-hundred-and-twenty men. In a fort ill-constructed for its original inhabitants, nearly four-hundred-and-fifty men were crowded into absurdly makeshift quarters.

Eagle Feather sniffed. "Smells bad," he remarked, making a face. No one could argue with Eagle Feather's

26

observation. The fort reeked not only of human odors, but also of horseshit.

"You want to go?" Gist asked his Indian companion.

Eagle Feather nodded and turned his horse away. There was no need for him to stay, and Gist knew he would be more comfortable outside the fort, where a number of his brother Seneca were camped in teepees beyond the confining walls of the stockade. Eagle Feather turned once and raised his flat hand in a farewell wave, then disappeared.

Gist dismounted and approached Washington's headquarters, knocking on the crude wooden door. The door was opened by another militiaman, and Gist was ushered in and motioned to an inner room. He stood at attention on the threshold of Washington's office. "Christopher Gist, sir. I have urgent news for the colonel!"

Washington frowned slightly and lifted a finger to his chin, scratching it distractedly. With his other hand, he motioned Gist to a straight-backed chair. Gist knew the routine. There wasn't going to be any small talk first.

His hand still on his chin, Washington looked into Gist's face. "How many? And when do you estimate they will arrive?"

Washington's expression was inscrutably deadpan. His voice held no sense of alarm, only a damnable tone that seemed to be saying, "I don't know why you look so harried, Gist. I can handle it if you'll just get the facts straight."

Gist cleared his throat. "I would guess there are five-hundred regular militia and some two-hundred Indians."

Gist scowled as he tried to remember the date. He had been riding night and day along a circuitous route from Fort Duquesne. Time had become telescoped for him. "Is this June 28?"

Washington nodded, displaying his irritation. Gist might be a good scout, but Washington disliked him. Gist smelled like an Indian. He was most unmilitary!

"I would guess they would arrive about the third of

27

July—yes, it will take them about five days. My guess, sir, is that they certainly intend to attack—in retaliation for your surprise ambush, sir."

Washington pressed his lips together, and Gist could see that his superior had not missed the true meaning of his last statement.

"It was not an ambush," Washington corrected him. "It was a preventive aggression."

Gist frowned. What the hell was a preventive aggression? Calling an ambush something else didn't alter the facts of the action or the result.

Washington tapped the table. "You would guess five-hundred men and two-hundred Indians . . . you would guess they might arrive in five days . . . *Guess?* Gist, guessing isn't good enough!"

Christopher shifted in his chair. "Five-hundred regulars, two-hundred Indians. Five days, sir. It's not a guess."

Washington stood up and shoved his chair backward. He folded his hands behind his back and looked out the window into the yard of the fort. "Mind you, this will cause some problems . . ."

"Maybe even a war . . ." Gist mumbled under his breath, "a long war."

Gist watched as Washington folded and unfolded his fingers.

"Our regular food supplies haven't arrived yet." With those words Washington turned back to Gist. "I'll want you to bring in the road-building units and keep me posted on the Canadian position."

Christopher started to stand up, but Washington stopped him. "Not yet," he said in a low voice. "I still have need of you. The Canadian position will have to be marked out on the maps."

Washington summoned his militiaman and ordered him to fetch Major Muse, his tactician, and Captain Mackay, his aide.

They were obviously going to have a meeting, Gist thought. But not necessarily a meeting of minds.

Christopher crossed his long legs awkwardly. Major

Muse could be argued with; he was what Gist called a "paper soldier." Although a masterful tactitian, he was in an odd position. Muse had taught Washington, but now Washington was his commander and Muse was merely "invited to give his opinions."

Captain Mackay was a competent soldier, albeit a severely overworked one. He was in charge of the fortifications.

The two men entered the room and formally greeted Washington. They sat down at a wave of Washington's hand, while Washington remained standing.

Somewhat officiously, Colonel Washington repeated Gist's news. He left out the word "guess."

"Gentlemen, we are in a difficult position." Washington's words belied the placid expression on his face. "We are dangerously short of food, we are outnumbered, and our defense situation is inadequate."

Washington's eyes fell on Mackay. "I want you to shore up some defenses outside the fort. Both you and Major Muse should look to expanding—as much as possible—the protective walls."

"May I suggest we institute food rationing, sir?" Major Muse craned his neck as he spoke, like a bird about to take flight.

"That goes without saying, and you are in charge of those arrangements." Washington's reply was curt.

"What are our chances?" Mackay asked.

Washington stiffened. "They're as good as we make them. Let's go to work, gentlemen.

The meeting was over. Colonel Washington turned his back on his advisors.

Major Muse and Christopher left together. Neither spoke as they walked across the muddy ground between two of the buildings. Once inside, Major Muse withdrew his maps and spread them out on the table. Master tactician Muse and master scout Gist worked there for a time in silence.

"Five days unless they speed up their column," Christopher repeated. He had marked the trails he thought the Canadians would take.

"Hard to move faster in that country," Muse commented.

"What do you think?" Christopher asked.

Major Muse whistled through his teeth and shook his head. "This fort is in a mindlessly chosen location, we don't have sufficient food, and we've got over a hundred men down sick. Morale couldn't be worse."

It was far from the answer Washington had given. "A hundred men sick!" It was the first Gist had heard of illness, though he wasn't surprised.

"Malaria," Major Muse answered. "This is nothing more than a swamp, the air's unhealthy."

Christopher nodded in agreement. "I have to bring in the road crews," he said, turning to leave.

Major Muse looked away sadly. "More mouths to feed."

Within the hour Christopher Gist was on his way. As he turned around in the saddle, he could actually hear the buzz of activity as men moved out of Fort Necessity to dig trenches as a defense against the advancing forces.

As Gist passed within proximity of the Seneca camp, he could make out a different kind of activity. The Seneca were moving out. It was more than the fact that the French were coming—it was the Indians' recognition that the fort was vulnerable. The Seneca were too smart to defend this specific spot. Loyalty was one thing, stupidity another.

Then, too, the Seneca had special reason for evacuating before the arrival of the Canadians.

It had been a Seneca chief, Tanacharisson, who had allegedly killed the French commander, Ensign Joseph Coulon de Villiers de Jumonville, during the sneak attack in May.

Chief Tanacharisson felt that the coming battle would be fought hard because it would be a battle of pure personal revenge. The man who led the advancing Canadian column was, according to Indian informants, de Jumonville's brother, Louis Coulon de Villiers. The white man was sometimes a good ally—if he was winning—but losers were to be avoided.

Christopher slapped his horse. There was no doubt about it—the Seneca were going to cut their losses. "Too bad Washington isn't so pragmatic," Christopher said aloud to himself.

But Washington was not at all pragmatic. In fact he was astoundingly set in his ways for one so young. He had recently experienced the flush of unearned victory, and he still savored an unjustifiable sense of glory. A dangerous man, Gist thought to himself. "Yes, a dangerous man."

"What do you think?" Janet opened the door of the drawing room and ushered Robert in. He nodded approvingly. It was a large room with a huge window that let in the morning sunlight. The furniture was draped, but one could tell it was well-designed.

"It's got a beautiful little courtyard. The roses are in bloom, too." Robert followed Janet through the house and out into the enclosed garden. He smiled and showed his approval in the special sign language they used to communicate.

"René and Pierre can have one bed chamber, Madelaine and Helena one, Mat and Andrew one, you one, and Mathew and I the other. It's got just the right number of rooms!"

Robert's soft eyes followed Janet. Her face glowed with delight. "It's going to be my first real home! I mean my very own!"

They had been staying with Madame Deschamps since coming to Quebec City, but Madame was unwell. She couldn't tolerate the noise her own grandchildren made, never mind the added Macleod clan. "It'll be much better if we have a place of our own—Mathew will be home at the end of the summer and we'll need privacy."

"What about me?" Robert asked in sign language.

Janet hugged him. "You're one of us!"

Robert kissed her on the cheek affectionately, bend-

31

ing over to do so. He was so tall now! There was a time when he had to stand on tiptoes to kiss her. Now at fifteen, Robert was nearly six feet tall, and his shoulders had broadened too. He was every bit the strapping Highlander, and handsome too. Moreover, Janet's adopted brother was something of a genius. If he couldn't speak, he more than made up for his muteness with understanding. He had mastered written Latin and could lip-read English, French, two Indian languages, and his own native Gaelic. Now Robert was studying Greek, and his Jesuit teachers praised his intelligence.

"The people who own the house are French. They're going back to France and I can buy it. We're extraordinarily fortunate. It's terribly difficult to get a house in the upper city."

Robert shook his finger at her mischievously. "It's because you have so much gold," he told her in sign language. "Aren't you glad I saved it for you now?" he asked, moving his hands rapidly.

"Of course I'm glad," Janet said, taking his hand. Then she became serious, "But I'd spend it all to have you speak again."

Robert squeezed her hand and shook his head. As it was, she had consulted every doctor in Quebec and Montreal. But they all said the same thing—his voice loss had been caused by severe shock and only severe shock could bring it back. Somehow it had ceased to matter to Robert. In a strange way, he enjoyed his silent world, his world of books. Of course, he also enjoyed the outdoors. He had lived with the Indians for quite some time and learned their ways. He still went on trips with Indians and half-breeds. Fou Loup often took him away for a few weeks. On such trips his silence was not a difficulty; in fact, it was an advantage.

Janet showed him the room that would be his. Robert nodded approvingly. "I like it," he told her.

"Shall I buy the house then?"

Robert nodded in the affirmative.

"I can hardly wait for Mathew to come back!" Janet breezed through the rooms of the bright airy house. It was July! He'd be home in September! Janet was counting the days.

A jolting crack broke the predawn silence and another cow fell to the earth with a thud, its ungainly legs askew, waving in the air as the last bit of its life twitched a farewell.

Captain Louis Coulon de Villiers, brother of the ill-fated Ensign Joseph Coulon de Villiers de Jumonville, who had been killed in May, gave his riflemen the order to begin shooting the cows and horses that grazed in the field. "One at a time . . . be methodical!"

Mathew Macleod turned away as each shot was fired. It seemed senseless. He would have preferred to see the animals simply rounded up and led away. As it was, fine horses were felled without mercy and milk-giving cows were being shot even as they fed their calves.

"Is this necessary?" Mathew questioned.

"*Oui*, engineer," came de Villiers's instant reply. "Those animals are food for the Virginians. If by some twist of fate we don't take that fort, I fully intend to starve the bastards out!"

Mathew nodded. He knew that was the reason, but he still hated to see senseless slaughter. But that wasn't the half of it. He hated to see war beginning again. The English and the French! The French and the English! He began to suspect there would never be an end to it. Moreover, he saw things he had neither seen nor understood before. Both the English and the French used the Indians—much as they had used the Scots. Mathew had no intention of shifting sides, but he was feeling more detached about national rivalries. On the other hand, he had to admit he respected de Villiers's personal anger. This was not war—not officially. This was peacetime, and it was a territorial dispute. It was French territory—Canadian territory—and the Virginians were moving in. The soldiers from Fort Necessity had wantonly attacked the Canadians, killing many and taking others captive. It was an infamous sneak attack —a dishonorable attack.

33

"Who commands Fort Necessity?" Mathew asked de Villiers.

De Villiers shrugged. "Some young idiot named Washington . . . George Washington. He's a man without honor, no military sense!"

Mathew raised his eyebrow. "Are you so sure of our own military position?"

"Quite," the wily Frenchman answered. "I will have my revenge." Another shot was fired, another cow dropped.

Above them, large clouds moved in to obscure the sun. Mathew looked up. It was going to rain. One day, he thought to himself, I'll take part in a battle when it doesn't rain. Memories of Culloden rushed back, but Mathew quickly put them aside. The situation here was entirely different. For once, the side on which he fought had adequate men and superior arms. Besides, he had seen Fort Necessity. There was no way it could withstand a battle.

The French troops were beginning to move now. Mathew heard shots ahead of him, and a large drop of water landed on his nose. Both the rain and the battle had begun.

Propelled by a high wind, the clouds thickened and filled the sky. Within the hour heavy rain began to fall, creating great puddles and filling the trenches with rivers of water. Dug in a zig-zag pattern, the trenches were manned by miserable, soaking-wet soldiers who had watched as their cattle and horses were slaughtered one by one. Every single one of the animals had been felled by sharpshooters hidden deep in the thick woods. The action had given birth to two emotions: the Virginians were angry as they watched their precious food supply killed, and they were apprehensive as they came to realize that the Frenchies could shoot accurately.

"Where the hell are they?" The voice belonged to seventeen-year-old Jeff Crothers, who was frustrated and angry.

"Ruddy, hiding cowards! Hey, Frenchie, come on out! Hey, pig, pig, pig! Come on out!" Crothers was nothing if not loud-mouthed. The illiterate son of a Virginia backwoods farmer, he called the Canadians as a farm boy would call his pigs. He let forth with another insulting cry.

"Shut up!" Will Anderson muttered. Crothers fell silent. Anderson was a big man, and if he told you to shut up, you did.

The French had finished off the livestock, and they were emerging from the woods, firing on the fort and the trenches as they moved forward. They had positioned themselves on three sides of the fort, easily catching the hapless defenders in the crossfire.

Washington scowled into the pouring rain and assessed the situation calmly. He could see that his men were at a decided disadvantage because they were on low ground. But there was something more worrying—the powder was wet and the trenches were flooding as the water ran down hill.

Colonel Washington was jolted when a man was hit nearby, letting out a wail of pain.

"Colonel!" Mackay struggled toward Washington, panting and wide-eyed. "Sir, we're holding fast—so far. We've five dead, thirty-five wounded. If this rain keeps up—"

Mackay didn't finish his sentence. He let out a scream that seemed to coincide with the whoosh of the bullet that just missed Washington and hit him. The missile penetrated Mackay's shoulder deeply, and the gaping wound gushed and splattered Washington with strings of flesh and blotches of blood. Washington dropped to his knees, catching Mackay in his arms.

"Get some help over here!" Washington shrieked to a terrified fifteen-year-old militiaman. The young man came tripping through the mud over the fallen bodies of his comrades-in-arms.

"Are you all right, colonel, sir?"

"Fine," Washington grumbled. "Get this man out of here, get him help immediately!" The young man

35

struggled with the unconscious Mackay. In a moment another man arrived and together they dragged Mackay off toward the barracks where Dr. James Craik was busy patching up the wounded.

A low, distant roll of thunder added to the noise of the battle. It seemed to be coming nearer, then a bolt of lightning crackled through the air. Everywhere muskets were being fired.

Washington felt ill. The powder was soaked, including the powder for the stockade swivel guns. Wounded men were drowning in the trenches. The weather was as much an enemy as the Canadians; it was, in fact, an abomination.

The battle continued intermittently for hours till darkness fell, bringing with it an eerie silence that was broken only by the occasional moan of an injured militiaman or the sloshing of boots moving along the trenches as Washington's men took stock of their situation.

"There's all but mutiny inside the fort," a young militiaman reported nervously. "The sick are clamoring for medication, and some of the men have broken into the rum supplies."

Washington only mumbled darkly and began picking his way back to headquarters. Once there, he sat in the darkness and stared into space for a full hour.

"Colonel, sir!" Almost in a daze, Washington looked up. Mechanically, he leaned forward and lit a candle. Before him was the contorted, grimy face of Major Muse. "We're in a hopeless position," Muse intoned. "Wet powder, sick men, a poor strategic position, barely three days worth of supplies left, and more than nine-hundred men out there, picking us off one by one. You know the only reason they haven't stormed the fort?"

In a kind of sullen shock, Washington shook his head dumbly.

"Because their powder is wet, too!" Muse said.

The door burst open and a panting Christopher Gist

nearly fell into the room. "Beg your pardon, sirs . . . Colonel, Major . . ."

Washington jerked to semiattention. "You could at least knock, Gist!" Washington's voice was high-pitched as he reprimanded his scout.

"Sir, my apologies, but the French want to talk. There's a messenger waiting for an answer."

Washington summed up his last reserves. He replied in a somewhat haughty tone, "Wait outside for a few minutes. I will inform you of my answer."

Washington glanced at Major Muse as the door closed. Then he stood upright. "Well, is there any way out of this situation?"

Major Muse looked sullenly at Colonel Washington. He simply shook his head in the negative.

Washington turned away and peered into a dark corner of the room. "We must surrender then—the day is lost." He paused and turned back. "But I'll surrender only if we're accorded the honors of war, agreed?"

Again Muse nodded.

Washington strode to the door and flung it open. "Gist!"

Christopher Gist moved out of the shadows and stood before his arrogant commander. "Sir?"

"Tell the messenger to go and prepare the documents of surrender for me to sign. But tell them that though this day is theirs, I want to surrender with honor. You tell them that!" Washington slammed the door.

Gist was still smarting from Washington's previous rude rebuff. He turned to Eagle Feather and mumbled, "Defeated, but not humbled."

Gist stomped off into the night to meet the messenger, still mumbling and cursing under his breath at the utter stupidity that had brought them to this moment. Aggressive, indeed! Washington had been more than aggressive. Washington had committed a useless aggression against the Canadians, and now they were all paying for it.

As Gist trudged through the darkness, he speculated

on what the French might ask for. Gist knew the Canadians well. De Villiers would want some sort of revenge, at the very least. The Seneca were right about that.

Diedre clung to life for a few days, then slipped away during the night, her body yielding to the high fever. Her heart had simply stopped beating, and she had died without speaking any further to Richard, who never left her bedside.

Megan was there too, but she had remained sitting in a chair, her eyes closed against the reality of her mother's sickness.

It was no secret to Megan that her parents had a strange and special relationship. Not that they hadn't loved her or shared with her. On the contrary, both parents had lavished their attention upon her because she was their only child. But Megan could not deny that at times she felt like an intruder between them, and she had frequently felt the sting of her mother's disapproval.

At twenty-five, Megan Marta O'Flynn was her father's daughter in every sense of the phrase. She was tall like her father and had his black hair and glinting blue eyes. Megan was full-breasted with a small waist and full rounded hips—a stunningly beautiful woman who was physically strong and possessed a kind of emotional security. Above all, Megan was outrageously independent.

Over the years, Megan had rejected one suitor after another in favor of a career in London's blossoming theater. Clearly, Megan's mother had disapproved, but her father had not. He saw in Megan the consummate actress, and naturally Richard O'Flynn considered Megan's talent an inherited characteristic.

Now Megan lifted the teacup to her lips. She and her father sat at the table in silence. It was early morning, and the first rays of light were beginning to stream through the front windows.

The table was set with a fine damask cloth and

damask napkins in silver napkin rings. The silver glistened in the early-morning light, and the stark white china looked elegant. The table was set as it always was, even though the silence of mourning had settled over the house.

"You should try to get some rest," Megan suggested.

"I don't think I could," Richard O'Flynn stared into his teacup.

Ellie walked in silently from the kitchen and put a small pot of fresh tea on the table. She bowed quickly to O'Flynn. "Kippers this morning, sir?" Her voice was lower than usual, and her sad little brown eyes were downcast. Diedre had been her special friend and beloved mistress. Little Ellie had been crying, and even now as she served breakfast, she was struggling to suppress her tears.

Richard looked up at her and abstractedly patted her arm. "Are they already prepared?"

Ellie nodded in the affirmative, and Richard motioned her to bring on the kippers even though he had no appetite.

"I don't think I could rest," he said, returning to his conversation with Megan. "Too much to think about. For me, activity is the better medicine."

Megan sighed. "So you'll go on till you drop."

"I'll go on till I'm so tired I have to sleep."

Ellie came back and slipped the platter of kippers in front of Richard. The fish floated in a milky sauce and were garnished with green sprigs of parsley. As soon as she put the food down, Ellie was gone, audibly sniffing as she disappeared back into the pantry.

Richard looked into Megan's weary, drawn face. "You're the one who should sleep," he advised.

"I intend to try." Megan paused, then added, "I suppose what bothers me is all that was left unsaid. I keep thinking of all the things I should have said to Mother, things I should have done . . ."

Richard did not react immediately. Megan had expressed his own thoughts exactly. She is very much like me, he thought to himself. Megan was so outgoing that no one ever thought she might be burying her real emotions. Moreover, Megan's unusually deep voice projected an aura of intimacy, while her careful articulation of every word and phrase made one aware of her intelligence. There was a worldliness about Megan as well, a worldliness that Richard O'Flynn himself did not want to question or even think about. Regardless of how many beautiful women he had experienced, he could not think of his daughter engaged in sexual encounters, though he was certain she did have them.

Richard stood up abruptly. "I'm going to wash now," he announced. "I'll get cleaned up and then walk a bit before I go to the Ministry."

Megan watched her father casually wipe off his chin with the white napkin. "You're going away again, aren't you?"

Richard was startled by her unexpected question. She was more perceptive than he had given her credit for. And she was quite right, of course. He intended to ask for an overseas assignment immediately. But something in Megan's inflection seemed to be accusing him of running away rather than simply considering a new and long assignment abroad.

"Perhaps," Richard answered vaguely. "It's not entirely settled yet."

Megan stood up and leaned across the long table. "When it is, I'll want to talk to you about it," she said firmly.

"But you know I have commitments." Richard was suddenly aware that he felt and sounded defensive.

Megan arched a well-shaped eyebrow. "I may want to come with you," she announced.

"That's impossible! You know my work is dangerous!"

Megan smiled slightly. "Oh, I do know," she answered. "But I intend to go. In fact, I intend to become involved in your type of work." Her voice had become slightly coy. "Consider the possibilities, Father. Consider all of them."

Richard O'Flynn felt his breath grow tight. He had

spent virtually a lifetime protecting Megan and Diedre from his "work." Now Megan was standing before him, announcing that she intended to take up the same profession. And there was no question that his superiors would hire her. She had all the attributes of a good spy.

Richard cleared his throat and looked at Megan with cold blue eyes. "We'll discuss this later," he said, then turned on his heel and moved toward the arched doorway.

"The Covent Garden Theater is good training," Megan called after him.

CHAPTER III

July 3, 1754

Washington's headquarters had been tidied up and made as comfortable as possible. Chairs were placed around the long table, and even though brandy was offered all around, the assembled group remained ill at ease and stiffly formal.

On one side of the table, Colonel Washington sat in his full dress uniform, rigidly leaning forward on the edge of the chair.

To his left, a stony-faced Major Muse leaned back, puffing clouds of smoke into the air from his curved, Virginia corn-cob pipe. And on Washington's right, trying to find a more comfortable position in the straight-backed chair, a weary and bandaged Mackay shifted about, painfully aware of his throbbing shoulder and pounding head.

On the other side of the table, the aristocratic de Villiers sat quite relaxed and stared at his enemy, Colonel George Washington. The others in the room did not concern him; indeed, he would have liked to meet Washington alone—preferably with pistols drawn at forty paces.

Two of de Villiers's officers sat on either side of him,

and at one end of the table Captain Van Braam, Washington's interpreter, looked nervously from Washington to de Villiers.

At the far end of the table, Mathew Macleod watched Van Braam. De Villiers had brought Mathew as a second interpreter.

Van Braam cleared his throat. *"Est-ce que tu as amené les documents?"*

De Villiers crinkled his nose and looked slightly disgusted, as did his two aides and Mathew. Van Braam had only asked, "Have you brought the documents?" But he should have said, *"Avez-vous amené des documents?"* Obviously, Van Braam had learned his French in a brothel! One did not use the familiar pronoun *tu* in this sort of conversation, except perhaps as a rank and vile insult. But de Villiers knew full well Van Braam did not mean it as such; he was simply ignorant, his pronunciation gave that much away.

He can't speak French, Mathew thought to himself. And as Mathew knew so well, Frenchmen have a special love of their language. Every Frenchman would rather try to speak bad English than listen to his own language murdered in the mouth of a foreigner.

"Oui," de Villiers answered. He glanced toward Mathew. "Tell him in English not to use *tu*, tell him we're not lovers!" De Villiers laughed at his little joke.

Mathew delivered the message, and Van Braam flushed deeply.

"We have a fine interpreter in Monsieur Macleod. Perhaps it would be better to utilize his talents." De Villiers spoke in rapid French, and Van Braam looked duly confused.

Washington looked blankly from one man to another. "What's being said?"

"He said something about their interpreter, sir?" Van Braam offered.

Washington shook his head firmly and pressed his lips together. "Tell them I don't trust their interpreter and I want to use you!"

Van Braam sighed and fought his way through the

long sentence in French. He continued to use the wrong pronunciation, and his meaning came out a bit twisted. But de Villiers only shrugged philosophically. History could not accuse him of any wrongdoing. He had offered Colonel Washington a fine and honest interpreter, but the idiot preferred his own incompetent.

De Villiers leaned back in his chair. He was finished playing games. It was past time to get on with it.

"Did you kill my brother?" He spoke in French but looked directly at Washington. His question was abrupt, and his eyes flashed.

Van Braam was startled by the question, and he stumbled through his translation of it for Washington.

Colonel Washington straightened his shoulders, and his hands tensed on the table. Then in a haughty tone that could be understood in any language, he answered, "I led the attack during which your brother was killed. I therefore take the military responsibility. I only follow the orders of my superiors as you do!"

Van Braam translated. It was such a bad job that de Villiers turned to Mathew in frustration and Mathew retranslated.

De Villiers narrowed his eyes and glared at Washington. "My brother was on a peaceful mission. He didn't even bother to post guards! You and your men—men of supposed honor—attacked without provocation! It was a sneak attack—no more, no less than cold-blooded murder. You're a murderer, and the day you killed my brother, that day will live forever as a day of infamy!"

De Villiers had fairly spit out the words, and when he finished speaking, he extended the sheaf of papers toward Washington. "Sign the surrender and admit you are an assassin!"

Van Braam struggled with the de Villiers ultimatum, fine beads of perspiration breaking out on his forehead.

Washington followed Van Braam's translation, his eyes constantly shifting from de Villiers to Van Braam. He scowled and clenched his hands together. "Assassin?" He bolted up. "I am not an assassin. I'm a soldier!" The scowl on his face deepened. "I did not kill your brother. He was a casualty of battle."

"But you led the surprise attack! We are not at war, therefore you killed him!" De Villiers was insistent.

He wants his pound of Washington's flesh and he wants it now, Mathew thought to himself.

"Assassinat!" De Villiers muttered.

Van Braam tried again, then paused, thinking over the words. "Sir," he interjected, "I believe *assassinat* means something else in French. I think it has . . . well, other connotations."

Washington unclenched his hands and began tapping the table with his fingers.

"May I," Mathew put in, intending to correct Van Braam's misunderstanding.

"You may not!" Washington snapped. "We are not fools! We are educated, and we have our own interpreter!" He shot Mathew a nasty look, and Mathew only smiled and shrugged. If the man wanted to misunderstand so badly, he felt no further obligation to let him in on the truth.

"What else does he want?" Washington wanted it over. All of it.

De Villiers patiently waited for the translation, even though he understood full well what was being said. Then he slowly read out all the terms of the surrender while Van Braam did his best.

"And we are to take our men—those who are still alive and the wounded—and we are to leave this territory flying full military colors."

Washington let out his breath. The government in Williamsburg wasn't going to like this, but what choice was there? This at least was surrender with honor. There would be no prisoners.

"I want to see the papers." Washington reached out, took the papers from de Villiers, and quickly leafed through them. Written entirely in French, he could understand nothing, but his eyes still fell on the word *assassinat.*

"You're sure this means something else?" he questioned Van Braam.

"Oh, yes sir. It has a broader meaning . . . I think it means *death* or *killing*, and covers a number of ways in which . . ."

Washington nodded and cut Van Braam off with a wave of his hand. He handed the papers to Van Braam. "Check them," he said wearily.

Van Braam's eyes traveled the pages, then he handed them back to Washington. "They seem in order, sir."

Washington spread them out and withdrew the quill from the ink pot. Ceremoniously, he scribbled his name on the papers and handed them back to de Villiers.

Crisply, de Villiers handed them to his aide. The French then stood up and marched out of the room in cold military fashion.

Midway back to their camp, de Villiers turned to Mathew and smiled. "You're a man of honor," he said. "Let it not be said that you didn't try to stop that bastard from admitting his guilt."

"They'll still say he signed without understanding," Mathew answered.

De Villiers made a slight face. "It's not my fault that the ignorant idiot doesn't speak one single civilized language and that his interpreter has the understanding of an undereducated child. I did offer him an interpreter . . . several times. My, my—so untrusting, these men of the Virginia Colony!" De Villiers laughed deeply under his breath. "Assassin! Colonel George Washington has admitted—in writing—that he is an assassin. He is self-confessed! Now if he would only admit to his own stupidity and lack of judgment."

"Perhaps he'll learn from this experience," Mathew offered.

"Not likely," de Villiers argued without the slightest hint of charity in his voice. "Those kind never learn."

Back in his quarters, Colonel Washington sat dazed. "I had no other choice," he muttered over and over.

"I'm going to resign my commission! I wasn't made for this!"

"Nonsense," Major Muse answered.

Washington doubled his fist and banged it on the table. "Well, as God is my witness, let me tell you this . . . I'll never get trapped by the enemy again! I'll never fail to lay in sufficient supplies! I'll never lose another battle!"

Major Muse didn't say anything. It was a bad promise for a soldier to make, and doubtless it would be impossible to keep.

The French had encamped on high ground and, together with the Indians who rode with them, had set up makeshift lean-tos, tents, and teepees. The rain two days earlier had long since sunk into the ground or run downhill. The ever-present mosquitoes remained, but were kept at a distance by the over one-hundred campfires that burned, each one sending billows of smoke into the air because the wood was still damp.

The guards posted for night duty moved about the camp, but they were relaxed and obviously felt secure. Colonel Washington had surrendered, and now these woods and this territory belonged to the Canadians and their native allies.

Mathew rolled over on his back, snuggling into his bedroll and inhaling the odors of the camp that even now, long after the troops had been fed, included roasting meat.

Mathew searched the bright night sky for the dog star and the bear star. A wave of nostalgia swept over him as he recalled his trip with Running Fox and his painful initiation into woodsmanship. That experience was standing him in good stead, he thought.

"Our destiny is in the wild country of New France," Mathew mumbled to himself as he savored the night air and the clear bright sky. In Quebec City there were too many Frenchmen—not natives of the colony. Unlike the Canadians born in Quebec, who no longer thought

47

of themselves as French, those born in France were administrators who attempted to transfer Paris society to the banks of the Saint Lawrence.

Fleetingly, Mathew wondered if it was the same in the English colonies. Did men like Washington still consider themselves British? It was a difficult question to answer. Certainly Washington acted British, assuming British ways—much more so than the Canadians assumed the ways of the French.

Mathew thought to himself that he would like to get away from Quebec City, and he recalled the large tract of land he had surveyed near Fort Niagara. It was just the right kind of place—a sort of crossroads where traders came and went and where the land was fertile enough for farming. Mathew made a vow to investigate the possibilities of obtaining the land.

I'll have to write tomorrow, he thought to himself. There was no way he could go back now. He thought of his assignment to Fort Duquesne. There was going to be a war, of that he was now certain. As Mathew closed his eyes, he imagined Janet and the children. She would be so upset when she found out he couldn't be back at the end of the summer. "Soon," he said, barely moving his lips, "soon we'll be together." But in his heart Mathew was not sure how soon.

Upstairs, Janet's three young children napped peacefully, while the Deschamps children played together out in the garden. They had become a single family. Madame Deschamps, the children's grandmother, was growing old and had left the Deschamps brood to Janet, who had taken care of them for over six years. Maurice, their runaway father, still lived in Montreal with his mistress, Antoinette, and visited only now and again. He still drank heavily, but not when he visited the children. His mother would tolerate neither his drinking nor the crude Antoinette. Maurice was a man both bitter and resentful. Nonetheless, he was willing to let Janet and Mathew act as adoptive parents to his children. He had been given the choice between his mistress and his children. Maurice had chosen his mistress.

"How long has it been?" Janet asked, trying to make conversation. "Two months, three?"

Maurice shifted in the deep-cushioned chair and avoided looking at her.

He has aged, Janet thought to herself. His once-dark hair was now flecked with gray, and in spite of his elegant attire, his round paunch was quite visible beneath his vest. His face was lined, and he looked dissipated and thoroughly worn.

Maurice Deschamps lifted the teacup to his lips and made a slight face. He preferred brandy, but Janet never served him alcohol since once he began drinking he didn't stop till he passed out.

"Three months," he admitted. "But the children don't seem to have changed much."

It was Maurice's perception that he meant nothing to his children. "But they miss you," Janet insisted. "They should see you more often."

"I'm not good for them," Maurice said, looking away.

"Good for them or not, you're their father!" Janet felt her irritation growing. Maurice did not believe what he was saying. He simply didn't want to be bothered. Moreover, his daughter Madelaine reminded him of Louise, and that caused Maurice to become bitter and morose each time he saw her.

Maurice ignored Janet's chastisement. He leaned back and looked Janet straight in the eye. "I'm going to see Louise on this trip."

Janet's mouth opened in surprise, she was truly taken aback. Louise was hopelessly insane and confined to a hospital. Maurice had not visited her in years.

"Whatever for?" Janet blurted out.

"To confront her," Maruice answered tartly. "I'm seeking a Church annulment to our marriage."

Janet leaned over and plunked her cup down on the table. "They're difficult to obtain—if not impossible!"

Maurice shook his head. "Money talks . . ."

"This is not France, Maurice. The clergy are not so corrupt. The Jesuit influence is strong. You were wed to Louise in sickness and in health, remember?"

"I can have no life!" Maurice whined. The color rose in his face, and he pressed his lips together.

Janet leaned back and tried to think. She reminded herself that no matter what Maurice had done, he too had suffered and was a victim of a cruel fate.

"If you got the annulment, what would you do?"

"Marry Antoinette, of course."

Janet shook her head in understanding. "And the children?"

"I would like you to adopt them—officially. I'd still visit, of course."

"Of course," Janet retorted coldly. She knew Antoinette did not like the children and the children did not like her.

"I know you don't approve," Maurice said defensively.

"It is not I who have to approve." Janet looked at him evenly. "I suppose I understand," she finally allowed.

Maurice mumbled his garbled thanks and sipped some more tea. "I'm apprehensive about seeing Louise . . . It's been so long."

Janet looked at Maurice seriously. "You'll find her much changed." It was an understatement that Janet cursed herself for making. She had visited Louise only a few months earlier; the woman was a horror beyond all description.

"I'll feel better when it's over," Maurice admitted as he stood up. "You see . . . it's a sort of formality. I have to go and see her so I can say I did . . . so I can testify about her reaction to me."

"Of course." Janet held out her hand, then added, "Maurice be careful."

She watched in silence as Maurice put on his jacket and prepared to leave. Louise Deschamps had gone mad after the Indians had attacked, tortured, and raped her—the same night Robert had been kidnapped and lost his voice for all time. Since that dreadful event six years ago, Louise had tried to kill every man who came close to her.

Hôtel de Dieu de Quebec was one of two hospitals in Quebec City. Founded in 1637 by Maire-Madeleine de Vignerot, Duchess d'Arguillon, it was a large stone building operated by bustling nuns who swept down the corridors with silent sullen efficiency, looking neither to the left nor to the right. The Hospitaliers Augustines de Dieppe who tended the hospital were a strict and unyielding group of women.

Maurice sighed as he followed the unsmiling nun along the first-floor corridor. The hospital had survived over one-hundred years and was still served by the same cheerless sisters who seemed to produce a new generation of unhappy frowning faces every year. From behind closed doors, one could hear the moans of the ill. The building smelled like all hospitals, vinegary with a hint of turpentine.

"She's confined on the very top floor," the nun informed him curtly.

Maurice nodded. It was a gray building populated by gray people. The only relief came from the wide white wings on the hats worn by the sisters. They flopped back and forth as they walked, giving the nuns the appearance of giant black and white birds sailing in for a landing. Holy geese, Maurice thought to himself.

They reached the top floor, and Maruice stopped to catch his breath. The nun turned back to look at him disapprovingly. "Monsieur should get more exercise," she suggested in a cold, clinical voice. "Three flights of stairs should not make a young man pant so."

Maurice ignored her. The top-floor corridor seemed even narrower than the one on the first floor. On either side of the hall, there were heavy, bolted doors with great steel bars.

"Are there many people up here?"

"Only the ones possessed of the most violent devils—the hopelessly insane."

She beckoned him to a door at the end of the corridor. Then with a key on a large ring that dangled from her waist, she undid the lock on the latch and crossed herself.

"It's unwise to see her alone," the nun warned. "She's extraordinarily violent. We can't even groom her, no one gets close to her."

"I want to see her alone," Maurice persisted. "I'm her husband."

"I really can't take the responsibility," the nun hedged. "Let me send for some attendants."

Maurice shook his head. "No! I pay you to keep her here and I demand to see her alone!"

The nun took a step backward. "As you wish," she replied sullenly. "I'll remain here. Knock twice on the door when you want to leave."

Maurice slid the long steel bolt and let himself into the darkened room. He heard the nun pull the door closed and replace the bolt behind him.

Maurice blinked, adjusting to the dim light. The room was dank and smelled of urine and feces. The only light came from a tiny slit about seven feet up the wall; since it was late afternoon, the room was heavily shadowed.

In the corner, huddled like an animal, Louise sat on the edge of her cot. Maurice blinked again. He shivered at the sight of her.

A great mass of dark tangled hair framed her hideously contorted face. Louise's once lovely dark eyes were sunken deep in her head and surrounded by great bluish circles. Her nightdress, tattered by her own extremely long fingernails, failed to cover the drooping, yellowed breasts that still bore the scars of her torture. Around one of her ankles was a great chain that was attached to the wall. On the floor, an overturned cup and an empty plate evidenced a recently consumed meal.

"Louise?" Maurice tried to keep his voice soft. He took a step toward her. "Louise, it's Maurice." He

52

took another step and watched her face. She moved farther up against the wall, her hands buried beneath the coarse wool blanket that covered the cot.

"I want to talk to you, Louise. I had to see you, see for myself . . ." Maurice's voice trailed off. She looked less than human, and as he came closer, he could see a great swelling abscess on the upper part of one thigh. Apparently lanced, it poured forth a thick greenish liquid.

Regardless of how inhuman she looked, Maurice thought her facial expression was one of fear, not hatred. He moved a bit closer, and when she didn't make any movement, he sat down uneasily on the end of the cot.

"Do you know me, Louise?" Maurice reached out a hand to her—a surge of sympathy passed through him. She had once been so beautiful! But there was no beauty left, only the fear of a caged animal.

Suddenly Louise withdrew her hands from under the blanket. Her long yellow nails were like sharp daggers. She seized his extended arm and sunk her nails into his flesh, ripping it.

Maurice let out a cry of pain as he tried to wrench his arm loose, but Louise lunged at him from her crouched position, letting out a subhuman shriek as she sunk her sharp teeth into his leg. Blood spurted forth from it as Maurice staggered to his feet, trying desperately to push her away. But Louise was all arms and legs, filled with mad strength. It was as if she had been saving her energy for this moment.

Louise's eyes were huge black pools that glittered with sheer animalism. Poised for another bite, her mouth was open, blood and spittle drooling from it. She let go of his leg and spit as if she were spitting out the taste of him. She made another subhuman sound and fell on his neck with all her might, again sinking her teeth in, clawing at his clothing, kicking wildly, and making guttural sounds from deep inside her throat.

Maurice let out a scream, then drew back his arm and

53

hit her. Louise staggered momentarily and fell back against the cot. Maurice ran for the door.

Louise quickly recovered and threw herself at him, waving her arms and making noises like a cat in heat. But her leg chain would only allow her to go so far. She stood, half off balance, and flailed her arms in the air, moving her fingers like the claws of a gigantic ocean crab.

Maurice wiped his neck with his hand. Blood poured forth, and for a second he thought he might faint. Then with his last ounce of energy, he pounded on the door and screamed, "Let me out of here! Let me out of here! In the sweet name of Jesus, open this door!"

The latch moved with maddening slowness, then the door swung open and a wounded Maurice Deschamps staggered out.

"She's inhuman, she's no better than an animal!" Maurice was grunting and panting. He felt dizzy, and the nun in her black and white garb seemed to sway before him. Maurice tumbled to the floor, his face ashen, his legs no longer able to support his bulk.

When Maurice opened his eyes again, he was in a white room on a white bed, being examined by a host of birdlike angels with gray faces. Around his neck was a large bandage. Smaller dressings adorned his legs where Louise had made a series of scratches as well as taken one good-sized bite.

"I warned you," the old nun said. "I told you not to get too near to her. She's very dangerous, possessed of a vile devil!" The nun crossed herself.

"You could get a serious infection from a human bite," one of the younger nuns intoned. "But we've washed it out and bandaged it, so you might be all right."

Maurice did not need to be told. He could feel the stinging vinegar. It felt as if it might burn through his neck and leg.

"Why don't you trim her nails? She has nails like daggers!" Maurice looked at the nuns accusingly.

The old nun wrinkled up her face and looked at him quizzically. "We can't get close enough to her," she answered finally. "She's a devil!"

"She's gotten worse! Will she always be that way?"

"We pray for her," the Mother Superior answered blandly. "We've had her exorcised repeatedly. We've given her all the medications available. We used to bleed her regularly." The Mother Superior shook her head. "What more can we do? There's no hope!"

Maurice caught on the nun's words, and in spite of the pain of his wounds, he sat upright and reached out pleadingly to the Mother Superior. "Will you write a letter to the bishop explaining her condition? Tell him how she attacked me! A woman should not attack her own husband! And you admitted it yourself, you said she was possessed!"

Maurice could not see clearly, but he sensed the change in the nun's tone of voice when she spoke. It was cold and without sympathy. "And for what purpose do you ask me to write to the bishop about these matters?"

"I want an annulment!"

"I think an annulment is out of the question."

"That's not for you to decide," Maurice shot back with irritation. "Will you write the letter?"

The Mother Superior paused. "Well, I'm not certain it would be wise."

Shrewd old witch! Maurice thought to himself. The Mother Superior was the first of several hurdles he would have to overcome. She was, to say the least, an exasperating woman. "I might see my way clear to making a donation—a sizable donation—to your work," Maurice said evenly.

The Mother Superior's eyes seemed to grow wider, and Maurice saw the glimmering of interest in them. "Perhaps forty louis d'or?"

The nun's mouth tightened. "Sixty," she said coldly.

Maurice was again dizzy and his head throbbed, but he nodded his agreement and sank back against the white pillows. "Sixty," he mumbled in dejection. "May God bless your work," he added with a hint of sarcasm.

George Anne Bellamy was younger than Megan O'Flynn by nearly five years, but even if they had been the same age, they would still have been years apart in maturity. George Anne passed herself off as seventeen, though in reality she was twenty.

George Anne would eternally be a "girl." She was small of stature, but well-proportioned with high full breasts. She was a flirtatious little minx whose chief education was in the art of coquetry. Her hair was a mass of golden curls, and she had limpid blue eyes that were perpetually wide, giving the impression that she was always surprised or delighted. In spite of her fair skin and light hair, George Anne had carefully made-up, dark eyelashes, which she fluttered often and always at the right moment.

A good deal of George Anne's command of the art of male entrapment had been learned from her mother. In her time, Dame Bellamy had been a fine actress as well as one of London's finest hostesses, albeit for an exclusive group of gentlemen and young ladies of dubious reputation. The gentlemen were members of the British military establishment—generals and admirals—and some dottering members of the House of Lords—elderly men whose great wealth rivaled their senility—plus the occasional spy, if he or she was in good social standing.

The ladies had ranged in age from sixteen to twenty-eight. Their function was to offer discreet ears for conversation, warm smiles for the maintenance of egos, and sympathetic and patient bedroom companionship to those men whose physical abilities were on the wane. In the latter endeavor, George Anne surpassed all. And for the best ladies the rewards were excellent: money, power, position, and influence.

Dame Bellamy's house on Brewer Street in Soho was a necessary establishment, a place where important men could discuss important matters without fear of having their conversation repeated. It was also a place where such men could fully enjoy themselves without fearing discovery or censure.

Megan O'Flynn and George Anne Bellamy had met in the theater, for both were actresses. But Megan knew a great deal about George Anne before they actually met. She knew about the house in Soho because her father was a frequent visitor, and she knew that George Anne's mother, Dame Bellamy, had once been the mistress of Colonel James O'Hare, Baron Tyrawley, who was at the time of their liaison Ambassador to Portugal and was said to be George Anne's father.

Dame Bellamy, George Anne, their influential friends, and the house in Soho had become a matter of fascination for Megan, and it was with some determination that she set out to find out more by befriending George Anne. It was not a difficult task. Both Megan and George Anne were Irish, both in the theater, and both young and extraordinarily attractive. It was, Megan concluded, only a question of time. Megan considered herself to be the perfect type of woman to help entertain at Dame Bellamy's and her judgment was correct.

On Saturday, August 31, 1754, Megan was invited to George Anne's for the first time. It was an invitation she accepted eagerly.

At seven P.M. Megan's carriage drew up in front of the three-story house on Brewer Street. Through the louvered glass windows, Megan could see the flickering candles, and from the front steps the animated voices of the guests could be heard. Megan knocked.

The butler admitted her, silently taking her fur cloak and motioning her toward the large drawing room where some twenty men and women mingled while they sipped their before-dinner drinks.

George Anne floated up to Megan, an older gentleman clinging protectively to her bare arm. Her blond curls were arranged on top of her head, but a few spilled down to caress her neck. She was wearing a light blue taffeta gown with a daring neckline that only managed to cover the nipples of her ample breasts, leaving little to the imagination.

"Oh, I was afraid you wouldn't come!"

"I'm a little late," Megan apologized. In fact she had come late intentionally in order to make a solitary entrance.

"This is Megan O'Flynn. Megan, let me introduce General Braddock."

Megan smiled and extended her hand. The general took it and bowed, planting a somewhat damp kiss on the ends of her fingers. Megan looked at General Braddock with interest. George Anne spoke of the general often, and she was proud to be his current mistress. A gentleman of great prestige, General Edward Braddock was sixty. He was overweight and had a face that might have been carved from stone. An excessively long straight nose, a narrow mouth, small eyes, and a bald head beneath his powdered wig all combined to give him an air of austerity. In terms of appearance General Braddock had little to recommend him to a beautiful twenty-year-old. But General Braddock was a prime player in the new game of empire. His prestige was growing with British military power and influence—a power and influence that extended from India to North America and would soon be strengthened and expanded.

General Braddock's smile was reserved for women. "Another stunning beauty," he announced appreciatively. "Let me present you. O'Flynn? O'Flynn? You wouldn't be any relation to the Chameleon, would you? Richard O'Flynn?"

Megan laughed lightly. "I'm his daughter," she answered in a throaty voice.

"My God! Where's he been hiding you?"

Megan did not answer his rhetorical question, but she did allow him to guide her to the side of a young officer, one who was unaccompanied and for whom, she guessed, she was meant. George Anne had a way of working these things out in advance.

"Lieutenant-Colonel James Wolfe, may I present Miss Megan O'Flynn."

Lieutenant-Colonel Wolfe bowed formally and kissed Megan's hand, but it was a far different kiss from the one General Braddock had given her. It was a peck, and she instantly knew he was a shy young man as well as a gentleman with considerable military decorum.

Lieutenant-Colonel Wolfe was rather thin and pale. He was fine-featured and fine-boned with light blue eyes. He stood stiffly, as if he had been called to attention and no one had followed that order with those vital words, "At ease."

"May I get you a drink?"

"Yes, please," Megan answered. Wolfe turned and went to get a glass of wine from a nearby table.

"You'll like young Wolfe," General Braddock assured Megan. "He has interesting tastes for a soldier—different."

With that, General Braddock turned instantly to George Anne. His arm immediately encircled her while his eyes fell on her cleavage. Megan wondered if the poor general would make it through dinner.

Lieutenant-Colonel Wolfe returned with two large glasses of rosé wine. "Do you wish to stand, or should we sit down?" He shifted nervously as if he were unused to talking with women.

"We can sit," Megan answered. They moved together toward a settee and sat down. Megan snuggled up in one corner, smoothing her gold brocade gown as she did so. Wolfe sat on the very edge of the cushion and looked at the tips of his black boots.

"Do you like poetry, Miss O'Flynn?"

"I love poetry, I'm an actress."

Wolfe looked up at her with some interest as well as consternation. Megan knew why. Actresses, for the most part, had reputations. Indeed, most of the women present were actresses. Just being at this gathering had certain implications. Wolfe looked like a man who had been dragged here by friends who had probably told him, "It'll be good for you, just what you need." He had no doubt hoped that he would be paired with a less experienced woman. At the moment he certainly did not look like a man seeking a bed partner. Wolfe appeared to be something of a challenge. Megan smiled to herself. She liked challenges.

"What poets do you like?" Megan asked, seeking to put Wolfe at his ease.

"Thomas Gray," Wolfe replied with a distant look in his eyes.

Ah, Megan thought to herself, a lieutenant-colonel with a sentimental, romantic bent. An unusual soldier indeed.

Megan and Wolfe continued their discussion, while the various couples around them grew more friendly with one another—embarrassingly intimate in some cases.

Here a young officer held fast to the knee of a pretty red-headed child of sixteen, there a young man allowed his hand to rest on a brunette's well-rounded buttocks. And as one might have expected, George Anne and General Braddock disappeared. They were, in fact, not far off. As Megan would later hear in great detail, General Braddock had taken his "pet" downstairs to the deserted game room where he sunk his large hands down her dress, begging her to relieve him instantly from his constant hunger for her. That the dear girl had accomplished on the billiard table, her head resting on its cushioned sides, her eyes fixed upon the multicolored balls.

By nine, a number of couples had gone to seek a modicum of privacy, and those who remained in the drawing room had grown somewhat drunk. Even Lieutenant-Colonel James Wolfe had begun to relax. He now leaned back on the settee with his arm around Megan's bare shoulders.

"What are you doing here?" Richard O'Flynn's voice was strained as he tried to keep it even.

Megan was startled. She and Wolfe had been deep in conversation, and she had not heard the front door open nor seen her father stride across the room in long purposeful steps.

Wolfe's arm swept back into his lap in one swift movement. The pale, young lieutenant-colonel looked like a child who had just been caught with his hand in a forbidden cookie jar. Wolfe knew O'Flynn by reputation and he also knew that the man was not the type to be amused with finding his daughter in a brothel, even an upper-class brothel. A few people nearby stopped talking to watch the little drama unfold.

Megan met her father's eyes and smiled. "I might well ask you the same thing," she answered coolly.

Richard glanced around the room and noted the sudden silence. It was neither the time nor the place for an argument. He had come on business, though he was hardly adverse to pleasure. He could not insult any of the men or women in this room by insinuating that Megan should not be here. She was, after all, twenty-five. Still, he had not expected this. Certainly he did not think of his daughter in the same way he thought of the other women who frequented this house.

Richard O'Flynn was well aware that his face had grown red and that his lips were pressed tight. "I think we should have a talk, Megan." He had lowered his voice, and he thought he sounded reasonable and controlled.

Megan stood up and smoothed her golden dress. It clung to the curves of her body and accented her full breasts and rounded hips. If I were objective, Richard thought to himself, I'd have to admit she's the most beautiful woman in this room.

Wolfe also jumped to his feet, almost as if he were standing at inspection. Somewhat awkwardly, he held out his hand. "Lieutenant-Colonel Wolfe," he stuttered.

"Richard O'Flynn," Richard answered curtly. How does one greet a man who only seconds before was relishing a night in bed with his daughter. He turned away from Wolfe. "I imagine we can find a place to talk. Isn't there a game room downstairs?"

Richard O'Flynn placed his hand on Megan's arm and led her away. "You'll excuse us, Wolfe." He said it without turning around.

As they entered the dimly lit billiards room, a startled General Braddock was just doing up his pants. George Anne was still sitting on the edge of the table.

Megan could not suppress a smile, but her father's reaction was less than amused. "You should lock doors if you want privacy," Richard said tersely as he took in the scene.

General Braddock looked up stupidly—like most men with their pants down, Richard thought to himself. George Anne giggled.

General Braddock turned and lifted George Anne down from the table. "I expected to see you here," he said to Richard coldly, "but not till later."

"I should like to speak with my daughter in private," Richard answered, ignoring Braddock's weak come-back.

General Braddock finished stuffing his ruffled shirt into his breeches. "We'll speak later about your assignment." With that, he took George Anne's arm and guided her out of the game room. Then looking back over his shoulder, he added, "The door doesn't have a lock!"

"Lost your sense of humor, Father?" Megan walked around the billiard table and picked up a cue. Artfully, she struck one of the balls, which in turn struck another that sank into a side pocket.

"Do you know what the ladies who visit this house do?"

Megan didn't look up. She was seeking another shot, another ball she might sink. "I supposed they go to bed with important men. Like you."

Richard shifted from one foot to the other. "Yes—and what are *you* doing here?"

"What are *you* doing here?" Megan repeated.

Richard expelled air through his lips. "I'm going to North America on a mission—I have things to discuss with some of these men."

Megan still did not look up. "I'm going with you," she answered. "One might even say I'm going to help you."

Richard closed his eyes. "You can't do that, it would mean—"

"It would mean I might have to act the way you do."

"You can't."

Megan straightened up and looked straight into her father's eyes. "I can and will. I come by this profession naturally, and I expect to do quite well at it. I also intend to enjoy myself. In exactly the same ways you have always enjoyed yourself."

Richard could not ignore the flash of Irish temper he saw in Megan's eyes. "At least I'm single," she added with some sarcasm.

Richard leaned against the table and sunk his fingers into its cushioned sides. He felt defensive and wanted to cry out, "But I always loved your mother!" He could not say it. He opened his eyes, looked at Megan, and suddenly thought he was seeing her for the first time. She was beautiful, intelligent, defiant, and headstrong.

"I suppose I can't stop you," he said weakly.

"Absolutely not," Megan answered.

Richard only nodded.

"I think I'll go see to Lieutenant-Colonel Wolfe," Megan purred. "One does need practice." She picked up her long skirts and sailed out of the room without so much as a backward glance. When the door had closed behind her, Richard picked up the cue. Taking it firmly in both hands, he cracked it in two. The grand plan was to conquer a world, and he could not even control his own daughter!

CHAPTER IV

September 1754

Louise crouched on her filthy bed and tried to make out
the details of her cell in the darkness. She drew up her
feet automatically when she heard the scampering on
the floor. The horrid little vermin had come again to eat
the crumbs of her dinner. She shivered and whimpered
in the dampness.

She could hear them—they were all around her in the
darkness. They always came at night. Pairs of little
eyes, sharp threatening teeth, and short, cold, little legs
that sometimes ran the length of her body as she slept.

Abstractedly, Louise began pulling at her chain.
Something dropped to her bed with a thud, and she
reached for it quickly, afraid that it was one of the
vermin. But it was not. It was cold and solid—a lump of
the old wall had crumbled. Louise felt it curiously, and
then began to use it to pick at the wall about her chain.
The chain plate eventually loosened, Louise tilted her
head and felt the plate as it moved first to the left, then
to the right. In an instant, she was back at it, scraping
the crumbling stone with her nails, prying loose the
heavy plate that bound the chain to the wall. She

gripped it tightly, and with one strong pull, the plate came loose in her hands.

She sat very still for a moment and contemplated her situation. Then she cried out hoarsely, "Water! Water!"

Louise waited and then called out again, this time more loudly. "Water!" Her cry echoed down the long corridor.

Louise got up from the bed and crouched behind the door. Presently she saw the dim light of a candle and heard the shuffling approach of the old nun on night duty. She would open the door and shove some water within Louise's reach. It had happened before, but tonight it would be different.

Louise listened as the key turned in the lock and the bolt on the outside of the door was slipped.

"Water!" Louise called out again.

"Hush!" came the irritated voice from the other side of the door. "I'm bringing it! No need to wake up everyone!"

Louise smiled to herself.

The nun opened the door and ventured in. She carried the candle in one hand and the water in the other.

Louise jumped the old woman from behind and forced the sharp-edged chain plate into her gaping mouth, turning it viciously from side to side as she pulled the chain around the nun's neck and choked all the life out of her. The nun did not even scream. The plate cut her mouth and stifled all but a few low guttural sounds. Then Louise released her victim, and the old woman fell to the floor with a thud, blood pouring from her mouth. One sharp corner of the plate had punctured the roof of the nun's mouth.

Louise stood up and kicked the body with her foot. It didn't move. Louise groped in the darkness for the extinguished candle, but it was nowhere to be found. She stopped looking for the taper and began fumbling in the darkness with the keys that hung about the nun's waist. She tried each in turn, seeking the one that locked the length of chain to her ankle. She found the right one on the fourth try and immediately freed herself from the shackle, putting it instead on the nun's leg.

Then Louise stood up and thought. She glanced out the door. There was no one in sight. Quickly she bent down and began undressing the nun. Just as quickly, she discarded her own rags and put on the nun's habit. Then fastening the keys to her belt, she slipped into the corridor, closed the door, and bolted it shut from the outside.

The corridor was empty, and Louise sailed down it, then down the winding staircase that led to the ground floor. There she paused and with an uncanny instinct made her way into the supply room. In the dim light Louise spied a row of lovely sharp scalpels. She picked up the largest and turned it over in her hand, admiring the blade. Then she turned and headed for the door.

Louise Deschamps ran down the steps of the hospital with her habit skirts lifted. She inhaled the night air and danced around three times in a great circle as she made her way across the front lawn. "I'm free!" she sang out to herself as she disappeared into the trees.

Janet lifted her skirts so as not to trip on them. The uneven cobblestones made climbing the steep hill to Madame Deschamps' house more of a misery than it might ordinarily have been. Quebec City was a very vertical place, and the richer one was, the higher one lived—literally.

Janet stopped momentarily to catch her breath. Leaning against the side of the building, she called out to the Deschamps children who skipped merrily ahead of her. "Wait up! Another few moments won't make any difference. I promise you, we won't be late!"

Pierre Deschamps, age ten, René, age nine, and Madelaine, age seven, stopped dead in their tracks and looked back at Janet.

"Can we help you?" Pierre called back.

"No!" Janet's lilting laugh rang through the air. "I'm not an old woman!" She waved them on, smiling as they darted about, playing their games behind the steps of the stone houses—hiding from one another, then appearing again like magic.

Janet began to trudge up the hill again. It was warm! Unusually warm for September. The sun was bright, and it reflected off the glass windows of the fine houses with their black wrought-iron fences and little balconies.

Janet sighed. She thought of Mathew for a brief moment and wished he were here. Madelaine's birthday would have been much nicer had they all been together.

Her own three children were still at home. They were still too young to walk from Janet's newly acquired house to Madame Deschamps' house on the hill. Robert would bring them later in the carriage.

What would I do without Robert? Janet asked herself. Especially now that Mathew wouldn't be coming home as expected. Silently she prayed it wouldn't be too much longer.

"Papa is already there!" Madelaine's voice called Janet back from her reverie. Maurice's carriage was indeed outside the house. He had returned to Quebec for Madelaine's birthday, and Madame Deschamps had agreed that Antoinette might also come for this occasion. It was a bitter compromise for the elderly woman, and she only made it for Madelaine's sake.

Maurice, now recovered from his visit to Louise, had simply refused to come without Antoinette, and so the "infamous whore," as Madame Deschamps called her, had also been invited.

"I can see the carriage," Janet called to Madelaine. Janet quickened her step. "Wait for me!" she called out again. The three children paused at the bottom of the steps and waited for Janet to reach them.

"Oh, what a climb!" Janet gasped. "Your grandmama lives on the steepest hill in Quebec City. Straight up one side and straight down the other!"

67

Together they climbed the steps to the house. The three children huddled close around Janet as she knocked lightly on the door.

No one answered.

Janet tilted her head and listened. She heard no approaching footsteps. She knocked again, this time more loudly.

"Madame Deschamps!" Janet called out. It was true that Madame was deaf, but surely her nurse Marie heard the knock. And if not Marie, Maurice and Antoinette were certainly not deaf!

"Maurice! It's Janet and the children!"

"Try the door," Pierre suggested. "Perhaps they're all upstairs or out in the courtyard."

It occurred to Janet that Madame might not be well. The old woman was often ill these days, and indeed, that was the reason why Janet had moved out of her house and taken the brood of young children with her. Madame simply could not cope.

Tentatively, Janet placed her hand on the wrought-iron door handle and pressed the latch down. The door swung open and Janet poked her head inside. "Maurice! Madame!"

Perplexed, Janet stepped into the foyer followed by the three children.

"Where can they be?" Pierre asked.

Janet shrugged. "Somewhere," she answered vaguely. Aware that something was not right, she fought the sense of foreboding that suddenly filled her. The three children stood in the hall, and Janet opened one of the large, oak double doors leading to the parlor. Looking into the room, she let out a gasp and slammed the door, falling against the wall and turning white. Janet's hands automatically went to her temples. "Oh, my God!" she cried out. The sight she had seen was staggering.

Pierre reached for the door handle, but Janet seized his wrist fiercely. "Don't open that door!" she shrieked, then shook the startled youngster. "Pierre!" she said urgently. "Don't ask questions—go quickly for the militia! Take your brother and sister with you! Get out of this house! Go now!"

René's mouth was wide open with an unstated question, and Madelaine's little face was knit in a frown. "But it's my birthday!" she protested. "I want Papa and Grandmama!"

"Not now!" Janet said firmly. "Do as I tell you! Go with your brother!"

Pierre was shaken by Janet's sudden command and the stern look on her usually tranquil and patient face. He took René's arm and Madelaine's hand. "After you fetch the militiamen, go home! Go home and stay there till I come!"

Pierre opened the front door and led his siblings out of the house. Janet waited till they were safely out onto the street. Then filled with horror, she again opened the door to the parlor.

There, sprawled in the middle of the light blue carpet, was Marie, the little nun who was Madame Deschamps' nurse. She was on her back, her thin white throat slit from ear to ear. Her clothing was drenched in blood; the red slime still oozed from her neck, soaking into the rich carpet. A large candelabra was overturned, and a vase of flowers had been thrown against the wall. Bloody footsteps led out of the parlor and into the dining room.

Janet stood frozen as she took in the terrible scene. Robbers? That was the only thought that crossed her mind, but she could see that the silver was still in place—the expensive urn, the tea set, and the goblets were undisturbed. Robbers would have taken them.

Janet listened but heard no sound. "Maurice!" She shrieked his name. His carriage was out front! He and Antoinette must be here! "Madame!" Janet's voice echoed through the house.

Nearly in a trance, Janet followed the bloody footsteps into the kitchen. When she opened the kitchen door, she shrieked again.

Antoinette's lifeless body had been flung face up onto the table. Her head was resting in Madelaine's birthday cake, and her throat was slit, too. Moreover, Antoinette's assailant had not stopped at just killing her. Her green dress was shredded, and her full breasts had been slashed to bloody ribbons of flesh.

Janet fell against the wall and shook. Antoinette almost seemed to have been murdered and partially devoured by some wild animal. In spite of her own terror, Janet moved toward the back staircase. There, lying on the steps, was Madame Deschamps, face down and spread out on the bottom five steps, a series of bloody wounds perforating her back.

Tears filled Janet's eyes at the sight of the old woman who had helped her so much and had been her friend for so long. She knelt beside Madame Deschamps. "Oh, Madame!" was all Janet could say as she hugged the old woman and cried. Janet felt herself going numb, growing cold with shock.

"Maurice is upstairs if you want him." Janet jumped at the sound of the low guttural voice behind her, then quickly rose to her feet and whirled around. Her tear-filled eyes grew wide, her mouth fell open.

Before Janet stood a vision of pure horror—Louise Deschamps in a tattered nun's habit splattered with blood. Her long dark hair was a wild mass of unruly tangles, and her face was contorted with her round mouth twisted into a sardonic smile. Her skin was white, and her dark sunken eyes flashed with madness. In her hand she held a long, glistening scalpel tightly.

In an instant, Louise's mad laughter filled the kitchen. It was animalistic, high and hysterical like the cries of a cat caught in a trap.

"Louise," Janet gasped.

Instantly, Louise ceased her mad laughter and her face returned to the contours of hate. "Maurice is upstairs," she repeated. They were the words she had spoken before, but her voice sounded farther away, as if only her body was in the kitchen while her mind wandered over things past. "But he can't see you," Louise said.

Louise turned the scalpel over in her hand and

70

looked at its blood-stained blade. "I've cut his eyes out," Louise whispered. "Now he can't see you anymore, he can't see anyone." Louise's tone belied her murderous intent. She sounded almost childlike and sweet. Then as if suddenly jolted back into the present, she looked at Janet with a stony stare. "I'm going to kill you, too," she said with detachment.

Janet stood absolutely paralyzed as Louise began her steady advance, the scalpel pointed directly at Janet's stomach.

In the same instant that Janet saw Louise swing the scalpel outward to make her first slash, she heard a distant male voice cry out. Then she vaguely heard a scream and was aware that it was not her own. The world went gray, then blackened.

General William Augustus Cumberland, the Duke of Cumberland and son of King George II, lifted a pudgy hand and straightened his white wig of tight little curls. His face was red from a recently quaffed goblet of brandy, and his white ruffled shirt was straining at the seams over his puffed-out stomach.

General Edward Braddock was Cumberland's senior by nearly twenty-six years, but Cumberland was the commander by virtue of birth. Braddock had served with the duke in the suppression of the Jacobite rebellion back in 1745–1746. Cumberland had only been twenty-four then. He had already been overweight, Braddock thought to himself, but now eight years later, he was obscenely fat—a bad example of self-discipline for his troops. Braddock quite naturally thought of himself as "portly"—portliness being a condition common among upper-class men of fifty-nine, a badge of fine taste in foods and liquor. But the duke was a slob—there was no denying it. There was also no getting around the fact that he was the king's son.

At General Braddock's right at the long oak table was the round-faced, thirty-year-old Lieutenant-Colonel Robert Clive. On one wall was a gigantic map of the world. Cumberland was standing, pacing up and down in front of it. He rubbed his sweaty hands together and looked steadily at the two officers.

"It's a bold plan," he intoned solemnly. Clive tilted his chair back and grunted. It hardly mattered what the duke was saying—Clive always grunted. Robert Clive was a wealthy man. A poor man who had done the same things he had done would surely have been hung by this time. Braddock hated the son-of-a-whore. He had bought his commission just as he bought his respectability. Braddock himself was not rich—every penny he possessed he had earned, and he had earned his commission as well. Clive was an arrogant young whipper-snapper. He would become a general by purchase rather than by performance.

"The colonists in British North America have entirely too much to say. We desire to bring them more into line, under greater control."

Cumberland was looking directly at Braddock. "They squabble among themselves too much. What's needed is a firmer hand. I intend to provide it. Braddock, yours is the most important assignment ever given a British general. It will give you more power than any British soldier has ever had in the colonies."

Braddock lowered his eyes to the table and tried desperately to look humble. "I'm honored," he mumbled. Of course they were going to give him this assignment. Who else was there? God only knew the defense of the colonies against France had too long been in the hands of incompetent colonials who had no real military education or training and no sense of military decorum. A few of them had achieved lucky victories over inferior French forces, but luck could not be counted on forever. It was time for a British general to take charge and whip things into shape.

"You will be commander-in-chief of all His Majesty's forces raised, or to be raised, in America. You will be in direct contact with London and with our spies in both France and Canada."

Braddock shifted again. "Raised and to be raised?

72

How many British troops will I be taking to form the basis of the army?"

"Two regiments," Cumberland answered. "And of course, you will command all the colonial troops."

"I doubt they'll be much help," Braddock said under his breath.

Either the duke did not hear his comment or he chose to ignore it. "Pitt and I have discussed it thoroughly," Cumberland ambled on.

Then he turned with a sweeping gesture and wiped his fat arm across the map. "Colonies will be just that in the future—colonies! The British living in Boston, in Philadelphia, and in Williamsburg must all come to realize that they're British and that for the good of Great Britain, they'll be united under one general. After all, they exist to supply us with needed imports."

The duke turned to Clive. "Naturally, your assignment in India is no less important, Clive."

Braddock felt his own resentment rise. Cumberland was all too casual with Clive and obviously regarded him as more of an equal than Braddock. And their assignments reflected that as well. Braddock was getting a nice chunk of prestige, but Clive was going to have the opportunity to make millions in India— trading under the table, so to speak.

"This, gentlemen, is the beginning of an empire!" Cumberland's little pig eyes narrowed. "They will no longer say, *pax Romana*. They will say that all roads lead to Whitehall, to London!"

Janet opened her eyes and looked into Robert's concerned face. She shook her head, and the rest of the room began to come into focus. Louise lay crumpled in a corner. Robert's Indian knife had been thrown with great accuracy from across the room, and it had sunk deep into Louise's shoulder. Although the wound oozed blood, the knife kept it from bleeding profusely. Louise's eyes were closed, her mouth wide open.

"Is she dead?" Janet asked.

"Only unconscious." The strange voice belonged to a burly militiaman, a member of the home guard. His face was ashen, his mouth tightly drawn. "Holy Mother of Mary, this is the most grisly crime I've ever witnessed! *C'est terrifiant!*" The militiaman crossed himself reverently and rolled his eyes heavenward.

"She should have a doctor," Janet suggested, indicating Louise.

The militiaman turned to Janet in amazement. "She's a murderess! She's killed her husband, her mother-in-law, that woman . . ." he waved vaguely toward the kitchen, ". . . the nurse, and one of the Holy Sisters at the hospital!"

"She's insane, she's been in the hospital for years . . ." Janet protested.

"She's possessed!" the militiaman replied. "She'll be tried for murder!"

Janet felt both faint and nauseated as the horror of the afternoon returned to her. The house reeked of blood and death. Janet's eyes seemed to glaze over again—she was on the verge of passing out or retreating into a catatonic state. "She's insane," Janet kept repeating.

She sat up, still leaning heavily against Robert, who helped her to her feet. "She's insane!" Janet said again, collapsing against Robert's shoulder. She began to sob and shake again.

"I feel sick," Janet sobbed. Then suddenly jarred out of her distraction: "My God! Oh, my God! Where are the children?"

Robert patted her arm. "Home, safe . . ." He spoke the words hesitantly, slowly forming them with his lips.

Janet lifted her head from his shoulder and stared at him. "W-what?" she stuttered, her eyes seeking his.

"Home and safe," Robert repeated. His strong arm supported Janet, and she suddenly understood— Robert had spoken!

"You can thank this young man that you're still alive." The militiaman was shaking his head and look-

ing about the room, the look of disbelief still on his
face.

"He's my brother," Janet said, returning her head to
his shoulder.

"We'll have to ask you some questions later, but you
can go now."

Robert nodded and swooped Janet into his arms. She
closed her eyes and leaned against him. Robert was
taller than she and broad of shoulder. He had grown
dramatically in his thirteenth year and now possessed
the same kind of marvelous physique as his Highland
relatives. As he carried her to the waiting carriage, she
was suddenly aware that they had changed roles. For so
many years he had leaned against her, but Robert the
child was now Robert the young man, a source of
protection and comfort. As she had led him away from
the horror after Culloden, he was now leading her away
from this house.

As Robert placed Janet on the plush seat of the
carriage, she looked around dumbly. More militiamen
were arriving, and the narrow street was filling with
curious neighbors as well as the onlookers who habitu-
ally followed the law officers wherever they went.

As they drove away, Janet felt hypnotized by the
sound of the horses' hooves on the stone streets. Her
mind was a dizzy muddle, still filled with the horror of
the last hour.

"You're sure the children are all right?" Her voice
sounded far away to her, and she looked at Robert with
wide eyes.

"I had brought them," Robert said slowly, "but
when we met Pierre on the way down the hill, I sent
them home with the driver."

Janet shook her head. It was strange to hear Robert
speaking. His voice sounded as if it were coming from a
million miles away. When Louise was coming at her,
Janet had heard a man cry out. . . .

"I heard you . . . just before . . ." Janet's voice
trailed off.

Robert nodded. "Yes" was all he said.

Tears of relief and sadness streamed down Janet's face. It was a miracle that Robert's voice had been restored, but it had happened at a moment when there could be no rejoicing. All Janet could think of was the Deschamps children—what could she tell them? How could she protect them from knowing what had occurred? Their mad mother had killed their father and grandmother! How does one tell little children something like that? But they would have to be told something, they would hear it from other children, they would be a spectacle on the streets of Quebec City!

The carriage drew up in front of their own house, and Robert jumped out of the carriage and lifted Janet down. As much as Janet knew she could count on Robert, she felt a sudden pang, a need to have Mathew to hold her, to take her away from Quebec City.

The Duke of Cumberland paced before his map, carrying a long pointer. General Braddock followed him with his eyes.

"Your first objective—and it should be an easy one for a trained British general commanding British regulars—is Fort Duquesne." Cumberland tapped the map, indicating a mark at the junction of the Allegheny and Monongahela rivers. "After that is disposed of, the Virginians think you should take this place, uh . . ." Cumberland paused. "Fort Niagara." He pronounced the word with difficulty. "And when you do, change the name." Cumberland cleared his throat. "In fact, change both their names to something British."

Braddock nodded wearily. The duke was often quite tiresome. Braddock felt like standing up and stretching, but Cumberland was not to be put off. He was going to stand there and continue to outline strategy even though Braddock had already thoroughly familiarized himself with the situation.

"There's something else," Cumberland said, frowning. "Something we consider important. But for reasons of colonial dissension, it ought to remain part of the British secret plan."

Braddock looked up, trying to disguise his boredom. "The Atlantic Coast?"

Cumberland grunted, and as he did so, several of his chins jiggled. "The capture of Fort Beauséjour. You are not to undertake its capture yourself. You are to correspond with and remain in direct contact with Lieutenant-Colonel Lawrence, who is currently in command of our troops in Nova Scotia. You'll see that he's reinforced with seven hundred or so colonial troops."

Braddock mumbled his reply. Parting with colonial troops hardly seemed like much of a sacrifice.

"Now only if there is some reason why Lawrence can't carry on are you to consider going to Nova Scotia yourself . . . understood?" Cumberland raised both eyebrows. Again Braddock nodded.

"Lawrence in Nova Scotia and Shirley in Massachusetts ought to be given full rein—they should have no difficulty wiping out the Canadians! Your job is to placate the Virginians by securing the Ohio Valley."

"Politics, politics," Braddock replied with a faint smile. "The colonists have been allowed to go far too long on their separate paths. No discipline!"

"Differences of opinion between our own colonies is not altogether negative," Cumberland reminded the general. "Let us remember Scotland!" Cumberland's eyes lit up when he mentioned his greatest military success. "After all, it was the division of the Highland Clans—a division that separated the Campbells and the MacDonalds—that made total British control of Scotland possible. Sometimes . . ." the Duke had a faraway look in his eyes, "sometimes it is easier to control the sum of the divided parts than to hold power over a united whole. Indeed! Let that always be the British motto: Divide and conquer!"

Braddock took in Cumberland's words, but he did not try to understand what the pompous duke was saying. After all, they were only talking about taking a few undermanned, small French forts—ye gods! The French didn't even have any regular troops in New France. Their entire defense system was based on home-grown militia and a bunch of ignorant savages. At least the British colonial militia would now have good British regulars and the advice of a British general—no, not just his advice, his supreme command! The Duke of Cumberland was too ponderous. That was it—not only was he fat, his mind was fat. But it was necessary to remain on his good side. Braddock mentally congratulated himself on his own forbearance. After all, he now had a most important assignment. Perhaps *the* most important assignment.

Cumberland temporarily retired from pacing in front of his map and seated himself at the end of the long table. His chair was wider than the others in the war room. It had been specially constructed to accommodate his bulk.

"Brandy?" the duke offered. "Shall we drink to your success?"

"Please," Braddock answered.

He watched as the duke poured two goblets of brandy from the silver decanter that sat on the silver tray at the end of the table. The duke handed Braddock an amply filled goblet.

"To your success!" the duke offered.

Braddock's eyes went back to the wall map. His gaze moved slowly from Nova Scotia down the coastline, then westward across the continent all the way to the Pacific. A huge portion of the map was labeled "Canada" and colored blue for the French. Another vast section was also colored blue. This was the Louisiana Territory. In the south and in the whole vast area of the unknown southwest, the map was colored a pale yellow for Spain. Braddock's eyes then fixed on the Virginia Colony. Unlike the other colonies, it had no western border. Black arrows pointed westward from Virginia and northeastward up the Monongahela River.

"Let's drink to people who don't draw borders," Braddock said, smiling.

The Duke of Cumberland immediately grasped Braddock's meaning.

"To British North America!" he replied, tilting his goblet toward the map. "All of it!"

Louise's trial began on December 1, 1754. As Janet had feared, the trial attracted a great deal of attention. The "infamous murderess" was the topic of all conversations.

Louise had been proclaimed possessed, and therefore the civil authorities had turned her fate over to the Church. Had Louise been an ordinary murderer—one who had killed while committing robbery, for instance—she would have been tried in a civil court. But madness was not judged an illness—it was judged the work of the devil and therefore fell under the jurisdiction of the all-powerful institution that together with the French crown governed New France.

The Ursuline Convent was an austere brownstone building. It was normally a girl's school, but for Louise's trial, it's main hall had been converted into a courtroom.

Despite the inclement December weather, the large hall of the convent was unbearably hot and stuffy. It smelled foul from the throngs of curious people who waited long hours to gain admission. Moreover, there was constant noise as people mumbled, chatted, and pointed.

Periodically, the courtroom was stunned silent as the hideous rag-clad woman in her iron cage let out a horrible scream or the shriek of a wild animal. Sometimes Louise Deschamps shook the bars of the cage and laughed hysterically before letting loose with a barrage of curses.

"A witch!" one woman would whisper to another. "A sorceress! A devil!" another intoned self-righteously.

Janet huddled up against Robert as if to bury herself in his sleeve. The sight of Louise in the iron cage was horrible, the comments of the onlookers cruel and stupid. Robert's face was contorted with pain.

"I can't stand this," Janet whispered, shaking.

Robert's hand covered hers, squeezing it gently. "It'll be over soon."

"Madame Janet Macleod!" Janet was startled as the officious voice of the priest rang through the air, bringing the noisy throng to silence. It seemed to Janet that every eye in the hall turned to look at her.

"You wish to speak for the defendant." The priest's voice was cold.

Janet staggered to her feet and took a tentative step forward. She felt the amazed stares of the assemblage on her. A slight buzz went through the crowd as she pushed her way forward, trying not to look at the ghoulish spectacle of Louise Deschamps in her iron cage.

Janet said a silent prayer for strength. She felt this ordeal would never end. First there was the publicity and the gossip! She had kept the children out of school, away from the ugliness of wagging tongues and pointing fingers.

When Janet reached the front of the courtroom, the priest led her to a makeshift witness stand. Previously, several of the militiamen had testified as well as the Mother Superior and three nuns from the hospital. Janet trembled as she looked out on the sea of curious faces, faces that looked twisted and hateful to her. Her eyes settled on a woman in the back of the hall who had actually brought her children. The woman was unwrapping food and handing it to them! It was like theater to her! The onlookers seemed to have no sense of the reality of Louise's suffering or of the magnitude of the suffering her madness had caused.

"How long have you known the possessed woman?" the priest's voice was flat; it seemed to come from far off.

"Six years," Janet answered. Her own voice also sounded distant and far away to her.

"When was she possessed?"

Janet looked dumbly at the priest. He was an all-black specter with a gray stone face. He didn't possess the rosy-faced kindness of the parish priest in Trois Rivières. He did not look like a man filled with the compassion of God, but rather like a man filled with anger and wrath.

Janet inhaled and steadied herself against the rail. "She's not possessed," Janet answered. There was a hum of negative comment through the room, low, hushed. "No, no . . ."

Janet met the priest's eyes. "She's ill. She's been ill since she was raped and tortured by the Indians."

The priest did not contradict Janet directly. "So she was possessed at that time." It was a flat statement. Janet opened her mouth to protest, but the priest spoke first.

"What is the duty of a woman to her husband?"

Janet looked at him and was aware that a flash of anger must have been visible in her green eyes. She knew perfectly well what he meant.

"Well?" The priest tapped on the wooden rail.

"To bear children," Janet answered, frowning, "and Louise did that."

"But not after her possession." The priest was hammering home his point.

Suddenly Janet felt as if she were alone with this man. The others in the room momentarily disappeared for her. She leaned forward.

"What is the duty of a priest?" she asked coldly.

The priest stared at her and arched his eyebrow. "The duties of a priest are many . . ."

Janet didn't wait for him to go further. "One duty is to show God's creatures—*all* God's creatures—compassion. Louise Deschamps is sick, she's terribly ill! She's not responsible for what she did. She doesn't even understand what she did!"

The priest moved back and ran his fingers along the folds of his cassock. He ignored Janet and looked past her toward the audience for approval.

"She is then possessed," he said flatly. "And she

81

would have killed her children just as she would have killed you. You sent her children away, didn't you?"

Janet nodded and another ripple of sound passed through the assembly.

"If she is harmless, why did you send the children away?"

"I didn't say she was harmless," Janet protested, realizing that she was on the verge of exasperated tears. "I said she was ill, not responsible."

"And what would you have done with this murderous, possessed woman?"

Janet looked at the priest and shook her head. She knew full well how Louise had been kept—it had probably driven her even more insane. "I would have her confined," Janet admitted, "but looked after with love and compassion . . ."

The priest folded his hands. He turned slowly away from Janet. "You're a good woman," he said, putting emphasis on the word *good*. "But you do not understand the dangers of possession."

He turned back to her. "You may step down."

Janet looked at his face and knew that he had chosen not to understand what she was saying. His mind was already made up—as were the minds of the people who buzzed as she walked back to Robert. There was no saving Louise. They wanted to punish her.

"Take me home" was all she could say to Robert. "Oh, please take me home."

Three days later, Robert brought home the news. Louise Deschamps would be hanged and her body displayed for twelve days in her iron cage. "Across the St. Lawrence at the crossroads near Pointe-Lévy," Robert explained.

Janet fought back her tears. "It's barbaric—it's inhuman!" Janet could no longer hold her tears as the tension of the past weeks drained out of her even as she made her resolution. "I must leave here," she said, looking at Robert. "I can't stand it! The Deschamps children can't stay here!"

82

Robert's strong hand was on her shoulder. "And you miss Mathew," he added.

Janet looked up at Robert with tear-filled eyes. "And I miss Mathew," she confirmed.

Robert pressed his lips together. "It's rough country —they say there'll be war with the British."

"There's always war with the British!"

"I'll take you," Robert volunteered.

"In the spring," Janet said with conviction. "I'll write to Mathew tonight."

CHAPTER V

December 1754

A cold December wind swept the streets of London. The sun hadn't shone for days, and it had rained more or less constantly, cleaning the streets of the contents of emptied chamber pots and freshening the air.

In the lavish bedroom of the house on Brewer Street in Soho, a fire still flickered in the hearth and a single candle burned in its pewter holder on the bedside commode.

General Braddock lay spread out on the bed in his white nightshirt, his gangly, hairy legs extended from his white boxlike figure. He was propped up against four puffy, down-filled pillows, watching the wiggling toes barely visible over his own paunch. The room was still surprisingly warm. The heat from downstairs still filled the upper reaches of the house. The guests had departed; his farewell dinner was a thing of the past.

In the adjacent dressing room, General Braddock could hear his beloved little girl, George Anne, changing into her nightgown. There was the occasional tinkle of bottles, and the aroma of her perfume drifted into the bedroom. His anticipation grew with every passing second, and he could close his eyes and envisage her before her mirror, running the silver brush through her darling blond curls. General Braddock twitched.

"Are you going to blow out the candle?" her voice almost sang from the next room.

Braddock frowned. "Not tonight!" he called back. No, this was his last night with George Anne before leaving for North America, and he decided that for once he would insist on some light. Ah, why did women always prefer darkness?

"You're a shameful person, Teddy," she stepped out of the dressing room and glided to the end of the bed. Braddock smiled slyly at her. She was wearing a filmy powder-blue nightgown that dipped low, revealing her magnificent cleavage. The gown was gathered up under her plump breasts, and its folds fell over her delightfully rounded hips. Her hair was just as he had imagined it moments ago—loose blond curls recently brushed. George Anne's huge limpid blue eyes looked at him lovingly. He held out his arms toward her. "Come, my pet!"

George Anne sat down on the edge of the big canopied bed and leaned over him. "Oh, Teddy, you're always in such a hurry!"

Braddock could feel himself tense. He could hardly wait to plunge his hands down her nightdress. God, how he loved her teats! She was like a great white-breasted swan, and when he fastened his mouth on them, a wonderful warm feeling of nostalgia swept over him.

He pulled George Anne down to him and rolled her onto her back, burying his face in her cleavage. She giggled as his stubbly face touched her tender skin.

"I can't wait!" Braddock could feel his own heart-beat quicken. He pulled the drawstring on her nightie, then pushed it away as he sought her large pink nipples. He tweaked them with his fingers, and she cooed pleasantly.

"Touch me!" Braddock panted with urgency.

He sighed with delight as he fastened his mouth onto the tip of one rosy breast and felt George Anne's experienced fingers on his member. It was heaven!

George Anne wiggled and giggled, moving this way and that, rubbing him till he felt it might last—indeed, he prayed that it might last. He pulled up her skirts and pushed her legs apart, sinking into her with a satisfied sigh. All the while Braddock kept his large hands on her breasts, kneading them. He could never get enough of her. But alas! Age will out. He began to feel himself slacken just as she arched her back and began the rhythmic movements of satisfaction. He became so distracted watching her, he went completely limp. She gasped and lay back, panting slightly. Lovely, precious little kitten, Braddock thought to himself. "Oh, pet," he murmured.

George Anne looked up at him sympathetically. Her full lips rounded in a little pout. "Oh, Teddy!"

George Anne expertly moved out from under his bulk and once again sought him with her hands. She gently massaged him till she felt him grow strong again, then in one swift movement, she turned over and crouched on her knees, pulling her gown up to her waist.

General Braddock rose immediately and mounted her from the rear, seizing her beautiful white buttocks in his hands, thrilled at the sight of her perfect bottom. He closed his eyes and plunged into her passageway. She rocked for him and even whispered how wonderful he was. General Braddock took a deep breath and felt himself pulsate into George Anne. Then he collapsed in a heap on top of her.

"Oh, pet! I'm going to miss you so!"

George Anne moved from underneath him and settled at his side, curling herself up. "Poor Teddy!" she whispered. "Oh, poor, poor Teddy."

They lay in silence for a time. Braddock's hand remained on her bosom, molded to its contours. It never ceased to fascinate him. He delighted in watching a woman's teats harden. He had had a wife once—

albeit not a beautiful woman—and he had acquired a number of mistresses and knew many ladies of the night. Their infinite variety was a wonder!

"I hope you won't be ill on such a long sea voyage," George Anne said, making a circle on his chest with her finger.

"Never have before," Braddock said confidently.

"But it's such a long voyage—and in December! I hear it's terribly rough!"

"Not as bad as being separated from you, my pet!" He had both hands on her breasts now. He considered the situation for a moment and decided he couldn't possibly do it again. But then . . . he could always watch George Anne. He began to play with her again, and she sighed, closing her eyes. Obviously an encore was in order.

In the darkness of her closed lids, Braddock's hands might belong to anyone. They moved over her, teasing her to respond, coaxing her to give herself up to pure wanton pleasure. Well, dear Teddy had changed his will, George Anne thought to herself, I'm going to inherit half his worldly goods. Not that they were considerable, but it all added up. At least poor Teddy cared about her well-being.

George Anne abandoned herself to her task and eventually was fulfilled, much to Teddy's delight. "Oh, I'm sleepy now," George Anne said, knowing that he was now satisfied that he was the world's greatest lover.

George Anne reached over and blew out the candle, settling back into Braddock's arms and snuggling up to him. "Is it dangerous in North America?"

Braddock squeezed her delicious little body. "I suppose so," he answered absently.

Megan was dressed in a gray wool dress trimmed in white linen. Her hair was drawn back and partially covered. She wore plain black leather boots that extended to mid-calf; the folds of her dress fell nearly to her ankles.

"Modest little outfit, isn't it?"

Richard cast an appraising eye on his daughter. "I can't say it does much for you."

Megan smiled coyly. "I don't think I can pass for the wife of a soldier dressed in laces and taffeta—not on the frontier, as you describe it."

"This is not woman's work," Richard blustered.

"It is exactly woman's work! I'm a poor young woman who's traveled all the way to Fort Niagara, searching for her soldier husband—who's been killed." Megan put on a mock pout and shook her head. "They'll take me in," she said in a totally different tone. Then I can meet the engineers and find out all there is to find out about the fort's defenses. Finding out things from men is ideally woman's work!"

"It's a hard trek and a dangerous task."

Megan shook her head. "Don't say it again. I know you don't approve."

"I've given up," Richard O'Flynn said, shaking his head. "It's a game, you know," Richard was stuffing his pipe, "and it's about to have added players."

"You mean the British regulars being sent under General Braddock?"

Again Richard shook his head. "No, my dear. The French also have dreams of an empire. My, such dreams! It's finally occurred to them that they are a trifle over-extended, that the Canadian militia cannot possibly protect Louisbourg, Quebec, and a string of forts that extends all the way to New Orleans."

Megan sat down and primly smoothed out her skirts as Richard lit his pipe and billows of sweet smoke filled the room. "We're going to be traveling with French reinforcements," Richard announced. "I've reactivated my cover, so to speak. Once we're in Quebec your change of identity will be taken care of and you can travel on to Fort Niagara."

Megan nodded. "I thought you told me the Canadians didn't want French regular troops and a French command in the province."

Richard smiled wryly. "But you just said the key word. It is a province, a province of France. Of course, the Canadians don't want French troops—no more than our colonists want English troops, I'll wager."

"Well, it's only to protect them."

Richard just looked at Megan. She might well make an excellent spy, but she had not yet mastered some of the basic politics of the day. He sought to change the subject. There was little enough time left. "How are you enjoying Paris?" he asked with a wink.

Megan tilted her head. "There's something about it. Nicer than London, I think."

"Ah, multiple talents and a continental taste. Why don't you change into something more appropriate so we can go out to dinner?"

Megan wandered into the dressing room. "How many troops is the king sending?"

"It hasn't been decided yet," Richard answered. It was a new development—a development he suspected would come to no good end. This was the first time both antagonists—France and England—had decided to send substantial numbers of troops to the New World. Canada was a province of France, but it had recruited its own militia after the withdrawal of French regular troops in 1695. The American colonies of Britain also had an army composed entirely of local militia. But now both England and France were beginning to exert their power. Both were taking the defense of North America away from their home-grown militia and sending both troops and commanders to North America. War was inevitable, but so were the problems of foreign armies in North America. Richard figured that the farmers along the St. Lawrence would be no more pleased with billeting French soldiers than the New Englanders in Massachusetts would be to billet British troops. There was no doubt in his mind that England would win the war for the continent, but he saw other problems on the horizon.

Richard turned his mind to Janet Cameron. He had hoped to find her in Paris, but no one seemed to know where she had gone. He had made inquiries, but the de Foches, who might have known, were away.

He shrugged inwardly. Why was he looking? Janet probably wouldn't have anything to do with him in the first place, and in all likelihood she was either married or the mistress of some wealthy man. Still, he found himself thinking about her occasionally. He was now free, and he fantasized about renewing his relationship with her.

Restlessly, Richard stood up and walked over to the table. He studied the decanters for a few moments, then chose one and poured himself a drink.

"Are you almost ready?" he called out to Megan.

"Almost!" she answered lightheartedly.

The overland convoy to Fort Duquesne had made camp. They carried supplies, added reinforcements of men, and brought some families. It was a rough, but not entirely unpleasant trek.

Mathew had been gone almost a year! Janet couldn't believe it. He had tried to get away, but it had proved impossible. There was so much to do and the militia was so short of trained engineers. When she had first written him about her coming, he had been hesitant in his reply, warning her of all the difficulties of life in a frontier fort. But his second letter was different. He had been up to Niagara and had purchased some land. They would have to stay in Duquesne for a time, but after that they would go to Niagara and, as Mathew wrote, "We will build."

Janet stirred the fire with a stick and hoped the babies would sleep a little longer. She checked herself. She would have to stop thinking of them as babies: Andrew was five, Mat three, and Helena just over a year. She was the devil of the lot! Toddling here and there, and forever falling down. She was even beginning to talk, albeit in her own unique language.

Pierre Deschamps and his brother René had long since been up and about. At ten and eleven, they were old enough to help the men. Both now carried long Indian knives, and Pierre shouldered a musket. Janet always hated to admit it, but Pierre wielded it well since he was tall for his age and well-trained. In fact, both boys were excellent shots, having been taught by Robert, a fine marksman and sharpshooter himself.

Madelaine, the dark-haired beauty of the Deschamps family, was seven. But unlike her brothers, she was a sleepyhead, still drowsing in the tent.

Janet examined the gruel in the pot over the fire and stirred it. Robert and the others would be back soon, and they would all be hungry. Within two hours they would break camp and set out on another long day.

Around the encampment some ten fires smoldered. The wood was still damp from the spring rains, and it sizzled and smoked excessively as it burned. The other women cooked for their men, and one special cook prepared food for the militia guard. Making camp, cooking, breaking camp, loading the canoes—it was all part of the routine and it was all shared work.

Janet looked up as Jeanne Choubert strode over. She was one of the several women making the trek to join their husbands at the fort. She had one child with her, a baby whom she carried papoose-style. Jeanne was an earthy-looking girl with long brown hair and practical clothing. Her wool skirt stopped a little beneath her knees, just touching the tops of her heavy boots. It enabled her to walk with a longer stride, and it also didn't get caught on prickly bushes so easily. In the cool morning, Jeanne wore a great hand-knit woolen garment and a leather vest over it. When the sun got hotter, the vest and then the wool garment would be stuffed in her pack, leaving only a blouse of dark-colored material.

Born of a habitant family who lived along the St. Lawrence, Jeanne had been trained to shoot a rifle well. "I've shouldered a musket since I was nine," she said somewhat proudly. Then if prompted, Jeanne would tell the story of how she and her family had defended their land against both the English and the Mohawk. Afraid to go to the Ohio Valley? Jeanne would just laugh. "I've already killed four men! Three flesh-eating Mohawk and a British soldier!" Both

Jeanne and Robert were a good source of entertaining campfire lore for the travellers.

"Your babies still asleep?" Jeanne asked in her deep-husky voice.

Janet looked up and smiled. "For a change."

Jeanne smiled back with glistening white teeth. "You've got enough children to fill an Indian camp! To populate the West!" She crinkled her nose. "Good woman!"

Janet straightened up and stretched. "My own little clan," she answered.

Jeanne looked Janet up and down appraisingly, the way French women did with one another. "Tell me sometime how to keep a figure like yours after six children!"

Janet laughed out loud. "You only bear three of them," she whispered back, an amused twinkle in her eyes. "That's the only way."

Then realizing that Jeanne did not understand, she added, "Three of them are adopted."

Jeanne shook her head in comprehension and laughed again, this time at her own misunderstanding. Then she sat down on the edge of a large rock and spread her legs apart, her skirt falling between them. Idly, she picked up the stick Janet had dropped and began tracing in the dirt. "You planning to stay with your husband?"

"Yes," Janet answered without hesitation. "We want to farm eventually, up near Fort Niagara."

Jeanne nodded. "I hear the land's good there. Pretty too."

"And you?" Janet inquired.

"Oh, we'll go back to Trois Rivières—back to the home of my father. He's just become a seigneur with his own land and his own habitants." Then Jeanne shook her head sadly. "But it's hard to farm the land . . . much lies fallow. My brothers are all away in the militia."

"They say we'll have a war," Janet commented.

Jeanne shook her head. "English, French? It's the

land that matters—it's what you give to your children. War! It's endless. They won't just let us be—that's all the Canadians want! Just to be left alone. Just to survive!" There was more than a hint of weariness in Jeanne's voice.

Listening to Jeanne made Janet think of Scotland and the land she had left because of war. Divided and redivided, it now belonged to the English. Janet thought that she could have remained on the seigneurie that the Deschamps had left to her, but she and Mathew did not feel it was truly theirs. Instead of claiming it, they left a habitant family in charge and placed the land in the name of the Deschamps children, who could return to claim it when they were grown. Janet wanted to go to the place Mathew had written her about, and though she could not envisage it, she already had a strange feeling for it. It would be the first land she and Mathew ever owned together, and war or no war, English, French, and Indians notwithstanding, they were going to build on it *together*.

"I'm hungry." Andrew poked his head out of the tent. "And I have to pee!"

Janet pointed off toward a clump of bushes. "Over there," she said. "But pull on your boots first, the ground's soggy."

In the distance someone let out a catcall. It was the scouting party returning. Jeanne stood up and brushed out her coarse skirt. "Time for some food," she sighed. "Lot of hungry men to feed."

An early-morning breeze began to blow through the encampment, causing the embers of the fires to flare up and billows of smoke to rise up into the air above the group of makeshift tents, lean-tos, and teepees.

Janet inhaled deeply as she watched Andrew plough into the bushes. Even though it was early April, there was still a little frost on the ground. But the new leaves were becoming larger with each day's warm sun. They had set up camp by a rushing river, and though its water was cold, the men washed in it. The encampment was in a clearing, but all around them the pine, birch, and maple trees formed a thick forest. This was the longest portage, Janet had been told. "We'll be back on water tomorrow," Robert had assured her that morning. "And from then on, the journey will take less time."

Janet began mixing the gruel, carefully stirring the lumps out of it.

She looked up as the scouting party entered the encampment.

"Gruel ready?" Robert cried out as he strode toward her.

"I've got a whole basket of berries!" René ran up enthusiastically. "Sweet berries!"

Pierre was carrying a dead rabbit by the ears. "And I've got supper!" he announced proudly.

Janet looked up at her men and felt a sudden sense of pride.

The French vessels had set sail from Brest on the first day of May. The French reinforcements on board were more substantial than Richard O'Flynn had imagined. There were six battalions of French regulars—over three-thousand men in all. They were commanded by Jean Armand, Baron of Dieskau, and the troop ships traveled in convoy under the protection of a squadron of war vessels commanded by DuBois de la Motte.

It was understood that Governor Duquesne of Quebec would send pilots to meet the ships and guide them down the Saint Lawrence. This, as Richard understood it, was less a protection for the ships than a show of force for the Indians of the region.

Unlike the British, who had appointed General Braddock Supreme Military Commander, the French intended to place their reinforcements under the command of the governor. And Governor Duquesne had strict orders never to be the aggressor—his task and the task of the reinforcements was to defend and only to defend.

Richard took careful note that the troops included the regiments of La Reine, Languedoc, Guienne,

Béarn, Bourgogne, and Artois. Four of these were being sent to Canada, two were going to Louisbourg.

That precious information Richard had smuggled out of France by courier along with the name and description of the ship he and Megan would travel on. It was fine for the convoy to be attacked, but not their ship. Richard knew full well that the British admiral, Edward Boscawen, had orders to intercept any French warships or other vessels with troops on board. Richard smiled to himself. France and England were not yet at war, but it certainly was an interesting peace!

The voyage had been long, but not as bad as it could have been. Richard leaned over the rail. Megan stood next to him. There had been no attacks by the British so far, and now Richard doubted there would be. They were near the entrance to the St. Lawrence, and the convoy had kept in close order for the entire trip. The only exceptions were the three stragglers, the *Alcide,* the *Lys,* and the *Dauphin Royal.*

"Where are we?" Megan asked.

"Somewhere," Richard answered, "near the mouth of the St. Lawrence."

"Somewhere is right!" Megan said tersely as she brought up her warm shawl and pulled it around her shoulders. The fog was so thick that, standing aft, one could barely see the stern of the ship.

Richard blinked into the soft white fog. Damn! The weather was certainly with the French. Fog patches covered all the western approaches, and there was no way the British navy was going to find the French in this thick soup.

Then from somewhere in the distance came the muffled sound of cannon. Megan tilted her head and listened. The French were manning their battle stations. Footsteps could be heard running below deck, and soon men scurried past them.

"All passengers below deck!" one of the sailors yelled.

Richard guided Megan back toward their cabin.

"Are we going to be attacked?"

"I doubt it," Richard answered. "Chances are the Brits have picked up the three stragglers. They don't know we're here."

Megan took one last glance over her shoulder. It was a white world in which the wind was chilly and the water murky. "I think I'm glad about that," she said, smiling.

Richard marveled at his daughter's cool attitude, not to mention her stamina. He hated to admit it, but she was going to do well. He had half-expected her to be seasick, but she was not. And she was right about another thing as well. A woman did find it simple to get information out of a man. The captain was utterly charmed by Megan, and so was Armand the commander. He chatted with her endlessly about French plans for the defense of Canada.

The captain of the *Alcide* had spotted the English ships and realized they were bearing down on him. When they were close enough, he called out to them in French and then in English. "Are we at peace or at war?"

Boscawen took the blower himself and called back across the water, "We can't hear you!"

The French captain shrugged and shouted again into his blower, "Are we at peace or are we at war!"

All the while the distance between the two ships was growing less and less. The fog was not quite as dense in this spot. Then the British crew finally responded in a loud chorus: "Peace, peace! We're at peace!"

The French captain relaxed slightly, and a nearby member of the crew wiped his brow and stepped back from his position at the cannon.

But when the English ships were closer—half a pistol shot away—they opened fire.

"Tabernac!" the French captain shouted. "Man the guns! The stinking bastards are trying to take us by surprise!"

The French cannon opened up, but the British had already done their damage. The *Alcide* moved crazily in the water, its rudder damaged from the first blast of English cannon.

A fire blazed across the deck and engulfed part of the rigging, and the *Lys*, which was quite close, struck her colors, surrendering before she too was severely damaged.

Farther away, the *Dauphin Royal* turned and escaped into the fog. Commanding one of the fastest ships in the French navy, her captain took full advantage of her speed to beat a hasty retreat.

The little captain of the *Alcide* spit on the deck through his yellowed teeth, then let forth with a string of oaths and curses. "*Merde!* The English bastards have no honor! They lied. They can't fight like men! They have to stab their enemies in the back!" He panted from the exertion of his swearing and, totally frustrated, kicked the rail.

"Strike the colors!" he called out, then went back to his cursing. "Sons of dirty dogs! May your mothers bite you! It was a sneak attack! And on a Sunday! You attacked on a Sunday!"

It was sheer treachery, and no matter how the British would try to cover it, the end of the so-called peace was clearly in sight.

Fifteen miles outside of Frederick-town in Maryland, Braddock and his men passed a dormer-windowed tavern called Dowden's Ordinary. Other than the tavern, the journey up the Potomac to Frederick-town was without interest—to Braddock's way of thinking it was without much of anything.

It was farmland, but the farms were not close together. Frederick itself consisted of a mere two-hundred houses, a stone tavern, and a court house still under construction. Fort Cumberland, where he would have to spend some weeks, was adjacent to Frederick. Clearly, Frederick had less to offer than Alexandria!

Braddock tried to console himself by thinking that the poor colonials did their best with what they had, which wasn't much. They were a people of no charm, without even the most rudimentary manners. It was true that they appeared to read a great deal, but somehow they still seemed to have inferior educations. They chewed tobacco and actually spit! And the militia was dreadful! The men of the Virginia militia had no military decorum at all! General Braddock missed London.

Braddock's mind wandered back to April 15, when he had met with the colonial governors to discuss strategy. He sighed, for it had been an unpleasant duty. There was no question of keeping the combined English and colonial forces in a defensive position. It had been decided in London to attack and then to remain in an aggressive position, taking as much territory as possible. Braddock had carefully relayed to the governors the strategic plans outlined to him by the Duke of Cumberland. But the colonial governors were such nits! They immediately rejected the idea that they should pool their resources to pay for the war, though they quickly agreed that Fort Beauséjour in the Chignecto Isthmus, Fort St. Frédéric on Lake Champlain, Fort Niagara, and of course Fort Duquesne should be attacked. What they wanted was a full-fledged war without paying for it!

General Braddock also pondered the colonial governors' insistence that the British regulars and the colonial militia utilize the support of the Six Nations. Braddock did not approve of using Indians. But the governors were adamant, and they asked that Colonel William Johnson should conduct the campaign against Fort St. Frédéric. It was argued that Johnson knew the territory, and owing to his fondness for young Indian girls—a perversion that made Braddock shudder—he had actually learned the jibberish of the savages and was said to have some influence over them.

Braddock had given it considerable thought before deciding that it was entirely wrong to use the savages as allies. He had gone even further. He backed up his belief by forbidding the men under his command to fraternize with any Indians—but most especially the females. One William Johnson was enough for any army! Mixed blood was bad blood as far as Braddock was concerned. The poor colonials did not, after all, need the Indians. They only thought they needed them because they had such inferior military training. "I will change all that," Braddock mumbled under his breath. "Sheer numbers can't defeat a *real* army—not a British army anyway. Neither the Indians nor the colonials have the slightest idea of how to fight."

On the other hand, Braddock did have reason to congratulate himself on the Alexandria meeting. I have a fine sense of compromise, he told himself. He had gone along with the idea that Governor Shirley of the Massachusetts Bay Colony ought to conduct the Niagara campaign. The poor man was so eager! And of course, giving in on this point did serve another purpose. Only the Virginians were concerned with Fort Duquesne—it was their special project, and they feared that the other colonies would try to share the victory and the long-term benefits of the victory.

Apart from who would do what, the only other problem Braddock had faced with the squabbling colonial governors at Alexandria concerned the route he would take to Fort Duquesne. But on that point he had been stubborn. Over the mountains it would be! His route had been decided in England by the Duke of Cumberland and Sir William Pitt. No one in the colonies had the right or the power to contradict the Supreme Military Commander—a title Braddock reveled in.

General Braddock moved restlessly in the saddle. It had been a long ride. Now he could only hope that the person named Franklin who was supposed to meet him would show up on time. Franklin's assigned duty was to obtain the necessary wagons and means for onward transport over the mountains. Braddock sighed again to himself. He wondered whether these people really knew what they were doing.

Braddock glanced sideways and took comfort at the sight of his newly appointed aide-de-camp, Lieutenant-

Colonel George Washington. Well, Washington seemed to know what he was doing. Very military for a colonial! Very military and obviously quite competent.

As they entered Fort Cumberland—the advance camp where the British regulars were to team up with and train the backwoods colonial militia units—Braddock turned to Washington.

"What's this Franklin person like?"

Washington was lost in thought, but he quickly turned to face General Braddock. His expression was unemotional, and Braddock guessed that Washington's assessment of Franklin would be equally unemotional and unbiased.

"A jack of all trades," Washington answered, slowly trying to decide just how one ought to describe Franklin. "A self-educated man, a journalist, and a master politician and diplomat. He has a rather strange humor, however." Washington looked thoughtful. "Yes, a rather strange humor . . . and he also has something of a reputation for . . . for the . . ." Washington's voice trailed off.

"For what?" Braddock insisted.

Washington cleared his throat, and his normally pasty complexion reddened somewhat. He actually glanced around furtively to see if anyone else was within earshot. "Well, uh, for young girls . . . they say he's quite . . ." Washington was trying to find the right words, ". . . a ladies' man."

Braddock smiled. Washington was a man of tact. "How old is he, this ladies' man who has such influence?"

Washington frowned. "I'm not certain—late forties, early fifties."

Braddock nodded again. He thought to himself that it would be nice to meet an older person. If any one thing annoyed him, it was that the government and affairs of the colonies seemed to be carried out by bare-assed youths in their twenties, none of them dry behind the ears. Of course, there were exceptions—

Washington himself was quite young, but his military outlook, natural reserve, and fine manners gave him the demeanor of an older man.

They finally entered the gates of Fort Cumberland, and Washington escorted Braddock to his quarters.

"Spartan but adequate!" Braddock exclaimed, looking around. There were two rooms—one large meeting and strategy room and a private bedroom off it. Both rooms were sparsely furnished by local craftsmen. The tables, chairs, and even the bed were carved with strange decorative curls and painted with grotesque little blue and red flowers. Braddock crinkled his nose as he looked about.

"What manner of furniture is this?"

Washington snapped to attention as he always did when spoken to. "Dutch," he answered crisply. "The people of Frederick-town are Dutch—Dutch farmers mostly."

"I trust the food is English!" Braddock's tone was disparaging. "I don't think I could abide Dutch food."

"I'll see that you have only English food," Washington answered.

A knock on the door startled both Washington and Braddock.

"Enter!" Braddock called out officiously.

A young red-headed militiaman poked his head in the door. "General Braddock, sir. Mr. Franklin is here—recently arrived from Philadelphia."

Braddock smiled and patted his chest. "Good timing. Punctuality is a virtue. Show him in!"

The nervous young militia officer opened the door wider, stepped to one side, and stood rigidly at attention, "Mr. Benjamin Franklin, sir."

Franklin stepped into the room and extended his hand, which Braddock accepted. "Mr. Postmaster," Braddock said formally.

Braddock indicated a chair near the long table, and when Franklin had seated himself, Braddock also sat down.

Franklin was built somewhat like Braddock himself —a trifle pudgy. Franklin's gray eyes had a twinkle, but he also seemed businesslike.

Braddock looked up at Washington. "Dismissed!"

Washington again jolted to attention and, turning on his heel, left the building, closing the door behind him.

"Shall we get right down to business?" Franklin suggested.

Braddock nodded his agreement. He felt a quick and sudden liking for Franklin. One could tell he was more worldly and more efficient than most of the colonial bumpkins.

"I'm told you can obtain wagons for my onward journey."

"I can and will," Franklin answered. "And other provisions as well."

"Good!" Braddock was impressed. Franklin was the most positive colonial he had met. The first one to say, "I can." The others seemed to have an unfortunate penchant for words like "maybe" and "possibly," and plain negative phrases like "It can't be done."

"You're a positive man! I like that!"

"It's my job," Franklin replied. "Now, what about additional men—colonial militia?"

Braddock screwed up his face. "Unfortunately, the colonials seem a bit indifferent. Men who are indifferent do not, in my opinion, make good soldiers."

"Well, let's see what we can do," Franklin said cheerfully. He did not take offense at Braddock's statement about "colonials." Indeed, he felt the same way. Franklin had learned the way to wealth. The people of the British colonies downgraded the British on the one hand, but on the other they paid through the teeth for anything remotely English. Franklin had earned considerable money and reputation by imitating and reproducing items that appeared English. More than half of what appeared in his almanac was carefully culled and edited, if not actually plagiarized from the English publication *The Tatler*. Yes, there was no doubt in Franklin's mind that his fellow colonials had a most peculiar relationship with their British masters. It was a love-hate relationship, and nothing illustrated that relationship more than the city of Boston. The Massachusetts Bay Colony had a most independent bent, but no place in North America was more British than Boston! If Franklin were to make a prediction about the future, it would be that one day the colonies would indeed seek independence, but that when they got it, the people of the colonies would still seek out a royalty and fall on their faces before kings or whatever they created to stand in the place of kings.

Franklin tapped his fingers on the table and looked at the impatient British general before him. "The army should be fully provisioned within the month."

Braddock again sighed. It was becoming a habit; since his arrival in Virginia, he had sighed a lot. He looked around him at the strangely furnished room. "A month?"

Franklin reached over and patted Braddock's arm. "We'll find something to do to pass the time," he said reassuringly. Then Mr. Franklin winked. "Some of the Dutch can be quite entertaining!"

CHAPTER VI

May 1755

"Ah! You are a man of influence!" General Braddock was in a state of total admiration. "I wouldn't have believed it possible!"

Ben Franklin smiled his sly old smile. He had brought Braddock to the stone tavern in Fredericktown and arranged for private dining rooms on the second floor. In his infinite wisdom, he had also arranged for private tavern maids—three little blond Dutch girls of seventeen, one more attractive than the other. They were all full of giggles and smiles.

Braddock finished his rare roast beef and quaffed down his ale. Although he ate heartily, his eyes seldom left the low-necked dresses of the girls. They were a buxom trio, plump and quite ready for enjoyment. Then he thought of George Anne for a moment—he did miss her, he thought wistfully.

Franklin's eyes fell on the plumpest of the three girls. She had a delightfully ample bosom that peeked out from her little blue dress. He turned and winked mischievously at Braddock, whose face was already red from the ale and whose eyes were wide with lechery.

"You fancy young ladies?" Franklin asked merrily.

"Oh, indeed! Will they . . . ?" Braddock patted his full stomach. "I'm not familiar with colonial customs . . ."

Franklin let forth with a roar of laughter. "They've been paid to! Of course they will!"

Braddock smiled broadly. "All three of them?" he asked with enthusiasm.

"The more the merrier. Are you up to three young cherubs?"

"I daresay, I daresay!" It had been a long while since his last night in London with little George Anne. Then there had been the tiresome and sickening voyage and the utter dullness of Alexandria. Now Braddock faced what seemed like an eternity—a few weeks ensconced at Fort Cumberland with only the overland trek through the mountains to Fort Duquesne to look forward to. Ready? Up to it? He was eager!

"Shall we partake of the delights of the bedroom?" Franklin stood up and brushed the crumbs off his breeches.

Adjoining the small private dining room was a larger bedroom furnished with a wide bed covered with a great puffy quilt. Braddock noted that the furniture in this room was also carved and flowered.

The three little Dutch girls followed the two elderly gentlemen into the bedroom. Their faces were flushed as they continued to pinch one another and giggle gaily.

Braddock undid his pants and fell onto the bed, letting out a cry of surprise as he sunk into the feather mattress.

Franklin undressed carefully, hanging his waistcoat over a chair and folding his ruffled shirt neatly. Franklin then escorted one of the little girls to the other side of the bed, where he sat down. He pointed to the laces on his breeches and motioned her to undo them, then glanced over his shoulder at Braddock, who had quickly been joined by the other two girls.

"Early to bed, early to rise!" Franklin announced

cheerfully. And rise Mr. Franklin did, for he was obviously not the little Dutch girl's first experience with a gentleman.

"I haven't enough hands!" Braddock laughed. He was utterly overcome with delight. "Come, come, my pretties!"

"*Ich weiss nact,*" one of them answered, her lovely blue eyes opening wide.

"They don't speak English—you'll have to make do with hand motions . . ." Franklin laughed at the second of his fine puns.

Braddock dipped his hand into the bodice of one of the girl's dresses, and she responded quickly by undoing it and exposing her full breasts. Greedily, he reached for her with both hands; she leaned over his face, allowing him to both suckle and fondle her.

Below, he could feel the other little charmer's warm hands enclosing him. Braddock panted anxiously as the girl on his lower half straddled him and teased his member against her opening. All the while he engaged in his favorite fetish with the other. Her swelling breasts were nearly smothering him, but it was the most wonderful sensation!

On the other side of the bed, Mr. Franklin panted as the Dutch girl sat on his lap and pushed him into her. Face to face with her breasts, he bit and pinched her nipples while she bounced up and down on him.

When at last Franklin and his girl tumbled exhaustedly back onto the bed and Braddock stopped moaning beneath the pleasures of double caresses, the two spent gentlemen set about satisfying the girls. They stroked, rubbed, and caressed each of them in turn till they shook with pleasure and throbbed with delight. After that, the five of them had a gay frolic on the mattress. Lovely white bottoms intermingled playfully with full bosoms. .

At last, both Braddock and Franklin collapsed with the girls on the bed. Franklin nestled into a pair of soft breasts and wearily exclaimed, "What goes up, comes down!" He laughed to himself, then almost immediately fell sound asleep.

Fort Duquesne was located near the junction of the Allegheny and Monongahela rivers. It was well-fortified by cannon, and its supply system had been greatly improved over the months.

Right at the fork outside the fort walls, there were large cultivated gardens where corn and peas had been planted. And both pigs and cows were kept nearby. These imported animals supplied the Canadian fort and the few families who lived nearby with fresh meat and milk.

In the distance, Fort Duquesne's watchtowers loomed up over the trees. Janet could feel her eyes misting over as their boats neared the jetty outside the fort.

A crowd had already gathered on the shore, but Janet was still too far away to make out faces. Then in the afternoon sun, she caught sight of Mathew's sandy hair. He was so much taller than the others that he stood out. The flotilla of canoes made for the shore, and Janet waved wildly, as did the children.

Pierre, René, and Madelaine were the first to scramble out of the canoe and run to Mathew. Next Andrew and Mat were in his arms, and Helena was toddling toward him.

Mathew bent down and kissed Janet, but it was not the kind of kiss he wanted to give her. There were too many people milling about, and the children climbed all over him, squealing in childish glee.

Mathew swooped Helena into his arms and kissed her. Her red hair fell in ringlets around her face, and her green eyes were wide with delight. Even at sixteen months, the resemblance was uncanny. "They'll never ask whose child this is!" Mathew joked. "My God! How she's grown!"

"I doubt anyone would question who their father was

either," Janet answered, pointing to Mat and Andrew. Both boys bore a strong resemblance to Mathew.

"My own clan!" Mathew exclaimed. "Our accommodation is a two-room cabin. A little crowded!"

Janet beamed up at Mathew. "As long as we're together, we'll manage."

Mathew picked up the bags and boxes, and with Robert's help they packed off toward the fort and the tiny cabin within its walls.

"Are you staying, lad?" Robert nodded, then broke into a full laugh.

At the sound, Mathew started. He had not heard Robert MacLean make a sound since the age of seven—in Scotland.

"That's our biggest surprise and our best surprise!" Janet's face was alive with happiness. "Robert can speak again!"

Mathew stopped dead and dropped the boxes to the ground. He turned and embraced Robert in a great bear hug.

"You didn't write that! You didn't tell me!"

"Some things should be heard," Robert answered.

The two men stood for an instant and looked at one another. Both had tears in their eyes. Mathew remembered the pitiful little boy Robert had been—the little boy who had witnessed such horror he had lost his voice, the little boy who had been kidnapped by the Indians. He remembered the day Fou Loup had brought Robert to Fort St. Frédéric and the two of them had been reunited with one another.

"What a present!" Mathew said, then shouted again, "What a present!"

Robert pressed his lips together and looked into Mathew's eyes. As much as Janet had been a sister to him, Mathew had been a big brother. They were a close-knit family, and in spite of being separated for slightly over a year, things were now exactly as they had been.

Robert and Mathew bent down and retrieved the

boxes and bags. René and Pierre carried what they could, and so did Janet and Madelaine.

"In answer to your question," Robert said slowly, "no, I'm not staying. I have to go back to Quebec with the supply canoes. I'm in the militia, and I suspect I'll be assigned elsewhere."

Mathew didn't answer. The persistent English aggression could only lead to the conclusion that there would eventually be a war. The Virginians claimed this territory, and the aggressive forces of the Massachusetts Bay Colony longed to control Fort Louisbourg again. If there was war this time, it would be along the entire frontier.

They reached the cabin, and Mathew kicked its door open with his foot. "First room!" he announced. "This one's for cooking, talking, and for us to sleep in." They set the boxes down, and Mathew led Janet to the door of the second room and opened it. There were bunks along the sides of two walls. "For the clan!"

Mathew turned to Janet seriously. "I thought it better to be cramped inside the fort . . . too dangerous in open country."

"I like it!" Janet answered. Mathew had been reluctant about her coming at first, but now he was full of apologies about the accommodations.

"I'll have to help with the unloading of the supplies." Robert sensed that Janet and Mathew wanted to be alone. "C'mon! You're old enough to help!" Robert led René, Pierre, and Madelaine away.

"Me too!" Andrew followed them out, but Mat and Helena remained. They were already in the bedroom, climbing up on the bunks and laughing together.

"Let me start a fire," Mathew offered. "Fix something hot to drink." He began placing the kindling in the hearth.

"What do you think of your daughter?"

"I think she's almost as beautiful as her mother!"

Mathew lit the kindling, and when it was burning, he put on a larger piece of wood.

Janet busied herself fixing the children something to eat, and while they were fed, she and Mathew talked, exchanging information, telling each other all the things they had not been able to put into their infrequent letters.

When the youngsters, tired from the long day and weary from the excitement of their arrival, had been put to bed, Janet and Mathew sat down before the fire together.

"You were afraid to have me come, weren't you?"

Mathew turned to her. "Only because it's dangerous, because you can't have the comforts you had in Quebec."

"I don't want those things. I couldn't stay in Quebec after the trial. But even if it hadn't happened . . ." Janet reached up and stroked Mathew's cheek, "I had to be with you."

Mathew took her hand and kissed it.

"We were separated in one war—I won't have it happen again. If anything takes me away from here, it'll have to be something important."

Mathew ran his hand through her red hair as it glistened in the firelight. Her wonderful green eyes were on him, and Mathew pulled her closer. "We have to make our own way," he said steadily. "When this is over, I want to go to Fort Niagara—the land's ours and I'm having a cabin built. It's a special place."

Janet nuzzled against him. "I want that too," she whispered. "I've had enough of Quebec City."

Mathew reached for her chin and cupped it in his hand, then he kissed her deeply. It was a long slow kiss, and her lips moved under his, yielding to the pent-up passion they both felt for one another.

Mathew lowered her to the cushions on the floor and kissed her neck while his fingers undid her bodice and released her heaving breasts. In moments they were both undressed and entwined in one another's arms. Mathew's hands roamed her cool white thighs and teased her flesh. Janet buried herself in his chest, seeking his body even as he sought hers. When his lips fastened on her nipples, she moved beneath him rhythmically.

As always, their lovemaking was slow and passionate, gentle and affectionate. Janet moaned as Mathew touched her, then withdrew his hand and returned to caressing her breasts. Again and again he touched her while Janet's hips undulated upward, waiting for him to enter her.

Mathew sunk into Janet and continued to run his tongue lightly over her tight nipples. They moved together slowly till Janet let out a little gasp and arched her back in throbbing pleasure while Mathew released himself into her. They lay against one another, clinging to the reality of the moment. All the longing of the past months was gone, all the terrible loneliness erased.

Hepzibah Trumbull was the widow of Major Trumbull of the Virginia Militia. Around Fort Cumberland, Hepzibah was jokingly referred to as "the Amazon." The name was indicative of her remarkable proportions. Dame Trumbull stood over five-foot seven-inches tall, and she was also magnificently endowed. Although no man could span her ample waist, Hepzibah had huge high breasts that were rumored to be at least forty-eight inches around and three big handfuls each. But it was her rear view that was most fascinating to General Braddock. Hepzibah had enormous wide buttocks.

The days at Fort Cumberland wore long for General Braddock, and as much as he enjoyed the little Dutch girls at the tavern, whoring every night was an expensive entertainment. Especially when General Braddock was broke, as was usually the case.

He had been at Fort Cumberland for only two weeks when he met the admirable Dame Trumbull. It was then that his sorties to the tavern ended. Why pay for what was offered free of charge? And in such oversized proportions! Dame Trumbull was certainly enough for any man.

Their first coupling had been an experience Braddock would never forget. Her teats were the largest he had ever seen in his entire life of womanizing, and her bottom reminded him of nothing so much as the rump of his mare. Moreover, the dear woman was quite pliable and more than anxious to join with him.

Braddock leaned back and lit his pipe. He had succeeded in finding a comfortable chair and having it installed in his quarters. He considered this his main accomplishment since arriving at Fort Cumberland.

"I'm going with you, Braddy." Hepzibah stroked his knee with her large hand. "I'm going to be there when you take Fort Duquesne! I won't take no for an answer!"

General Braddock looked at his newly acquired mistress in awe. Gad! What a woman! "It's a most difficult journey," he protested.

"I insist! Besides, you said yourself it would only take a day or two to rout the Canadians."

"But I'll have to continue on to Fort Niagara."

"I'll go with you," Hepzibah announced with a wave of her hand. "Other men are taking their wives—why can't you take me?"

General Braddock thought about it for a moment. It was true that some of the other officers had their wives with them. Heaven only knew what it was going to be like at Fort Duquesne. Braddock had an image of no women at all—save for the Indians with whom he had forbidden fraternization. And Hepzibah was, without question, a strong woman. She rode like a man and certainly handled a musket well. These colonial women were quite remarkable, even if they did take some getting used to.

"Do you really want to come?" Braddock couldn't believe his great good fortune. First the little Dutch girls, now Hepzibah.

"Of course, I want to come," she purred.

Braddock smiled at her and patted her head. "You may come then," he agreed.

Braddock puffed on his pipe and watched as the smoke drifted up toward the beamed ceiling. The

112

wilderness of the colonies was not so bad. In any case, it seemed to have its compensations.

Chaussegros de Léry arrived from Fort Detroit to consult with Mathew and the commander of Fort Duquesne on the fort's defenses. Claude-Pierre Pécaudy de Contrecoeur, the commander of Fort Duquesne, had sent for the senior engineer on Mathew's advice. It was advice that Contrecoeur had readily accepted. He was a weary and nervous man and wanted no more than to return to Montreal now that his replacement had arrived. But nothing ever worked out! His replacement was to be Liénard de Beaujeu, but Beaujeu had received new orders to serve under Contrecoeur. "War is imminent," the dispatch informed him. "Remain in command."

Léry, to Contrecoeur's relief, inspected the fort thoroughly and complimented both him and Mathew on its defenses.

"Too bad Fort St. Frédéric is not as defensible," Léry commented.

Mathew nodded and thought back on his time at Fort St. Frédéric. Both he and the engineer, Louis Franquet, had recommended new defenses for St. Frédéric, but at the time the French were unprepared to spend the money.

"We could use more cannon over there," Léry indicated the western walls of the fort. The two men began a walk around the outside walls.

"What do you think?" Léry questioned. "You helped build it."

Mathew shook his head. "If the English have cannon, the walls won't withstand a prolonged attack. But I must admit, I don't believe in trying to defend a fort from the inside in any case."

Léry smiled. It was a meeting of minds. "It's a stupid, stilted way to fight. We have to count on the Indians, and that's not their kind of warfare."

"Glad to see you've mastered the English weakness," Mathew said, putting his hands in his pockets and looking at the ground. "The Virginia militia might be all right, but the British regulars won't understand the Indian way of fighting; they won't be expecting an ambush."

Léry laughed sardonically. "They might not expect it, but they certainly deserve it. It is they who have lied and cheated, they who have wantonly attacked us, they who have broken the peace." Léry's fists automatically doubled and his teeth clenched. "They're on their way here to perform yet another treachery, and war has not even been declared! Let us arrange an ambush. Let us give them a taste of their own medicine!"

"We have good intelligence sources," Mathew informed Léry. "We're undermanned and we're going to have to count on the Shawnee and the Delaware."

"Have you thought about the best place for such an ambush, a place where the Indians' talents can be made the most of?"

"I have a spot," Mathew admitted. "Let me show you. I think it's ideal."

Léry laughed and slapped Mathew across the back. *"Bon ami!"* Léry exclaimed. "Take me to it!"

General Braddock's army had moved over the high land toward Great Meadows and the Youghiegany River. It was late June when the long columns of marching men, supply wagons, farm animals, and artillery reached the ruins of the palisades of Fort Necessity. There, weary, depressed, and anxiety-ridden, the mixed army of British regulars and Virginia militia camped for the night.

The British regulars were mainly Irish, and they mingled uneasily with the Virginians.

This was not the kind of environment in which the superstitious Irish were used to fighting. The forest was thicker than any they had ever seen. There were no towns in which to seek pleasure. It was a dark, lonely, forbidding wilderness filled with stinging, biting, man-eating insects. Moreover, it was populated by half-dressed savages.

The Virginians, on the other hand, had been born in the wilderness, and to some extent they had conquered it. They found the Irish to be complainers, and as punishment for their more or less continual whining, the Virginians delighted in telling the goriest stories they could about the Indians.

Tad Williamson was typical of the lads in the Virginia militia. He was a lanky farm boy with sun-blond hair and dark eyes. He carried his musket easily—slung over his shoulder—and he walked in long strides, seldom talking as he marched. Tad Williamson had been in the area of Fort Necessity before, so he knew the Indians and how to survive in the woods if he had to.

Sean O'Brien was Tad's physical opposite. He was short and stocky with jet-black hair and blue eyes. He was gregarious and seldom quiet. He sang as he marched along, and he talked and laughed half the night with his fellows. To Tad's way of thinking, the Irish regulars were too noisy to be good soldiers and they had a peculiar sense of humor—always laughing at things that were not funny. Moreover, they were boastful to the point of annoyance.

"This is no way to fight a war!" Sean said loudly as he tossed a pebble into the fire. "It's taking us a month of marching just to get to an enemy we can whip in a matter of hours!" Sean slapped one of his fellow Irish on the back. "The French can't fight! And the Canadians are French, right? Their savages can't fight either! They're no match for the likes of us!" The whole group of Irish soldiers laughed. The Irish were gathered on one side of the fire, the Virginians on the other. That was the way it had been since the march to Fort Duquesne began.

Tad looked into the fire. He was fed up with the Irish and their boasts and bellyaching. After all, the Virginia militia had been defeated by the French, and if the French couldn't fight, what did that say about the Virginians? The British regulars were just like their fat commander—disdainful.

"You just haven't fought Indians yet," Tad warned in

his maddeningly slow drawl. "You have to shoot at nothing, 'cause you can't see 'em. And if they catch you, they slice you to bits slowly 'cause they like to hear the white man scream. Then they slice the top of your head right off while you can still feel it!"

The Irishman Sean O'Brien laughed as if to ward off any thoughts of the reality of Tad's words.

"May yourself go stone blind so that you will not know your wife from a haystack!" Sean called out mockingly. It was an old Irish curse, and all the Irishmen laughed.

Tad looked at them and shook his head. "I don't have a wife," he answered, stone-faced. "And glad of it. I've no desire to leave a widow!"

"Ah! We know how to fight! We're trained soldiers. Been in lots of battles, won them all. Don't worry, little Virginia boy, we'll take care of you!" Sean laughed again.

Tad shook his head. He was finished trying to get through to these dolts. The march had been long, and it had taken its toll on the wagons and the livestock. Moreover, they had been forced to abandon some of the heavy artillery, and the morale of the men was not what it should have been. If the Irish fools didn't realize what a mess things already were and didn't care to know what might happen, there was nothing he could do.

Tad rolled over in his bedroll, turning away from the fire. The hell with them! Let them find out in a week's time when they got closer to Fort Duquesne. But it still bothered Tad. Overconfidence could easily cause defeat, and Tad knew exactly what that meant.

General Braddock sat in his tent with Hepzibah. They had just finished dinner and were sipping some fine Irish whiskey. Braddock could only marvel at Hepzibah's stamina. No matter how hard and difficult the day's trek, she never seemed to tire.

"We're getting close to our destination," Braddock said, poking his tongue into the whiskey. "God! Will I

116

be glad when this is over! I look forward to sleeping in a bed at Fort Duquesne!"

Hepzibah looked a trifle doubtful. "I imagine they'll protect those beds." Hepzibah had reason to doubt it would go so easily. Her husband had died at Fort Necessity, and however much she admired her "Braddy," she felt it her duty to remind him of the realities of colonial life.

"Pshaw!" Braddock answered. Then he crooked his finger at his comely Amazon, beckoning her to his side. "There are things you don't know," he confided in a whisper. "We do have spies . . . one in Quebec City, one who will soon be in Fort Niagara, and one right inside Fort Duquesne. The one inside Duquesne is a hostage named Robert Soho, and he prepared a map and had it smuggled out by an Indian."

As Braddock spoke, he opened a small, square, metal strong box, taking out a crumpled piece of parchment. He unfolded it on the table and showed it to Hepzibah. "See here, he's drawn a map of all the defenses of the garrison." Braddock moved his finger around the map. "I know exactly what to do," he announced. "I have every detail worked out."

Hepzibah studied the map in the candlelight and felt her spirits grow. Her general was not just cocky after all!

"It's wonderful!" Hepzibah reached out and touched Braddock's arm. He withdrew momentarily and re-folded the precious paper, returning it to safekeeping in the strong box, which he locked and slipped back into his bag. Then he returned to Hepzibah.

"It's a long journey tomorrow," he hinted. "Ought we not go to bed?"

Hepzibah smiled knowingly and without further encouragement began to undo her clothing, which she tossed aside with gay abandon. General Braddock fairly dribbled each time she behaved in such a manner. Her mounds of white flesh glimmered in the candlelight. He reached for her hand across the narrow little table, leading her around it toward their makeshift bed.

As they tumbled down onto the mounds of quilts, Hepzibah undid the strings of his breeches.

Braddock seized her breathlessly and marveled at the fact that his two hands were barely equal to the task of encompassing only one of her huge breasts.

Eagerly, Braddock mounted Hepzibah. It passed through his mind that even if the quilts on the floor of the tent offered little in the way of comfort, Hepzibah herself provided a fine mattress on which to rest one's weary body.

Tad Williamson and Sean O'Brien were part of the advance scouting party. When they reached Turtle Creek, a small river that ran into the Monongahela, Tad pointed off into the woods and said, "We're about eight miles from Duquesne."

Tad and Sean were not very far ahead of the rest of the long column. A large group from the advance party was already ambling along the riverbank—the whole long column was stretched out behind them on the road.

It was Tad's trained ears that first heard the sound of horses approaching the clearing. He held up his hand, and the column came to a full stop behind him, pulling up their horses in surprise. Tad pointed, but it was too late.

"It's the Canadians!" Tad bellowed.

"Open fire! Open fire!"

The troop of men immediately took up positions and opened fire with blasts of grapeshot.

Louis Liénard de Beaujeu had intended to lay ambush for the British, but he was as surprised as the British. "Return fire!" Beaujeu cried out in French.

Mathew had been riding at the rear of the Canadian column, and he took in the scene at a glance. He knew full well that the entire British colonial army could not be far behind. He turned his horse abruptly and rode toward Charles-Michel Langlade, who was in charge of the large number of Indians who rode with the Canadians. "Take the high ground!" Mathew advised breath-lessly.

"So we can attack the enemy flank!" Langlade had already seen the advantage and was on his way to seize it. The French regulars took up positions in the front, while the Indians spread out.

Mathew looked upward. The sun was shining, and there wasn't a cloud in the sky. "That's a good omen," he said, pointing to the clear blue sky. Langlade looked puzzled.

Mathew only shook his head and waved Langlade on. It was no time for explanations of things past, but this was the first battle Mathew Macleod had ever fought in when it wasn't raining.

A cry from the British soldiers could be heard clearly above the gunfire. Mathew and the French regulars around him froze.

"Long live the king! Long live the king!" It rang out across the field. Then someone shouted, "Beaujeu's been killed!"

Both sides now were employing their full troop strength and deafening volleys crashed on all sides. Down on the field, Captain Jean-Daniel Dumas took over from Beaujeu. It was immediately obvious that Dumas was a man with extraordinary leadership skills. He wasted no time after Beaujeu fell. He rallied the regulars and bought the necessary time for the Indians to take cover in the dense woods.

Within minutes, the Indians opened fire on the enemy columns. The British fell back in screaming confusion.

The bulk of the British and colonial troops were jammed together on the narrow road. They were suddenly deluged by retreating soldiers.

Wagons were overturned as their drivers attempted to turn them around. Disorganized, shrieking Irish troops ran off in all directions, trying to seek shelter, and artillery officers fought against their own men, attempting to get the cannon in position. But there was no firing because the British and colonial forward troops were between the cannon and the enemy.

"Where the hell are they?!" Fearful soldiers sought a target, but they saw only faceless trees spewing forth bullets.

"I'll never get back to Belfast!" Sean O'Brien screamed. Disorganized British soldiers cried out curses in their frustration, but they could not see their enemy and the murderous fire continued.

Braddock was thoroughly confused. This was no way to fight a battle! He had expected an orderly line of enemy approaching him in a clearing. How was one to show one's superiority if one could not see what one was shooting at? He rode about trying to organize his terrified army of British regulars, most of whom shrieked their fears about not wanting to be scalped as they tried desperately to get away.

Braddock was utterly staggered. His troops had been well-trained in the art of formal battle, but not in the art of backwoods ambush. Moreover, to Braddock's great shock the Indians were precise marksmen. His troops were literally being mowed down by Indian gunfire.

"Holy Mother of God!" Langlade pronounced. "Look how they run!"

Mathew did not look at Langlade. He had his musket trained on a target he knew. Long live the king, indeed! Mathew trained his musket on the portly British general who was trying so idiotically to rally his men— none other than General Braddock, veteran of the British victory at Culloden and one of the men most responsible for the rape of Scotland, both literally and figuratively! Mathew fired, mumbling under his breath, "One for the MacDonalds, the Camerons, and all the Jacobites you slaughtered!"

Langlade looked over at his engineer. Mathew Macleod's face was normally kind and placid. He had the kind of openness that made him a friend to almost any man. But at this moment, Langlade saw something quite different. He saw that Mathew Macleod remembered his enemies and suspected that he had just been released from an old vow. "Is that the famous General Braddock?"

Mathew actually smiled as he nodded in the affirmative. He raised his musket over his head and yelled, "For Bonnie Prince Charlie!" Mathew's incongruous holler rang through the woods.

"Something personal?" Langlade inquired.

"Very personal," Mathew said, aware that tears were forming in the corners of his eyes. "As personal as five thousand hacked, murdered countrymen!"

"For Bonnie Prince Charlie!" Repeating the phrase, Mathew rode off into the heat of the battle. He saw that the felled General Braddock was carried from the field. Suddenly Mathew Macleod felt even. This day was his own retribution for Culloden. The field quieted down. The British, or what was left of them, were in full retreat, running to save their scalps from the vengeful Indians. Mathew looked up at the blue sky and smiled to himself. He was free of his hatred at last.

The Canadians cleaned up, and by nightfall most of them were headed back to Fort Duquesne, eight miles down the trail. Eight miles! It was as close as the British got.

Dumas walked around the fort and inspected the treasures of war as they were brought in from the field of battle. Guns—the big brass and sixes, howitzers and mortars. A fine addition to the artillery the French already had. And there were abandoned wagons and farm animals—more pack horses than could be put to work. Ah, the British were so generous! They left clothing, utensils, furniture, and a wonderful store of Irish whiskey!

Dumas made his way to the officers' mess. While his anxious men watched, he plopped down a large strong box on a long oak table.

"Over twenty-five-thousand pounds—and this!" Dumas triumphantly opened General Braddock's captured war chest. Inside it were copies of all his correspondence with London, his orders, the map of Fort Duquesne, and the British plans for attack on Fort Niagara and Fort St. Frédéric.

"My, my!" Dumas intoned. "For a nation that has not yet declared war, General Braddock seems to have had very interesting orders!"

"What shall we do with the prisoners, sir?" The young French officer pointed out toward the fort yard where a group of naked, shivering prisoners were huddled under guard.

"Take them to the stockade!" Dumas ordered. He was a happy man. There were over five-hundred British and colonial dead and hundreds more who were wounded or now on the run from the Indians. The Canadians had lost a total of three officers, three members of the Canadian militia, two members of the Troupe de Marine, and fifteen Indians. The French, Canadian, and Indian forces combined sustained a mere twenty-three casualties in all. Dumas smiled. "Considering we were outnumbered, I'd say we had a fine day!"

Mathew did not hesitate to join his fellows in more than one round of the captured Irish whiskey. But the wounded left on the field troubled him.

"What about the British wounded?" he asked after a time. Mathew knew he had left his intense hatred for the British out on the battlefield, and he didn't regret the loss. The fate of his fellow countrymen at Culloden and the subsequent rape and pillage—Janet's rape—had gnawed at his soul for over nine years. Now he felt the luxury of human kindness. The men lying wounded on the road eight miles away may have been British, but they were also human.

"Leave them to the Indians!" Dumas replied coldly. "It's part of our agreement with them—we don't ask what they do with them, and I personally don't want to know."

Mathew looked at Dumas carefully. Dumas had certainly not lost *his* hatred for the British. Mathew sipped his whiskey and considered the situation. War was war, but Mathew sensed it might be difficult for him to continue to fight with the French—not that he had any intention of fighting for the British. The question he was asking himself was simple: Did one have to be as bad as one's enemies?

The whiskey warmed Mathew's throat, and he tried to push his many conflicting thoughts out of his mind.

"I'd like to send you to Fort Niagara" Dumas said, interrupting Mathew's thoughts. "We have the British plans and I suspect Niagara will need some additional fortifications."

"I expect you're right," Mathew answered. It was not the perfect solution, but it was the offered solution. Mathew suspected that it would be a long time before the British mounted another attack. Fort Niagara and his land would be quite safe after today's rout. He wanted to go there in any case. "We can leave in a few days' time," Mathew said thoughtfully. But in the back of his mind he nurtured a fear too. The mountains, the Alleghenys, had been a shield, protecting the French from the English. Now those mountains had been crossed and they might be crossed again. They might become a bitter shield.

CHAPTER VII

July 9, 1757

Hepzibah had run blindly into the woods, brandishing a
musket and screaming curses at the top of her mighty
lungs. In a small clearing about half a mile from the
main fighting, she had stopped frozen in fear and
horror.

A dozen or so red-eyed Indians had surrounded her,
and whooping and yelling their ungodly cries, they
dared her to shoot.

Hepzibah had bravely fired one shot, but an arrow
pierced her shoulder and felled her. The Amazon
passed out on the ground while the braves danced
about her, shouting and screaming.

When she awoke, Hepzibah found herself tied to a
flat board. As she began to focus, she saw that she was
still surrounded by screaming, shrieking warriors, who
waved their tomahawks about her wildly.

For an hour or more, they danced around her—a
whirling blur to her disoriented eyes and shattered
nerves. They began their ritual with a series of slashes
on her arms and legs—deep slashes made with long,
glistening hunting knives. Hepzibah screamed in pain

and several times lost consciousness, only to awake to more torture and more pain.

Next they slashed at her huge breasts, then at her stomach. The wounds poured forth blood, and Hepzibah screamed for mercy, begging them to kill her quickly. But she was a strong woman, and she lasted many hours before the Indian chief ordered the final blow. This was delivered on the head—an act of mercy—before she was scalped.

Hepzibah's body, bearing no less than one-hundred separate knife slashes, was then carried to the fire. There, the women of the tribe artfully butchered her. As was the custom, her womb and buttocks were cooked first. These were consumed by the women of the tribe, who hoped that eating them would increase their own fertility. Then the rest of Hepzibah was also cooked and eaten, and portions of her fatty meat were given to all.

Janet and Mathew nestled together in their bedroll. All the young children slept. Robert had left several weeks before to return to Quebec City. The evening fire still burned in the hearth, and the main room of the overcrowded little cabin still smelled of food from the evening meal.

Mathew slipped his arm under Janet's shoulders and pulled her to him.

"You're quiet tonight," Janet whispered.

Mathew squeezed his wife lovingly. "Battles don't make me talkative."

"It was quite a victory," Janet answered. She was well aware that Mathew's mood was not the kind of triumphant one to be expected after victory.

"It's difficult for me to put it into words," Mathew said thoughtfully. "I killed a man today . . . a British general who fought at Culloden . . . a man responsible for much of what happened after . . ." Mathew paused. "I'm not sure I can make you understand—I'm not certain I understand myself."

Janet pulled herself up on one elbow and looked into Mathew's serious face. "Try," she urged. "Try to tell me."

"It's as if I evened the score. I don't love the British or their colonial allies—but something's happened to me. I don't hate them as I once did." Mathew shook his head. "I don't like leaving the wounded out there to be scalped or eaten by animals . . ." For a moment Mathew watched the shadows made by the fire as they danced across the ceiling. "Some of the Indians practice cannibalism," he added.

Janet leaned over and hugged Mathew. "I do understand," she assured him. Janet reflected for a moment. She did not really hate the British either—except for one man. That man was the ugly, brutal sergeant who had raped and beaten her after the Scots defeat at Culloden. Her negative feelings were focused on that one man; inside Janet felt no animosity for the faceless colonists and British soldiers who were now the enemy.

"We are in New France," Janet said, then with determination continued, "we do have to defend ourselves and our land." She bent over and kissed Mathew's cheek. "But we don't have to hate," she added softly. "We don't have to behave the way either the French or the English do." Janet's mind strayed back to Louise's trial and the harsh and inhuman verdict that was handed down.

Mathew pulled Janet still closer, pressing her body into his. He knew that she understood and that he didn't have to say any more. They were one, as always.

François Bigot was the intendant of New France, making him the second most important man in Canada, which had the status of a French overseas province. The intendant's source of power was drawn from his role in government. He was in charge of all economic affairs, a situation from which Bigot knew how to profit immensely.

Buying and selling, awarding contracts, making certain appointments—these activities fell within Bigot's jurisdiction. Bigot's motto was quite simple: "You receive after you give." In other words, Bigot never gave out a government contract without receiving a personal payment from the contractor. In this way, Bigot had greatly increased his personal fortune.

But Bigot was a generous man—both with the fortune he came into honestly and with his ill-acquired wealth. Indeed, he was so generous with his inheritance that he was more or less forced into acquiring additional funds fraudulently. Bigot fancied himself as a man of impeccable breeding. Born in France, he was related to a marshall of France and to the Comte de Morville. Bigot held court in Quebec City much the way Louis XV held court in France, though on a lesser scale. Bigot was renowned for setting a fine table, for playing the grand seigneur, and for keeping a beautiful mistress. It was at Bigot's home that the upper class of Quebec met and dined; it was at his home that the most incredible parties took place.

Robert MacLean found himself at one such gathering more by accident than by design. In fact, he was ordered to attend. The reason for the gathering was to celebrate the great victory at Fort Duquesne, albeit three months after the event. Robert had just returned from the fort, and though he had not been present during the battle, he nevertheless had firsthand information and bore messages from the officers in charge.

Much to Robert's embarrassment, his reputation preceded him. Though he had only just turned seventeen, he had been given a commission. His childhood experience among the Mohawk enemy and his talents as a trained scout added immeasurably to his value. He was also multilingual, speaking French, English, Gaelic, and the Mohawk tongue. To these, he was adding two other Indian languages. He had lived with the Deschamps, a well-respected family up until their demise at the hands of a madwoman, and he had been reared by the wealthy Janet Cameron Macleod, who had arrived in Quebec rich with gold and who was now the guardian of the equally wealthy Deschamps children.

Robert MacLean was not the only Scot serving the government of New France. Indeed, there was an entire Highland regiment in Quebec—a regiment of former Jacobites who had fled Scotland and settled in Canada.

Having returned from Fort Duquesne, Robert found himself the object of polite curiosity. Quebec society was isolated from the population of Canada, and most of the members of that society hung on tales of the frontier, gaining a vicarious feeling of participation from them. They doted on the heroes of New France, regardless of whether the heroes were real or imaginary.

Robert shifted from one foot to the other. His scarlet uniform was new and stiff, but at least it kept him from having to wear evening clothes. One could not be incorrectly dressed while wearing the scarlet uniform of the militia, and for that Robert was grateful.

As he looked around, he could not help thinking of the late Madame Deschamps. Her home had been richly appointed, but it did not compare with the Bigot mansion, which was entirely furnished in the style of Louis XV. Everything appeared to have been imported directly from Paris.

The Bigot mansion boasted many fine rooms, all carpeted with deep, thick rugs. The walls of the central drawing room were paneled with a dark wood and groupings of fine paintings hung on each wall.

Lit by a proliferation of ornate silver and gold candelabra, the drawing room was alive with the tinkle of expensive European crystal. The decor, the people, and the conversation all had an unseemly elegance—incongruous given the realities of Quebec's fragile economy.

The other men in the drawing room all wore fine clothing: dark velvet trousers, bright waistcoats trimmed in gold, and white ruffled shirts with hand-made lace. The women dressed as women in Paris might dress—certainly as Robert remembered women in Paris dressing. The necklines of their lace, silk, taffeta, or brocade gowns dipped sufficiently low to be daring. Compared to the average habitant women, the women in the Bigot drawing room would be considered brazen.

Robert took a sip of his rosé wine and looked into the eyes of Madame Lupien, who smiled much too coquettishly for a woman of her age. Her pinched little face was framed by an elaborate coiffure, and her voice was strangely high-pitched as she said, "I can't imagine life outside Quebec! It must be dreadful at the frontier forts!"

Robert forced himself not to mention that it was, in fact, dreadful only several miles away from where they stood. The harvest had been bad, so food was short, and the Indian attacks continued. Moreover, sanitation in the lower half of the city left much to be desired, and the attitude of the people could be described in a single phrase: "In the name of God, leave us alone!" This phrase might have been addressed to the British, the Indians, or their own government.

But, speaking of such things with a woman like Madame Lupien would be of no earthly use. Instead, he went on to describe Fort Duquesne while her eyes grew large and cowlike.

"Oh, it must be terrible, I know you weren't there when the attack took place, but can you imagine such a thing?! Oh! Those colonists are such—such barbarians!" Madame Lupien sniffed. "Yes, barbarians! Uneducated, uncultivated barbarians! Do you know I've heard they won't even negotiate properly for the release of our hostages? And we're not even at war!"

Several responses went through Robert's mind, but he resisted. "You get used to the frontier," he answered noncommittally.

"But my, you've had such an adventurous life!" Madame Lupien was gushing.

"Much of it unsolicited," Robert answered dryly. It

was nearly ten o'clock and dinner had not yet been served. He felt his empty, gnawing stomach and wondered if the before-dinner drinks with their accompaniment of small talk would ever come to an end. Sometimes he wished he had not regained his voice. At least when he was mute, he was spared the obligation of meaningless conversation.

"Oh, do come with me," Madame Lupien urged. Her drooping bosom heaved with a deep breath, and her face was flushed with wine. She took Robert's arm firmly and began leading him through the crowded room. "I want you to meet my niece!" She turned her head, "Come, come . . ."

Robert allowed himself to be guided among the mingling guests. "Here she is!" Madame Lupien placed her arm on the young girl's shoulder and pulled her about.

"Monsieur MacLean, I would like to present my niece, Marguerite Lupien."

Robert's eyes widened with delight. Suddenly, he thought to himself, the evening had begun to look somewhat brighter.

Marguerite curtsied prettily and smiled up at him. She was a small girl, not more than five feet. But she was perfectly proportioned, with warm hazel eyes and a mass of dark brown curls framing her face. Marguerite seemed to be his own age, perhaps a year younger.

"Mademoiselle . . ." Robert bowed and kissed her delicate hand.

"I feel you two should get to know one another," Madame Lupien said meaningfully. Then in a whirl of silk, she spun away to mingle with the other guests.

Marguerite blushed deeply. "My aunt is . . . is a very enthusiastic person."

Robert grinned. "I'm glad," he replied, a hint of mischief in his voice. "Do you suppose it's possible to find a place to sit?"

Marguerite looked around quickly and spotted an empty settee in a far corner alcove of the room. "Over there?" She tilted her head, and Robert took her arm, guiding her toward the brocaded refuge.

"I've not seen you before in Quebec," Robert commented. It was an absurd thing to say: there were a great many people in Quebec he hadn't seen. But how did one begin a conversation with a beautiful young woman?

"Oh, I've only just come from France," Marguerite answered seriously. "On the same ship as the new governor, Monsieur Vaudreuil."

Robert inhaled and let out his breath. "You are fortunate. Had you been traveling a little later, your ship might have been attacked."

Marguerite pressed her lips together and met his eyes. "I wish I had not come at all. Now I can't go back to France . . . and terrible things are happening everywhere."

"There are some victories," Robert said, trying to cheer her up. "Except for Acadia we're holding our ground."

Robert was only too aware of the events that had taken place in June while he was on his way back to Quebec from Fort Duquesne. At almost the same time that General Braddock was attemtping to take Fort Duquesne, Governor Shirley of the Massachusetts Bay Colony had taken a force of colonial militia and some British regulars and taken Fort Beauséjour. By all accounts it had been a terrible battle. But the loss of Fort Beauséjour was not the only tragedy. What was happening now was nothing less than an atrocity.

When Fort Beauséjour had surrendered, it was agreed that the Acadians would be pardoned because the French regular army had more or less forced them into fighting. But the dishonorable governor of Massachusetts had left almost immediately to take over from Braddock following his defeat and death on July 9. Shirley had left Governor Lawrence of Nova Scotia in command and Lawrence had not kept the terms of the surrender. He was deporting the Acadians. The cruel and unnecessary deportations had begun in September, and they continued even now as Robert and Marguerite were speaking.

Some fifteen hundred of the ragged, pitiful Acadian refugees had run away and reached Canada, but the others had been rounded up and placed in camps. As quickly as ships could be provided, the Acadians were distributed throughout the southern colonies where, being outnumbered, they would be absorbed if they didn't starve first. Worse yet, the Acadians were close-knit and family-oriented, so the most inhuman and atrocious thing about the deportations was the splitting of families. Small children were sent on one ship, their parents on another.

Marguerite shook her head again in sadness. "I've been helping with the refugees—in the hospital," she said. "I hear the stories of what's happened to them— it's inhuman!"

Robert was quite taken aback. Marguerite was not only delicate and beautiful, she was compassionate as well. She was the loveliest girl he had ever met and the first he felt anything for.

They continued to talk, then Robert paused. "I should like to ask your aunt's permission to call on you," he finally managed, "if that would be agreeable to you."

Marguerite blushed again. "Most agreeable," she replied.

"It's not much," Mathew said, opening the door of the three-room cabin. "But it's got two fireplaces, and we can build on it."

"But it's ours!" Janet said with delight. "It's our beginning."

Pierre and René were already unloading the wagons. They trudged into the cabin, carrying what they could, mostly the smaller parcels and boxes.

"It's close enough to the fort," Mathew said, putting down a large carton. "But not too close."

"It's wonderful land," Janet answered. She looked

132

out on the blaze of October colors. In the background one could hear the rushing river as it thundered through the gorge that marked the end of their property.

"If the winter's not too bad, I can get some more land cleared before spring."

"That gives you two jobs," Janet reminded him.

"Nobody attacks in the winter," Mathew assured her. "I'm still uneasy about leaving you out here when I'm at the fort."

Janet laughed. "It's what we decided! We decided to live in our own house on our own land and to farm that land. Mathew, I've lived in more dangerous places. Besides, I won't be alone!" Janet looked lovingly at the children. Pierre was so tall, and René only a little shorter. Mat and Andrew were getting big too, and eight-year-old Madelaine could certainly help. "Look, I have four fine men to protect me!" René and Pierre beamed.

"I'm almost old enough to be in the army," Pierre boasted.

Mathew ruffled Pierre's brown hair. "Not quite yet," he said, smiling. Nonetheless, he could hardly deny that Pierre was nearly full-grown and a fine shot.

"The land's in a good location," Mathew commented.

"It's perfect! Mathew, one day we'll have a proper house on this land."

"And one day I'll build a bridge across that river!" Mathew laughed and hugged her.

"At the falls, I suppose?" Janet was laughing too.

"A bridge should have a good view," Mathew said, still smiling at the grandiose plans. Then with a sudden burst of love, he lifted Janet into his arms and turned her around. She leaned over toward him and kissed him. "Enough of this. We need to get a fire started, it's damp in here!"

Mathew set her down. "Right away!"

Janet gathered up the boxes the children had brought in and began opening them. Things had to be put away

133

and temporary beds arranged. At the moment she faced three empty rooms and two wagons of household and personal belongings. But they were hers, Janet thought to herself as she got down to the work of getting settled. "It's our land," Janet kept saying under her breath. "Ours—Mathew's and mine!"

Mathew came back and forth, carrying the heavier items, and each of the children carried what they could till almost everything was inside.

Janet shoved their table into place and began to unpack the utensils she needed to cook with. By six o'clock Mathew had come in with the last load of furniture.

"This place is a mess!" Mathew said cheerfully.

Janet looked at him with misty green eyes. "I've lived in castles, on farms, and even in a palace. None of them was as nice as this. This is our home!"

Mathew grinned and began rummaging in one of the boxes.

"What are you doing?" Janet laughed. "There's time to unpack later."

"Well, this is something special," Mathew said as he withdrew a large, flat parcel wrapped carefully in cloth. "Something I had made for the front gate when we have a front gate."

Janet looked on curiously as Mathew opened it. Inside was a wooden plaque with a hand-carved inscription. "The name of this land—your land," he said, handing it to Janet. It said: LOCHIEL . . . FOUNDED BY JANET AND MATHEW MACLEOD, OCTOBER 1755.

Janet ran her finger over the engraved words, and tears flooded her green eyes. Lochiel . . . for the Camerons of Lochiel who had lost their own land to the British!

"Oh, Mathew!" Janet leaned against him. "This Lochiel will always be ours!"

It was a proper courtship. Robert came to call on Marguerite once a week and sometimes, his training schedule permitting, twice. At first their visits had been

134

awkward and stiff, with Madame Lupien acting as a chattering chaperone. She droned on endlessly while they all sat on the edges of their chairs, sipping wine or eating little pastries.

After a time, Madame left them more to themselves, allowing them to walk in the garden and finally to go out together within the safe confines of the upper city. The lower city had come to be a dangerous place, and the countryside was unfortunately less than secure.

Robert grew more in love with Marguerite each time he was with her, and when they were separated, he thought about her constantly. They attended a constant round of parties given by the first families of the upper city, at which they danced, met with other young couples, and talked to one another for hours.

When Robert kissed Marguerite and she returned his passion, his courage grew. And after a year and a half—the socially required length of time, having courted her for over a year—Robert proposed marriage in the spring of 1757.

The bells of the church of Notre Dame des Victoires were just striking four, and the weak May sun was lowering itself in the western sky. The garden of the Lupien house was alive with early-spring blossoms, and the air was unseasonably warm, as sometimes happens when a soft breeze blows out of the south.

"I'll speak to your uncle and aunt tomorrow," Robert promised. "I want to marry you now, but it's better if we wait—I'm sure to have orders soon."

Marguerite pressed herself to his chest. "I'm so afraid . . ." As she shivered against him, Robert felt the urgency of his own love for Marguerite. It was, nonetheless, an urgency he vowed to control. The war with the English went on—Robert could not bear the thought of leaving a widow to fend for herself.

"I would lock you up somewhere to keep you safe. I don't want to leave you."

Marguerite's hazel eyes flickered with fear, and Robert put his arms around her and kissed her lips and then her warm neck. "My God, I love you," he whispered.

135

"And I you," Marguerite answered, stroking his cheek. "Please come back to me, please don't let anything happen."

Marguerite sat down on the stone bench and pulled Robert down next to her. The garden was well-hidden from the house, and anyway Madame Lupien was away, leaving only Monsieur Lupien who, having drunk too much brandy, slept peacefully in his chair in the study.

Robert put his arm around Marguerite's shoulder, and she snuggled up to him, peacefully resting her head on him. It was a day without chaperones, a summer's day in early spring.

They sat for a time in silence, then Marguerite encircled Robert with her arm, drawing herself even closer to him.

"Robert . . . if you don't come back . . ." Tears welled in Marguerite's eyes, and she looked up at him pleadingly. "If you don't come back, I'll never have known you . . . I mean, really known you."

Robert felt another surge of fevered desire. It was a desire made more urgent by the threat of battle and separation. They were both virgins, but Robert had vowed to be honorable, to take Marguerite as wife. She was young and innocent, a lady, a girl from a fine family, a girl raised in a convent.

Robert leaned over and kissed her neck again. Marguerite's hand dropped into his lap where a fire burned.

She breathed heavily against him, and Robert knew she could feel him rising, even as he kissed her neck and then her cleavage, boldly burying his face in her. They remained in that position for a moment. In that instant Robert thought he would die of desire.

Finally, the two young lovers lifted their heads, and Robert looked into Marguerite's tear-filled eyes. Her full lips were parted, her cheeks flushed.

"I want you now," she whispered.

Robert trembled. It was not right, not proper. It was wrong. Still, a thousand images moved through his mind. He would soon be leaving the relative safety of Quebec City and going into battle. There were no assurances, no promises one could make, no future one could look forward to.

As if she'd read his mind, Marguerite pleaded with him, "I want you . . . I'll always want you, only you. Oh, Robert, we don't know . . . the past is dying! The future might never come." Marguerite pressed herself to him again. "We only have the present. Oh, Robert, we have this moment." She kissed his lips, and Robert's desire grew as his resolve melted before her urgent pleas.

"Come," Marguerite murmured. She stood up and took him by the hand to the little summer house in the garden. "Here," she whispered. "We can be alone here . . . for a little while."

In the humid stillness of the small house, Robert could hear himself breathing as he fumbled with the ties that held her bodice. Then he touched her beautiful bare breasts almost as if they were sacred, and her nipples hardened under his fingers and then his lips.

Marguerite's flesh grew warm under his unsure groping movements, and she moaned and moved beneath him. Carefully, Robert lifted her skirts and removed her undergarments. He felt her soft white thighs. Urgently, with shaking fingers, Robert fumbled to free himself.

Marguerite touched him curiously, feeling what seemed to be a bone. Tingling with excitement, Robert jumped at the touch of her fingers. "Spread your legs," he whispered hoarsely. Then with boyish excitement, he pressed into her. Marguerite let out a cry and shook against him. Again Robert thrust and she cried out as he penetrated her, painfully breaking her maidenhead and causing her to shake violently with the temporary hurt.

His eyes closed, his senses concentrated, Robert throbbed into her, unable to control himself. Then he collapsed against her. "Oh, my God! I've hurt you." He fairly gathered her up in his arms, whispering over and over, "I didn't mean to hurt you, I didn't mean to hurt you."

Marguerite clung to him, afraid that if he withdrew the pain would be even greater. "Don't leave," she gasped. "Don't move . . ." Then after a time, the ache disappeared. "It's all right," she finally said.

Robert carefully withdrew, feeling the embarrassment of his own youthful clumsiness and the quickness of his spent passion.

"I'm sorry," was all he could manage to say. Then he tenderly kissed her breasts again and again.

"It's all right," Marguerite answered. Her arms went around his neck, her body moved under his kisses, and she found that in spite of her pain, she longed to have him touch her more.

Instinctively, she moved Robert's hand to the most sensitive part of her body. And sensing that she enjoyed the movements of his fingers, he stroked her till her face flushed and she threw her arms around him and cried out in the release of pure pleasure.

Robert watched her as her face grew pinkish, her eyes closed, and her lips opened. He saw her tense, and he saw her fall into a shivering release. Then he pressed her to him and rocked her back and forth. "It'll be better next time," he promised. "We'll learn together."

"I love you," Marguerite whispered.

"And I you," Robert answered.

Robert rocked Marguerite and thought about his coming assignment. Would he come back?

The regular supply convoy arrived at Fort Niagara in the first week of May 1759. It was an easy eight-day journey from Montreal, down the St. Lawrence and along the south shore of Lake Ontario, with only one portage to avoid the great falls at Niagara.

The supply convoy carried seeds for planting, some small farm animals, military supplies, and women and children who had come to join their husbands for the summer months.

As the central junction for the fur trade, the fort was

of strategic importance, and a small community had grown up nearby. It was composed of a few scattered farms and the shanty cabins of the middlemen who bought and sold furs.

Among the wives arriving to join their husbands was a comely young Irish girl who traveled under the name of Megan Coulon. Megan had obtained the name of a dead soldier from informants in Montreal. It had taken some time to arrange, but her cover was complete. It would be assumed that she had left to join her husband before the notification of his death reached her.

Megan stood in the acting commandant's office and received the sad news that the husband she sought to join was dead. "*Mon Dieu!*" the acting commandant muttered. "And you have traveled so far to receive such bad news!"

Megan O'Flynn, the consummate actress, forced tears into her magnificent blue eyes and sank into the hard-backed chair opposite the commandant's desk. Covering her eyes with her hand, she sobbed quietly and mumbled in French, "What shall I do? Oh, monsieur, what shall I do?" Megan paused briefly in her portrayal of grief and sniffed. "I can't go all the way back to Montreal! I have no family, monsieur, they've all been killed! I am quite alone in the world! Alone!"

The commandant fidgeted with his belt buckle and tried not to cry himself. He was a man of high emotion and unused to the sight of a sobbing woman in his office. Still, as he looked at Madame Coulon, he could not put it out of his mind that a woman so beautiful would surely not remain alone or single long. In the civilized areas of Canada, men outnumbered available women at all times; here on the frontier the ratio was preposterous. There were more than one-hundred single young men—men who would gladly marry a beautiful widow and look after her. Indeed, he himself was quite available.

The commandant cleared his throat several times before a puffy-eyed Megan removed her hand from her eyes and looked up at him.

"I'll find some sort of employment for you," he offered. "Obviously, I can't send you back to Quebec alone."

Megan sniffed. "Oh, monsieur—you're too kind!" The commandant blushed a deep red. He was a rotund little man who had lost his own wife two years before when she had succumbed to consumption. The young woman before him was an exquisite creature, albeit distraught at the moment. It vaguely occurred to him that the problem of his loneliness might be solved. "Can you cook?" he asked.

Megan nodded. "*Oui, monsieur.*"

He cleared his throat again. "I need a cook." Then it suddenly struck him that Madame Coulon might take his suggestion the wrong way. She looked like a proper young woman—modestly dressed in plain woolen clothes, her dark hair partially covered with a scarf. "Strictly a cook, madame. I didn't mean to suggest . . ." He reddened again. "I'm a man of honor—" he stuttered.

Megan smiled shyly. "Oh, monsieur . . . I would never think a man of your stature, of your importance . . . a man so kind would—would have anything else in mind!" Her great blue eyes were wide in worshipful wonderment, and the commandant dissolved before her, his words reduced to embarrassed, incoherent mumblings. "A sort of hostess . . . uh, you understand . . ."

Megan bowed her head. "*Oui, monsieur,* I understand."

The commandant congratulated himself. She was a proper young lady, no doubt a good, convent-bred woman and above reproach. "I'll make arrangements for you to live with one of the families."

Again Megan nodded silently. It was all she could do to repress a smile. The old dear was a simple little man—a man easily manipulated.

The commandant stood up and smoothed out his rumpled uniform. "Let me show you around," he suggested. "You can leave your things here."

He cursed himself for his unmilitary appearance and wished he had taken more care with his attire on this particular day. But how was he to know that this would be the day an angel would come into his life?

Megan stood up and adjusted her dark scarf. Eyes down, she followed the acting commandant, Monsieur Godé, out of his office. He led her across the main yard of the fort and up to a smaller building where he knocked on the door.

Mathew started at the sound of the knock. He was deeply absorbed in reading engineer Léry's suggestions for improving the fortifications and adding his own suggestions to Léry's notes.

"Monsieur Macleod?" Godé poked his balding head in the door.

Mathew stood up quickly, and Godé entered with a young woman. She stood shyly a few feet behind him.

"Monsieur Macleod, I want to introduce Madame Coulon. Madame Coulon is a widow, but she will be remaining here . . . at least for the summer. I bring her to meet you because you have your wife here. There are so few women . . ." His voice trailed off.

"Madame," Mathew smiled at the shy-appearing young woman. She was unusually beautiful.

Megan lifted her eyes and held out her hand gracefully—perhaps too gracefully for a Canadian woman allegedly the widow of a young army officer.

Mathew kissed her hand. "Let me welcome you to Fort Niagara," he said politely.

Megan could not been more pleased. He was an engineer! One of the very men she had to get to know, a man who would know everything about the fort and its construction. But more pleasurable still, he wasn't French! He was a tall, exceptionally good-looking Scot. It did not matter that he was married. What, after all, could a frontier French wife look like? Doubtlessly a dowdy little woman with no charm and no education.

Megan looked at Mathew Macleod. She knew that there was another engineer, Léry, who was in full charge of all defenses and that Monsieur Pouchot, a third engineer, was in charge of the defenses for this fort. But both these men were currently away, and Megan, after a moment of consideration, decided that this civilian assistant might indeed be more useful.

"Thank you, monsieur," Megan replied, lifting her eyes to meet Mathew's curious look.

Mathew raised an eyebrow. Her French was perfect, but she had a slight accent that betrayed it as her second language rather than her mother tongue. Moreover, it was the French spoken in France, not the French spoken by most Canadians.

"You are not Canadian, madame?"

Megan smiled and shook her head. "An immigrant —an Irish Jacobite," she answered. "But my husband . . ." She paused to blink back tears. "My late husband, Pierre Coulon, was Canadian. From Montreal."

Mathew nodded knowingly. "I'm Scots," he admitted. "Also a Jacobite refugee."

"We have something in common," Megan replied carefully.

"Perhaps you can come to dinner sometime. When you are settled, madame. My wife will be glad to have female companionship."

"I should be pleased," Megan answered. Then she turned obediently to her benefactor. "Would that be all right, monsieur?"

"But of course," Godé beamed. Then considering the matter for a second, he added, "But it would be more convenient if you all came to my quarters."

Mathew nodded his agreement. It was true that the journey back from the farm to the fort was better taken during daylight hours. He and Janet could stay in the fort and return in the morning.

"Well, that's arranged," Godé sighed. "Come along . . . there's more to show you." As he guided Megan away, Mathew followed them with his eyes. Madame Coulon was an enigma. There was something about her . . . something Mathew could not fathom. He watched them walk away across the fort yard. "Well,

142

it's no business of mine," he said to himself as he closed the door.

After Megan's perfunctory tour of the fort, Godé returned her to his own quarters. "I don't know where you'll spend the night . . ." He looked around uneasily. His quarters had only two small rooms. A large one for cooking and entertaining—such as he did—and a sort of alcove for sleeping. Now if he had actually been the commander, he would have had larger headquarters.

"I must apologize, madame. My quarters are not large. You see, I'm only the acting commandant."

Megan again had to force back a smile. Actually she had known that all along and preferred his situation. Attempting to become the wife or mistress of the head man was too conspicuous. Her relationship with Godé would not be so obvious.

"But you are an important man!" Megan praised, her eyes opening wide. She reached out and touched his arm. "I can stay here tonight. I know you are a man of honor."

"Oh, but madame, that would not be proper." Godé again blushed. He ran a nervous finger around his collar and was suddenly aware he was perspiring.

Megan formed her perfect mouth into a little pout and tilted her head becomingly. "What we and God know is proper, *is* proper, monsieur. I trust you completely."

Godé shrugged and gave in instantly. Who could refuse such a beautiful angel? Who was he to contradict either her sweet words of praise or her trust?

CHAPTER VIII

May 1757

Robert sat stiffly on the edge of the settee. Monsieur Lupien sat on his right, and Madame Lupien sat in a soft, yellow brocaded chair opposite. Both Madame and Monsieur Lupien looked bemused at Robert's obvious discomfort.

"Marguerite will be down soon," her aunt promised in a bland tone. "Isn't the weather magnificent?" Her eyes strayed outside.

"Oui, madame," Robert answered, aware that he sounded uncomfortable and must have looked as ill at ease as he felt.

He cleared his throat, "Madame, monsieur, I have a most important matter to discuss with you." Robert felt an urge to get it over with, even to blurt it out. But he restrained himself. Form was important—to the French, manners were the sign of good upbringing, a proper background. Here in the wealthy district of Quebec City, people like the Lupiens had done everything possible to create a little Paris. Of course, outside Quebec City—amoung the habitants and even among some of the seigneurs—there was quite a different attitude, an easier attitude with less formality. The people of New France were distant from the upper class of Quebec City, and in spite of the war, they resented having to billet French regular troops in their homes. The Canadians longed to rid themselves of the vestiges of the French feudal system and the colonial government.

Though the Lupiens and their ilk were imitators of the French royalty in the new land, Marguerite was different. She was compassionate and intelligent, young enough to be flexible. Nonetheless, Robert knew he would have to go through the motions with her guardians.

"I would like to request the hand of your niece in marriage," Robert finally managed to say. He leaned back a little and tried to assess their reaction. Surely they expected his proposal. He had been calling on Marguerite for over a year, always acting the ardent suitor.

"And your prospects?" the proper Monsieur Lupien asked.

It was an expected question. Robert recited them along with a list of his assets. He had charge of the house left by Madame Deschamps, even if at present French officers were being billeted there. He also had more than half the gold that Janet had guarded so carefully over the years, which she insisted he take. Moreover, Robert was in charge of the large land holdings of Maurice Deschamps near Trois Rivières.

Monsieur Lupien was most impressed. Like much of the government aristocracy of Quebec, his wealth was more show than substance. And times were undeniably terrible. Crop failures had resulted in famine and food riots in the lower city. The situation on the farms along the St. Lawrence was scarcely any better. Life was difficult, and growing worse.

"Does Marguerite agree?" Madame Lupien asked.

"*Oui, madame,*" Robert answered.

Monsieur Lupien smiled and revealed two rows of yellow, crooked teeth. "We would not stand in the way of Marguerite's happiness! I can see no objection to this union."

Robert knew what was expected of him. He stood up and bowed to Monsieur Lupien and then to Madame, whose hand he kissed. "I cannot express my gratitude," he said.

That done, he sat back down.

Monsieur Lupien looked away and ran his hand along the material that covered the settee. From his sudden nervousness, Robert could guess what was coming, though he had suspected it all along.

"Marguerite is, as you know, an orphan," Monsieur said slowly. "Madame and I have already married two daughters and given two dowries. I'm afraid . . ." His voice trailed off and he didn't finish his sentence. It would have been bad form indeed to mention his financial status openly.

Doubtless the Lupiens assumed that it would be simple to find a husband for their niece, but a husband of equal standing certainly would have expected a dowry. No surprise then that the Lupiens were anxious for Marguerite to marry Robert, who had money and prospects as an officer in the military.

Robert smiled and sought to put Monsieur Lupien at ease immediately. "A dowry is of no concern to me," he said quickly.

A look of relief passed over both the Lupiens' faces.

"And when will the marriage take place?" Madame was cooing now.

"Madame, regrettably I have orders to join General Montcalm as a scout. But as soon as I return . . ."

"Perfect!" Madame said breathlessly. "I'm certain it won't be long."

Robert let out his breath. He wished he could be so optimistic. The situation as to both food and arms was critical. Montcalm's troops had their task cut out for them. The English fort on which Montcalm set his sights was known to contain considerable arms and large food supplies. It was part of the French strategy to fight the British with their own food and weapons—

in other words to capture as much as possible and use it against them.

Robert did not doubt for a moment that General Montcalm could take his objective; what he doubted was that the French could control their Indian allies, the Abenaki. Indeed, relations with the Indians were a part of Robert's specific assignment.

But sitting here in this comfortable drawing room in this stone house overlooking the lazily winding St. Lawrence, it was impossible to explain his inner fears. People like the Lupiens could not conceive of the brutality of war or the possibility of Canadian failure. Only the habitants whose farms along the St. Lawrence had been burned and looted by the Mohawk and whose children had been kidnapped or killed could understand. Of course, the Acadians knew—they had been sent into a wilderness, their families broken up. They too could understand.

Robert thought for a moment of his own childhood, and the contrasts he had experienced. It was true that the French had supported the Scots Highlanders in their battle to restore the rightful king to the throne of England, but no person in the French court could have conceived of the aftermath of Culloden. It was outside their realm of experience, just as this war was outside the experience of Quebec's aristocracy. For the most part, the well-born and the wealthy were always protected from the realities of war. Their loss was seldom as great as that of the common people if only because they began with more.

Right now the war might be called a draw. But how long could it remain a draw? The French regular troops were far too cocky, considering they were so few in number compared to the British and their colonial allies.

The French settlements were strung out from Quebec to the Ohio Territory and beyond that to Fort Detroit and all the way down the Mississippi to New Orleans. They were, to say the least, overextended.

"Oh, here she is!" Madame Lupien's sudden comment snapped Robert out of his thoughts. He looked up to see his beautiful Marguerite coming down the spiral staircase. Her russet gown trailed behind her, and there were ribbons in her curly brown hair. Robert held out his hands to her, and for the first time he kissed her in front of her guardians.

Marguerite knew it was the signal. The marriage had been agreed to. But because of Robert's duties with General Montcalm, it would probably not occur till the fall of 1758.

"It smells wonderful!" Monsieur Godé raved. "Oh, I'm overcome with the aroma!" In reality, Monsieur Godé was more overcome with the sight of the lovely Irish girl who, once she had changed her clothing and removed her scarf, transformed from a mere beauty to a delectable goddess.

As if reading his mind, Megan turned to him wide-eyed. "Do I look satisfactory?"

"Mais oui! Madame, mais oui!" What words of praise could he possibly muster to describe her? Megan's little blue dress was more than becoming, it was revealing as well. Monsieur Godé could not remove his lustful eyes from the supple contours of Megan's body. All this in the wilderness! She was a dream come true.

"It's the only party dress I have," Megan pouted, "but I suppose it will do."

Monsieur Godé could hardly contain himself. He was proud of Madame Coulon, and he did not care what anyone thought—indeed, if they thought he had taken a mistress or seduced her, it could only be a compliment to his taste and a testament to his manhood. Monsieur Godé had already decided to propose marriage to this angel as soon as possible. After all, a widow—a woman alone—needed protection. Monsieur Godé saw himself as a man with much to offer.

The knock on the door jolted Monsieur Godé out of his fantasies.

"Oh, they're here!" Godé exclaimed. "Oh, you will like Madame Macleod."

Megan ran her hand through her hair as Godé opened the door. She took one look at Janet Macleod and nearly let down her guard. The woman who walked through the door with Mathew Macleod was certainly no daughter of a peasant farmer! She was astoundingly attractive—a well-endowed redhead of twenty-five or twenty-six. She too must be Scots, Megan thought. Her heart and hopes sank. The woman who moved into the center of the cabin was competition indeed, and Megan was intelligent enough to know it. Her easy task had just become difficult.

Janet smiled and extended her hand in warm welcome. She drew Megan to her and kissed her on the cheek. "Welcome to Fort Niagara, Madame Coulon."

She *is* Scots, Megan thought to herself. She and her husband had doubtless come together to New France. Moreover, Janet Macleod's own security was obvious in her warm, friendly manner. This, Megan guessed, was a woman with so much self-confidence that she could not be jealous.

Janet stepped back and Megan thanked her. There was some aura of familiarity about this young Irish girl—Janet was puzzled by this sensation of recognition.

"Excuse me, madame," Janet asked. "But you seem so familiar to me."

A slight chill ran through Megan. She quickly searched her memory for everyone she had met since arriving in Canada. No, this woman was not among them, of that Megan was certain. Nor had she ever met her in London. Perhaps Janet Macleod had seen her on the stage? No, that was an utter impossibility. Besides, she could not ask and reveal her English past.

"I'm sorry, madame," Megan stumbled.

"It's nothing then," Janet smiled. "Nothing at all."

"Some wine?" Monsieur Godé held up two glasses. He handed one to Janet and the other to Megan. Then he poured two more for Mathew and himself. "To peace!" he toasted, raising his glass.

They sat down at the table, and when they had finished their first drinks, Megan served dinner while Monsieur Godé poured more wine.

The conversation was light. Like most people just getting to know one another, they exchanged stories, seeking out one another's tastes and interests. Janet tried not to ask Megan too many questions; she sensed that the Irishwoman was hesitant to talk about herself —probably because she had recently learned of the death of her husband.

"I should be pleased to have you come and visit me," Janet said to Megan toward the end of the pleasant evening. "Do you know many Irish folk tales? My children are fond of Celtic stories, and I'm running out of Scots stories. But the Irish have such a rich lore . . ." Janet's voice trailed off. Richard O'Flynn had just crossed her mind; Richard and his beguiling tales, tales that hypnotized Robert in his childhood.

"Have you known many Irish?" Megan responded, a twinkle in her blue eyes.

Janet tilted her head. "Only one. A Richard O'Flynn . . . a long time ago."

Megan's expression fairly froze on her face. She turned quickly to look into the fire. It took all her self-control to turn back around and smile.

"Is there something the matter?" Janet asked, sensing Megan's sudden discomfort.

"No, no," Megan answered quickly. "Just a bit of homesickness. But really, we must get together for an evening of storytelling."

"That's a winter entertainment," Mathew laughed. "That's what we do out here. We spend all summer getting ready for winter and in the winter our entertainment is storytelling."

Megan nodded. She wanted to change the subject, in fact she wanted them to leave. It was going to take her some time to get over the shock of Janet Macleod's offhand reference to her father. No wonder Janet thought she looked familiar!

Megan watched as Janet stood up and wrapped her light shawl around her shoulders. "Please come soon," Janet said warmly.

"I shall try," Megan answered.

"There are only six women living at the fort or nearby. It's a lonely life," Janet said, holding Megan's hand. "We have to stick together."

After they had left, Godé was lavish in his praise. "You are a wonderful hostess, simply wonderful!" Megan only bowed her head slightly and blushed.

"I don't entertain much," Godé sighed. "One goes further in the army if one has a wife to plan social functions."

Godé thought to himself that a beautiful and charming wife would be even more of an asset.

Megan watched the look in Godé's eyes. She had steeled herself for the moment he would make his advances toward her. Monsieur Godé was so obviously lonely.

Godé looked at Megan with round, warm puppy eyes. "I hardly know you, madame. But you are both beautiful and charming. Madame, I know this is presumptuous . . . but a woman should not be alone on the frontier. A woman should be properly married."

Megan lowered her eyes. "I know, monsieur."

Godé cleared his throat. "I would be most honored if you would . . . would become my wife." Godé could hardly believe he had gained the courage to speak the words. "Oh, madame, do not misunderstand . . . I know it will take time for you to get to know me. . . . We would not have to . . . to be intimate. I mean not right away. For now, for the moment, ours would be a marriage of convenience."

Megan looked up at him, and it took all her acting skills not to burst into laughter. He did indeed look like a lap dog—one that had been cast out into the cold and was now seeking a home.

Megan considered Monsieur Godé for a second. A marriage to him would certainly distract any suspicions Janet Macleod might have—if indeed she had any. Marriage to Monsieur Godé would also be an excellent cover for her real activities. In any case, if all went as planned, she would be widowed in a short time.

Megan held out her hands to Godé. "You are most generous, monsieur. I accept your protection."

Monsieur Godé's eyes lit up. He pulled her into his arms and hugged her, quivering with anticipation as he did so. "Oh, madame! Oh, madame!" was all he could manage to say.

At the end of July 1757, the French army commanded by General Montcalm began to move in force. Their first objective was Fort William Henry, located on the Hudson River north of Saratoga and the important fur trading center of Albany. Their second objective—if possible—was the less isolated British Fort Edward, which was south of Fort William Henry.

The entire army assembled at the French Fort Carillon. There, after careful planning, the army was divided. The first division of Montcalm's army was commanded by Lévis and Senezergues. They began to move south from Fort Carillon with de Villiers' Indians and the Canadian militia as the advance guard. They numbered two thousand and traveled lightly because they were to march overland to act as a cover for the main body of the army, which was to move by boat.

The main body was commanded by Montcalm himself and consisted of the La Reine and La Sarre brigades, an additional contingent of Canadian militia, Indians, and a number of cannon. The group under Montcalm marched to Lake St. Sacrement and left its shores by *bateaux*, specially designed vessels for carrying large numbers of troops, a kind of barge with sails.

It was, Robert reflected, quite a colorful sight. There were 250 *bateaux* in all, and they were preceded by 1,500 naked Indians in birchbark canoes. As they paddled in unison, their skin gleamed in the sunlight, and Robert could see the flexing of their well-toned muscles. Many of the bronze-skinned Indians wore colorful beads around their necks or headbands with single feathers. A few had donned war paint and their faces were masks of grotesque lines in red ochre. Robert glanced backward —it was by any standards an armada. Twenty-five hundred men by land; 3,600 by water.

They had sailed early on the morning of August 1 and continued without interruption till the evening of August 2. If there were scouts or Indian spies from Fort William Henry about, none were detected.

On the evening of August 2, the troops camped at a place chosen by Lévis. It was a thickly wooded glen some three miles from Fort William Henry—ideal striking distance.

The following morning, August 3, the guns arrived. Then Lévis moved his men south and around to the woods that lined the rough road from Fort William Henry to Fort Edward. Here Lévis remained. This action was intended to keep new supplies of men and arms from reaching Fort William Henry.

Montcalm took his men and calmly and deliberately surrounded Fort William Henry.

Robert marveled at General Montcalm. He was a fine strategist, but he was also a proper general from the old French military establishment. Montcalm had joined the French army at the age of twelve. When he was twenty-one, he fought against the Austrians in the War of the Polish Succession. Later in his career, during the War of the Austrian Succession, he won fame and honors during the defense of Prague.

Montcalm had inherited his father's lands and properties and was a proper gentleman as well as a "traditional" general. A well-groomed, soft-spoken man with wide-set eyes, a long nose, and rather full lips, he had a youthful appearance.

Robert was well aware that General Montcalm had

clashed with the new governor of Canada, the Marquis de Vaudreuil, but Robert could not help admiring Montcalm. In point of fact, both Montcalm and Vaudreuil had much to commend them. But of the two, Montcalm seemed the more humane.

As soon as all the cannon were in place around Fort William Henry, Montcalm formally demanded the surrender of the fort. He was not a man to engage in messy and unnecessary battles if they could be avoided.

"Why are you smiling, MacLean?" Montcalm asked Robert.

Robert immediately sobered his expression. He was one of the general's aides, and when the general had sent forth a messenger at precisely three o'clock, Robert could suppress himself no longer. Earlier in the afternoon the Indians had done some aimless shooting at the fort. Their real target had been a large herd of grazing oxen that they wanted for fresh food. But other than that, not a shot had been fired. The British and the colonial militia were holed up in the fort. They had no idea they were surrounded by such a large force. Robert was smiling at Montcalm's notion that he could take the fort simply by informing its commander that his "situation was hopeless."

"I'm sorry, sir," Robert replied.

Montcalm softened his expression. "Well, I don't like to be left out of a joke, MacLean. Why were you smiling?"

Robert flushed. "A matter of national understanding, sir."

Montcalm raised an eyebrow. "Oh, will you explain?"

"Well, sir, the commander of Fort Henry is Colonel George Monro . . . Scots, sir. Sir, a Scot would never surrender on the basis of his enemy's assessment. He'll prove stubborn, sir."

Montcalm stood somewhat stiffly. "You mean he would not accept the fact that a French general, a man of honor, would tell him the truth? Good heavens, his situation *is* hopeless! The poor bugger's totally surrounded by a superior force, and he's cut off from all supplies."

"I know, sir. But Monro is Scots. All Scots—Catholics and Protestants—share stubbornness as a trait. Also, he's been fighting with the British and their colonial lackeys. He doesn't see much honor, sir."

Montcalm smiled. He certainly remembered the treachery of the English naval commanders when they captured the French vessels by pretending to be friendly. Not to mention General Braddock's orders to take every French fort when war hadn't even been properly declared—indeed when the British ambassador in Paris was lying through his teeth trying to buy enough time for a sneak attack of major proportions.

"I see your point," Montcalm allowed. "You Scots certainly get about."

It was Robert's turn to smile.

"And I might add you have quite a way with the Indians."

Robert agreed. "It may be that we come out of a tribal society ourselves, sir. We seem to adjust easily to other cultures and peoples. Perhaps because of our history."

"But once a Scot, always a Scot, eh?"

"Yes, sir," Robert answered.

It was a prophetic conversation. In fact, Colonel Monro did not surrender.

Montcalm was a man of some patience. He set about refining his own fortifications and let Fort William Henry simply sit for five days under siege.

On August 5, General Montcalm once again summoned his young aide. An Indian stood before Robert and the general.

"I require your services as a translator, MacLean."

Robert heard the Indian out and then turned to Montcalm. "The Indians spotted a night runner trying to make it to Fort William Henry from Fort Edward, sir. They killed him, but he was carrying this note."

155

Robert took the crumpled, blood-stained document from the Indian and gave it to Montcalm.

Montcalm squinted and handed it back. "I can't read English," he admitted.

"It's from Commander Webb at Fort Edward, sir. It says . . . 'Do not expect help or supplies from here. Hold out as best you can. Expected militia reinforcements have not yet come. Good luck.' That's it."

Montcalm shrugged. "Send another messenger with another demand for surrender."

"Shall we mention the interception, sir?"

"Not yet," Montcalm answered.

Again Monro refused. On the morning of August 6, the first French battery of eight cannon opened fire, and on the next day the second battery was also commanded to fire. After a full day of shelling, Bougainville was sent into Fort William Henry again. This time, in addition to the demand for surrender, he carried the intercepted note from Fort Edward. Monro, as Robert had explained, was Scots to the core. He thanked Montcalm for his "generosity," but still refused to surrender.

The following morning Monro sent out a sortie of some 500 men, but within two hours they were brutally beaten back by de Villiers' Indian warriors.

Robert stood before Montcalm in his hastily erected quarters. He tapped his fingers on the desk. "Sir, this situation is—well, not the best, sir."

Montcalm looked at Robert innocently—but it was more than just a look, Robert thought to himself. The general really is innocent of attitudes; he is innocent of the Indians.

"Sir, the Abenaki have special grudges against the British and their colonists. For many years the British and the colonists have employed the Mohawk against them. Sir, the Abenaki grow angrier by the hour."

Robert felt that he was lost the moment he tried to explain to Montcalm. Montcalm did not understand—could not understand—the alliances between the Indians and the Canadians. Montcalm could not grasp the

156

fact that the Indians did not consider themselves under his command.

"Don't worry," Montcalm kept saying. "All will be well . . ."

Robert spent an uneasy night tossing in his bedroll. The Indians simply could not be controlled any longer. They were preparing their own attack, and Montcalm would not be able to stop them, despite his grand plan to have the fort surrender with no more loss of life. It was with some relief that at seven o'clock the next morning Robert awoke to see a white flag flying over Fort William Henry.

The surrender ceremony was formal in the extreme. Indeed, both Monro and Montcalm fought to outdo each other with military decorum, honor, and general politeness.

Montcalm's demands were not unreasonable; if anything, they were far too generous. Montcalm was ready to yield the honors of war to Monro and allow Monro and his 2,000 men to return to Fort Edward. The proviso was that they agree not to make war against His Most Catholic Majesty for at least eighteen months.

It was further agreed that the British would release all the French and Indian prisoners they held at Fort Edward—indeed, all the prisoners they had taken since the beginning of the war.

Robert was spared translating during this discussion. Monro, like so many Scots, spoke French and did not need an interpreter.

Montcalm immediately took up headquarters at Fort William Henry. The British and colonials would be taken to Fort Edward the following morning.

By four-thirty Robert was again in Montcalm's quarters. "Sir, the Indians are not leaving the prisoners alone. They're robbing them and fighting with them."

Montcalm looked annoyed. "I've warned the British and colonials to dump their liquor supplies—that's all the Indians want. We dumped our supplies, why can't they dump theirs?"

"It's more than that, sir. The Abenaki hate them.

They've been building to a fever pitch since this entire operation began. Sir, they clearly want a massacre, and we're going to have difficulty controlling them."

"A massacre!" Montcalm was outraged. "But those men surrendered! They have my word promising good treatment and safe conduct."

"I understand, sir. But you must try to understand the Indians and the nature of their alliance with us. Sir, your terms for surrender are, to the Indians' way of thinking, much too trusting. They say that none of these colonials or British will wait eighteen months to take up arms against us. They say they'll be back in uniform and back fighting and killing the Abenaki by the time you turn around and head for Quebec City."

Montcalm twitched his nose nervously. "They gave me their word! Their sacred word as soldiers! The Indians are under my command!" he finally said with some firmness.

"But not under your control, sir."

"I want you to take the march to Fort Edward, MacLean. Good God, can't you make them understand?"

"I'll try, sir. Sir, may I quote you something an Indian once said?"

Montcalm nodded.

"He said: 'The English behave like cowards and the French like fools.' Sir, the Indians are in truth allied only with themselves. They did not fight this battle for us, but only for the pleasure of killing their enemies. Our code of ethics is denying them that, sir. And we'll have trouble with them."

"What are you suggesting? Do you want me to turn over the British, who have surrendered honorably, as a living sacrifice to some tribal code I don't even understand . . . don't want to understand?"

"No, sir. I want you to understand what our alliance with the Indians means. Had they been able to fight honorably, sir, this problem would not have arisen. Had they seen us march the men off as prisoners—or as

158

they understand it, slaves—even if we released them later, it would have been better."

Montcalm put his hand on Robert's shoulder. He looked deeply troubled as he began to understand the implications of his actions. He was not angry at Robert's honest assessment. "Do what you can," Montcalm replied thoughtfully. "I'll give your words some thought."

"Thank you, sir."

Robert left with a feeling of terrible foreboding. Tomorrow's march to Fort Edward was nothing to look forward to.

The August sun was already hot. Robert searched the sky and assumed it must have been near nine o'clock when they left Fort William Henry.

The road to Fort Edward followed the winding, lazy Hudson River—lazy this time of year, but not at flood tide in the spring. The road itself was a narrow, rutted, dusty path with a thick pine and birch forest on either side.

The long scraggly line of British and colonial prisoners had barely left the fort when the Abenaki came running out of the woods on both sides, their voices raised in hideous death cries, their tomahawks slashing.

Robert raised his hand and let out a cry for them to halt, but the line of prisoners had scattered and the Indians—most of them dead drunk on liquor given to them by the British as bribes the day before—were too angry, noisy, and disorganized to listen.

Robert drew in his horse and looked about frantically for their leader. It was hopeless unless he could persuade their leader to call them back.

To his dismay, Robert saw that three of his own men, French grenadiers, had been wounded in the melee. The Indians were scalping, chasing, and bludgeoning the prisoners. Some were being dragged unconscious into the woods, others were killed on the spot, while still others were being chased back to the Indian camp like so many sheep being herded.

The air was filled with screams of fear and agonized shrieks, as well as curses from the braver of the prisoners and pleas from those who still sought to buy mercy.

The noise was so great that some French troops came forth from the fort, riding furiously. Among them was a distraught General Montcalm.

Robert felt the pain of a stray arrow graze his shoulder, leaving a deep cut. "Shit!" Robert mumbled under his breath.

"Black Hawk!" Robert screamed out the Indian chief's name even though he didn't see him. Then noticing that the majority of the Indians were either dragging or herding prisoners back toward their camp, Robert rode after the retreating Indians and their terrified prisoners, yelling the name of Black Hawk as loudly as he could.

Cursing the entire way, Robert followed the Indians and their 500 screaming captives all the way back to the Abenaki encampment.

"Where is Black Hawk?" he insisted.

The Indian chief emerged from his wigwam with a look of something like sweet placidity on his face. "Who speaks my name?" he said in Abenaki.

Robert sat straight in the saddle, but did not dismount. He tried to look official. "I come in the name of General Montcalm—great warrior and chief of my people. He asks that you release these prisoners. At once!"

Then Robert dismounted and stood facing the Indian chief. Black Hawk's face had turned to stone. He was shorter than Robert and young for a chief, but he was certainly a strong man and a well-trained warrior. Black Hawk's stance revealed his unyielding attitude. He stood with his legs wide apart, his lips pressed together, and his eyes narrowed.

At that moment, Montcalm and his aide Bourlamaque rode into the Indian camp with a group of French officers.

"Let your chief speak for himself," Black Hawk said sarcastically.

Montcalm dismounted and came quickly to Robert's side. "Try to explain it all to him," he urged.

Robert shook his head. "I'll explain, sir. But after that—no matter what happens—you must not interfere."

Montcalm looked totally puzzled, but he agreed.

Robert turned back to Black Hawk. "It's a matter of honor," Robert explained in Abenaki. "My chief has given his word that these men will be returned unharmed. You stand between my chief and his honor." Robert spoke deliberately, letting all the emphasis fall on the word *honor*. It was possibly the one European value they truly understood.

"And I promised my braves that they would have their retribution. Your chief's honor is in the way of my honor."

"My chief is a greater chief," Robert said boldly.

Black Hawk narrowed his eyes and glared at Robert. Since Robert had spoken Abenaki, all the braves nearby heard and understood what he had said. They made no sound, but the looks on their faces spoke their thoughts.

"My chief is so much greater that I—who stands in the place of my chief and who speaks with the tongue of my chief—will challenge Black Hawk, who has defeated his own braves for the honor of being chief. I do battle for my chief. I am greater than you and therefore my chief is much greater." With those words, Robert stepped up to Black Hawk and snatched one of the arrows from his quiver. He snapped it in half, dropped it to the ground, and stamped it into the dust.

Montcalm's eyes grew large, and his mouth dropped open. He knew enough to realize that Robert had just openly challenged Black Hawk. The entire camp, including the whimpering colonial prisoners, fell silent. Every pair of eyes fell on Black Hawk and Robert MacLean.

161

The chief took a wide step backward and lifted his tomahawk. Robert placed his feet wide apart and held open his weaponless hands. Instantly, as was demanded by custom, one of the braves ran forward and handed Robert his tomahawk. Robert inspected it for a second, then grasped it tightly. If the Mohawk had not taught him well, he thought to himself, this was the moment he would find that out.

The chief and Robert moved silently and almost in unison to the clearing in the middle of the camp. There for a few moments, they stood assessing one another at a distance of some five feet. Then Black Hawk jumped forward, brandishing his tomahawk and letting forth a startling war cry.

Robert easily dodged the first blow and in one single leap was in back of Black Hawk, the two having quickly changed sides with the artfulness of two experienced dancers. The Indian tried another blow, this time from the side in a circular motion. Robert stepped back, and just as quickly he was behind Black Hawk. He seized him at the nape of the neck with his left hand and used his right to control Black Hawk's tomahawk. Robert broke Black Hawk's balance and whispered a Mohawk war cry into his right ear. Black Hawk stiffened, and Robert, using the power of his whole body, flashed his own tomahawk in Black Hawk's face and thrust him backward and away from him, having in an instant illustrated that he could have killed him but did not.

Black Hawk rolled backward and got up on his feet again. The tall one who spoke for the French chief handled his tomahawk with obvious skill. Moreover, he had spoken Mohawk. That meant he was trained by the Mohawk!

Robert saw the expression on Black Hawk's face, and he knew the Indian was frightened. The Abenaki had been beaten too many times by the Mohawk not to respect their skill.

But Black Hawk tried again. Again Robert sidestepped him and, moving in the opposite direction, seized the Indian by the neck. This time Robert continued to hold him. It was a position which could be fatal. The chief went slack and dropped his weapon.

Robert released the stunned chief. "We'll take our prisoners now," he announced in Abenaki. Black Hawk did not look up, but stood sullenly, staring at the ground. He gave his arm a wave.

Robert gave the order in English so the British and colonials would understand. "Fall in! Look smart!" The terrified prisoners lined up and slowly left the Indian camp. Robert had recovered 400 of the original 500. The remainder had paid Black Hawk's debt to his warriors—for them it was too late.

"Don't look back, sir," Robert said to Montcalm.

"You're a brave man," Montcalm commented in a low voice. "I congratulate and thank you."

Robert was embarrassed. "Thank you, sir."

"Your shoulder is hurt."

"It's only a scratch, sir. Stray arrow."

"Naturally, you'll be decorated. And no doubt promoted."

"Thank you, sir." Robert paused and then drew in his horse. "Sir?"

Montcalm drew in his horse as well, seeing that his interpreter wanted to talk with him.

"Sir, I would like to go back to Quebec City for a short time. I'm engaged. I should like to be married."

Montcalm smiled. "I'll arrange for you to be transferred to my headquarters there as soon as possible."

Robert nodded back and smiled, thanking the general. The two men rode off together quietly. It had been a horrendous day, and both of them knew that the victory at Fort William Henry was deeply marred by the Indian massacre of the prisoners. It was just the type of incident that the colonials and the British would whip into an atrocity tale . . . the kind of story that raised ignorant men to high temper.

Janet had straightened up the cabin, put the children to bed, and finished the dishes. What a day! she thought to herself. And where had another summer gone? It was the end of September 1758, and the first bite of autumn was already in the air. All day, every day was now spent in preparation for winter.

The eggs had to be candled and stored. The meat had to be dried and salted and hung in the cold house. The corn also had to be stored, and the carrots and potatoes put away carefully in the root cellar. Everyone had a job, and everyone had to do it.

Butchering, drying, and salting the meat was the task of Mathew, Pierre, and René. Madelaine was in charge of the eggs, while Mat and Andrew cleaned and prepared the vegetables for storage. Even three-year-old Helena had a job. She was to string together pieces of washed apples. Once strung together, the apples were hung from the beams of the cabin to dry. Janet sank into the comfortable rocker in front of the fire once again and unfolded the precious letter from Robert in order to reread it. Outside, she could hear the steady rhythm of Mathew's ax as he chopped for their winter store of firewood. Mathew must be even more exhausted than she herself was, Janet thought.

Robert's handwriting was smooth and even. Janet examined the letter, smiled to herself, and let it drop into her lap. Robert was getting married! It seemed to Janet that it was only yesterday that Robert was a boy, only yesterday that they had made their escape together from Scotland. How could the years have passed so quickly? Where had the time gone?

Janet sighed to herself. The sound of Mathew's ax ceased, and she heard his footsteps on the cabin's wooden front steps. Mathew opened the door and came in, wiping his brow.

Mathew's eyes fell on his wife and on the letter in her lap. He had read it with her some hours ago, but they had not had time to discuss it.

"It's good news," Mathew said happily. "You should be pleased."

Janet looked up, "I am, but I'm sad too."

"You want to be there?"

Janet nodded. "So much of our lives have been spent

164

together . . . Robert and I are so close—but I don't
need to tell you that."

Mathew bent down and kissed her forehead. "It's not
such a long trip to Quebec City. You should go."

Janet's face knit into a frown. "Oh, I can't leave you!
And the children—no, it's all impossible."

Mathew studied his wife's concerned face. The trip
from Fort Niagara to Quebec City was mostly by water.
Upstream, it took no more than three weeks. Coming
back was even faster. "Fou Loup's heading back with
supply requests in a few days' time. He's taking some
soldiers. There aren't many men I'd trust with my wife,
but Fou Loup's the best scout around."

Mathew thought fondly of his old friend. The rotund,
jolly half-breed was the one who had taken him to Fort
St. Frédéric and then brought him Robert, whom he
had rescued from the Mohawks. Fou Loup was a
trustworthy friend, and although he was widely acknowledged as an adventurer, Mathew knew him as a
man of kindness, humor, loyalty, and shrewdness.

"You could go now," Mathew suggested, "and return in the early spring."

Janet stood up and put her arms around Mathew's
neck. He kissed her ear. "You really want me to go,
don't you?"

Mathew nodded. "Pierre and René are men now,"
Mathew said proudly, "and Madelaine often looks
after Andrew, Mat, and Helena. It's only for a few
months."

"But there's a war, Mathew, I promised never to
leave . . ."

Mathew pulled Janet back and looked steadily into
her green eyes. "The war's a stalemate. We've turned
back the British and the colonials before. We'll do it
again. I'll be safe; the children will be safe." Mathew
paused. "We could get that woman—uh, Megan—to
help look after the children. And I'll be here."

"Do you want me to go?" Janet's questioning eyes
revealed her inner conflict.

"I'll miss you—God, will I miss you!" Mathew's

165

voice was firm as he pulled her to him. "But we'll be all right. And it won't be for so long."

Janet managed a faint smile. "Do you think Megan would look after the children? I wouldn't want Madelaine to have all the responsibility."

"She seems like a friendly sort. And I'm certain she's bored enough."

"You'd move them to the fort?"

"I imagine. We're going to start reinforcing some of the outer walls, so I'll have to be there more often in any case. There's a half-breed who can be hired to look after the livestock." Mathew squeezed Janet. "Yes, being at the fort would be better. Besides, Megan wouldn't want to leave her new husband."

Janet tilted her head and smiled. "I wouldn't be certain of that," she answered playfully. "I suspect theirs is a marriage of convenience."

"Obviously," Mathew laughed. "But it's for the best. A woman shouldn't be alone out here."

"I agree. It's just that it was so sudden."

"Poor Godé," Mathew said, chuckling. "He's enchanted by her."

"But it's not mutual," Janet answered. "Megan's too smart for him, and too beautiful."

"Well, she's got a home, and she probably feels more secure with a husband. Godé's not a bad sort."

Janet pressed herself to Mathew. "Besides, the best man in all of Fort Niagara—maybe all Canada—is taken!"

Mathew swept Janet into his arms. He kissed her on the nose and laughed. "What do you mean, *maybe?* Come here, my lovely wench!"

Janet's arms were around Mathew's neck, and she leaned on his broad shoulder. "So now I'm a wench?"

"A saucy wench!" Mathew corrected.

"I'm a matron and a mother," Janet said in a mocking tone.

Mathew carried her to the bed and dropped her there, then fell alongside her. He buried his face in her

166

bodice and nuzzled her breasts. "Matron, mother, mistress—you're my woman!"

Janet's arms were around Mathew's neck even as she felt him undoing her dress. "And you're my man," she replied as he pressed himself on her. Then more seriously, "Do you really want me to leave?"

Mathew's hand rested on her bare breast. "I'll never want you to leave, but I think it's right that you do."

Janet ran her long fingers through her husband's sandy hair as his lips fastened on the tip of her breast. She felt the heat of excitement pass through her and wondered if it was the same with him. They were so good together, so much a part of one another. When they made love, it was always like the first time—always exciting, always new.

A few months, Janet thought to herself, it's only for a few months . . .

CHAPTER IX

September 1758

"I'll be delighted to look after them," Megan's eyes shone brightly. Janet Macleod was going to be gone for some months, and no greater opportunity could possibly present itself. Megan looked on the prospect happily. Caring for the children would not only offer her company but also give her unlimited access to Mathew.

Megan also rationalized that the children would be safer with her. When the time came, she could offer them her considerable protection. Megan did not believe that the punishments of war should be inflicted on mere children.

Then, too, there was Mathew. He was good-looking, intelligent, and charming. It would take planning, but with luck she would be able to protect him as well. In the meantime, Janet was going on a trip from which she might well not return. Mathew would be lonely—but not alone.

"The situation in Quebec City is not at all good," Megan warned. "There are severe food shortages, and French troops billeted all over the city."

"I know," Janet answered, although in truth she

could not picture what Megan described. In spite of the tales she heard, Janet still envisaged Quebec City as she had left it—a prosperous community with a fine cultural life.

"I'm sure I'll be fine," Janet assured Megan. "I've seen and known hard times before. Besides, this trip is a matter of great personal concern. My brother's getting married, and I wouldn't feel right if I wasn't there." Janet did not bother to explain to Megan about her relationship with Robert. She always called him her brother, and in every emotional sense of the word he was.

Janet consoled herself with the certainty that she would return in the spring and that the children would be well cared for till her return. They would have Mathew and Megan and other children. Fort Niagara, of all forts, seemed impregnable. It had been attacked, but the attack was easily repulsed. Perhaps the prolonged war would even come to an end before she returned.

Janet looked down at Helena, who was playing with some crude wooden blocks Mathew had made her. "This is difficult for me," Janet stumbled. "They're so important to me . . ." Words failed her, but finally Janet looked up at Megan. "I trust you, Megan. And I thank you for helping."

Megan smiled back, and again Janet sensed the familiarity she had felt at their first meeting. Why did she feel she knew Megan before . . . had known her for a long time?

The trip back to Quebec City took three full weeks. It was early October 1758, and although the days could be quite warm and the changing leaves gave the thickly forested banks of the river a warm orange and golden glow, the nights were crisp and in the early mornings the ground was covered with white frost that crackled underfoot. The fires of their night encampments were smoky because the wood was often damp. Everywhere small animals scurried about making rustling noises as they gathered stores for their winter hibernation. But it was not only the animals who would hibernate—the people of Canada and those who warred against them also hibernated. Every year since the fighting had begun, hostile activity ceased during the winter months. Neither the defenders nor the aggressors would brave the snow, ice, and wind.

When Janet reached Quebec City, it was late October. All the stories of the traders proved true: Quebec was a city divided.

The farms along the St. Lawrence were short of manpower; the fields lay fallow because the men were away. The crops were reduced even further by inclement weather and by constant Indian raids. The towns produced little, and those who lived in them suffered severe shortages.

The lower city was a mass of poverty, though the upper city where the Quebec government society lived functioned much as it always had. As the situation grew grimmer for the average Canadian, the Intendant Bigot gave more and more lavish parties.

To Janet it seemed that half the city was in want and the other half was deaf and blind to what was happening. The rich comforted themselves with the happy thought that they did their part—they housed high-ranking French officers in their homes, they did some volunteer work, they made economic plans for the time when peace would come.

Janet's home and Madame Deschamps' were filled with French officers. But in any case, Madame Lupien was adamant—Janet was to stay with them. It was equally clear from the moment of Janet's arrival that Madame Lupien desired a lavish wedding, however out of place such an event would be, given the situation.

Robert's arms were around Janet, and she relaxed against him, tears of joy running down her face. Mercifully, they had been left alone in the Lupien drawing room for a time. It was the first time they had been given the chance to talk alone together since Janet's arrival two days earlier. "I'm so glad you're well. . . . I've been so worried about you . . ." Janet was aware that she was reciting all the clichés one recited when reunited with a loved one.

"What do you think of Marguerite?" Robert's soft eyes twinkled when he mentioned her name.

"She's beautiful and sweet," Janet responded. "A lovely girl."

"Her aunt and uncle are . . ." Robert hesitated, seeking the right words, "more concerned with society than she is."

Janet had met the diminutive Marguerite and immediately warmed to her. Janet blinked back her tears. "Married! I can't believe it! I can't believe you're getting married!"

Robert squeezed her again. Man and boy, he was the same Robert to Janet. He held her at arm's length, looked her in the eye, and asked for details of Mathew and the children. Janet told him everything.

"You'll love Lochiel," Janet said dreamily. "And soon we're going to build a proper house on it—our house!"

"Niagara's bound to become an important community," Robert commented. "It's the crossroads of the fur trade."

Janet leaned back against the light blue cushions of the settee. Her eyes fell on the ornate crystal candelabra and then ranged over the room. She had seen it often in the last two days, but now it was as if she were seeing it for the first time, comparing it with the three-room cabin she called home. "This is a dying and isolated world," Janet said softly.

"And a much changed one," Robert allowed.

"How are the Ian MacDonalds and the MacCoys?"

Janet thought of her old friends, the many Scots who had found their way to Quebec just as she and Mathew had found their way. Many Highlanders who had retained their Catholic sympathies had settled in New

France. They had, for the most part, gone into banking. The Scots were good merchants as well, and they now formed a solid part of the community.

"The MacDonalds have moved," Robert answered. "Roy MacCoy's in the army—there's an entire company of Highlanders. Bagpipes, kilts, and all, they're fighting for the French."

"And just as many Scots on the other side," Janet said seriously.

"Bagpipes and all," Robert replied pensively. "I met a British colonel only recently—a Highlander."

"Was he a prisoner?" Janet inquired.

Robert shook his head. "Not anymore . . . he was the commander at Fort William Henry. He's been returned."

Janet shifted around a little and, seeking to change the subject, asked, "When will you and Marguerite marry?"

"Madame Lupien is a proper French lady. She desires a proper wedding and engagement. Quite early in the spring . . . I insisted on that because I know you can't stay longer."

Janet took Robert's hand and held it tightly. "Good," she agreed. "I do have to get back in the early spring—I miss Mathew and the children already."

Winter came with a vengeance to Fort Niagara. The winds howled across the open country, and snow drifted in huge mounds against the walls of the fort. A few miles away at the great falls, the torrents of water froze even as they fell and the white spray seemed to be suspended in midair as it glistened in the ice-cold January sun. All around the falls, the spray froze on the straight, tall, bare trees, making them look like a fantasy in crystal. Beneath the ice, the waterfalls still poured from the Niagara River into the deep gorge. But the appearance of the falls in winter was a misty illusion of stillness.

In January 1759, the world of the French defenders,

like the falls of Niagara, seemed suspended in time and space.

Mathew had begun coughing nearly a week earlier. His head pounded, and his face was red and flushed. He continued to work, counting on his constitution to throw off his illness, but his physical strength failed him, and after several days, a high fever overcame him.

"You are going to stay right there in that bed!" Megan ordered authoritatively. "You should have been there a week ago!"

Mathew tossed feverishly and was only vaguely aware of Megan's presence. She seemed to float across the main room of his quarters, a swaying image in the half-light.

"I'm fixing you some tea, you must try to drink it."

Mathew couldn't answer. His throat was dry and raspy, his mouth had that rancid taste that accompanied fever. In the last twelve hours, time had simply disappeared. He knew it was sometime in the evening because it was dark outside, and he was sure he had heard the crier on the far guard post call out the hour. Megan's swaying image approached the bed and pressed a hot cup of tea into his shaking hands. With one arm, she lifted his head slightly.

"Drink this," she murmured.

Mathew took a gulp and moaned slightly. "You should go home to your husband," he mumbled. "I'll be all right. I'm causing you too much trouble."

"Hush!" Megan answered as she again pressed the cup to his lips. Mathew tried to drink, and then, weak from the effort, he waved his hand at her and sunk back against the pillows.

Two hours passed. Mathew vaguely felt a cool hand on his brow, but his eyes couldn't focus and the room wouldn't stop moving. He was also aware of being hot and cold at the same time. Again the cool hand was on his forehead. He seized the lovely narrow, white wrist.

"Janet, Janet . . ." Mathew's voice was slurred, and Megan stroked his cheek, trying to comfort him.

173

"So cold . . ." Mathew moaned and shook violently again.

Megan studied Mathew's handsome face and fearfully felt his fevered brow. He was still shivering uncontrollably, and no amount of blankets seemed to warm him.

Megan shook loose from Mathew's grasp and went outside, returning quickly with a snow-filled bucket. As the snow melted, she soaked rags in the cold water and made compresses that she applied to Mathew's head, arms, and chest in an attempt to break his fever. Again Mathew cried out for Janet.

Megan closed her eyes when Mathew gripped her hand. Although it was not her name that he spoke, he caressed her hand warmly.

She was transfixed by Mathew's touch and admitted to herself that his touch aroused her. She felt herself flush with deep longing, and in spite of the fact that she had obtained information from Mathew and passed it on to the British, she realized she was in love with him.

For some three months now, Megan had cared for Mathew's children. Sometimes she had cooked for him, and they had often talked. Now his hand grasped hers, and even though he called out for Janet, Megan's desire grew. She blinked back tears of frustration, "Damn you, Janet Macleod," she mumbled under her breath. "Damn you for being!"

Then almost in a trance, Megan undressed slowly. When she had dropped the last of her clothing, she eased back the quilt on the bed and crawled in, pressing her cool, nude body to Mathew's feverish flesh.

Mathew moved slightly at her touch, and after a time his hand came to rest on Megan's breast, causing her nipple to rise and harden, causing her to want him even more. But she realized he was too ill to respond, too ill even to know who she was.

She felt an agonizing longing fueled by the touch of his hand and the pressure of his body against her. Megan closed her eyes and, lost in her own pleasure, took Mathew's hand and placed it on her most sensitive area, rubbing his fingers against the center of her pleasure till, unable to hold back any longer, she pressed his hand down and pulsated against him even as he called out Janet's name.

During the night, Mathew's fever began to subside. At dawn, he opened his reddened eyes and tried to focus. His head pounded, and his ears rang. Blindly, in the darkness of the winter dawn with his mind still in a muddle, Mathew felt across the bed that he normally shared with his wife.

"Janet," he whispered urgently. Then Mathew remembered that Janet was gone. Mathew pulled back the covers with a sudden jerk and beheld the ravishing, tempting nude body of Megan.

Mathew shook his head. "My God!" he whispered.

Megan's intense blue eyes opened, and for a long moment she looked sleepily up at Mathew, who loomed over her.

Megan held out her long white arms. "Make love to me again," she said in a deep throaty voice. Her hands were on his arms, gently caressing him. She did not try to hide her wonderfully full breasts with their hardened tips or her rounded buttocks and her long white thighs.

"Please do it again," Megan pleaded. Mathew shook his head and closed his eyes against the sight of her. Megan's hands moved away from his arms and down his body. Mathew could feel himself stiffen even before he felt Megan's hands fold around him and begin to move up and down slowly. His head pounded, and he was racked by confusion. He couldn't remember anything . . . neither how this ravishing female got into his bed nor his having slept with her before. But he was aware of her hands on him now and of the feel of her next to him.

Megan was too expert and her touch too sure. Mathew gasped and suddenly shook, feeling the sudden release as he pulsated in response to her intimate caresses.

175

Megan wiggled against him. "Please . . ." Her voice was deep, she pressed herself to him, pleading.

Mathew shook his head, and with all his strength pushed Megan away. "No!" he said firmly as he edged off the bed, "No!" Mathew staggered from the bed and braced himself against one of its posts. The room was unbearably cold—the fire had gone out during the night. Guilt and confusion swept over him. Had he slept with her? He had dreamed of Janet!

Mathew's head grew dizzy, but he watched as Megan got up and began dressing. Then he collapsed across the bed.

"Get under the covers," she said matter-of-factly. Mathew struggled, and Megan threw the quilts back over him. He closed his eyes and tried to remember, to clear his head.

After a time, Mathew opened his eyes and saw that Megan was stoking the fire. She turned and looked at him. Her dark hair was still in disarray, her eyes seemed strangely sad. She turned to Mathew and looked at him for a long moment. "I'm sorry."

Mathew shook his head against the pillow. His fever had left him, but he couldn't remember. Moreover, he still felt weak. "I don't remember," was Mathew's only reply to Megan's strange apology.

Megan shrugged. "It's all right," she mumbled even as she avoided looking at him. "It won't happen again."

Mathew leaned back and watched her go about the morning chores. He cursed his memory and his illness. Why had she been in his bed? What had happened between them?

But Megan offered no further explanation. From that moment on, Megan was all business. She went about the cooking and cleaning with the help of the older children. Neither of them spoke of the night they'd shared his bed, though both thought about it. Mathew watched Megan carefully, and sometimes their eyes met briefly. At those moments, Megan knew Mathew was still trying to comprehend exactly what had happened and Mathew read her feelings of desire with embarrassment.

"It's a miracle the French supply ships even got through!" Robert paced the room, his face showing deep concern.

It was an incongruous setting for their conversation. It was May, and spring was in the air. Outside the drawing room, birds were singing, and every tree and every bush was bursting forth with new life.

Janet sat rigidly on the edge of her chair. She felt as if she were entering a nightmare world—one she recognized from past experience. Louisbourg had fallen! The supply ships sent under private charter had broken through Vice-Admiral Philip Durell's blockade, but there was no doubt as to what would happen next. No doubt at all.

Robert sat down on the edge of a chair opposite Janet, his legs spread wide apart. He brought his hands together and steepled his fingers. "There's no leaving Quebec City—none."

Janet inhaled. "Is there any news from Fort Niagara?"

"The latest dispatches indicate it's quiet there." Robert's voice was low and serious. Had the decision been his he would have evacuated half of Quebec City the month before. But it was not his decision. "This place is well-located," he said of the fortresslike walled city, "but we're not prepared for a siege." Robert paused and shook his head. "We've even had major reinforcements—three regiments and some militia from the Richelieu Valley."

Janet's face was tight with concern, and Marguerite sat in another chair like a statuette. The wedding had been put off because Robert would now be on constant duty. Quebec society was grinding to a terrified halt. People waited, knowing that the English fleet was on its way and the British and colonial troops would not be far behind.

"We have over fourteen-thousand men," Robert

said, trying to give the women more hope than he himself actually had.

Marguerite was frightened, but Robert knew that was not Janet's problem. Her concern was for her children and for Mathew. She wanted to be with them, and now there was no leaving. Communications were all but cut off.

Janet considered the situation carefully. "It won't do me any good to sit around thinking about the children," she said, standing up. "Having nothing to do, having too much time to think will only make matters worse." Janet's face hardened, and she looked from Robert to Marguerite, holding out her hand to Robert's intended. "We'll find something to do," Janet told her firmly. "The more active we are, the better. If Quebec is going to be under siege—if this is where the British choose to fight—we can't be idle. Preparations will have to be made at the hospital. Useful things can be done!"

Robert stood up and kissed Janet's cheek. "You're the strongest woman I know," he said with admiration.

Janet looked into Robert's soft eyes. "Strength comes from purpose," she replied. "I know Mathew will keep the children safe. I must do something!" Then Janet turned to the silent Marguerite. "We must do something," she repeated firmly.

The British picked their way down the St. Lawrence, navigating by night, slipping between the islands with a skill that surprised even the troops they carried. The huge fleet anchored off the Ile d'Orleans on June 26, 1759. They dropped anchor opposite St. Laurent on the south side of the island, and on the twenty-seventh, Major-General Wolfe and his engineer, Major Patrick Mackellar, went ashore to study their position. It was there that they were met by Richard O'Flynn.

Richard greeted Wolfe formally. He smiled and thought to himself that the young pup who had fought at Culloden, and whom he had watched trying to seduce his daughter, had been well-promoted. "You've come a long way," O'Flynn said in an almost teasing tone.

Wolfe blushed when he saw O'Flynn. A vivid memory of Megan flashed across his mind, and although he was now engaged to another woman, he had not—indeed, could not—forget Megan O'Flynn.

"I've been fortunate," Wolfe replied, ignoring O'Flynn's flippancy. It was on the tip of his tongue to ask after Megan, but he held back when he saw that the expression on O'Flynn's face had changed. This was, in any case, no time for pleasantries.

"I expect the French will try to attack the fleet," O'Flynn revealed. "But there's no strength there—what ships they have are commanded by incompetents. We have no worries on the water. French strength is on the land."

O'Flynn pressed his lips together and pointed upward toward the hills. "We should go for the high ground directly opposite the city."

Wolfe nodded knowingly. "Brigadier Monckton will see to that part of the operation."

O'Flynn studied Wolfe carefully and decided that Wolfe's promotion was one of those mindless acts of the hierarchy. He was a strange young man, and clearly he preferred poetry to war. It was just as clear that Wolfe was a poor physical specimen—underweight, unseemly pale, and slight of build. Indeed, Wolfe had a number of feminine characteristics, and had he not seen him trying to seduce his own daughter and learned more recently that Wolfe was engaged, O'Flynn would have seriously wondered about him. Certainly it was not that unusual! The British army—indeed the government—was riddled with men who favored other men to women. But that aside, Wolfe did not look capable of the task ahead.

"This will be a long siege," O'Flynn warned Wolfe. "Quebec was built to defend."

"They must be lured into a proper battle," Wolfe commented. His voice seemed far away, and O'Flynn

179

knew that young General Wolfe was thinking of Culloden. When a man was stymied, his mind always returned to the scene of success. Culloden had been the decisive battle against the Scots; it had brought a rapid and total end to the hostilities and the Jacobite uprising. Wolfe wanted a decisive battle in Quebec. He longed to bring this protracted war to its completion.

"That won't be easy," O'Flynn informed Wolfe. "Those bluffs are over 350 feet high. I would think a siege—"

"I don't like sieges!" Wolfe interrupted him. "What other way is there?"

Richard shrugged. "There are some risky accesses—up over the bluffs and around the back, coming down on the city from above, across the plains behind it . . . but that's not possible now. It's the kind of move that would have to come later . . . much later, when morale is low, when the defenses have been weakened."

Wolfe looked distressed at the prospects. He seemed to be an indecisive man of little patience. It was a bad combination.

"Are you going back to the city—infiltrate the high command?"

Richard O'Flynn shook his head. "My usefulness in Quebec is at an end."

Wolfe appeared to be something between pleased and surprised. O'Flynn sensed he made Wolfe uncomfortable, and truth be told, Wolfe made him uncomfortable.

"What happened?"

"What happens to most of us. I was to be transferred to Montcalm's command, but I found there is someone on the good general's staff who knows me—from another time and place."

Wolfe looked nonplussed and disinterested. Richard O'Flynn pictured Robert MacLean in his mind. He had seen him fleetingly from a distance—Robert had not seen him. Robert had grown into a fine young man, and Richard could not help wondering if Janet Cameron were still in France. Richard smiled to himself. Robert had been eight when he had last seen him. Chances were that Robert probably wouldn't have known him, but it wasn't worth the risk. Fate, Richard thought, shaking his head. He had nurtured and taught Robert, now they were on different sides.

Wolfe frowned. "Have you new orders?"

Richard O'Flynn looked up toward the beautiful old fortress of Quebec and answered in a faraway voice, "I'm headed south."

Wolfe stepped forward and shook O'Flynn's hand limply. Richard thought to himself: You can't trust a man with a limp handshake.

A few days later, the French ships did indeed attack, but it was an abortive attempt that was easily beaten back. Richard O'Flynn, as usual, was quite correct.

Brigadier Monckton took the high ground on the south shore of the St. Lawrence, and in spite of a ground attack by the Canadian militia, Monckton consolidated his position on the Lévis shore.

On July 12, a second French attack was sustained and beaten back. That night it began. General Wolfe ordered a rocket fired into the sky and aimed at Montmorency. It was a signal for the gunners at Point Lévis to open fire on Quebec. The relentless shelling was to last for two solid months almost without interruption.

Megan left Fort Niagara with Mathew's children on July 5. Without consulting him, she simply wrote him a note and took the children back to Lochiel where, in her estimation and based on her advanced knowledge, they would be safer.

Throughout the long day, Mathew had worked with the fort's commander, a fellow engineer named Pierre Pouchot. When he returned to his quarters and found Megan's note, he reacted with anger and irritation, then followed Megan to Lochiel, just as she had hoped he would.

Mathew arrived well after dark, but it was a warm

181

evening and the moon shone brightly over the rows of corn he had hired the Indians to plant. The cabin, with smoke curling up from the fireplace, was easily visible as he made the bend in the road.

Mathew dismounted and went to the door, thinking it silly that he was actually about to knock. It was, after all, his house. Why had Megan brought the children out here alone? Surely she realized it was safer at the fort. Mathew was puzzled. Megan was an enigma—she had been one since the morning he had found her in bed with him.

Megan opened the door, and her facial expression was calm. She didn't seem in the least surprised to see him.

"I thought you'd come," Megan announced.

Mathew strode into the room and looked around. Megan had unpacked the utensils and uncovered the furniture.

"I don't understand," Mathew said with bewilderment. "Why did you leave the fort? Why did you bring the children here without my permission or knowledge?" Mathew's voice was tense, his words had an edge to them. "Your husband's distraught—I promised I'd bring you back tonight."

"I'm not going back," Megan said stubbornly. "And neither are you."

Mathew steeled himself for the argument he sensed was coming. "Would you care to explain?"

"Some things are not so easily explained," Megan answered, trying to hedge in order to gain time. "Would you like something to drink?"

Mathew sat down at the table and put his elbows on it. "You're quite a hostess in my house," he said, somewhat sarcastically.

"I'm quite a good mother to your children," Megan snapped back.

"Well, you did volunteer. And it won't be for much longer." Mathew had thought to add that Janet was expected some weeks ago, but he didn't say it. He had put it out of his mind, telling himself that the wedding must have been delayed. Still, the lack of communications from Quebec had made him tense. "Janet will be back soon," he said confidently.

"Not too soon," Megan answered. "Perhaps not at all."

Mathew jolted upright in his chair. His face contorted with intensity. "What do you mean by that?"

"I mean the English fleet is on its way to Quebec—is probably there by this time. Louisbourg has fallen." Megan leaned over the table. "Your beloved wife can't get back—even if she wanted to come."

Mathew fairly lunged at Megan. He seized her wrist and held it fast. "How do you know this?" His brown eyes flashed, and as Megan winced with pain, he realized he was hurting her. Mathew dropped her hand. His eyes searched her beautiful face for answers.

Megan shook her hand and rubbed her wrist as she looked at Mathew. His love for Janet was so strong; she felt the same sinking sensation she had felt that night in bed with him. As long as there was the slightest hope that Janet was alive, Mathew would never look at another woman—even if she were dead, he might not.

"Do you want something to drink?" Megan repeated. "Let's make a little more civilized conversation."

"You tell me that Quebec is under siege, or about to be . . . you tell me all of this military information, which you should have no way of knowing, and you want a civilized conversation! Who are you? No! *What* are you?" Mathew struggled to keep his voice even and not to shout.

Megan walked across the room to her satchel and withdrew a bottle of brandy. Then she went to the cupboard and took out two tin mugs.

"If you don't want something to drink, I do," she said, sitting down.

Megan poured brandy into both mugs and shoved one at Mathew. "This isn't going to be easy," she said, pushing the brandy toward him. "Not for me to tell you, nor for you to understand."

Mathew lifted the mug to his lips. He took a gulp and

leaned back. It burned his throat. "Try me." He looked at her with determination. But it also seemed to Mathew that the woman he was facing was not the same Megan he had known all these months. There was something different about her. A thousand suspicions mounted in his mind. She could not know the things she claimed to know unless . . .

"I'm not what I seem," Megan confessed.

"I'm not certain what you mean," Mathew replied, trying to read her thoughts.

"I have special information," Megan looked him in the eye unflinchingly. "Very special information."

"You're a spy!" The words slipped out of Mathew's mouth, and he knew they were true. A thousand small pieces to the puzzle of Megan began to fall into place.

"Of sorts," Megan answered forthrightly. "But I didn't count on falling in love with you."

Mathew felt the color drain from his face. Somehow he had hoped she might never mention that night again. He had pushed both that night and the morning after to the farthest reaches of his mind.

"I love Janet," Mathew said defensively. "I don't remember sleeping with you . . ." His voice trailed off. It all sounded absurd. In any case, he certainly remembered the morning—he remembered responding to her touch all too clearly. He hadn't been able to hold back. And it certainly wasn't that he hadn't been tempted by her, it wasn't that he hadn't found her wonderfully attractive. It was that he and Janet had something special, even sacred.

"I know you love your wife," Megan answered without bitterness. Then in an almost kindly gesture, she put her hand on Mathew's. "Unfortunately for me, you've always been faithful to her as well."

"I don't understand," was all Mathew could manage. His confusion at this moment cluttered his every thought. He gulped down some more brandy and watched her carefully.

Megan stood up and brushed out her long skirt. "Oh, you don't have to feel guilty. You didn't sleep with me—you don't have a thing to remember." She turned to him and smiled seductively. "Let's just say I enjoyed being next to you—let's just say I wish you had slept with me."

Mathew felt his face turn a deep red. "It isn't that I don't find you attractive . . ."

"It's just that you love your wife. An admirable trait, fidelity. It's an excuse I don't often hear."

There was a twinkle of humor in Megan's eyes, and Mathew felt himself relaxing. No matter what else she was, Megan was quite a woman. Quite a rare woman, in fact.

"I doubt you ever hear any excuses," Mathew said, letting a bit of his admiration show through.

"You're the first," Megan allowed, sitting back down.

"But you are a spy?"

Megan nodded. "Of sorts."

"Well, you can't expect me to sympathize." Mathew's voice had grown cooler. He felt certain that what Megan had told him was true, and his mind filled with anxiety for Janet. He could only pray that she would be safe and that Robert would find a way to get her home.

"What you tell me about Quebec is one thing," Mathew said, returning to the moment, "but you haven't explained why we're here or why you brought the children here."

"Because Fort Niagara is about to be attacked." Megan spoke the words so matter-of-factly that Mathew was caught unawares. "My God!" He stood up abruptly and reached automatically for his jacket. "There are nearly five-hundred men there! And women and children!"

"It's too late," Megan said resolutely. "You couldn't get through the lines if you tried. Besides, this farm will be spared because my whereabouts are known. You and your children will be safe because I'm here."

Mathew looked at Megan coldly. The enormity of her duplicity overwhelmed him. He stood frozen for an

185

instant and tried to think. How could he leave the children with this woman? How could he not warn the people in the fort? He knew instantly and instinctively that Megan would not hurt the children. "I'm going to warn the troops." Mathew narrowed his eyes and looked at Megan. "I can't let this happen! I couldn't live with myself!"

"You will stay here," Megan answered.

"And what in your twisted mind made you decide we're worth saving? Why are my children more important than other children? Why am I more important than those other four-hundred-and-ninety-nine men?"

"Because I love you," Megan answered simply.

"Well, thank you! But I'm going anyway!" Mathew shouted at her as he flung on his jacket. He turned his back on her and took a step toward the door.

"Stop! You're not going! Take another step and I'll kill you!"

Mathew whirled around to face Megan now holding a pistol in her hand. She must have had it in the table drawer all this time. She trained it on him.

"I'm going," Mathew said evenly. He turned his back. Megan's lips parted, and she took careful aim. Her fingers squeezed the trigger, and a shot broke the stillness of the cabin.

CHAPTER X

July 1759

Searing pain ripped through Mathew, but he still managed to take three steps. Then everything went black, and he fell face down in the doorway.

Megan inhaled and glanced toward the two rooms where the children slept. Then she quickly bolted both doors from the outside. Pierre and René were both quite strong. She waited fearfully, but there was no sound. Miraculously, none of the children had stirred, and Megan congratulated herself on her foresight. She had drugged their food, and while she hadn't liked doing it, she convinced herself it was for their own good.

Megan quickly turned her attention to Mathew. She dragged him back over the threshold where he had fallen and locked and bolted the door. His left leg was bleeding badly. She had shot him in the back of the thigh.

Nothing I can do about the bullet, she thought to herself. It will have to wait for a surgeon. Megan bandaged the wound carefully and stopped the flow of blood. Then she propped a pillow under Mathew's head and covered him with a blanket.

Mathew awoke to the sound of distant gunfire and a horrible ripping pain in his left leg. He groaned as he tried in vain to move.

Megan stood over him and shook her head. "You see," she said softly, "when I decide to save a man's life, I won't tolerate any gallant foolishness."

"Let us out!" There was a great banging on the door—indeed on both doors—as the children raised their voices in strong protest.

"Tell them to be quiet," Megan said crisply. "The others are all right, but I'll have to keep Pierre and René locked up. Either of them could have a fit of your gallantry."

Mathew raised himself up slightly with great effort. "It's all right!" he called out huskily. "René! Pierre! It's Mathew . . . trust me, it's all right. Please be still!"

The banging stopped instantly.

"What's happening?" Pierre's voice was strong and clear.

"I can't explain now," Mathew called back. "Just trust me." The noise ceased altogether.

Megan smiled and went to the other door. A pale-faced Madelaine and a frightened four-year-old Helena came out hand in hand. Both of them ran to Mathew.

"You're hurt!" Madelaine's dark eyes were large. She whirled about and looked at Megan accusingly. "What have you done to Papa?"

"It was an accident," Megan answered coldly.

Madelaine turned back to Mathew questioningly.

Mathew nodded his head in agreement. "An accident," he confirmed.

Madelaine seemed on the verge of tears. "What's happening?" she sniffed, burying her face in Mathew's chest.

"The fort's being attacked," Mathew answered. "But we're safe." He stroked her dark curls.

Megan said no more, but she gathered up the muskets and emptied them of their shells. Then she locked them in the far room.

That done, she let René, Pierre, Mat, and Andrew

out. They ran immediately to Mathew, each of them full of questions.

"What's happened?" Pierre asked. At fourteen, he was the eldest and spoke for all of them.

"I had an accident," Mathew lied. "The fort's under siege. We have to stay here."

"I want my gun." Pierre looked about. "Where is it?" he demanded.

"No guns," Mathew said firmly. "We'll be safe."

Megan had returned to the fire to dish up bowls of warm gruel. "Breakfast," she announced calmly.

Twelve-year-old Madelaine took Helena to the table and helped her sit down on the bench.

"Go eat," Mathew told the boys. Sullenly they sat down and began eating in silence.

"I'd like to get you onto the bed," Megan said. "Do you think you can make it if you lean on René and Pierre?"

Mathew could only feel numbness in his leg. But the other leg was fine. "I think so," he answered.

The two boys came instantly, and with their help Mathew struggled to his feet and was dragged to the bed.

"After you've eaten," Megan told the children, "I want you to go back in your rooms and stay there."

There was a collective mumble of protest. "No arguments," she added.

"No arguments," Mathew added his voice to hers. Mystified, the children finished eating and returned to their rooms.

Megan closed the door behind them. "I appreciate your cooperation," she said, looking at him. "It's better this way."

Mathew looked at her dully. "Do you realize you've made me a part of this?" He was incredulous at Megan's calm.

"It's better than being dead, you know. If by chance Janet does get home, it would be nice if there *was* a home."

"How do you know I won't kill you?" Mathew's eyes

189

remained on her. "Wring your lovely white neck," he added.

Megan smiled. "Because it would be a waste of time and effort. The damage is done. Besides, Mathew Macleod, you're not the type to wring my neck or kill a woman in cold blood." She sipped her tea. "And you have doubts. Too many doubts."

Mathew raised his eyebrows. "That hardly means I'm the type to sell out my friends."

"You didn't sell anybody out. I did. And they weren't my friends. Why don't you face the fact that you're on the wrong side? The losing side. The French are finished in North America—they're finished in Europe!"

"I've been on the losing side before—it's what the side stands for that's important."

"And what do the French stand for?" Megan threw back her head. "That's a question you can't answer. One side's no better than the other! You're not French —you're no more French than I am! You ought to be able to live well and prosper in British North America!"

Megan handed him a cup of tea. She had hit Mathew's weak spot. "Deny that both sides use the Indians brutally? Go on—deny that?"

"I can't," Mathew answered. "But I can't be disloyal either!"

"Oh, you haven't been. But you owe it to your children to stay here under my protection," Megan said evenly. "For that matter, you owe it to them not to wring my neck. Mathew, your battle's lost. Stop fighting it."

Mathew looked at Megan. His leg throbbed with pain. His emotions were mixed; he felt at once hostile and grateful to Megan. Hostile because she had prevented him from warning the troops, and grateful because she was protecting the children while Janet was trapped.

"Spies are loathsome," Mathew mumbled, narrowing his eyes.

"And both sides use them," Megan retorted.

Mathew looked up at her steadily. "Janet will come home."

Megan shrugged. "Perhaps," she allowed. "Janet is not my concern."

Fort Niagara capitulated on July 26. Pouchot surrendered when he learned from the British commander, Sir William Johnson, that the reinforcements had been caught in an ambush and were all but annihilated by Johnson's bloody Mohawk warriors. Some two-hundred Canadians did escape by boat and headed for Fort Detroit. The trading center at Little Niagara was destroyed, and the few settlers there had their homes burned. But, as Megan had promised, Lochiel was spared.

Janet led Marguerite through the rubble-strewn streets of Quebec. By this time she knew the safest path to the makeshift hospital where they both worked.

"I could stand it if they would only stop for a while! It's the continuous thunder . . . the fires . . ."

Another blast echoed through the air, but Janet did not pause. They were not in the area currently being shelled. Marguerite sniffed and went on mumbling about the explosions. She was often tearful and frightened, having never experienced war, and she missed Robert terribly.

All around them the beauty of Quebec City seemed to lay in ruins. Small fires smoldered here and there; volunteers dug survivors out of tumbled buildings. The streets were strewn with garbage, with human waste, with loose stones, and sometimes with wounded or dead bodies.

For over three weeks now the two women had been sleeping by themselves in the basement of the Lupien house. Monsieur Lupien had been forced into uniform and had engaged in an abortive attack against the British. He had not been among those who escaped, so it was assumed that he was a prisoner or that he had been killed.

Madame Lupien had bundled up her silver, her gold, and her crystal into a great white sheet and simply disappeared. Either she had found a safe place or, as Janet suspected, she had been driven mad by the shelling and the collapse of her house. She had doubtless joined the legion of fearful wanderers who walked through the streets, carrying their belongings with them, trying to find enough food to stay alive. Janet and Marguerite had moved the belongings that had not been destroyed into the basement, or that part of the basement not caved in. During the day Janet and Marguerite worked side by side with the nuns in the hospital, where they received one meal a day—usually a weak soup and some heavy, dark brown bread.

Another blast hit somewhere to the west. Janet closed her eyes and paused momentarily. Marguerite was quite right—the unceasing torment of the constant shelling was the worst.

"We're almost there," Janet said, pointing down the street. It's only a little farther." Marguerite nodded and stepped over a great loose stone. Somewhere a dog howled a song that seemed to herald the next blast.

Poor Marguerite. She was all right during the day while they worked at the hospital. As long as she was among people, she seemed strong enough. But even then, she searched every face, terrified that Robert would turn up on a bloodied makeshift stretcher. Janet also felt that fear, but she tried not to let it show. Marguerite needed all the support Janet had to offer.

At night, Marguerite crumbled. While they slept in the dark, blown-out basement, rats scampered about and cats followed them, their eyes gleaming in the blackness. Marguerite would sob herself to sleep in Janet's arms, crying for the city to surrender, praying the nightmare would end.

General Montcalm paced his office. He could clearly imagine the clouds of smoke rising from the burning villages along the St. Lawrence and the bright-colored flames that landed on the very rooftops of the houses of Quebec.

Robert watched the general. The man was torn, utterly torn. He had sought in every way to avoid just this battle; he had erred on the side of caution.

Montcalm wrung his hands together nervously. "How can I be certain? How can I be sure? I can't move all my men and march them to Quebec and the plains beyond. What do you think?"

It was partly a rhetorical question. One that Robert had already answered twice and quite clearly.

Robert was certain that the British troop movements indicated General Wolfe's plans to attack the city from behind, however improbable the route. Montcalm, on the other hand, was convinced that the British troop movements were a ruse designed to inveigle him into moving his own troops away from the place of attack.

"I think Quebec should be protected." Robert gave his advice as requested, even though he knew Montcalm would not take it. General Montcalm was confused by the various British maneuvers. Moreover, he was outraged by the manner in which French prisoners of war were being treated. Rumors of British barbarism had reached headquarters, and everyone knew they were more than rumors. General Wolfe was turning men who had surrendered honorably over to the Indians to be brutally tortured and scalped while still alive. Such atrocities did not surprise Robert MacLean. He knew enough Scotsmen who had fought at Culloden to have heard of the infamous Wolfe. In the aftermath of Culloden, which Robert remembered personally, Wolfe had been nothing more than a common murderer and looter. It was said that he read poetry to his soldiers—songs. Music soothes the savage beast, Robert thought to himself, and Wolfe certainly seemed to be a beast. An appropriately named man—a man who fought like an animal and treated other men as vanquished prey.

"I see no way the heights can be scaled," Montcalm reiterated. He regarded Quebec City as impregnable.

Robert disagreed silently. It was not impossible to scale the heights with men—he had done it himself. It was a long and arduous climb, and it might be extremely difficult to achieve with any kind of artillery. Certainly the British could not hope to win any battle without their prized guns. Robert puzzled it over—if they came, how would they come? How could they have the advantage of complete surprise?

Robert saw himself as a creature of the New World. Unlike either General Montcalm or General Wolfe, he had no particular love of set battle and the formalities of war so common to Old World military strategy. Both General Wolfe and General Montcalm were at odds with their own colonial militias, which were composed of men like himself, men who had grown up in North America and who realized the advantage of Indian strategy. If they could, both Montcalm and Wolfe would set an hour and then line up two opposing armies to fight it out. But surprise played as large a role as strength here. Robert had a sinking feeling that it was the French who were going to be surprised.

General Wolfe suffered from great indecision, making and re-making plans. On September 1, the pale Wolfe moved his troops from Montmorency to the south shore of the St. Lawrence near the Etchemen River. He considered and reconsidered the best place to make his crossing. He finally decided on a point between Point-aux-Trembles and St. Augustine.

Wolfe's first plan was to feint a crossing at Point-aux-Trembles in order to fool Montcalm. In fact, Wolfe planned actually to land the bulk of his troops at St. Augustine. This first plan was foiled not by the French, but by the weather. It rained sheets of water, and the wind whipped up the river, making impossible a crossing of any kind.

Wolfe returned to the original plans made by Washington and the information given him by O'Flynn. He considered the possibilities and selected Anse-au-Foulon near St. Michel.

O'Flynn had assured him the heights could be scaled by large numbers of men. Moreover, it was suggested that the navy be in charge of getting the artillery up the hill. They had the winches and the know-how to move the cannon up the heights. Wolfe closed his eyes and tried to envisage what lay ahead. It *is* possible, he told himself.

Robert tossed in his cot, then rolled over, opened his eyes, and looked up at the ceiling. Its beams were just visible in the half-light. He wondered why he'd awakened suddenly with his heart pounding. It was the silence! The shelling from Point Lévis had stopped. Robert inhaled and listened to the blessed quiet.

Robert sat up. The feeling that came over him was not one of comfort, in spite of the silent guns. It was a quite different feeling—an inexplicable gut feeling of great foreboding.

Robert sat for a moment on the edge of his cot, then got up silently and pulled on his breeches, his boots, and finally his shirt and coat. He tiptoed across the floor so as not to wake his fellow officers, and looked out the window. It was September 12, and a light layer of early frost covered the barren ground.

Robert left the overcrowded sleeping quarters and, arming himself with knife and pistol, slipped out of the building and headed across the open space between the buildings toward the trough where his mare was tethered. He untied and mounted his horse, only to be challenged as he left Fort Beauport. Robert gave the guard his identification and destination.

"Bonne chance!" the guard called after the well-known scout. Robert waved back. He would need good luck. This was a mission of pure instinct.

Captain du Pont Vergor commanded a piquet—a sentry point on the cliffs above Foulon. Foulon, which lay below, was a small inlet on the St. Lawrence. It was an exceedingly steep climb up the cliffs from Foulon to the plains that stretched out behind the city.

It was across those plains that Robert now rode. Had he been stopped and asked to give cause, he would have been able to give only the feeblest of excuses— Louis du Pont Vergor's sentry post had not been checked for days—but that was not the real reason in any case.

The real reason was Robert's dream—or nightmare. He did not fully remember it till he was riding on the flat Plains of Abraham—so named for the wealthy Scots farmer, Abraham L'Écossais, who owned the land and whose last name meant Scot in French.

It was now that Robert recalled his vague dream with an eerie feeling of discomfort. In the dream, Robert had envisaged a battle—a battle that took place here! Robert shook his head and spurred his horse on. He reminded himself that a dream was only a dream and that riding through this dark September night was a reality. It was quiet; it could not have been more peaceful.

Robert reckoned it was between three and four o'clock in the morning when he reached Vergor's piquet. It was not a heavily staffed sentry post, and Robert well-remembered the discussion that had taken place concerning it. Someone had asked if it should be reinforced. The answer had come with a sneering laugh, "What for? The English can't fly!"

As Robert approached the sentry post, he heard considerable noise. He froze for a second and then rode hard for the place where Vergor's guards were.

"Halt!" one of them called out in the darkness. Robert drew in his horse and responded in French. The guard relaxed.

Robert identified himself. He pointed off into the darkness toward the cliffs. "What's all that noise?" he demanded.

The guard rubbed his eyes sleepily and shrugged with

boredom. "Supply ships below—we've been expecting them."

Robert frowned. "Were they challenged?"

"Of course! They answered in French—they're ours!"

"I answered in French," Robert said crisply. "But I'm not French! The French are not the only people who speak French!"

The guard glared at Robert. "Relax, they're our supply ships."

Robert would have liked to think so. God only knew, the besieged city needed supplies—most of all it needed food.

"Has Vergor been awakened?"

"What for?" the guard answered with a note of irritation. All he needed was some smart scout from Montcalm's staff asking dumb questions in the middle of the night.

Robert felt a sudden flash of temper. He knew it wasn't justified—yet. "Well, look a little sharper!" he warned the guard. "I'm going down there to see what's going on."

Robert knew the steep path that led down to the river. It was heavily wooded on either side. He tied his mare and made off on foot into the woods, moving silently downward on a route that ran parallel to the actual path. He had not gone far when he froze in horror. The low cursing voices he heard from beyond the bush were those of British foot soldiers. Robert didn't wait to hear more than a few sentences.

Robert turned and quickly made his way back on the route he had come. There was some sort of machinery in use below, and the noise he had heard indicated a large number of men. Robert couldn't quite imagine it, but he was certain the grunting and the cursing he had heard were related to the machinery. That was it! They were using winches!

As Robert took the last step over the top of the cliff, he bolted for his mare, nearly knocking over the bewildered sentry.

"Wake up Vergor! Man the guns! The British are coming!" Robert was still shouting as he threw himself across his horse and took off into the night. His chest ached from the exertion of his rapid climb and the long run back to the sentry post. His mind reeled at the reality of his discovery.

Robert let his horse open into a full stride as he hit the flat plains. Behind him he heard gunfire, and he knew the first of Wolfe's troops had come over the top of the cliff. Vergor would not be able to repulse them.

Robert burst into Montcalm's headquarters at Fort Beauport. "Wake up the general!" Robert steadied himself against the desk and panted, trying to catch his breath. The moments seemed like hours—no one seemed to be paying him the slightest bit of attention.

In a moment, General Montcalm appeared. His eyes were still heavy with sleep, and he was wrapped in a red velvet robe.

"The British have scaled the cliffs at Foulon!" Robert blurted out his message. "Vergor is under attack!"

General Montcalm frowned, but much to Robert's amazement, he looked only mildly distressed. Then rubbing his eyes, he shook his head. "It can't be, that's an impossible climb!"

"They've done the impossible!" Robert retorted. He knew his voice was becoming shrill with irritation.

"Well, there can't be many—Vergor will repulse them. He does have the high ground."

Robert could feel himself begin to shake. He suddenly felt like hitting this general he had once respected so much. He certainly wanted to grab him and shake him. "It's more than a few!" he said, trying to keep his tone even so as not to reveal his anger. "It's the main force! I think they've used the ships' winches to get the artillery up the hill."

Montcalm held out his hand in a gesture of patience. "I'll send Dumas to investigate," he finally allowed. Then looking at Robert solicitously, "Why don't you get some more sleep?"

Robert knew his mouth was open, but he forced back a curse.

Montcalm gave the order to send Dumas to Foulon, then he calmly retreated into his bedroom.

Robert turned on his heel and walked out the door. The cool predawn breeze blew in his face, and for a long moment he leaned against the side of the building, trying to think.

Robert considered his limited options. He could go back to Quebec City and try to escape with Janet and Marguerite. But how far would they get? There would soon be troop movements everywhere. Escape was going to take planning, for there was an immediate danger of running into groups of Mohawk or British troops, or both. And to try escape now would constitute desertion. In that case he would have to watch out for the French as well. If one was going to get out of the city, it might be better accomplished after the battle. "Be safe," Robert mumbled under his breath. "I'll come back for you." He said the words to Janet and Marguerite.

Robert wondered if he should remain here and wait for reality to dawn on Montcalm, or if he should head for the units of the Canadian militia and Indians who fought with them. Not being addicted to the absurdity of set battle, they might at least stand a chance of survival.

Robert swore and kicked the ground. Then remembering the necessities of life, he undid his breeches and pissed on the frost-covered earth. As his warm urine hit the cold frost, it sent up a weak steam. "Shit!" Robert said out loud. He turned to one of Montcalm's guards. "When the general receives his confirmation, tell him I've gone to warn the militia!" With that, Robert remounted his horse and rode off. A thin ray of light was just breaking in the eastern sky. It would soon be sunrise.

General Montcalm had returned to his bedroom, but he did not return to bed. Instead he ordered tea. After a time, he finished the tea, dressed in full battle dress, and left his headquarters. He was near the bridge that crossed the Charles River when he received confirmation from Boishebert.

The color drained from General Montcalm's face as he realized the panic-stricken message delivered by his scout was one-hundred-percent accurate. "I didn't want this battle," Montcalm mumbled.

He straightened himself up, striking an aristocratic pose. Then he searched the sky with his eyes. It must be between six-thirty and seven, he thought to himself as he looked at the rising sun. General Montcalm turned to his aide. "Have the troops assemble on the Plains of Abraham . . . at nine o'clock."

Robert looked out between the branches of the low shrub. He was with the Canadian militia at the top of the hill, and his position offered him a good view of the assembled armies. It was also a fine position from which to fight, especially for the Canadian sharpshooters; the Canadians and the Indians and half-breeds who fought with them were fine hunters, who seldom wasted bullets.

The militia extended their line into the bushes where Robert was located. To their left were the French regular troops of the La Sarre, Languedoc, Béarn, Guienne, and Royal Roussillon divisions. On the extreme left were the Indians and some more militia who moved through the woods along the cliff.

Two cannons were on the left in front of the St. Louis gate. Montcalm himself took up a position in the center with Montreuil; Senezergues was on the right and Fontbonne on the left. The French had gathered some 4,500 troops; Robert had intelligence reports that suggested Wolfe had managed to assemble his entire army of some 5,000 men. As Robert could see, Wolfe had also gotten his precious artillery up the hill.

Robert shook his head as he surveyed the British cannons. He knew the cliff where the big guns had been brought up. "Damn the British Navy and the winches! But he gets full credit!" Robert said of General Wolfe. "Whatever else he is, the man's a persistent son of a whore!"

Robert's fingers were already on the trigger of his musket when he heard the distant sounds of bagpipes on the Plains of Abraham. For an instant, he closed his eyes and listened. There was no sound so beautiful, no instrument so stirring! Sadly, Robert realized the sound of the pipes was coming from both sides.

Behind Montcalm was a regiment of Scots Highlanders, most dressed in battle kilts and war bonnets. But General Wolfe had Scots behind him too. The Frasers played their own tunes. For Robert it was an eerie sound, and with it came a thousand boyhood memories and all the stories of Culloden.

"History repeats itself," Robert mumbled under his breath.

Part of the Canadian militia had begun to move ahead to exchange sporadic shots with the enemy. Robert watched as the September sun rose in the sky. The two armies—the British and the French—were waiting for the official signal to go at one another. By Robert's calculation, it was nearly ten o' clock before Montcalm gave the order to advance. When he raised his arm, the French regulars ran forward as if in slow motion, stopping now and again to fire at the enemy.

Their muskets were long and awkward. They had to be loaded from the barrel. The soldiers ran forward, fired, dropped to the ground to reload, got up, and ran forward again. . . . But the French were totally disorganized. Their center line began to crumble and fall apart under the return British fire. This exposed the phalanx to the regular volleys of the British infantry.

Robert dropped the butt of his musket to reload. He was well behind the trees when he saw the French lines begin to break up. The men who were able to, simply turned and ran.

General Montcalm had been felled by a load of

grapeshot and was carried from the field. His chief commanders, Brigadiers Senezergues and Fontbonne, were taken prisoner.

Robert lifted his musket and again took careful aim. The British were now charging with fixed bayonets, and the Scots on both sides had discarded their guns and were fighting with their traditional weapons. They slashed at one another with their broadswords.

The one group of Canadians holding their ground was Robert's. Their constant well-placed shots from the bushes were making it possible for some of the French troops to retreat across the Charles River to temporary safety.

"*Mon Dieu!*" The Canadian marksman who was standing near Robert threw his broad-brimmed, feathered hat in the air.

Robert's eyes widened as he saw what had happened. The unknown Canadian had shot General Wolfe, who was now surrounded by his men. *Vive les Canadiens!*" the marksman shouted. "That's one British general who won't fight again against *les Canadiens!*"

But Wolfe or no Wolfe, it was clearly too late.

"Time to get out of here," Robert said to his compatriot. It was not a moment too soon. The British were sending in reinforcements to clean up the snipers in the bush.

Robert stealthily made his way around the main body of the fighting. It was more than clear that this battle was lost. The French forces were utterly crumbled, and Quebec City would now surrender. But he was damn well going to get back to Janet and Marguerite in one piece.

"He's dead, I know he's dead!" Marguerite Lupien leaned against Janet and sobbed uncontrollably. Her entire body shook, and tears ran down her face from her swollen eyes.

Janet held Marguerite close and tried to think. She could not think of Robert dead any more than she could think of Mathew dead. But days passed, and while many soldiers straggled into the besieged city and the hospitals were overflowing with wounded, there was neither news about Robert nor a message from him.

Five days after the battle had begun the population was starving! The city was ready to surrender, and promises of good treatment had been received.

"He'd come back if he were alive!" Marguerite sobbed.

"Perhaps he can't come back," Janet tried to comfort Marguerite. "Robert's a resourceful person—he may be waiting for the right moment."

"Maybe he's lying wounded somewhere! I can't stand not knowing."

Janet stroked Marguerite's hair. "I wish you would try to get some rest," she urged, easing Marguerite down onto the makeshift bedroll. "I'm going to the hospital. I'll look around, ask people."

Marguerite nodded, and Janet covered her frail body with the blanket. "Just try to sleep," the older woman advised.

Janet brushed herself off, drew her shawl around her shoulders, then stopped momentarily.

After the house had been hit, she and Marguerite gathered all the belongings they could find and stored them in the corner of the basement where they now took shelter.

Janet began rummaging through the piles. There, among the things she had retrieved from the kitchen, was the hunting knife. The fine, long, sharp, strong-bladed knife was secure in its own leather sheath. Janet put the knife down her dress and adjusted it between her breasts. Then she pulled up her shawl again and left.

Tonight Quebec City would be in British hands, and promises or not, Janet knew the British all too well. She would not go unarmed through the streets of Quebec City.

CHAPTER XI

September 1759

Sergeant Will Stanley had never been promoted. He had been a sergeant at Culloden when he had served under Wolfe, and he was a sergeant now. Commissions were normally bought. Stanley was a common man from a common family; there was no hope of him having the money to buy a commission.

Will Stanley was nearly fifty now, with small beady eyes and pock-marked skin that had yellowed with age, like his teeth. With his superiors Will Stanley was subservient—a good soldier. With his underlings he was cruel. But in spite of his cruelty, Sergeant Stanley had a reputation—the kind of reputation that only soldiers considered admirable. Prisoners turned over to Sergeant Stanley for interrogation either produced answers or died.

Sergeant Stanley was personally outraged by the terms of surrender offered the French. It was bad enough to be fighting in this godforsaken part of nowhere, but the terms of surrender did not allow for harassment of the population of Quebec City or the pleasure of looting. Stanley willingly admitted, however, that there probably wasn't much to loot in any case. Months of continuous shelling had left the city a pile of rubble, and the population was already starving. Winter was coming, and although Quebec had surrendered, the French had not. The war would go on. Indeed, it was the fact that the battle on the Plains of Abraham had not caused total capitulation that irritated Stanley. Too many French soldiers and Canadians had escaped and were now headed downriver to Montreal and other points west. For Sergeant Stanley that meant only one thing—more fighting. He had looked forward to certain entertainments in Quebec City— particularly the little French girls—and now that type of entertainment would be forbidden.

Just why the British had been so generous Stanley could not figure out. Why to the French and their Canadian allies? Were these North American French any different from the French of France? He could not fathom the terms of the surrender or the orderly way the government was to be handed over. It seemed totally stupid. After all, the city and its inhabitants were at the mercy of the British.

Stanley was still cursing his higher-ups when he received orders to go into Quebec City. He was to be part of a small group that would verify the damage done by the shelling. His orders were strict, and his assignment specific. Nonetheless, Sergeant Stanley smiled to himself. Who could know what opportunity might present itself? Certainly going anywhere was preferable to remaining at Beauport.

"You can write a succinct report on conditions, can't you?" The lieutenant looked at Stanley with some disdain.

Stanley saluted and assured him he could.

The lieutenant unrolled a large map of Quebec City. "We've divided the city into areas . . ." the lieutenant said in a low, flat drone. He pointed to a section of the city. "You take this area. It's quite a simple task really. Just count the number of houses standing, the number partially destroyed, and the number completely destroyed."

Stanley nodded. "How many men shall I take?"

The lieutenant shook his head. "None. That's the arrangement we've made. One man to each section. No arms either."

"You mean I'm to go unarmed?"

"Yes. All we want is some simple information so we can compare it with that given by the city authorities."

Stanley grunted and then saluted. "Yes, sir!"

It was hardly a military task, he thought to himself. But still, it was better than nothing. Fantasies of lovely, frightened Frenchwomen moved across his mind. It had been a long time.

It was September 20. The smells and sights of fall were very much in the air. Janet had left Marguerite just as she did every day, but she too was beginning to despair. There was still no news of Robert. His body had not been returned for burial and he was not among the wounded. But of course the British did have prisoners. Janet thought Robert might be among them.

As she made her way along the rubble-strewn streets, she was thankful only that the shelling had stopped and the air had cleared. September 20! Janet repeated the date to herself again and again. It had been a year! She'd been away almost exactly a year. Her heart ached to see her children; she yearned to have Mathew's arms around her. Janet would entertain no thought that any harm had come to them. "They are well, they are safe," she kept telling herself.

As she headed toward the hospital, Janet was aware of the gnawing hunger that was becoming a constant. There was little food left anywhere. She and Marguerite had finished the last of their own food the night before. Janet had given most of it to Marguerite. Rumor had it that the British would allow the landing of foodstuffs soon. Janet wondered what "soon" meant; for many tomorrow would be too late.

Janet went through the hospital carefully. She stopped and spoke to the wounded, asking after Robert MacLean, as usual. Janet paused near the bed of a wounded militiaman. The smell of vinegar and turpentine was overpowering. The nuns were scrubbing down again, trying to prevent disease from breaking out in the crowded quarters.

"Does it hurt much?" Janet asked, placing a cool hand on the man's face.

He shook his head and smiled up at her.

"Do you know a Robert MacLean?"

The man shook his head in the negative.

"I know him!" The voice came from the adjacent bed.

Janet whirled around and shuddered. The boy was young, perhaps no more than fifteen. His left leg had been blown off, and his young face was etched with pain.

Janet took his hand and pressed it in hers. "When did you last see him?" she asked anxiously.

The young man inhaled. "In the woods . . . he was with Goudet."

"Where's Goudet?" Janet pressed.

"Wounded . . . in the church on the far side of the city. He was taken there, too crowded here . . ."

Janet gasped. It was her first real clue to Robert's whereabouts.

"Oh, bless you!" She bent down and kissed the young man on the cheek. He blushed and pressed her hand. "Thank you, oh, thank you," Janet added.

Janet fairly ran out of the hospital, repeating Goudet's name under her breath so she would not forget it on the long walk to the church.

Sergeant Will Stanley had been riding the streets of his assigned area for over two hours. Up one hill and down the other. The cobblestones were uneven, and the task was boring.

Stanley ambled up to the ruins of the Lupien house

and looked around. He added it to his list of destroyed structures. The street was empty; the sun was beginning to set.

Stanley pressed his lips together. He was thirsty. Daydreaming for an instant about some ale, he then dismounted.

Stanley moved around toward the side of the demolished house and kicked some rubble.

"Janet?" A woman's clear voice from somewhere inside the tumbledown house startled him. He moved in the direction of the sound without answering. There in the dim light of an underground doorway, he saw Marguerite. She was a pretty little cunt! Albeit a bit grubby and on the thin side.

Marguerite stared at him, and her lips parted in surprise. She backed into the basement. Stanley followed.

"Come here!" His voice was deep and angry-sounding.

Marguerite peered out at him from behind a post. Her brown eyes were large with fear, and Stanley could see she was quite alone.

"Come here!" he repeated harshly.

"Je ne parle pas l'anglais."

"I don't care if you don't speak English!" Stanley answered sneeringly. His long-awaited moment had come. She was alone, and he was not expected back for a while. Ah, he had found a sweet and helpless little French girl! He felt himself harden as he looked into her frightened face.

"Come here!" Stanley lunged at Marguerite and grabbed her by the wrist, pulling her toward him.

Marguerite opened her mouth to scream, but no sound came out. She was mesmerized by the man's beady eyes and the sheer ugliness of his face.

Stanley twirled Marguerite around and with one fast move stuffed his dirty rag of a handkerchief into her mouth.

Marguerite kicked and struggled, but Stanley was far too strong for her. He forced her to the floor with one hand and tore open the front of her dress, exposing her lovely breasts.

"Sweet little bitch, aren't you!" Stanley straddled the struggling Marguerite. He pinched her nipples and began to squeeze her breasts.

Marguerite flailed at him, but his weight held her down firmly, as he was tearing off her skirts and trying to force her legs open.

Holding her flat, Stanley sat up long enough to undo the strings on his pants, releasing his organ and letting it forth into her face.

Stanley grinned as he watched his prey struggle. Then falling on her lengthwise, he pulled out the handkerchief.

Marguerite gasped as he pulled and twisted her breasts cruelly, and then she let out a long, agonized scream.

Stanley grew harder—it was her scream, he loved to hear them scream! But then Stanley remembered his situation. His horse was out front. He roughly clamped his hand over her mouth even as he plunged into her.

Marguerite's entire body convulsed as he ripped into her brutally. Stanley threw his head back as he felt release, then sat upright on his torn victim and looked down.

Marguerite's face was a ghastly white. Her terror-filled eyes stared at him. Stanley thought for a moment. He couldn't let her live.

Stanley bent down and ran his hands over Marguerite's breasts. At his touch she let out another scream, but he seized her throat and, pressing his thumbs against her windpipe, squeezed as hard as he could, shaking her head as he did so.

Marguerite's horrified face turned bright red, then white as Stanley choked the life out of her. Then he shook her inert body as if she were a small rag doll.

Janet had been at the base of the hill when she heard Marguerite scream. She had begun to run, but the hill was steep. Janet tripped in the darkness and scraped her knee. Struggling to her feet, Janet continued onward as fast as she could. It was now pitch black, and every step was impeded by the rubble that still littered the road. Janet's lungs hurt with the effort of her climb.

She stopped dead for a second when she saw the horse. Then she heard Marguerite scream again. Janet was only half-aware of having drawn the knife from its sheath. She grasped it tightly as she neared the doorway; some instinct told her not to call out.

Janet fumbled in her pocket with her right hand. Her left grasped the knife. She found the candle and flint. She lit it quickly and peered into the room.

Marguerite's nude body was on the floor. Janet almost shrieked when the burly man who was hitching up his pants turned suddenly, a look of surprise on his ugly pock-marked face.

"You!" Janet uttered. "You!" It was the same pock-marked face, the same beady piglike eyes. It was the face of the man in her nightmares, the man who had beaten and raped her, the man she had vowed never to forget.

Stanley's eyes seemed to grow larger. She was older, but there was no way to forget one's only virgin. Her red hair was still bright and flaming, her green eyes still flashed.

A sickening, lecherous smile crossed Stanley's ugly face. "My little runaway Scots cunt!" His eyes fell on her high, full breasts, her narrow waist, and her rounded hips. Much more beautiful than the woman he had just had. Janet set down the candle, and Stanley took a step toward her. He didn't seem to see the knife gripped tightly in her left hand and partially hidden in the folds of her dress.

He took another step toward her. What had Robert said? How had he instructed her? Janet watched Stanley take another step. Between the ribs . . . up and under . . . that was it! Between the ribs, up and under.

"Come to me!" Janet said in a low, seductive, throaty voice. "Come to me!"

Stanley's face twisted and twitched. He felt for his gun and then remembered he didn't have it. But his eyes didn't leave Janet's face. Her full lips were parted, and she was inviting him. "Come," she repeated.

Stanley reached her. He was going to kiss the full, inviting lips. She looked incredibly seductive! She seemed to want him!

He felt almost limp as he looked into her clear green eyes—eyes like jewels, hypnotizing him, pulling him forward. His arm went around her neck and he leaned down to kiss her. Janet plunged the knife in with a shriek . . . under and up!

Stanley reared back, and Janet pulled the knife out. Blood spurted from his heart, his pig eyes bulged, and one long moan escaped his lips as he tumbled in front of her.

Janet sank to her knees and with both hands plunged the knife into his stomach. "You!" she screamed. "You killed Marguerite!" Janet plunged the knife in again and withdrew it again. "This is for Robert's sisters! This is for Queen Maggie! This is for me! God damn you! You've killed Marguerite!" Blind with anger and tears, Janet shook as she sunk the knife into the dead man over and over. "I'll kill you!" she shrieked irrationally. "Die!"

Robert had made his way off the Plains of Abraham, and by hiding during the day and traveling at night, he had made his way back to the city. But owing to troop movements and to the signing of the surrender papers he had been delayed, waiting till today to enter the city and head for the Lupien house.

It was past midnight—even in the broken city the church bells peeled out the hour.

Robert knew the house had been destroyed. But he hoped that Janet and Marguerite were still living there.

In his pack Robert carried some food. He had stolen rations from a British soldier. Clothes were a more serious problem. He had stripped what he could from his uniform, but there was no mistaking his boots, shirt, and jacket. If they were going to get out of the city, he could not look like a soldier.

The crumbled house loomed ahead of him. Robert paused. There was a horse outside. Robert moved carefully and quietly toward the animal. It was tethered to a post and moved about in an agitated way.

Robert looked around furtively. The street was quiet. But there was no mistaking the saddle. The horse belonged to a British soldier! But occupation of the city was not within the terms of the surrender—he had heard that.

Robert rummaged through the saddle bags for a second. There was nothing of value. He undid the horse, thinking that if there were a British soldier in the house, he would have to kill him. An untended horse could bring those searching for him to the house. With a slap on the rear, the horse took off aimlessly.

Robert moved carefully around to the back basement door. As he stepped into the pitch blackness, he could hear someone breathing.

"Janet? Marguerite?" There was a groan.

Robert fumbled in his pack for a moment and withdrew his candle and flint. He lit the candle and gasped. "My God!"

Janet was hovering over a British soldier—a soldier in a pool of his own blood from the numerous stab wounds. Behind them, Robert saw Marguerite. He knew instantly she was dead, just as he knew Janet had killed the soldier.

Janet looked up at him. Her green eyes were glazed as if she were in a trance.

"Janet!" Robert spoke her name and bent down, shaking her shoulders. "Janet!" Her eyes flickered, and she let out a deep, guttural sob and threw herself on his shoulder. Robert held Janet, patting her back as she began to sob.

He pulled her back and kissed her on the cheek. There were tears in his eyes too, tears for Marguerite. He stood up and kicked the British soldier. The fat body rolled over, and Robert looked with amazement into the face of Sergeant Stanley. The man's eyes stared at him—two pig eyes in an evil face. But the face was known! The face was frozen in Robert's memory just as it was frozen in Janet's. It was the face of the man who had ordered his mother and sisters killed, the man who had raped Janet. Robert sank to the floor with the realization that this evil creature had raped and killed his beloved Marguerite as well.

Robert looked at Marguerite. In the dim, flickering light of the candle, she looked like a child. Tenderly, Robert covered her body with her dress, then he bent down and kissed her forehead.

"I got here too late!" Janet sobbed. "Oh, I got here too late!" Robert bent down and lifted Janet up. The British sergeant was a terrible sight. Janet must have stabbed him a hundred times. Robert shook his head sadly and pulled Janet into his arms. "He's never going to hurt us again!" Janet cried, her voice muffled as Robert held her to his chest. Janet kept repeating these words as she heaved against Robert and he caressed her hair, trying to calm her. Finally, Robert pulled her back and looked into her eyes.

"I have to take you home," he said softly. "Janet, we're going home."

Janet opened her eyes to see Robert cleaning the hunting knife. The bodies of Stanley and Marguerite were both gone.

Janet looked up at Robert questioningly.

"I buried them in the rubble," Robert confessed. "It wouldn't do to have a British soldier found dead here."

Janet nodded.

Robert put the knife back in its sheath and handed it back to her. "Better keep this," he advised.

Robert opened his pack and handed her some biscuits. "It's not much, but it's something."

Janet took one and began eating. She had forgotten how empty she still was.

"Did you salvage any clothes from upstairs?"

"Over there," Janet answered, pointing off toward

some trunks in the corner. "I thought you were a dream last night . . ." Janet's voice trailed off.

"One deserves a dream at the end of a nightmare."

"I heard Marguerite scream . . . I tried to get here. I'd been at the church looking for you . . ." Janet's words tumbled out of her mouth in rapid succession. Robert stopped for a moment and listened. When she finished, he had her begin again and recount the story from start to finish. Then he held her close. "It's not your fault," he kept repeating to her.

Then after a time, Robert drew her back and looked into her eyes. "We're going to leave tonight," he said firmly. "While there's still a certain amount of confusion." Janet nodded in agreement.

"We have a lot to do," Robert informed her seriously. "This is going to be a rough journey . . . at least till we get to Lake Ontario." Robert bit his lip and looked about thoughtfully. "I want you to find the very warmest men's clothes you can. Some for you, some for me."

"Some for me?" Janet looked at him quizzically.

"The woods are full of marauding Mohawk. I want you dressed like a man because you'll be less interesting to them and women's clothes are impractical for portage. Boots—try to find some good warm boots."

"Some of Monsieur Lupien's clothes are here . . ." Janet glanced toward the things she had salvaged from the upstairs bed chambers.

"Janet, this is a dangerous trip. If we're caught by the Mohawk, I want you to kill yourself with the knife."

Robert's eyes were so steady Janet felt mesmerized by them. But she understood the gravity of his warning.

"I'll fix some bedrolls and make the packs. Only the warmest clothes . . ." Robert reminded her. "It's going to be cold before we get home."

Janet tried to smile at Robert. "Home," she repeated.

Robert immediately set to work. Janet went to

gather up suitable things from among Monsieur Lupien's clothes. She glanced over at Robert once and watched him preparing earnestly for the journey ahead.

It was an irony of the strangest kind! As she had smuggled Robert out of Scotland, he was now taking her out of Quebec. In thirteen years their roles had been completely reversed. The protectress had become the protected.

"We'll make it," Robert said confidently.

Janet looked into Robert's soft brown eyes and knew it was true. Robert would take her home.

Janet and Robert left Quebec City under cover of darkness and moved through the woods toward the St. Lawrence. The night was crisp and cold; the moon and the stars shone brightly. They kept to the dense woods, staying close together and remaining silent.

It took them all night to walk to the spot where Robert had hidden a canoe after the battle, for he knew it would be needed to carry out his escape plan.

Robert turned the canoe over and pushed it quietly into the waters of the St. Lawrence. He beckoned Janet and, placing his paddle across the gunnels, steadied the canoe so she could climb in. Then he took his own position and put his paddle into the dark waters.

"The river's full of English ships," Janet said in a whisper.

"But they're used to seeing canoes," Robert answered. "If we pass any other canoes, just keep paddling. Let me give a signal in Mohawk."

Robert silently stripped off his shirt and bared his chest.

"You're going to freeze," Janet said, shivering.

Robert turned his head and smiled at her. "The silhouette has to be right in the moonlight. I'll play Indian. You can be my British passenger."

Janet could not help laughing.

"You're right," Robert said in a loud whisper. "Better to hope we don't run into anyone."

Within two hours Janet and Robert were well beyond the place where the British ships were at anchor. The St. Lawrence glimmered in the moonlight, and the paddles cut through the water silently.

"We'll stay on the St. Lawrence and travel at night," Robert told Janet. *"But* when the river joins Lake Ontario, we'll stay on the north shore and come into Niagara from behind. It's longer, but it's safer. There are too many troops on the south shore."

On the second day of their trip, after Robert had beached the canoe but before they had gone to sleep for the day, six canoes filled with fleeing French troops passed them on their way to Montreal.

Robert watched them and bit his lip thoughtfully. "We'll have to skirt Montreal," he said carefully. "The British will move on it sooner or later—there will have to be a lot of troop movements in that area."

"Will it take much longer?"

"Perhaps only a week, depending on the weather. We'll portage north of Montreal to the Ottawa River, go up the Ottawa and then south back down to the St. Lawrence. There are lots of smaller rivers that flow from the Ottawa to the St. Lawrence. We'll take the one that seems best when we get to it."

"Have you been this way before?" Janet questioned.

"Twice. It has the advantage of getting us into friendlier Indian territory. Less danger of running into Mohawk."

Janet automatically felt for the hunting knife when Robert mentioned the Mohawk. The woods on either side of the river were dense, and the shoreline was littered with large rocks. Some of the larger trees dipped right into the water, and here and there, by the light of the waning moon, one could make out a sandy cove. There were no friendly campfires to be seen, no flickering lights from farmhouses, no curls of white smoke reaching for the sky. It was an uninhabited wilderness, and only the eerie cry of the loon across the river interrupted the silence of the night.

After three nights of travel, Robert and Janet made camp on the shores of the Ottawa River. Robert roasted a wild hare he had snared during the night. Bits of fat fell into the fire, causing it to crackle. It was the first meat they had even tried to trap since leaving Quebec.

"We're lucky to have Indian summer," Robert said, smiling.

"We're lucky to have food," Janet answered, suddenly realizing how hungry she was.

Janet looked at Robert thoughtfully. "Are you sorry not to be fighting with the army?" It was a question she had thought of asking before. Robert had literally deserted to take her home—and home was now in British territory.

Robert shook his head solemnly. "It means nothing to me." His face was pensive. "I have no respect for either side. If I go back into French territory, it will only be because I want to travel in that territory, not because it's French."

Janet looked away from the small fire on which the hare sizzled. She stared into the tangled bush and bit her lip. "You're not going to stay with us?"

"For a short time," Robert answered. "It's difficult for me to explain."

"Because of Marguerite . . . ?" They had barely spoken of Marguerite's murder or of Robert's loss. Janet was afraid he was bottling up his feelings, burying his emotions.

"Partially," Robert answered vaguely. "Call it wanderlust, but I have no reason to settle down now." Robert wiped the soot from his brow. He had been leaning over the smoky fire turning the hare. "Something happened to me on the Plains of Abraham . . . it was seeing the Scots divided, seeing the Highlanders, hearing the pipers play on both sides, watching the way the French and the English set their armies on each other. Those men weren't fighting for what they believed in, they were fighting for the eternal glory of Wolfe and Montcalm! If they'd been fighting for themselves, they'd have fought differently. I'm through fighting for the glory of some general . . ." Robert's voice trailed off.

Janet understood what Robert meant for she had heard Mathew say the same thing. Robert seemed suddenly older to her, more mature.

"I'm of this land!" Robert said with conviction. "I'm no longer a part of what we left behind when we came here!"

Janet nodded. "Mathew feels the same way. He says we have to build a new life here . . . whatever happens."

"And you will," Robert answered, "because you and Mathew are Scots, because the Scots are neither French nor English, because when you come down to it, the Campbells and the MacDonalds have more in common in this land than the English and the French. I realized that when I talked with the Scots commander at Fort William Henry. He was fighting with the British, but we two had more in common than I had with Montcalm or he had with his British superior. Do you understand? Am I making any sense?"

Janet leaned over and kissed Robert's cheek. "I understand," she answered.

"You see," Robert explained, "I can't stay with you and Mathew. I have to find my own Lochiel."

Janet smiled tenderly at Robert. "Where will you look?"

"I'm going to head southwest, into the Louisiana Territory. I may not find it there, but when I find it, I'll know."

Janet's eyes were moist and so were Robert's. In silence he took the hare off the wooden spit and divided it with her. When they had finished eating, Robert extinguished the fire and buried the traces of their camp. It was early evening, and soon they would be on their way again, silently moving along the river.

Mathew and Megan kept a cool distance, and though Megan still came to help the children, she spent more time at the fort, consulting with the British.

Mathew busied himself by adding a new room to the cabin. The children continued the daily preparations for winter. As always, there was wood to be chopped, dried, and stored; candles to be made; meat to be salted; vegetables to be prepared; and wild cranberries to be collected.

When Mathew and Megan spoke, it was about the children or some household need. The British surgeon had, at Megan's request, removed the bullet from Mathew's leg. Though it had healed well, Mathew limped slightly, and at night his leg often throbbed.

Mathew placed an armload of logs in the bin next to the fireplace.

"You shouldn't work so hard," Megan commented. "You're still limping." She was stirring the soup.

"Winter's coming," Mathew answered. "It'll come whether I limp or not. There are things that have to be done." Mathew turned away from Megan's piercing blue eyes. He was resentful toward her and felt trapped by her continued presence. He could not deny that Megan had assured the safety of the children and the farm, or that she had saved his own life. It was just as true that she took good care of the children and avoided discussing politics within their hearing, carefully protecting them from the undercurrents of the household. But still Mathew resented her—she had made him a traitor at gunpoint, she had used his own children, and now she remained with them as if she were waiting for something.

"There's news today," Megan said.

"How nice that you have news," Mathew answered sarcastically. "One of the advantages of living with a spy, I imagine."

Megan wiped her hands on her apron. "Unfortunately, we don't live together," she corrected him. "We exist under the same roof."

Mathew didn't answer.

"Quebec City has surrendered," she said matter-of-factly.

Mathew looked up at her. His eyes flickered with apprehension. "Tell me . . ."

Megan shrugged. "The British terms are said to be generous. The civilian population is quite safe."

Mathew let out his breath. "Janet will be coming home."

Megan looked at him. It was a long, questioning look. "You'll never like me, will you?"

"Like you?" Mathew's voice rose.

"Well, you'll be pleased to know that I'm leaving."

Mathew's eyes widened. He had wanted her to say that, he had in fact been waiting for her to do so. But as always his emotions concerning Megan were mixed.

"Oh, don't worry. Nothing will happen to you or this farm or your children. The British are really quite grateful you didn't warn the French. They suppose you're a sympathizer. I've done my best to encourage that supposition."

"And I'm to be grateful?" Mathew's voice held the edge of his bitterness.

"Gratitude is not what I wanted from you!" Megan snapped back, her blue eyes flashing.

Mathew leaned toward her, his own brown eyes searching her face. "You tried to buy love, Megan— you tried to buy it by offering me my life and offering me safety for my children. You can't buy love, you can't force it."

Megan looked away. "I suppose I did place you in an impossible position."

Mathew sat down and buried his face in his hands. Impossible was hardly the word to describe the mix of emotions he felt. Throughout the long weeks he had tried to concentrate on the children, on the need to protect them. At the same time, it was impossible to ignore the slaughter at Fort Niagara. He couldn't get it out of his mind or cast away the thought that he could have prevented it. Megan's act of duplicity had torn him completely, and his inner struggle of conscience was more complicated than he could admit. He'd certainly had doubts about both the French and the English, doubts that had surfaced long before Megan's appearance. But he had not made the decisions! Megan had made them—she had prevented him from warning the French.

Mathew looked at Megan evenly. Half of him wanted to explode, the other half was weary of the whole incident.

"When are you going?" Mathew asked.

"Day after tomorrow," Megan answered crisply. "To meet my father."

"Where are you going?"

"I really can't tell you. Perhaps to Boston, perhaps to Virginia."

Megan sat down at the table and looked across at Mathew. Her face was softer, her eyes sadder. "We could have had a great deal together."

Mathew met her eyes, and for the first time he did not feel complete bitterness toward her. He shook his head slowly. "No, Megan. We couldn't have had anything."

"Papa! Papa! Someone's coming! Someone's coming!" Andrew's voice rang through the crisp October, early-morning air.

Pierre and René were bundling twigs, and Madelaine was in the cabin, preparing a pot of stew for the noon meal while Mat watched her curiously.

Mathew was in the barn, milking the cow, and six-year-old Helena leaned over his shoulder, giggling with fascination as Mathew squeezed the milk from the cow's teats into the bucket.

At the sound of Andrew's voice, Mathew stopped milking instantly and picked up his musket. "Stay here!" he told the green-eyed Helena.

Mathew opened the barn door and looked across the

open field that led to the river. Two figures approached. One carried a musket. The other walked too gracefully for its male attire. Mathew stood for a second, aware that both Pierre and René were behind him, muskets in hand. Then Mathew turned. "It's all right!" He broke into a limping run.

The graceful figure on the left removed its dark cap, and Mathew saw Janet's red hair tumble to her shoulders. She began running toward him. "Mathew!" her voice sang across the distance between them

"Janet!" Mathew ran on until they met and fell into each other's arms. "My God! It is you!"

Janet pressed herself against her husband and hugged him tightly. "You're all right," she gasped breathlessly. "Oh, thank God, you're safe!"

In another second the children were all there, each clinging to their mother and claiming a share of her affection.

Janet buried herself in them. Her heart pounded with relief, her long-held fears sped out of her.

"And nobody cares about me?" Robert grinned. The children were on him at once. "Uncle Robert! Uncle Robert!"

Robert kissed Mat, Andrew, Helena and Madelaine. He hugged René and Pierre, both of whom had grown tall and strong. "I've paddled a canoe all the way from Quebec City," Robert said playfully. "Can you go back down to the river and secure it and bring up our packs?" The two boys ran off toward the river without hesitation.

Arm in arm, Janet and Mathew walked back toward the cabin. It was a joyful reunion that lasted all afternoon and well into the night.

In the days that followed, Janet told Mathew about Marguerite and the sergeant. Mathew told Janet about Megan.

"What a strange woman," Janet said thoughtfully. "But how can I hate her, Mathew?" Janet's green eyes were filled with questions. "How can I hate a woman who saved my children's lives and yours too?"

"She saved my life and destroyed my honor," Mathew protested. "But I don't hate her . . . I don't know how I feel."

"But she forced you not to warn the fort—she shot you! You didn't behave dishonorably."

"And now we accept the British—we accept their protection. And if not their protection, their willingness to ignore us."

Janet moved into Mathew's arms and rested her head against him. "You said it yourself," she reminded him. "We're neither one nor the other . . . we're of this land, Mathew. What's important is this land and our home. I have no desire to fight for either one side or the other. Damn both of them! What we have here is what we will build on. And, Mathew, French or English, woe to the person who tries to take it away from us!"

Mathew felt her shaking against him. He knew she was right. It was only this land they would ever defend, and it was here they would build.

Spring came early in 1760, and the drenching March rains left the land fertile and ready for planting.

Robert had remained with Janet and Mathew over the winter months, but now he was leaving.

"You're welcome to stay," Mathew told him. "There's more than enough land, more than I can work alone."

Robert looked at the Macleod clan—René, Pierre, Madelaine, Andrew, Mat and Helena. The oldest was sixteen, the youngest seven. "You're hardly alone!" Robert laughed.

"You're a part of us," Janet insisted.

Robert took her in his arms. "And I always will be, no matter where I go. But it hasn't left me . . . I have to satisfy my wanderlust. I have to find what I lost when Marguerite was killed."

"Still going south?"

"Maybe to New Orleans," Robert replied as he put the finishing touches on his pack.

"I'm going to be a voyageur!" Andrew chimed in.

Robert pointed to the dwindling fire. "Then you had better learn to build a proper fire," he teased. Andrew sheepishly went back to stoking the lethargic blaze.

"Come back to us," Janet pleaded.

"Of course I'll come back," Robert answered, holding her close. But his thoughts were elsewhere. They were already on the wide open country of the Illinois and the great Mississippi he had heard about. "The Louisiana Territory," Robert said under his breath. "It's waiting."

CHAPTER XII

March 1760

Robert MacLean began his solitary journey in late March of 1760. At Janet's insistence he carried some gold sewn into his clothing. Other than that, Robert took only his woodsman's pack, his knife, his pistol, and the clothes he wore.

His canoe was made of birch bark, strong enough for rapid rivers and white water, light enough to portage alone.

Robert traveled along the shores of Lake Erie to Fort Detroit, which he avoided because of the continuation of the war. From there, he canoed and portaged across inland waterways to Joliet and then onward to La Salle, where the great Illinois River began winding its lazy path to join the legendary Mississippi at Fort St. Louis.

For nearly two years Robert wandered the Illinois Territory, leading the precarious existence of a voyageur. He trapped and passed his fur pelts on to those who headed down river. He wintered with friendly Indians, and he mastered the network of rivers that led to the Mississippi.

In March of 1762, Robert returned to Fort St. Louis

and made plans to follow the Mississippi all the way to its vast delta and the famed port of New Orleans.

By the time Robert left Joliet, the huge evergreens of the north country had yielded to the low-lying scrub bush and the soft-wood poplars. The hills rolled more gently than in Canada, and the bluffs above the river were often smooth. The lakes were no longer the crystal-clear, spring-fed lakes of the north; they were lakes fed by the river, and though the water was clean enough to drink, the river's silt made the lakes brown in appearance.

Fort St. Louis was a thriving fur-trading center populated mostly by raucous traders and the Indians they lived and worked with.

Robert settled himself down on the wooden steps of the trading post. He had just bought a skin of rum, and as he lifted it to his lips, he thought about how long it had been since he had tasted anything but water. The rum burned his throat and filled his chest with a warm feeling. In spite of the noise inside the post, Robert began to relax.

"Give me a drink or I'll slit your ribs!" A knife point was dead against Robert, and he jerked around quickly at the sound of the low voice that spoke in broken French. The startled anger on his face changed instantly to a wide grin. "Fou Loup!" Robert boomed out.

"Eh! You know I hardly recognized you!" the Indian exclaimed.

"Fou Loup!" Robert embraced Fou Loup. "What are you doing here? What the hell are you doing here?"

Fou Loup shrugged in his classical French way. "One woods is pretty much like another . . . not so much shooting in these woods."

Robert laughed and passed Fou Loup the rum. Fou Loup, trader and scout, was a practical man. He knew how to live off the land—and live was what he intended to do. He was nearly fifty now, and clearly he'd had enough of war.

226

"Now I'll ask you—what are you doing here?" Fou Loup took a generous swig of rum.

"The same as you," Robert answered.

"You staying here to trade furs?" Fou Loup asked.

Robert shook his head. "I'm headed down to New Orleans."

"You got business in New Orleans?"

"No, I've just never been there."

Fou Loup spit and made a face. "Never did like rum," he mumbled as he withdrew his own skin of raw whiskey.

"I hear there are pretty French women in New Orleans," Fou Loup said with a tone of appreciation.

"I hear there's money to be made," Robert replied. That was not the only reason for his heading south. In fact, it had just occurred to him.

"You got a loose foot?"

Robert looked so perplexed that Fou Loup felt obliged to rephrase his question. "You can't settle down . . . got to keep moving . . . you know, a loose foot."

Robert laughed. Fou Loup's French was enough to confuse most people. "Two loose feet," he answered.

"Me too," Fou Loup confessed. "You know, I got a big load of rich furs. Bet they'd sell good in New Orleans." Fou Loup rubbed his chin, and beneath his untidy mop of graying hair, his narrow Mohawk eyes twinkled mischievously. "But it's not good for a man to travel down the Mississippi alone with a load of furs."

Robert took the hint. "How about two men?"

Fou Loup took a swig of whiskey and wiped his mouth on his stained buckskin sleeve. "Two men's good . . . 'specially if one of them's a big fellow." Fou Loup let out another bellow and slapped Robert across the back. "Them furs buy us plenty in New Orleans!"

Robert looked at the flat barge suspiciously. It was nearly as large as the main room of a cabin, and it had a sort of crude shelter built in the middle. Attached to it was a rope to measure the depth of the river. There were long poles to punt with. "We'll tie the canoes on just in case," Fou Loup announced as he continued to pile the furs on the flat surface of the barge. "Then we tie down the furs and cover them."

"I'm impressed," Robert answered. "Do we sleep in there?" He pointed to the structure in the center.

"Only if it rains."

"That goes too . . ." Fou Loup pointed off toward a round metal bucket. "It's to cook in . . . cost plenty out here. Bought it from a starving Seneca."

Robert threw their packs on board with their supply of rum and whiskey. Then he helped Fou Loup tie down the furs and cover them. Within the hour they were off.

"I'll say it's easier than paddling," Robert admitted. The current was in fact carrying them along without much help.

"Well, you gotta watch where you're going."

Robert laughed and shook his head in amazement. Fou Loup, he thought to himself, always watched where he was going.

Fou Loup hit the flat, wooden surface of the barge with his hand. "Heavy! Good thing it's all water. Wouldn't want to portage this!"

With that Fou Loup stripped off the grimy top of his buckskins and stretched out on his back in the hot sun. "This is a lazy man's way to travel," he announced, lifting his whiskey skin to his mouth again.

Robert stood with the long punt and watched the river and the course of the barge. The river ran brown, as did the lakes and streams. It was incredibly wide in some places and narrow in others. At times it seemed to split in two and then rejoin itself farther downstream.

The shoreline varied. Sometimes it was wide and sandy—at those places there were often large sand bars in the middle of the river as well. Huge white birds collected on them, and when the barge approached, they all took flight with terrified squawks, circling around in the air till the barge had passed their domain. At other times, the shoreline was dense with low shrubbery that gave way to rolling hills covered with wild flowers. The farther south they traveled, the more gradual the roll in the hills and the fewer the bluffs. Now the trees were almost all poplars with some graceful willows that hung over and dipped right into the water. The sun grew warmer, the air heavier with humidity.

On one occasion they passed an Indian village. Fou Loup called out a welcome, and the children of the village all stood on the shore and waved at them.

"Friendly," Robert commented.

Fou Loup shrugged. "Not always. But as long as we're on the river, they won't bother us. They're used to it. We French and half-breeds have been traveling this river since old La Salle found it."

"It's hot!" Robert said, taking off his shirt.

Fou Loup laughed, his gold tooth sparkling in the sun.

In 1762, New Orleans was as exotic a place as Robert had ever seen or for that matter imagined. The French engineer, Adrien de Pauger, had laid it out in sixty-six squares with Bourbon Street running more or less through its center.

Some of the earliest structures still stood, and these now housed the poor. They were made from bark, reeds, the refuse of old Spanish galleons, and boards that washed up the river.

"Good enough most of the time," an old man told Robert, pointing toward his shanty. "When the hurricane come, she knock 'em down. We just set 'em back up. And in the summer, they good—the wind, what there is of it, she blow in and out. Not cold like Canada here. Warm most all year."

The old man who revealed all this was stooped with age and of indeterminate heritage. His eyes were almost golden, and his skin was the golden tan of buckskin, but aged and lined like old leather. He called himself a "Cajun," which was how he pronounced "Canadian" when he tried to say it. He spoke a peculiar dialect of French—even more peculiar than Fou Loup's French. It was mixed with a little of the Indian tongue and expressions from some lost African language.

Nonetheless, the old man, whose name was José Goulet, was a mine of information, having been born in New Orleans even before it was New Orleans. It turned out his father was a Canadian adventurer—a voyageur —and his mother was half-Indian, half-African.

New Orleans, Robert learned, had been founded in 1717 by John Law's Company of the West, which had taken control of Louisiana the same year. The French had envisaged it as a port of deposit where future trade from upriver would be sold and then resold to ships on their way to Europe.

The inhabitants of New Orleans were, like José Goulet, as varied in origin as they were in interests, breeding, and vocations. New Orleans was a mixture of Canadian backwoodsmen, many of whom were the sons of the original craftsmen brought to the colony in the 1720s; troops; some convicts who worked as indentured servants; African slaves; Spanish privateers and their offspring; and a good many women of uncertain virtue.

Robert's ears were constantly assaulted by the noisy charm of the city. Fishmongers sang out about the superiority of their wares, and one heard French, Spanish, English, mysterious African, and a mixture of Indian languages, as well as the common patois. The people of New Orleans had solved the problem of communication by inventing their own language; it seemed to incorporate a little bit of everything.

But New Orleans was more than just noise and a thousand tongues. The aromas of the city tweaked the nostrils. Here shrimp was king, and rich French-style soups were flavored with the spices of the Caribbean.

The city's main exports were tobacco and indigo, but since the beginning of the long war with the English, few French ships came. It was more often the Spanish who traded, albeit surreptitiously.

Robert noted that unlike Quebec, New Orleans had no food shortage. The bayous were a constant source of food from both the sea and the river, the delta was rich with rice, and on higher ground fresh vegetables grew easily under the southern sun.

Fou Loup's rich hoard of furs was sold to a squint-eyed, sallow-skinned Spanish sea captain who spoke with a lisp, but negotiated the price as if he were trading his own skin for the furs.

"*Madre de Cristo!*" He shouted when Fou Loup first gave the price. "I'm not a prince! I'm not the king of Spain!"

Fou Loup's face hardened. His narrow Mohawk eyes—his one legacy from his father besides his woodsman's skill—became small slits. "And I am not the king of France!"

"I didn't know you spoke Spanish," Robert said, amazed at Fou Loup's sudden use of the tongue.

Fou Loup shrugged. "It's easy. Just like French, but you pronounce all the letters."

"*Ciente!* Not a sovereign more!" the Captain lisped.

Fou Loup eyed the gold pieces and sneered. "Nine-hundred!" he insisted. Then turning his back on the Spaniard, he began to pack up the furs that had been spread out on the crude trading table, shaking his head with disgust and mumbling.

The captain also turned away momentarily, but Robert saw that he sneaked a look at Fou Loup out of the corner of his eye.

Finally, the captain threw up his arms and shouted, "French pig! Cheap bastard! Son of a whore! Cur! Six-hundred-and-fifty!"

Fou Loup looked nonplussed. He continued to pack the furs, albeit with maddening slowness.

Robert wiped his brow. They were in the heart of the market, an area of ramshackle buildings that looked as if they might fall into the river at any moment. The smells were incredible, and the heat was overwhelming. The air was heavy with moisture, and Robert was perspiring profusely.

"Eight-hundred-and-seventy-five," Fou Loup said without looking the captain in the eye.

"Grave robber!" the Spaniard screamed. "Seven-hundred!" With that he stomped his foot on the ground.

A considerable crowd had gathered to watch the proceedings. Such matters were a source of general entertainment.

"How long have they been at it?" a fat woman asked cheerfully. "Have I missed much?"

"About three hours," Robert said, glancing up at the sun and wishing he had something to drink.

"Pirate!" Fou Loup replied. "You would steal from your mother, from the mother of God! You probably sleep with nuns!"

Robert blinked and fought back his laugh. Fou Loup looked deadly serious.

"Eight-hundred! I won't take less than eight-hundred!"

"Bastard!" the Spaniard lisped. "Your mother must have been a wolf and your father a fox! Seven-hundred-and-fifty."

Fou Loup shook his head, and this time he began to pack the furs in earnest.

The captain lifted his arms to the heavens and shrieked, "Eight-hundred!"

Fou Loup turned to Robert. "How does that sound?"

"Sounds good," Robert said as he winked.

Fou Loup turned to the captain. "Spanish thief! Slaver! Sacrament stealer. I'll take it!"

The captain smiled, Fou Loup smiled, and the two men embraced like brothers, kissing each other on the cheek and suddenly laughing. The crowd gave out a round of applause and yells.

The captain shoved the piles of gold across the table,

and Fou Loup nodded toward the furs. "They're all yours!"

At that, the captain signaled to his two surly crewmen, and they began piling up the furs to take them away.

"We can buy lots of good times with this!" Fou Loup winked. He counted out half and shoved it toward Robert.

"I can't take this—they were your furs."

"I gonna carry all those furs to New Orleans alone? Fair's fair. You help me, half the gold's yours."

Fou Loup was insistent, and when they had bundled their money, Fou Loup slapped Robert on the back and let out a whoop. "C'mon! So far I've only heard about the women!"

Together Robert and Fou Loup walked along the dusty street. The air down by the river market was a fine mixture of sweet, southern blossoms and dead fish, of acrid smoke from the houses of the tanners and rice cooking in outdoor pots.

Fou Loup raised a bushy eyebrow. "Watch your money with these women," he warned. "They have a sweet-talking reputation."

Robert followed Fou Loup up to what had to be a bordello. A little black girl answered the door and ushered them into a parlor, motioning them to sit down.

Robert inhaled. Unlike the air outside, the air in this room was heavy and pungent. There was something erotic about it. The furniture was a mixture of old French and Spanish and hand-crafted French colonial. The many candles were subdued by hoods of colored glass, and the drapes were a bright blood red.

The little black girl disappeared immediately, and a woman of ample proportions appeared. She was, Robert guessed, about Fou Loup's age. But maturity had not made her modest. She wore a bright red taffeta dress that was cut low enough to reveal her heaving breasts.

Robert thought she must be heavily corseted—no one could have had such a shape by nature. Her waist was tiny compared to her great girth of hips. Her hair, though gray, fell loosely over her shoulders, and she wore a red hair ribbon, as a young girl might.

"Madame!" Fou Loup bowed with a grace that surprised Robert. Fou Loup's eyes flickered with anticipation.

"You've come to see my girls!" Madame cooed as she shook out her handkerchief. Then her soft, motherly face hardened. "Have you got money?" she questioned.

"*Oui, madame!*"

Madame's face broke into a smile that revealed two rows of yellowed teeth. She set her handkerchief in her lap and clapped her hands.

A line of young women passed into the parlor—five in all. They seemed to range in age from fifteen to thirty.

Robert was about to say something, but Fou Loup interrupted. He was the consummate trader.

"How much?"

"A Louis d'or for the night," Madame exclaimed proudly.

Fou Loup did not look impressed. "A quarter of that!"

"For these girls! They're wonderful girls! They're all clean, and they're all good! You insult me, monsieur. You insult them."

Fou Loup bent down and started to shoulder his pack. The madame looked at him and said, "Half."

As she spoke, a sixth girl entered the room. Robert looked up to see a creature so lovely he nearly gasped. She was statuesque with a magnificent figure and tawny golden skin. Her eyes were the huge yellow eyes of a beautiful cat.

Fou Loup ignored Robert's obvious newfound interest in the negotiations. "A third!" Fou Loup offered.

At that, the madame gave in. "Agreed," she said,

shrugging. "Though how you expect a decent woman to make a living is beyond me!"

"Which one?" Fou Loup asked.

"Her," Robert said, nodding toward the beautiful Creole woman.

Madame motioned to the Creole woman and then turned to Fou Loup. "And you?"

"You, of course!" Fou Loup answered, chuckling.

"Me!" Madame was clearly shocked. She stood up, and her face actually flushed. "You," Fou Loup repeated as he casually swatted her across the fanny. "I got strange French tastes—I need a woman of experience!"

Robert fought back a rude comment, but he could not suppress the smile on his face. The Creole woman took his hand, and Robert eagerly followed her.

She led him to a medium-sized room where the drapes, chairs, and bedcovers were not the jarring red of the parlor, but rather more subdued shades of yellow, buff, beige, and brown.

The window gave way to a tiny wrought-iron balcony that overlooked a small inner courtyard. It was open wide, and a mild breeze from the river gently stirred the filmy curtains. In spite of the ventilation, the room smelled of musk—the same pungent and arousing aroma that filled the parlor.

The Creole woman moved with a graceful flow, her golden gown rustling as she walked across the room. She was without question the most beautiful creature Robert had ever laid eyes on. Her hair was a warm chestnut color and was piled elaborately on her head, held in place by a large tortoise-shell comb. Her eyebrows were dark and well-arched. Her lips were full, and her throat was long and shapely. But it was her eyes that fascinated Robert most. Like her skin, her eyes were golden. Their pupils were great dark pools.

For a moment, Robert just looked at her. He realized she was older than he had originally thought—not a girl, but a woman in the full-blown beauty of her prime. She was perhaps thirty—though it was simply impossible to tell with certainty. The woman was the most magnificent product of cross breeding one could imagine. She had the high cheekbones of an Indian, the coffee-colored skin produced by mixing white and African bloods and the hair of the Spanish.

For the first time in his life, Robert felt the rush of real sexual desire, and he realized that however much he had loved Marguerite, he had not felt the same animal desire to possess her.

Their fleeting moments together—stolen moments on the eve of battle—came back to him in a rush. They had both been novices! Children playing at lovemaking. But the woman who faced him now—who gestured him toward the bed—was a woman of real experience, a woman who could fulfill him totally.

As Robert began to undo his clothing, he was aware that the Creole beauty was watching him with admiring eyes. Her look so filled him with anticipation that even before he removed his breeches and boots, he felt himself swelling.

"Mademoiselle, comment t'appeles-tu?"

"Juliet," she replied, smiling seductively.

Robert sat down facing her on the edge of the bed.

"You are most handsome, monsieur," Juliet said in a low throaty voice. "Most strong." Her golden cat eyes fell on his manhood, but Robert did not blush.

Juliet began to disrobe slowly, beginning at the top. She wore no chemise beneath her golden gown, which she pulled down slowly to reveal two voluptuous breasts—coffee-colored mounds tipped with taut brown nipples. Juliet stepped out of her gown and removed her white petticoats. Her waist was small, and her hips were well-rounded. She had wonderfully long, slim thighs and shapely legs that tapered down to comely ankles.

When Juliet stretched out beside Robert on the feather mattress, he thought that her movements were as catlike as her eyes. For a moment she lay languidly beside him, flesh to flesh, body to body.

Robert rolled onto his side and touched one of her erect nipples.

"Kiss it," she whispered, moving her whole body against his in one movement.

Robert touched the nipple with his lips while Juliet held his head gently. "Again . . ." she purred. "Keep doing it . . ."

Under the pressure of gentle sucking, the nipple grew larger and firmer. With one hand, Juliet directed Robert's hand to her other breast. "Touch me too," she said, pressing against him.

Robert continued, amazed at the incredible urgency in his loins. It had been so long—too long.

"You're anxious," Juliet said, nuzzling him. Robert nodded affirmatively. He felt he should make excuses, but she seemed to understand. "Relax first," she whispered. "Then we'll really make love." She moved beneath him with ease and spread her long legs wide, allowing Robert to enter her. He closed his eyes and tried to think of something else, anything else. But it was no use. The vision of her undressing remained firmly in his mind, and the feel of her body undulating beneath him was more than he could stand. Robert tensed and felt himself rush into her. His breath came in short gasps, and in a few seconds he collapsed on her soft, dewy body.

Robert lay on Juliet for a few moments, then he felt her hands on his back. Her fingers moved lightly from the back of his neck down to his buttocks.

Juliet moaned slightly as he withdrew from her, then she opened her eyes and looked at him with pleasure. "Now," she uttered in a low voice, "now we will do it more slowly . . ."

Juliet placed her warm, delicate hands on his cheeks and guided his lips back to her swollen breasts. "Caress me," she breathed, "slowly and for a long, long time . . ."

Robert's tongue moved in slow circles while his hand toyed with her free nipple. Her flesh tasted sweet, and

237

she groaned with pleasure as he continued. "That's good, yes, that's good . . ."

While Robert caressed her, Juliet's expert hands were on him, causing him to rise again.

When Juliet slithered down in the bed and took him in her mouth, rounding her lips and applying a gentle pressure, Robert thought he would die of the sensation, but she withdrew too soon for him to complete his pleasure. Instead, she moved over Robert, bidding him to tease her as she had just teased him. "Oh, no, no . . . not that way . . ."

Juliet guided his hands and lips; she pressed against him and moved with him. "Ah, yes . . . like that . . . that's better."

Robert felt her grow damp and heard her small sounds of pure animal pleasure as she squirmed beneath him. Then Juliet climbed on top of him, lowering her breasts so he could take one into his mouth and easily place his hand on the other. Then she straddled Robert, allowing him to push up into her. With agonizing slowness, Juliet moved up and down. She placed one of his hands on her most sensitive area and groaned as Robert gently touched her, losing himself in the dizzying slowness of their lovemaking. Just as Robert could hold back no longer, Juliet arched her back and tossed her head backward, letting out a moan of pure pleasure as they throbbed against one another.

Robert held her in his arms when she rolled off onto her side, nuzzling into his broad chest. They slept in each other's arms for a time, but Juliet did not hesitate to awaken Robert for more pleasure. Throughout the night and for part of the morning, Juliet taught Robert the art of lovemaking. "Always slowly," she told him. "You must learn to give pleasure as well as to take it."

Fou Loup lifted the bitter whiskey to his lips and slurped it down, allowing a slight dribble to run out the side of his mouth and down his chin. Then he plopped the mug down on the tavern table and looked at Robert with a puzzled expression on his face.

"Since yesterday you've looked like a love-sick wolf." Fou Loup shook his head in mock disgust. "You're not supposed to fall in love with a whore."

"She's the most beautiful woman I've ever seen," Robert said in his own defense.

"And you're going back and spend some more money on her."

"Probably," Robert allowed. Even as he said it, he knew it was more than a probability—it was a certainty.

"I knew you'd need half that gold. Young men always need more money for women."

Robert laughed. "Three months in the bush is a long time."

"Me, I've had enough to last three months! That madame has a cunt the size of a seven-year-old mare who's had six colts!"

Robert laughed again at his partner. He was used to Fou Loup's crudeness. In any case, Fou Loup was no less crude than any other backwoodsman—they were all a tough lot, made so by the country they conquered and the way in which they lived. Such men did not consider women much more than animals to be used—and, Robert thought to himself, a great many used animals and women in the same manner.

"You want to go back upriver in the spring for more furs?" Fou Loup asked, raising an eyebrow. "Good money, but I need a partner."

Robert contemplated the idea for a few moments. Fou Loup was quite right. The war between the English and the French droned on, and its miserable continuation had caused a partial cessation in the fur trade. There was indeed money to be made, and that money could form the basis of a more permanent business venture.

"You have a partner," Robert agreed. And the whole idea had another advantage. There wasn't much shooting around Fort St. Louis. It was the Ohio Territory that the British wanted—the Louisiana Territory was peaceful.

"We winter here?" Fou Loup questioned. "You

going to spend the whole winter in bed with that Creole whore?"

"Not the whole winter," Robert said, tossing back his head with a laugh.

The two of them left the tavern and walked the streets for a while. Winter would obviously be more pleasurable here than in Canada. The days were longer, and it was always mild.

They paused and watched the lazy river with its sand bars and estuaries stretching out in all directions.

Robert looked at Fou Loup with amusement. He had discarded his buckskins in favor of black boots, bright red breeches, and a puffy shirt. He had talked the Spanish captain out of this outfit for a little gold. As part of the bargain, Fou Loup had obtained a broad-brimmed black hat with a feather as red as his pants.

"They say a man can live forever up them bayous . . ." Fou Loup pointed off down the river. "Lots of birds to shoot . . . shrimp to catch and those little crayfish and crabs."

"With those pants and that hat, you'd be lucky if someone didn't shoot you for a bird." Robert smiled.

"Too hot for buckskins. Anyway, I'm a bird, a tough old Canadian bird."

"You want to hunt in the bayous?" Robert could tell Fou Loup was growing tired of the town.

"I want to hunt a mean old animal called an alligator . . . but they say she's got a fine skin! Lot meaner than a beaver!" Fou Loup laughed under his breath. "Lot meaner."

Robert shook his head in partial agreement. He inhaled and was again struck by the peculiar combination of odors that always seemed to engulf New Orleans with its mixed-blood population of some nine-thousand souls. Suddenly he knew what it was: magnolia blossoms and fish!

"We could winter on the bayou . . . catch some alligator . . ."

"Not just yet," Robert answered. Poor Fou Loup. He didn't much like sleeping in a bed. He'd rather be out with the stars and the mosquitoes. But Robert's mind strayed back to his ravishing Creole beauty, Juliet. "Not just yet," Robert repeated.

Robert sat in the ornate bathtub with his knees bent. The water was steaming, and in spite of the excessively warm weather, Robert found this hot bath quite relaxing.

Juliet knelt beside the tub, scrubbing Robert's back with a stiff brush. When she had finished with the brush, she massaged him with a soft cloth that she wrung out again and again, allowing the warm water to run down Robert's back.

Juliet was nude, and her breasts moved temptingly with the stroking motions of her arm. Her body glistened with dampness, small beads of perspiration ran between her breasts.

Robert withdrew a wet hand from the tub and caressed her, watching her grow taut.

"Get in," he invited, "c'mon."

Robert folded himself up to make room. Juliet smiled coquettishly. "Do you really want me to?"

Robert winked and signaled to her by tilting his head. Juliet stood up, lifted a long, lovely leg, and stepped into the tub. She crouched before Robert, facing him.

Robert took the soap and began lathering her bosom; Juliet quivered beneath his touch as translucent suds dripped erotically from her tight nipples. The ends of her long hair were wet and curling into ringlets.

"I love you," Robert whispered as he pulled her toward him, touching her most sensitive area. "I love you, and I want to marry you."

Juliet pressed herself against him, moving her hips in order to gain the most pleasure from his explorations, but she laughed too. It was a high, musical laugh.

Robert pulled away slightly, though he did not remove his hand, causing Juliet to squirm under the growing pressure of his caress.

241

"I want to marry you." Robert's soft brown eyes were serious and steady as he looked into her face.

Juliet stopped laughing. Her expression changed to match his.

"You flatter me," Juliet answered softly. "But one does not marry a whore."

"You're not a whore! I love you!" Robert did not, could not think of this woman with another man—when he was with her, she was completely his.

"I'm a whore," Juliet answered with conviction. "And older than you, my magnificent young stallion . . . quite a bit older." Juliet lowered her long dark lashes and looked down at the water.

Robert renewed the pressure, and his fingers continued to explore her. Soon she was clinging to him as he massaged her slowly, drawing deep sighs from her and then a throbbing groan of pleasure. She sunk against his wet, hairy chest.

"You've learned well," Juliet murmured. "But my pleasure does not mean I love you."

Robert was startled by her statement. Juliet withdrew from him and looked him in the face. Her eyes were large, almost luminous, and her expression was serious. "You are one of my best customers, but I don't love you." Her voice had taken on a sudden hardness that Robert had never heard before. He hated her use of the word "customer." He had thought of himself as more than a "customer."

"How many men do you . . ." Robert couldn't complete his question. He could not think of her being caressed by another man; he could not tolerate the idea of another man drawing pleasure from her or giving it to her.

Juliet arched her well-shaped eyebrow and thrust out her lower lip. "When you're not here . . . a great many, yes. Juliet has many men." Juliet looked away. "In fact, you're taking up far too much of my time. I could be making more money."

"I thought we had something that went beyond money!" Robert was hurt, and suddenly he felt his

242

anger rising. No, he thought to himself, it was not all anger or hurt. He felt used. He was suddenly seeing a side of Juliet he hadn't dreamed existed. He had thought of her only in terms of their erotic lovemaking; he had romanticized her, idolized her.

"You're a pleasurable young man," Juliet said with a chill in her voice, "but almost anyone can be if taught."

"I wanted to take you away from this! Away from selling your body!" Robert was aware that he sounded a bit childish. He cursed himself for his naïve petulance, but his desire for her had blinded him—it still did.

Juliet stepped up and out of the tub. She wrapped a large length of cloth around her. "I don't want to be taken away! Why do you presume I do?" She turned her back to him and began drying herself.

"This is no life for you!" Robert protested. "It's no way for a lady to live!"

Juliet turned on him suddenly, the pupils of her cat eyes enormous. "Understand this! My mother was a slave."

Robert's mouth fell open; he didn't know how to respond.

"The man who owned my mother was a savage. He beat her to death! Understand that I'm free, and my daughter's free. I have money, and I intend to have more money. Much more money. I don't give away what can be sold!" Juliet's eyes narrowed. "I sell, and I'm not a slave. A wife is a slave . . . marriage is just another form of slavery!"

Robert's face contorted with pain. Juliet had never mentioned her daughter or her mother. He felt a crushing defeat, an emptiness and a hurt. The reality of Juliet's hatred for men pierced him deeply.

Juliet stood up straight. Her dark, wet hair tumbled to her shoulders; her golden cat eyes were set. She was proud of herself. "I don't want love," she said coldly. "Love is slavery. I don't want it now, I don't want it ever!"

Robert pulled himself from the tub as Juliet left the

room. He dressed and cursed himself for not grasping the reality of their relationship. She had hurt him with her rejection, and she had stunned him with her bitter confession.

As Robert finished buttoning his shirt, he looked up at Juliet, who had returned wearing her petticoats. Her cat eyes were larger now and softer. Their pupils were great dark pools. "You're a romantic," she murmured. "A young, handsome man. An unusual man, but you're naïve."

Robert looked at Juliet and felt he was seeing her for the first time—she was lovely, but she was cold.

"Good-bye," he mumbled, looking down. The words stuck in his throat.

"One day you'll thank me," Juliet said in a low voice. She walked over to him and sought his eyes with her own. "It's a hard lesson," she advised, "but don't confuse the need created by your loneliness with love."

Robert nodded silently. For all he had experienced in life, for all he had learned, he was still a novice with women. He felt a fool now, all too aware of the pitfalls of youthful passion.

Fou Loup met Robert in the tavern. It was, as always, crowded with men who boasted loudly in a variety of languages, drank far too much, and cursed at every possible opportunity.

Fou Loup looked into Robert's face and read it like an old book. He sucked in and snorted. Then he spit on the dirty floor and lifted his tankard of whiskey to his mouth.

Robert sat down dejectedly and looked around him. The customers were a motley lot. Men who plied their living from the sea. They were wily Spanish and the refuse of New France—displaced Canadians, voyageurs, refugees, convicts.

A robust, quick-moving black woman set down a tankard of rum before him. Her half-exposed breasts glistened with perspiration, and her black hair clung tightly to her head. Robert pressed some coins into her hand and picked up the tankard. The rum trickled down his throat, relieving the dryness.

"You done in bed for a while?" Fou Loup asked.

"Yup," Robert answered.

"You ready for some alligator pie?"

Robert smiled at the thought. He had seen an alligator in a cage—it looked slow and ferocious. Like a pock-marked log with jaws of steel.

"I'm ready," Robert answered. For the moment he too wanted to sleep under the stars to the accompaniment of birdsong and the scurrying of small animals. Anyway it was money, and it offered something to keep them busy over the winter.

CHAPTER XIII

December 1762

The *Norden* was a slave ship, an ancient vessel pressed into service to meet the economic demand for more slaves in the English colonies. Its stinking hold gave off the vile odors of rotting flesh, human wastes, disease, and death.

It was a Dutch ship chartered by one James Plimpton, a well-known slave trader in the Carolinas. But the ship sailed under a Spanish flag, and its crew was mixed—Dutch officers, Spanish sailors.

The *Norden* followed a well-traveled route. It left Holland and proceeded down the west coast of Africa to the Gold Coast, laying anchor at Elmina. There, the master of the ship traded a load of cotton, trinkets, and weapons for 300 slaves sold by the Ashanti warriors who rounded up the unfortunates from the interior.

From Elmina the ship sailed directly to the Carolinas where the surviving 260 men, women, and children were sold.

In Charlestown, the ship took on another human cargo—a huddle of Acadian deportees. Again, the ship was on a double journey. The Acadians would be put ashore and a cargo of indigo taken on in the Port of New Orleans.

The orders were simple: "Scatter the Acadians. No one cares where. Just scatter them."

The *Norden* had anchored off the bayous, and one by one or in family groups, the weary, frightened Acadians were rowed to different locations and left on high ground to fend for themselves.

Among the last to be taken off the *Norden* were the Comeaus: Jean Comeau and his two children, eighteen-year-old Angelique and her three-year-old brother, Martin.

Angelique closed her eyes as the wretched longboat slipped through the black water into the darker night of the bayous. Scattered clouds covered the moon and obscured the stars.

Four stocky, squat Spaniards pulled at the oars of the longboat. They babbled to one another in rapid Spanish, their conversation liberally scattered with obscenities and vile curses. Their bodies were heavy with sweat, and they smelled foul even in the fresh night air.

Angelique pressed her younger brother to her and thanked God that he was so weary he was sleeping soundly. Her father coughed and stared blankly into the night.

"There's no light on shore! Where are you taking us?" Jean Comeau demanded in a raspy voice. It was one last attempt at futile protest.

"No habla francés!" one of the sailors replied angrily.

Angelique shivered even though the night was warm. From the dark, forested shore, one could hear the sounds of strange animals, the weird sounds of night birds.

"We gave you all we had!" Angelique joined her father in trying to rouse some human pity in the animals who sullenly rowed the boat.

"Everything!" she repeated. "You promised—your captain promised!" Tears were welling in her eyes. The past years had been a never-ending nightmare.

247

First they had been watched. Then their houses were broken into and ransacked by cursing British soldiers. Then their neighbors had begun to disappear—dragged away in the night for imaginary crimes. Finally they too were taken and herded with a hundred others into camps—horrible stockades where they were guarded by soldiers who shot at anyone who tried to escape. Food had been scarce, and the water was putrid.

And the British! The British burned their home, trampled their fields, killed their livestock. "They'll let us out soon," her father kept saying. "We've done nothing. They'll let us go home." He was wrong. After a time, they had been loaded into the hold of a Yankee schooner and transported south to the Carolinas. There, in abject poverty, they had remained for nearly a year. Angelique's mother, the soft-spoken Teresa Comeau, had died; for weeks she had coughed up blood just as Jean Comeau did now.

After a time, they had been gathered up again at gunpoint and loaded into the *Norden*. "You're going to fine new homes," they were told. "Fine new homes where you can farm and grow prosperous."

But they had lied. They had all lied. Angelique's father had given the captain the last of their money. The captain had taken it, promising good treatment, but he too had lied.

All that was left was one lone trunk—a small trunk with some clothes and a few embroidered table scarves made of threads spun lovingly at their spinning wheel by Teresa; scarves that had once decorated the pine table of their cottage in Acadia.

Angelique shivered with apprehension and wondered why she didn't leap out of the boat into the black water and end it now. Could it be that she still had some kind of hope? It had all been so gradual: her life, the life she had known, had slipped slowly away till there was nothing left now.

"*Aquí!*" one of the sailors called out. The others lifted their paddles out of the water, and the longboat drifted toward the shore.

Angelique crossed herself. It was an uninhabited wilderness full of wild animals. It was the end of their journey.

The sailors lifted their lanterns and surveyed the shore. Then they clambered out of the boat and dragged it onto the sand, securing it to a nearby tree with a rope.

One of them carried the trunk, and the others motioned for Angelique and her father to follow. Their pistols were drawn, and in the flickering light of the lanterns their faces looked evil.

The little procession followed the path for some distance, then came to an abrupt halt in a small clearing.

"Aquí!" the one in command repeated. Angelique assumed the word meant "here."

The sailor with the trunk dropped it with a thud in the middle of the clearing. The lanterns created dancing shadows on the earth as the trees shuddered in the warm breeze.

Angelique turned pleadingly to one of the sailors. "You can't leave us here!"

They all laughed, and one ripped Martin from her arms, dropping the sleeping boy on the ground. Martin's eyes opened as he let out a wailing cry of surprised pain.

Angelique started to run to her little brother, but one of the sailors seized her wrist, jerking her back.

"Leave my daughter alone!" Jean rushed into the fray and grabbed the sailor by the shoulders, trying to shake loose his grip on Angelique.

A shot crackled through the air, and a nest of birds shrieked in the night and took flight. Angelique screamed.

"Papa!" she screamed again, and the woods echoed it through the night as her father fell to the ground, blood gushing from his chest. One of the sailors kicked his stomach while another bent down and checked his pockets. He found nothing and kicked the body again in pure disgust.

"You've killed him! You've killed him!" Angelique struggled against the man who held her. "Murderers! Assassins!" She kicked the Spanish sailor in the groin as hard as she could. He let out a shriek of pain, grasping himself and cursing in Spanish. The other three laughed loudly.

Angelique whirled around, but one of the others caught her in his arms while another grabbed her feet. They forced her to the damp ground, one holding the upper part of her body, the other two her legs, which they spread apart.

Angelique struggled bitterly—kicking, biting, and screaming. But there were four sailors, and three held her fast while the last tore off her clothing.

"Kill me! In the name of heaven, kill me!" The one who held the top part of her body put his free hand on her bare breast and squeezed. Angelique screamed again. She looked up into his dark face, and he grinned at her with yellow, crooked teeth and spit in her face.

The fourth man straddled her and, dropping his pants, plunged into her. Angelique let out a high-pitched cry of pain, then moaned as the man continued to pierce her. "Oh, dear God!" She felt the hands on her naked breasts; another pair roughly rubbed her thighs. She struggled, but the more she did, the more they laughed, the more they pawed her and taunted her.

Angelique closed her eyes and tried to say prayers as they changed places and another of the vile creatures fell on her.

On the rim of her consciousness, Angelique heard Martin crying out, and a sudden vision of him wandering off alone into the blackness of the strange forest obliterated the horror and reality of what the men were doing to her.

"Martin!" she called. "Martin, stay here!"

Even as she cried out, another of the sailors fell on her. She thought her skin must be ripping apart. "Oh, God in Heaven. Oh, sweet God!" Their hands were still on her, their hungers were still unsatisfied.

250

Angelique panted heavily as the fourth man replaced the third. They were all laughing—laughing in the night. For a moment Angelique truly wanted to die, but what about Martin? If she died, he'd be alone! Her fingers dug into the damp earth as the fourth sailor let out a cry and rolled off her.

"Martin!" she cried once again just before she lost consciousness.

The barge that Robert and Fou Loup chose to explore the bayous was smaller than the one they had brought down the Mississippi, but it was of essentially the same design.

It was, according to Fou Loup, essential to sleep on the barge since the ground near the shore was often marshy and a man could sink into it up to his waist or even farther.

Moreover, sleeping on the barge—in the shelter of its little center hut if it rained—offered safety from snakes. "They hang from the trees," Fou Loup told him solemnly. "It's not like Canada where you just have to watch the ground." Fou Loup's source of information was an elderly Cajun who spent long months in the bayous, then emerged in New Orleans only to drink and tell tales to the curious.

As they punted along, Robert studied the shore. Their barge was gliding down one of thousands of waterways: the bayous were a maze of inlets, islands, sand bars, and jungle. Great, graceful, green cypress trees dipped into the dark waters and seemed to drink through their leaves. Every inch of solid land was overgrown with lush vegetation, and there were birds of every possible description. Delicate, statuesque flamingos, white-winged birds, and even nesting Canada geese.

Fou Loup pointed to one of the geese with its distinctive green-and-blue neck banded with a white ring, and he let out a whoop that sent a treeful of small red birds into frantic flight. "See! Winter and war makes all Canadians go south!"

Robert laughed, but his eyes were not on the geese. On the shore there was a clutch of alligators that had dragged themselves out of the muddy waters to sun themselves on the warm rocks.

"They look like logs," Robert commented. But he had seen them in the water, and in the water they moved.

"That's where we have to get 'em," Fou Loup advised. "They say they're fast in the water and a lot stronger there than they are on land."

Robert had already surmised as much. They had passed quite a few of the creatures sunning themselves on the shore. They looked dead, genuinely like misshapen trees lying askew. They had passed them in the water too, where they slithered at incredible speeds as they searched for prey.

They floated on for a time, allowing the current to carry them. After a while they came to a sand bar where three alligators lay sleepily in the sun.

Fou Loup pointed to the alligators and slowed the barge as they approached the sand bar. In New Orleans they had been shown how to catch the beasts, but they both knew how to do it only in principle. "Don't use bullets on gators," they had been told. "Use the big stick! Quick, you have to be quick!" The idea was to distract the gator with the stick, jamming it into his mouth if necessary, while the other person clubbed the animal.

Robert and Fou Loup took their weapons and climbed onto the sand bar well away from the resting gators. As they approached, the alligators made no moves.

Fou Loup slapped one of the alligators over his long nose with the pole. The alligator snapped at it wildly. The other two alligators slithered toward the water and immediately disappeared. Robert tried to club the animal, but it was too quick. Fou Loup jabbed the gator with the stick, and for a few minutes it was a furious battle of flapping tail and snapping teeth. Twice the alligator managed to pound its tail so hard that Robert was partially blinded by flying wet sand.

"Now!" Fou Loup yelled as he finally succeeded in jamming the pole down the alligator's mouth. Panting, Robert struck the beast with his club, but its vicious tail kept flapping. Robert clubbed it again and again. Finally, on the fourth clubbing, the alligator lay still.

"Christ!" Fou Loup said as he expelled his breath and fell onto the sand, panting.

Robert sunk down beside him. They were both trying to recover their dignity as woodsmen.

After a few moments Robert sat up and tapped Fou Loup on the knee. "Do you suppose there's more to this than we think?"

Fou Loup sat up and brushed the clinging sand off his bare chest. "Sure as hell is meaner than a beaver," Fou Loup answered as he looked at the wicked animal. "Hell of a lot meaner!"

Robert looked at the beast admiringly. "You have to admire a thing that fights that way—hissed like a mountain lion and it even seemed to roar."

Robert walked around the alligator. It was nearly seven feet long, and its eyes were in the top of its head, little beads staring at the hazy sun.

"Ugly!" Fou Loup admitted. "But we gotta skin it."

"I hear the tail makes good eating," Robert suggested. "Pity to waste the whole animal just to get its skin." Robert walked around the alligator's tail—the instrument that had nearly swatted him to the ground like a fly.

Fou Loup made a face, but he was willing to try alligator tail. He set about slitting the tough skin. "Wonder what it tastes like?"

"We'll find out," Robert answered as he joined Fou Loup in the skinning.

When they had finished, they loaded the skin on the barge and Robert began a fire in the iron container they used for cooking. The barge was again set afloat on the water.

253

"It's sweet meat," Fou Loup said, gleefully chewing on some alligator tail. "You wouldn't think a thing that ugly and mean would have such sweet meat!"

Robert ate in silence, stopping now and again to swat at the persistent bugs drawn to the barge by the fire that burned in the cooking pail.

When they had finished eating, they lay in their bedrolls under a mosquito net and listened to the sounds of the night. They were incredible sounds—crickets, frogs, and the shrill shrieks of unknown night birds.

Since it did not look like rain, Fou Loup and Robert slept with their feet inside the barge hut and their heads outside under the mosquito netting. This arrangement allowed them to see the stars and benefit from what breezes stirred the sultry air.

The bayous, Robert thought as he looked upward, were a world of their own; they hardly even seemed to be a part of this earth.

The barge gently rocked Fou Loup and Robert toward deep sleep. The sounds of the bayous had been strange the first few nights, but now they seemed like a familiar lullaby.

Robert was close to deep sleep when he heard the ungodly sound. He sat bolt upright and listened. Fou Loup also jumped up, and even by the subdued light of the moon Robert could see that Fou Loup's eyes were large and held a fearful glint.

It was a long, agonized wailing—a scream that sounded half-animal, half-human amid the other night noises. Fou Loup crossed himself three times. "Blessed Virgin!" he mumbled as the wailing continued unabated.

Robert looked out into the night. The moon shimmered off the water, but the shore was pitch black on either side.

"It's coming from over there!" Robert pointed off toward the shore, trying to determine exactly where the weird noise was coming from.

Fou Loup continued to mumble and utter a string of

prayers, which he alternated with French curses. To these he added some special Mohawk incantations—just to be on the safe side.

Then the wailing stopped. "I don't think that's an animal," Robert said with conviction.

"It's a devil!" Fou Loup stated in a low, almost reverent whisper.

Robert nodded out of politeness rather than belief, remembering how truly superstitious his companion was.

They both sat up wide awake, and the time passed slowly. There was no continuation of the noise. Uneasily, they both lay back down, but within the hour the weird wailing began again. It continued as before, and then it again ceased. It went on through the night, on and off, on and off.

An hour before sunrise the sound began again, but this time it was mixed with the predawn sounds of a million birds waking and taking flight. Everything in the bayous seemed alive. Robert tossed restlessly—he had hardly slept. The haunting sounds emanating from the shore had kept him awake most of the night.

Fou Loup looked around. The length of rope was tied to the trunk of the huge cypress tree. They were twenty or thirty feet from shore, but the rope kept them from drifting off during the night.

The wailing began again. "Devils don't cry out in the daytime," Fou Loup said with conviction.

"I'm going to find out what it is," Robert said in a determined voice. "Man or beast, I'm going to find out!"

Fou Loup grabbed the rope and tugged the barge toward the shore.

"Luckily, the ground looks solid." Fou Loup tested the ground by keeping one foot on the barge and the other on the leaf-covered shore.

The huge, graceful cypress trees shaded the area, and there were no alligators visible.

Robert took out his pistol and checked it. Then he gingerly leapt onto the solid ground and stepped into the thicket of dense bush with Fou Loup close on his heels.

"There's a path," Robert pointed to a narrow trail, and both he and Fou Loup started to follow it. Robert watched the ground; Fou Loup kept an eye out for hanging snakes. Small oily green lizards scattered across the path in front of them. The light from the sun barely penetrated the dense trees; it seemed to filter to the forest floor, casting strange shadows that created the effect of finely cut, deep-green lace. With each breeze the treetops rustled and the lacy light seemed to shiver. Moving through the bush was both beautiful and eerie, Robert thought.

Animal life scattered, and even the plants seemed to move. Then the wailing, much closer now, began anew.

"Who's there?" Robert called out in a husky voice.

The wailing instantly ceased.

Robert looked down at the ground. There were distinct boot prints in the soft earth. Silently, Robert pointed to the many prints. "Devils don't wear boots," he whispered to Fou Loup.

Again there was a long wail, and this time it sounded definitely human.

"Who's there?" Robert called out in French. His voice echoed through the woods, and more birds took flight from a nearby clutch.

"Oh, God help us!" The words were spoken in French, and the distinctly feminine voice was terror-stricken.

Robert bounded down the half-cleared pathway after the sound. "We're friends!" he called out in French.

Fou Loup loped along behind, mumbling, "How do you know it's a friend?"

Robert reached a small clearing and took a deep breath. The sight before him was horrible.

A girl wearing a tattered blue dress, a black apron, and a mud-caked white cap sat on a small sea chest. She lifted frightened, tear-filled eyes to him.

Beside her a small child clung to her skirts and

sucked his thumb. Face down on the ground a few feet away was the body of a man. Large red ants crawled over him and through the pool of his congealed blood.

"Oh, my God!" Robert said in a low voice.

Fou Loup crossed himself as he always did in the presence of the dead.

The girl's long black hair hung to her shoulders in dirty strands, but her gaze had a strange composure. Her fists were clenched tightly. "Don't touch me!" she said firmly.

Robert stopped. "Don't be frightened."

The girl began to shake violently, and as Robert drew closer to her, he could see that her white skin was a mass of raw insect bites. The child's tender skin was even worse. Instinctively, Robert lifted the little boy into his arms and hugged him. His little pants were soaked with urine.

"It's all right," Robert said, rocking the little boy in his arms. Then he handed the child to Fou Loup, who quipped, "I figured you'd take the girl."

Robert held out his hand to the terrified girl.

"Mademoiselle, we won't hurt you. What are you doing here? Where are you from?" Questions poured forth from Robert in a torrent.

The girl stood up and seemed to hear his French for the first time. She threw herself against him and began sobbing wildly.

Robert allowed her to vent her fears. When her sobs subsided, he drew her back from his chest and looked at her. "Come along," he urged. "There are too many insects here."

Robert guided her gently along the path toward the shore. She squinted in the sudden sunlight as they emerged from the bush.

Fou Loup carried the child onto the barge and immediately began stripping him. Like an old Indian mother, he washed the baby boy down with water squeezed from a rag and then bundled him into a bedroll.

The girl sat with her feet under her and her arms hanging limply at her side.

"What's in the trunk?" Fou Loup asked.

"Clothes . . ." She looked down at her torn dress and fingered the shreds absently. "More rags . . . all we have."

Fou Loup wasted no time. He set back after the trunk, mumbling about naked children in the woods.

"My name's Robert MacLean," Robert spoke slowly. "Tell me yours."

She looked at him with soft hazel eyes—eyes that still looked dazed and a bit frightened.

"It's all right," Robert assured her. "We'll protect you."

"Angelique," she replied, studying his face.

"Where are you from?"

"*Acadie,*" Angelique answered painfully. She could not say the name of her homeland without feeling the agony of loss. "*Acadie,*" she repeated with tears in her eyes.

Robert covered his eyes with his hand for an instant. He had seen the Acadian refugees coming into New Orleans—he knew they had been scattered throughout the Carolinas from where many had been deported or chosen to make the overland trek into French territory. Robert also knew that just as many had been killed en route or died from hunger and cruelty. The Acadians were a people deeply rooted in their land, their families, and their language. Now they were uprooted, wandering deportees in a strange and hostile land.

"But how did you get here?" Robert pressed. "How did you get into the bayous?"

"They brought us here," Angelique answered. "We paid them to take us to New Orleans, but they brought us here. They put us ashore, they killed my father and, and . . ." Angelique's voice trailed off as the horror returned to her eyes. Robert didn't have to hear the rest. He had seen women like this before—he had seen Janet, he had seen Louise and Madelaine.

"They hurt me," Angelique began crying again, but

258

no longer in convulsive sobs. Her silent tears rolled down her cheeks.

"They took our money, they left my brother and me to die . . ."

Robert patted her arm gently. "How long have you been out here?"

"Three days . . . four nights . . ."

Robert shook his head. It was a wonder they had survived. "I'll make a fire, fix you something to eat and drink."

Robert got the fire started and retrieved some tea from his stores. He handed Angelique some dried biscuits, and she tore at them like a starved animal. When the tea was ready, Robert gave her a steaming mugful. "We'll feed the child when he wakes up," Robert assured her.

Fou Loup staggered out of the brush, panting. He dragged the trunk behind him, and lifting it with a grunt, he plopped it on deck.

"I disposed of the body," Fou Loup said. "Buried it as best I could, but you can't dig out here—the water comes right up into the hole."

Angelique murmured a thank you.

"They've both got a lot of nasty bites," Robert observed.

Fou Loup nodded and rummaged in his pack for assorted Indian salves, finally producing a dreadful red paste.

"Try this," he offered.

"Put it on your bites," Robert advised Angelique. "It will stop the itching and help them heal."

Robert glanced toward the sleeping child. "What's your brother's name?"

"Martin—he's only three."

"And your mother? What became of your mother?"

Angelique looked into the muddy water. "Dead— died of a fever."

Robert patted her gently on the arm. "We'll take you back to New Orleans."

Fou Loup shrugged and raised an eyebrow.

"Back to bed, eh?" he mumbled under his breath.
In return, Robert shot him a silencing glance.

The sun rose in a hazy mist, and dark clouds shifted ominously in the southern sky.

Angelique fed her brother and then ate with Robert and Fou Loup. Her hair was matted and her face dirty. She had managed to crawl into the barge hut and put on a faded dress, one of the few things that was in one piece. But her skin was swollen with bites, and despite her night's rest, her eyes were still puffy from crying.

Nonetheless, Angelique seemed to warm to Robert and Fou Loup. They had rescued and fed her and Martin. They seemed kind, and neither of them bothered her. Having spent the night on the barge with them without incident, Angelique had begun to relax and trust the two men.

"How far is it to New Orleans?" she questioned.

"Three days," Robert answered.

Angelique looked ahead—the jungle was dense, but somehow it now seemed less frightening. To her the waterways they followed seemed like never-ending paths that wound in circles.

"Are you still afraid?" Robert asked.

Angelique looked at him sadly. "Only for my brother," she admitted. "He's so small . . . I don't know what I'll do, or what will become of me. We have nothing."

Robert patted the flat deck of the barge and bade her to sit down next to him. "Don't worry," he assured her. "I'll find you a place to stay in New Orleans. I'll see you're taken care of."

"I can't let you do that," Angelique replied. "It's not right. I can't pay you back."

Robert looked at Angelique seriously. "The dispossessed have to stick together," he replied. "I don't want to be paid back, it's not necessary."

"You're very kind," Angelique answered shyly.

Robert understood her protestations only too well. She was clearly afraid he would want payment with her body. Moreover, she had just been through a horrid experience, an experience it would take some time to overcome. He wanted to tell her that he had no intention of demanding her body in payment for help, but he could not decide how to phrase it. Not touching her, not approaching her was surely the best way. And as he looked at her, he had to admit that he did not feel particularly attracted to her in any case. In point of fact, he could hardly imagine what she might look like cleaned up.

"I don't want anything in return," Robert stressed, that being as much as he could bring himself to say. Then he added, "I was once in a similiar situation."

Angelique tilted her head. "You were?"

"I'm not French," Robert confessed, "I'm Scots." Then Robert told her about Scotland and the crushing defeat of the Highlanders. He told her how he escaped with Janet and about his life in Quebec and in the militia. He even told her about Louise and how he had been kidnapped and then rescued by Fou Loup. "We go back a long way!" Robert said, gesturing toward Fou Loup, "a long, long way."

Angelique was fascinated. She listened intently, and as Robert revealed his past, she grew less shy.

When Robert had finished, he turned to her. "You're a strong woman to have survived as much as you have. Don't be afraid to accept our help."

Angelique nodded silently. She was in awe of this sensitive, handsome young man, and she was grateful. He clearly understood because he too had been uprooted and dispossessed.

Angelique patted Robert's hand gently. "I trust you," she said softly.

CHAPTER XIV

January 1763

Grande Mama was a fat, down-to-earth woman of fifty. She had come from France in her youth—some said on a convict ship. After a successful career in a New Orleans brothel—where, it was rumored, she stole gold coins from pirates and stuffed them inside herself—she had opened a sort of boardinghouse. "Not as lucrative as whoring," she would tell her friends, "but more relaxing."

Grande Mama's house was made of a yellowed cement and boasted a wide downstairs veranda as well as the typical little wrought-iron balconies outside the upstairs windows. It was a large, square house with an inner courtyard that had a large weeping willow in its center and scattered magnolia trees around the edges.

In one corner of the courtyard, obscured by a sweet-smelling magnolia was an ancient outhouse. The odors from the outhouse mixed with the blossoms under the southern sun, and the resulting aroma—if the wind was blowing in the right direction—was both sweet and acidic.

Once a week, Grande Mama filled a huge tin tub with hot steaming water in the middle of the kitchen and invited her roomers, one by one, to bathe in it. Grande Mama was a fair woman. The bathing order was rotated so that once every two months each roomer got to use the bathwater first.

Grande Mama stood in the middle of her kitchen with her great hands on her even greater hips and looked at Robert as if he were entirely mad. "Fill the bathtub?" she exclaimed in amazement to the tenants she had just rented a room to. "Fill the bathtub? It's not even Friday! It's only Tuesday!"

Fou Loup eyed the tub suspiciously. He agreed with Grande Mama. He could certainly wait.

Robert feigned exasperation. "How much?" he queried.

Grande Mama assessed Angelique and the small boy. God knew they looked like they needed a bath. She screwed up her face and mumbled a pittance of a sum. "But you'll have to carry the water!" she warned. "I only do that on Fridays!"

Robert agreed and pressed the coins into her fingers.

Fou Loup grunted. "I usually get paid to bathe," he said, making a face.

"Well, I'll pay you—especially if I have to sleep in the same room with you. C'mon, get the fire started," Robert laughed.

Fou Loup looked at the fire with disdain. It was bad enough to have to take a bath, but to have to prepare it yourself was adding insult to injury. God only knew what might happen to you! Fou Loup had always considered his personal odors his only defense against the world of disease and insects.

Robert took Grande Mama's hand and led her aside. "I want you to go out and get some clothes for the woman and the baby—I'm not very good at that sort of thing." He was aware of his blushing when he said it.

Grande Mama raised an eyebrow and gave him a knowing look. "Is that girl your mistress?" she questioned in a demanding whisper.

Robert shook his head. "Just an Acadian refugee I intend to take care of."

Grande Mama shot Angelique a quick glance. She could see that the girl was painfully shy and certainly in horrid condition. She wondered how Angelique would look cleansed and dressed properly. Certainly much different from the way she looked now. "I'll go," Grande Mama agreed. "But I'll need to measure her."

The elderly woman sighed and folded her hands over her fat belly. "Why don't you leave all this to me. Go on. Get out of here. Shoo!"

Robert gave Grande Mama some more money and smiled at her warmly.

Grande Mama giggled girlishly at his look and mumbled under her breath, "Men, men, men!" Then she added, "Come back later. You get the bathwater when she's finished."

In deference to Angelique's modesty, Grande Mama closed the kitchen curtains and locked the doors. "Now you can have your privacy, honey," she told the girl. "Get out of those rags!"

Angelique undressed quickly, and Grande Mama noted that the naked young Cajun girl had a fine figure that had been totally obscured by the loose-fitting, faded dress she had been wearing.

Angelique sank into the tub of hot water, and Grande Mama washed her back and then her hair, rinsing it with clear water.

"How did you find that unlikely pair?" Grande Mama questioned, referring to Fou Loup and Robert, who had rented the large upstairs room.

"They found me," Angelique answered. Then she told Grande Mama her story.

"Men!" Grande Mama muttered again. She squeezed out the washrag and handed it to Angelique to finish scrubbing herself.

With difficulty Grande Mama unfolded herself and stood up. "The young one's good-looking," she commented, rubbing her hands dry on her white apron. "Mighty good-looking!"

Angelique smiled up at Grande Mama. Her dark hair was wringing wet, and it fell in dripping curls over her alabaster shoulders. "And kind," Angelique said, "and a gentleman too."

After a time, Angelique stood up and Grande Mama wrapped her in a huge towel. "You scoot upstairs," she advised. "Dry your hair and wait for me."

Grande Mama plopped through the kitchen and out to the veranda where Robert, Fou Loup, and little Martin were sitting.

"The baby next," Grande Mama said authoritatively. "Then you," she pointed to Robert. "And you last!" She looked at Fou Loup and sniffed. "Definitely last!"

With those instructions given, Grande Mama shuffled off with Robert's gold pieces. She wouldn't have to go far. The girls at the brothel down the street had plenty of gowns and buying a few wouldn't be difficult.

"What we gonna do now?" Fou Loup asked as he wiggled his toes in the water. "We all gonna stay cooped up in one room—Jesus! We got a ready-made family!"

"The room's for them," Robert answered as he put on clean clothes. "We're going back upriver for furs."

Fou Loup breathed a sigh of relief. He had not relished the idea of settling down in New Orleans. He climbed out of the bathwater and complained, "I feel all itchy. It's that damn lye soap. I tell you bathing's unhealthy!"

Robert laughed and pointed to Fou Loup's clean clothes. Fou Loup clearly longed for his previous state. He swatted at a passing insect. "See," he said ruefully, "the goddamn things bite when you're clean!"

Fou Loup put on his clothes while Robert dressed Martin. The three of them emptied the well-used bathwater, tidied up Grande Mama's kitchen, and went back out on the veranda.

The sun was falling off the western edge of the earth

in a blaze of bright red. Overhead, the sky was still blue except for groupings of fluffy white clouds. The fragrance of exotic flowers hung heavy in the southern air.

"She's ready!" Grande Mama's voice rang out from behind the front door. "Now here's a transformation!"

Robert looked up, startled. Angelique's dark hair sparkled and hung long and full over her bared, white shoulders. Her hazel eyes were beautiful and warm; her skin was snow white and smooth. Robert saw what he had not noticed before—Angelique had a beautiful figure. The green silk gown that Grande Mama had chosen revealed just enough to make Angelique a real temptation. How could he not have realized how exquisite she was!

Feeling Robert's eyes on her and seeing his obvious admiration, Angelique blushed deeply. "This is not the kind of dress a good Acadian woman wears," she said.

Robert took her hands and pressed them in his. "This is New Orleans," he said. "And you're breathtaking!"

Again Angelique blushed deeply.

"I'd say it's time for dinner!" Grande Mama announced.

"Past time!" Fou Loup grumbled.

Grande Mama turned to him sharply. "You smell . . ." she said, crinkling her nose, "good for a change!"

After dinner Robert took Angelique into the enclosed courtyard, and they talked for a long while.

"We won't be staying," Robert advised her. "We're going back upriver for furs."

Angelique's beautiful face clouded over and filled with apprehension and unanswered questions.

"You're not to worry," Robert assured her. "You and Martin will stay here with Grande Mama. I've paid in advance for the room and for all you'll need."

Angelique's clear hazel eyes sought Robert's. "You're kind," she whispered. "We'd have died if you hadn't found us . . ."

266

Robert ran a hand through her mass of dark hair and drew her to him. She rested her head against him. "I'll come back," he assured her. "Believe me, I'll come back."

Fou Loup patted his stomach and burped appreciatively.

"More?" Grande Mama poured another helping of fish stew into his bowl.

"You're a bottomless pit!" she said, grinning. "A woman could go broke feeding you! Good thing you're leaving—I'd have to raise the rent!"

"You like feeding me," Fou Loup answered with an air of confidence. He winked at her, and surprisingly Grande Mama blushed.

"How old are you?" she questioned. It was impossible to tell. He was gray and round and balding, but his skin was taut. He reminded her of a bear.

Fou Loup shrugged. "Don't know," he answered. "But the priest says I was born around 1710."

"That would make you over fifty," Grande Mama answered, counting on her fingers.

"How old are you?" Fou Loup's eyes fell on her enormous, drooping bosom.

"You're not supposed to ask a lady her age," Grande Mama answered with a haughty air.

"A lady!" Fou Loup let out a whoop of laughter that could be heard all the way out into the courtyard.

Grande Mama stood up and looked around. The other boarders were all gone. They always disappeared right after dinner. She bent toward Fou Loup. "Forty-eight," she lied.

Fou Loup did not reply. He only lifted the bowl to his mouth and drained it. Then he patted his stomach again and let out a great belch. "You got any whiskey?"

Grande Mama shook her head in mock disapproval. Then bending over, she confided, "Not in here."

Fou Loup's eyes narrowed. He stood up and took her hand. "Where?"

"In my room."

"Well, let's go to your room."

Grande Mama straightened up and attempted to look shocked. "A lady does not take men to her room to drink whiskey!"

"A lady doesn't keep whiskey in her room for men to drink," Fou Loup retorted. "I hear you got the best ass in New Orleans!"

Grande Mama's mouth flew open, but after a moment she decided it was a compliment rather than an insult. "Well, they don't call me *Grande* for nothing, honey," she replied with a wink of her own.

Grande Mama then motioned to Fou Loup knowingly, and he followed her upstairs to her private room. She went immediately to the cupboard and removed a decanter of raw whiskey. Fou Loup took it from her and drank a great swig. A dribble ran down his mouth.

"I want to see the best ass in New Orleans," he announced.

"I usually charge," Grande Mama replied. "It used to be my profession."

Fou Loup laughed. "You're past charging, and I'm past paying."

Grande Mama grinned and disrobed without another word, revealing huge loose breasts and a fine wide bottom.

Fou Loup undressed quickly and pushed her roughly to the bed. He slapped her ass and let out a whoop. Then he mounted her, grasping her wide buttocks and laughing loudly as he plunged into her with relish.

Grande Mama groaned beneath him, clawing at the bedsheets. "You don't waste any time!" she gasped.

"At my age—our age—there's no time to waste!" Then he added with considerable admiration in his voice, "You remind me of my horse."

Janet Cameron Macleod stood outside and looked at her newly completed house. It was a far cry from the log cabin she, Mathew, and the children had been living in for three years—it was a mansion by comparison.

It was two stories high, a magnificent stone house with four chimneys and eight louvered windows. Mathew had modeled it after Léry's house near Fort Beauséjour. Since both men were engineers, they both had sturdy houses of excellent design.

Mathew rounded the side of the house and walked up to Janet. She's a handsome woman, he thought to himself. Still tall and straight, with her russet hair blowing in the wind and her green eyes fastened on the horizon, she almost looks like a model in a painting.

"Happy?"

"More happy than I've ever been."

"It's over," Mathew said. "The peace treaty's signed, and it's finally over."

Janet put her arm around Mathew's waist. They had known the treaty was imminent, but this morning a messenger had come. Now it was final. Janet looked back on the seven-year war and remembered all the changes it had brought. So many settlements had been burned, so many people killed.

"There will be new settlers now, new farms."

"British colonials," Mathew said with a faraway look in his eyes. "British North America! We live in British North America!" Mathew kicked the soil with the toe of his boot. He was still trying to get used to the reality, though he had accepted the idea when Fort Niagara had been taken.

Janet looked up at him with determination. "No, we live here," she said flatly. "On this land." Janet reached up and put her soft hands on Mathew's cheeks. "And our sons will live on this land, and our grandsons. This is our Lochiel, our home."

Mathew smiled joyfully at her. He picked her up in his arms and cast out all thoughts of the peace treaty and its meaning. "C'mon, Grandma!" he joked. "Let's go eat in our house, on our land."

Mathew strode toward the house, carrying Janet easily.

"Grandma! I'm not so old!" Janet protested. She

wondered if this might be the moment to reveal her secret.

"Haven't you been a mother to Pierre?" Mathew questioned, a mischievous look on his face.

"I hope so," Janet answered. "What's that got to do with it?"

"Well, men discuss things," Mathew teased.

"What things?"

Mathew set Janet down inside the threshold and closed the front door. "He's getting married."

Janet's mouth opened in surprise. "Genevieve? The daughter of the blacksmith? Across the river?"

Mathew nodded. "Who else? He rides over there three times a week."

"Oh, the devil! He didn't tell me!"

"But you knew." Mathew playfully slapped Janet across the bottom.

Janet impulsively whirled around and threw herself into Mathew's arms, kissing him. "Oh, Mathew! You're not the only one with a secret."

Mathew held her at arms' length and searched her eyes.

"I have a really shameful secret," Janet confessed, a smile crossing her face. "Of course, you should be just as ashamed as I. Come to think of it, you should be more ashamed."

Mathew looked at her and tried to figure out her meaning. She seemed on the verge of breaking into laughter, but her tone was half-serious, half-mocking. "What should I be ashamed of?"

"You should be ashamed that I shall have to attend Pierre's wedding great with child! A disgrace for a woman of thirty-five!"

Mathew burst into happy laughter and pulled her to him.

"Oh, Mathew. We've found such happiness," she murmured.

Mathew kissed her hair and held her lovingly. "Yes, we have," he answered thoughtfully. But Mathew suppressed his inner thoughts. The Indians were demanding Niagara—except for the fort. There was a possibility they would have to give up Lochiel. No, Mathew decided. He would not tell Janet. Not yet.

Robert and Fou Loup returned to Fort St. Louis and spent the entire summer gathering furs. In September when the leaves began to turn, they loaded their shipment onto the large flat barge and headed south again.

They followed the river as Jean Baptiste Le Moyne, the Sieur de Bienville, had done in 1716 when he had first claimed this territory and named it Louisiana. Le Moyne had founded two cities—Fort Rosalie, which was now called Natchez, and New Orleans, on the delta.

At Fort Rosalie, Robert and Fou Loup put ashore for supplies. As in New Orleans, the air was heavy with magnolia blossoms, but the settlement beyond the fort—Natchez—was an embryo town in comparison. It was half-city, half-frontier.

Thirty years earlier, Natchez had been nearly wiped out by the Indians, who resented the French incursion on their land. Somehow it survived the massacre and was now an area of settlement.

"You know," Robert said to Fou Loup. "This area is a mid-point for trade . . ." Robert's mind was wandering. "When the war's over, this place will get both the overland east-west trade and the Mississippi trade."

"We gonna become traders now?" Fou Loup asked.

Robert shrugged. "The soil's rich—it's located in just the right place."

"You asking me to settle down?" Fou Loup questioned.

Robert raised an eyebrow. "I'd like to build here, but it's too much for one man."

"Maybe," Fou Loup answered, scratching his chin.

Robert slapped his partner's back. "It's high time you planted your feet," he chuckled, "and I like my

271

partner!" Robert motioned to Fou Loup. "Let's go see what gold can buy," he suggested.

It was late October when Fou Loup and Robert approached New Orleans. They were fifteen miles upriver of the city when Fou Loup pointed south and shook his head. "We'd better head for shore," he cautioned. "Cover the furs and take shelter."

The air was thick and still, and the black clouds on the horizon blotted out the setting sun and seemed to extend in a semicircular configuration with the greatest density in the south, out over the gulf and the bayou country.

Fou Loup guided the raft toward shore, and Robert swore under his breath. He had hoped to be in New Orleans by early tomorrow; now they would be delayed.

"You been away five months—another day can't matter!" Fou Loup shouted.

Robert scanned the shore with irritation. Fou Loup was right—there was no point risking the furs over a few hours' delay. He reprimanded himself for daydreaming about Angelique. She might have found someone else, any number of things could have happened in five months. Still, Robert longed to see her. Juliet had been right. He was a romantic.

The late-afternoon stillness was ominous. The ubiquitous birds that usually nested on the shore of the river had apparently all taken flight and an unseemly silence had fallen over the countryside.

Fou Loup pointed up. High above, a formation of seagulls swooped and dived, moving northward. "Bad storm coming," Fou Loup muttered. "Big blow!"

Robert pointed off toward the shore. There was a small inlet and large willows to which the raft might be secured. Up the hill there were some large boulders.

"This looks like a good place," Robert suggested.

In moments they had the raft secured.

"We better get the furs ashore and covered." Fou Loup took an armload and hopped ashore. He struggled partway up the hill and found a spot among the rocks. He motioned to Robert, who followed with more furs.

They worked laboriously for over two hours before the furs were piled, covered, and tied down.

"What now?" Robert asked as he looked toward the river. The usually lazy Mississippi seemed to be rising angrily.

"We wait up here too," Fou Loup confirmed. He was taking their only other piece of canvas and making a lean-to between the rocks. "I've heard tell of winds so strong they can lift a man right up like a feather," Fou Loup announced gloomily as he continued working. "I got a feeling we're going to get pretty wet!"

"Hurricanes," Robert said abstractedly. His mind was still on Angelique and the land he and Fou Loup had just purchased across the river from Natchez.

Fou Loup stood back and looked at his creation. "It's not much, but maybe it'll help."

Robert followed Fou Loup into their shelter amid the boulders. Leaning back, he felt he had a great deal in common with Angelique. And even if he had known her only for a short while, the time they had spent together had been intense. They had talked a great deal, and she seemed to like him. Robert was uncertain as to whether Angelique would marry him—he had made her a promise, but she had not said she'd wait.

Robert closed his eyes and tried to picture her in his mind—she was beautiful and sweet. She was strong like Janet, but had she recovered from being so brutally attacked? Robert did not have to be told what scars such a terrible experience could leave. He knew all too well from Janet and Louise.

Robert crouched down lower when the first few droplets of rain began to fall. He was so uncertain! He wasn't even sure if Angelique would allow him to make love to her—she might still be afraid. Robert began to ache for her again, daydreaming about making love to her, imagining her responding to him.

"Is there something the matter with you? You look

love-sick." Fou Loup had caught the expression on Robert's face.

Robert altered his expression. "No," he answered sullenly.

Fou Loup laughed and slapped his knee. "The rain and wind will cool you off," he announced, looking upward.

"You have a raunchy mind," Robert shot back with a half-smile.

"It's more comfortable than what you got," Fou Loup replied blatantly.

Robert blushed. Fou Loup was right—this was no time for fantasies.

The rain came in little droplets at first, then grew to larger pellets of water until the sky seemed to split apart. It grew as dark as night, and the wind came up with a vengeance.

As Fou Loup had predicted, this was no ordinary wind. Robert had to brace himself between the rocks as all around them the wind bent poplar trees to the ground while the less flexible trees snapped in half as if they were tiny sticks. The only relief to the darkness came when the sky was split by a thunderbolt and the landscape was temporarily illuminated. The wind blew on, and after a time the rain ceased as if the wind had chased the sheets of water away.

An hour passed, and the ground beneath them turned to mud as rivulets of water plunged downhill toward the Mississippi. The winds went as suddenly as they had come, and the rain returned. But this time it was a softer rain. Another hour or two passed, and the rain stopped. Robert glanced over at Fou Loup. He was immersed in his bedroll and apparently sleeping. Robert could not bring himself to pull the soaking-wet covers of his bedroll around him, but he leaned back against the rocks and closed his eyes. Overcome by weariness, he fell into a light sleep.

When Robert opened his eyes, a stillness had once again fallen over the shore, and the air was clearer and fresher than it normally was on the lower river. The sun was shining down on a muddy world, and the Mississippi was flowing rapidly toward the gulf.

Robert jumped up and wondered how he had managed to sleep. "Fou Loup!" he called out.

"Over here!"

Robert emerged from the tattered lean-to and looked around. His clothes were caked in red mud, and he was still soaked to the bone.

Fou Loup was laying out the furs to dry on the rocks. "They're all right. Wet, but all right! It's not as if a beaver never gets wet!"

Robert laughed. "They're wet most of the time!"

"We gotta dry these out before we can pile them back on the raft."

Robert picked up some furs and began spreading them out the way Fou Loup was doing. His heart sank. The pelts were soaked. It would take at least three days to dry them out so they could be restacked.

"What a mess!" Grande Mama surveyed her parlor and shook her head. "First the Spanish and now this! One hurricane is worse than a ship full of sailors in a whorehouse on a Saturday night! Look at that chair! It's soaked!"

Grande Mama was moving around the parlor, picking things up and shaking her head. The front window had been blown out, and water had poured in along with what seemed to her half the magnolia leaves in New Orleans.

Angelique brought in a pail of water and began to wash the floor.

"You're a good girl!" Grande Mama praised her. "You're my only tenant who cares to live in a clean house. The rest of them wouldn't mind living in a pig sty! They'd just leave everything the way it is right now—let the next big wind pull down the house around them and they'd sleep right through it!"

Angelique watched Grande Mama with a smile. In

spite of her crudeness, Grande Mama was a wonderful woman. She baked special sweets for Martin and told him stories.

"You don't look like the happiest girl in the world," Grande Mama commented as she watched Angelique scrubbing. "You've been unhappy lately, and it's more than just this mess. What's the matter?"

Angelique sighed. "I didn't know I was so transparent." It was difficult to hide anything from Grande Mama.

"I'm afraid he won't come back."

Grande Mama put her hands on her hips and laughed. "He'll come back!" she pronounced.

"It's almost the end of September," Angelique reminded her. "He said he'd be back earlier."

"Men are the strangest of all animals," Grande Mama explained. "But when a man gets a certain woman in his head, he behaves like a bird coming back to the nest. What makes you think he won't come back?"

Angelique shrugged and looked perplexed. "Maybe because this territory is now Spanish. I don't know."

Grande Mama considered the comment. "No, that wouldn't stop him. I doubt if he cares whose territory it is. Anyway, it hasn't made any difference to us. The French come and go. Spanish or no Spanish, the French are still the masters of the river."

Angelique pulled herself up and wrung out the rag she had been washing the floor with. "I hope you're right."

"You're in love with him?" Grande Mama asked the question out of courtesy. The answer was all too obvious.

Angelique's lips parted. She shook her head affirmatively.

"And he loves you?" Grande Mama asked.

"I don't know," Angelique answered truthfully. "But I'm afraid . . ." She didn't finish her sentence, and her hazel eyes filled with sadness.

"Afraid of what?" Grande Mama persisted.

"I'm afraid he won't want me because . . . because of those men and what they did." She looked down and away.

Grande Mama dropped the pillow she was shaking and sat down on the damp settee. She patted the cushion next to her and motioned for Angelique to come sit beside her.

Grande Mama patted Angelique on the knee. "Honey, you're as innocent as the day you were born—dirty Spaniards or no dirty Spaniards. That young man's not the kind to care about that sort of thing. I saw the way he looks at you. That's a fine young man. Grande Mama has seen a lot of men. That Robert MacLean is one of the good ones, and he'll be back."

"I hope so," Angelique whispered.

Grande Mama put her large arm around Angelique. "Lovemaking is mighty nice when you're in love," she assured her. "Nothing like what you went through, nothing at all like that. Grande Mama knows. That young man will come back, and that young man's going to make you cry with joy! I'm never wrong about men—never!"

Robert and Fou Loup looked around the river market. The streets were littered with broken glass, parts of houses, and uprooted trees. The shanty town was in virtual ruin, and two ships that had put into port had their sails badly damaged. But in the river market, business went on as usual. The traders had merely reerected their shacks, found their trading tables, and gone back to commerce as usual.

Fou Loup frowned and tugged on Robert's sleeve. "Lots of Spanish ships. And flags . . ." He pointed out toward the undamaged ships. He was right—every one of them was Spanish. "Not a French flag around."

A funny feeling swept over Robert as he realized Fou Loup was right. "Maybe something's happened we don't know about," Robert said cautiously.

277

"After five months in the bush, all we do know about is skinning beaver." Fou Loup eyed the traders again. "All Spanish," he confirmed.

A fat, bustling black woman moved past them with a basket of white eggs. Her head was covered with a red kerchief, and she picked up her skirts so they wouldn't drag in the mud. Robert caught her elbow. "Excuse me, ma'am . . ."

The woman stopped, and her face broke into a wide, toothy grin.

"Why are there so many Spanish flags?" Robert pointed around.

The woman smiled, then broke into a full laugh. "Where you been, honey?" She was convulsed.

"In the woods!" Fou Loup chimed in irritatedly.

The woman stopped laughing, but a smile still dominated her face. "Why the French signed a peace treaty, and New Orleans and Louisiana Territory now belong to the Spanish!"

"The war's over?"

The woman nodded.

Robert turned to Fou Loup. "The war's over!"

Fou Loup looked nonplussed. "Spanish, eh?" He smiled as he looked back at the trading tables. "The Spanish are the best bargainers," he announced with a relish he could not conceal.

Robert felt absurd. He wanted to yell and scream that the bloody war was over, but who would care? Everyone in the river market already knew.

Fou Loup was already tugging the cart with their furs toward a likely-looking Spaniard. "You don't need me for this," Robert announced.

Fou Loup raised an eyebrow. "The trouble with people your age is you have no patience!" He threw up his arms and rolled his eyes heavenward. "All right! All right! Go rock your bed!" Then he winked slyly. "Tell Grande Mama to get out her whiskey and take off her pants! Fou Loup's coming!"

Robert's face reddened. "You're incorrigible," he

278

muttered, hoping in vain that no one had heard the lewd comment.

"Go along!" Fou Loup said, waving Robert off with his hand.

Robert laughed and hurried off through the muddy streets of New Orleans. As he approached Grande Mama's, he could see that part of the veranda had been ripped off and several windows broken. He stepped over the debris and struggled toward the front door. The furniture in the parlor was askew, and most of it looked wet. But clearly someone had begun to clean up, for the broken glass had been neatly swept into one corner.

"Angelique! Angelique! Grande Mama!" Robert's voice echoed through the rooms.

"Out here!" Grande Mama's voice called back from the courtyard. Robert bolted down the long hall.

The tall cypress tree was still standing, sheltered as it was by the surrounding house.

Grande Mama was in the middle of the courtyard, stirring a pot that hung over an open fire. "The fireplace is all stuffed up with leaves," she said by way of explanation.

Martin was sitting under the magnolia bush, playing with bits of wood. Angelique was under the cypress, and when her eyes met Robert's, they glistened.

Angelique hesitated for a moment, then ran into Robert's arms. He swept her up, kissing the lips that moved beneath his own.

Grande Mama went on stirring, an impish look on her face.

When Robert released Angelique, Grande Mama looked up and grinned. "See, I'm never wrong."

Grande Mama took in Robert's filthy clothes and muddy boots. "You're a mess," she commented. "There's some water in the kitchen. Why don't you clean up!"

Robert pressed Angelique's hand. "She's right, I am a mess."

"There are clean clothes upstairs." Angelique smiled.

Robert leaned over and kissed her on the cheek. "I have a million things to tell you," he whispered in her ear.

Robert headed into the kitchen. In the corner there was a large bucket of water. He stripped down and washed away the mud and perspiration of the last week. When he was finished, he wrapped himself in the large bath towel and went upstairs.

In the room Robert had rented for Angelique and Martin, clean clothes had been laid out on the bed. Robert began dressing. He had just finished when there was a light tap on the door.

"Come in," Robert called out.

Angelique entered and walked over to him. Robert turned and took her in his arms, kissing her again and again, feeling her response.

"What is Grande Mama never wrong about?" he asked, referring to Grande Mama's comment in the garden.

"Men," Angelique answered, pressing her head to his chest.

Robert smiled and looked into her exquisite face. Angelique's hazel eyes seemed full of love.

"I love you," Robert whispered. "I love you, and I want to marry you."

Angelique quivered as he kissed her again, her arms now around his neck.

As she pressed herself to him, Robert felt his own need growing—it had been so long, and he had thought about her so much. Robert devoured her throat and bare shoulders with kisses, then his hand fell on her full breast. Angelique stiffened and pulled away.

Robert's face was flushed, and he was breathing hard. He looked at her steadily. "I'm sorry," he murmured. "I've missed you, thought about you."

Angelique hung her head, and her eyes filled with tears. "And I of you," she said softly. "I want you," she looked up and met his eyes, "but I'm afraid . . ."

Robert opened his arms and enclosed her in them. "I'll be gentle," he promised.

She did not pull away, but leaned against him. "I might not be able . . ." she said after a moment. "I'm so afraid I can't make you happy or be a good wife."

Robert bent down and kissed her neck and shoulders again. "You will be," he promised her.

Robert wordlessly led Angelique to the bed and pressed her downward. He kissed her mouth and her shoulders; he held her in his arms and tried to close his thoughts against his own desires. But as he held her and longed for her, Angelique moved her hands along his back. Again Robert kissed her bare shoulders, and then he kissed the top of her breast softly.

When he lifted his head, he looked into her eyes.

"I must know," she murmured. "I must know if I can let you love me . . ."

Robert closed her mouth with another long, deep kiss. He undid the ribbons that held her bodice fast and slipped his hand inside her dress, gently touching her soft flesh.

When Angelique moaned slightly, Robert pulled away the material and kissed the tips of her breasts. They grew taut beneath the gentle movement of his lips.

Robert struggled out of his shirt and breeches. He carefully removed the rest of Angelique's clothing and stretched out beside her. He returned to kissing her softly, making himself go slowly, while all the time he hungered for her.

He lingered over her till she returned his kisses and pressed herself against him, lost in pleasure and responding to the movements of his fingers and mouth. She shivered beneath him, and when Robert returned to the tips of her breasts, she pressed herself upward, allowing him to enter her.

Robert felt her surge beneath him, but he did not allow himself full pleasure till he felt Angelique throbbing against him, her hands clutching his back. When she gasped and the undulating movements of her hips

281

momentarily stopped, Robert closed his eyes and released himself.

For a long moment they both breathed in short, quick inhalations. Robert did not move at first. He remained joined to her, stroking her beautiful hair.

Then Robert withdrew slowly and lay down beside her, pulling Angelique into his arms. She rested her head on his chest. "I love you," she murmured.

Robert kissed her hair. "I love you too!"

They lay in silence, eventually drifting off into a short, happy sleep.

It was the slamming of the front door that awakened them.

Robert sat up, and Angelique stirred.

Fou Loup's voice thundered through the house. "Doesn't anybody care about gold?!"

"We'd better go downstairs," Robert said as he kissed Angelique on the cheek. "We have tonight and a thousand nights to come."

Angelique blushed.

They got up and quickly dressed.

Fou Loup and Grande Mama watched them from the first-floor landing as they came out of the bed chamber and down the winding staircase. Both had smirks on their faces, and both shook their heads.

Angelique's face was bright red, and Robert flushed too.

Fou Loup put his hands on his hips and shook his head in mock disgust. "Good thing we got more patience!" he intoned, winking at Grande Mama.

Grande Mama looked at Robert mischievously. "You look like you just lost something."

Robert took Angelique's hand and looked from Fou Loup to Grande Mama and then back to Angelique.

"No, I found something." Robert had a faraway look in his eyes. "Something I thought I lost in Quebec . . . something I wasn't sure I'd ever find again."

Grande Mama beamed. "Love," she mumbled under her breath.